D1626034

SUSAN

DOWN OUR STREET

Also by Lena Kennedy
MAGGIE
AUTUMN ALLEY
NELLY KELLY
LIZZIE
LADY PENELOPE

Susan

Down our Street

LENA KENNEDY

BOOK CLUB ASSOCIATES LONDON

This omnibus edition published 1987 by
Book Club Associates
by arrangement with Macdonald & Co Ltd

Susan © Lena Kennedy 1984
Down Our Street © Lena Kennedy 1986

Set in 10/11 pt Times, Compugraphic
by Colset Private Limited, Singapore
Printed in Great Britain by
Richard Clay Ltd,
Bungay, Suffolk

Contents

Susan

Prologue

With a yawn, Sue stretched out her long slim shape over the pink silk divan. Lifting one of her legs high into the air, she casually surveyed the jewelled slipper balanced precariously on the end of her painted toes.

Sue was an extremely beautiful woman in her early thirties. At first glance you might think that her face and figure were flawless but if you looked closely you would just be able to see a faint scar, which a highly skilled surgeon had all but erased, running down her cheek from her eye to her mouth. And in those wide dark eyes, behind the seductive gaze, you might see a sadness hidden away from the rest of the world. Or you might see an occasional bitter twist of her pink lips. But on the whole, she looked like a woman who enjoyed her work and who was in control of her life. Certainly the luxuriously furnished flat was an indication of her success.

Suddenly the door opened and a tiny, wizened woman came into the room. Her strange hooded eyes were so deep set that it was impossible to tell what colour they were. She was neat and tidy in a black dress and natty white apron with a little piece of fancy lace on top of her frizzy hair. And when she opened her mouth in a perfectly straight line, she exposed little black stumps which might once have been teeth.

Sue stared at the maid through a veil of false eyelashes. 'Shut the shop, Gladys,' she said. 'Take the phone off the hook. I don't want no more clients today.'

Gladys' wide mouth gaped in astonishment. 'But you've got two more to come, Sue.'

Sue shrugged. 'I don't want them today,' she declared. 'You'll have to send them away. I'm quitting for the day – I've got things on my mind.'

This seemed to please Gladys tremendously. She clasped her hands together and looked eagerly at Sue. 'Are we going to have a chat?' she asked.

'You know we are, you crafty old devil,' replied Sue. 'Go and get the nosh and a bottle. You and I will talk over old times.'

Soon the velvet drapes were drawn across the tall windows. Sue still lay on the pink divan but was freshly bathed and dressed in a frilly housecoat. On the rug beside her crouched Gladys looking like an excited child. The remains of their satisfying meal lay on the table by the wall.

'I can still hear my damned old stepmother's voice,' said Sue. 'It still comes to me, clear as a bell: "You'll come to a bad end, you will",' she mimicked in the high-pitched voice. 'Bad end!' she said scornfully. 'Look at all this!' She swept her arm around to indicate the lusciousness of the room. 'I hardly call this a bad end.'

The gnome-like figure at her feet nodded in agreement. Gladys' brown cheeks were flushed red from the effects of the strong sherry they had shared. 'Go on, Sue,' she giggled. 'Talk about those days when we was poor orphans at St Augustine's.'

With a serene smile on her lips, Sue closed her eyes and let her mind drift back in time to unfold the story of a little girl who never had a chance . . .

Chapter One

A Bad Start

Sue's thoughts drifted back to the earliest days of her childhood, when she played barefooted in the slum back streets, and pushed a shabby old pram full of babies to the park during the school holidays. She vividly recalled the squabbles and fights with the other kids, and particularly the bigger boys who swore every other word, told filthy jokes and exposed themselves behind the bushes, beckoning the girls to come and have a look at them. Yes, she could remember all that very well. But most of all she could remember a particular day, which came back to her now like a bad dream, when the police came charging through the house after her lively Cockney father who tried desperately to escape from them by scrambling over the roof tops. Young Sue had watched the chase in bewilderment but then she knew that an accident had followed, because of the commotion – the crowds milling about, the white ambulance that came and went and, most of all, her little mother screaming hysterically. No one bothered to explain to that skinny little girl what had happened, but she, quietly minding her twin brothers in the kitchen, knew that it was something bad.

The following day, her grief-stricken mother had collapsed down on the bare floor-boards, gasping and clutching her swollen belly. 'Get the midwife, Sue!' she cried.

On long thin legs Sue had run down the street to fetch the old crone who returned with her, shuffling in old carpet slippers and carrying a large straw shopping bag.

Later that day, the ambulance came to the street once again, and her mother, covered with a red blanket, disappeared to hospital. For some hours afterwards, the neighbours stood about gossiping; some wept.

So then it was goodbye to the drab slum house with its dirty linen and faded wallpaper. How often since, she wondered, had her heart ached for that squalid room, where she used to sit up in bed surrounded by her grubby brothers and sisters, and share a

11

sticky piece of nougat with them while she told them fairy tales? But it was no more. The back street home was replaced by a hard white bed, painted walls and three substantial meals a day, with a prayer before and after.

Nine years old, with her dark hair hanging on two long pigtails, Sue had stared insolently at the matron of the children's home, and carefully sized up the situation. Her cheeks had been so well scrubbed that they tingled, and rebellion seethed in her young breast. Let them start, she thought angrily; she was ready for them. They had taken the twins away from her earlier, without even letting her see them. Tears welled up in her eyes but she forced them back. She was not going to cry, she would not let them see how much they had hurt her. She hated these Nosey Parkers, and they were not going to keep her in this rotten school, she vowed, no matter how hard they tried.

'She's quite intelligent,' explained Miss Woodcote, the welfare officer, to the matron. 'It's a pity she came from such a bad home, with the father in and out of prison.'

'Well, we get all kinds here,' the matron replied placidly. 'She'll soon settle down.'

Sue spent three years at Barham House. She absconded twice and was brought back by the police on both occasions. How she hated the place! It never changed. Every day was dreary and monotonous. They did the same things at the same times in the same places. They ate the same old food, read the same old books and played with the same old jigsaw puzzles. Sue grew big and very tall, and her dark eyes became angry and brooding. It was not that anyone was unkind to her, it was just that she was starved of affection when her young heart was crying out to be loved and to give love.

Nearly twelve and her figure had begun to fill out. She had long, perfectly formed legs, and her small breasts were like spring buds as they pushed shape into the sack-like gingham dress she had to wear. Her dresses always had the same faded light-blue checks. Sometimes they were too long, sometimes they were too short but always they were too tight around the bust for Sue. But Sue had seldom seen herself in a full-length mirror, and was quite unconcerned about her shape. When she walked, she leaned forwards slightly and took long, boyish strides. And her face always had a surly, hang-dog expression.

'Sue has settled nicely,' remarked Miss Woodcote on one of her infrequent visits.

'Yes,' replied the new young matron. 'The staff all agree that she has changed considerably since I came.' She beamed.

Miss Woodcote sipped her tea in an absent-minded manner. 'I'm pleased to get a good report of Sue. She was a big problem here at first.'

'She likes to see you,' said Matron. 'No one else has ever visited her.'

'I'm afraid that this is my last visit,' replied Miss Woodcote. 'I'm leaving the service, and going to Africa on mission work, something I have always fancied.'

'How nice,' replied Matron, 'but Sue will really miss you.' She paused. 'I must say, she is very handy with the small children.'

'That's just as well,' replied Miss Woodcote. 'If she hadn't settled down here it would have been reform school for her, after the trouble she has caused.' She placed her tea cup carefully on the table beside her. 'A slight hazard has cropped up concerning Sue,' she said. 'Her father will shortly be paroled. He is a very embittered man and permanently crippled by the fall he had while being arrested.'

Matron nodded and sighed. 'Oh dear,' she said, 'what troubles lie ahead for Sue, then? If her father claims her, I'll be forced to let her go.'

'Yes,' replied Miss Woodcote,' and most of our hard work will have been for nothing.' She picked up her gloves. 'I have to admit that I won't be sorry to leave the welfare service. Will you say goodbye to Sue for me? I don't think I can face it.'

Thus Sue's only friend from the outside world was preparing to abandon her. Miss Woodcote had been the one who brought sweets and talked to her about that little back street called home. At first Sue had been waiting anxiously in the corridor for her, but then she had gone outside to listen to the women's conversation at the half-open window. Now she had heard enough. Sullenly, she hugged her long arms tight about her. Tucked under the faded cardigan, her nails bit viciously into her skin. She kicked her heels against the wall and her dark eyes squinted. 'Beasts!' she muttered. 'Mean, evil beasts!' She seethed at the fact that they were making plans and talking about her like that after all the work she had done for them, each morning sitting the little kids on pots which she then had the dirty job of emptying. Blast them! Who wanted to see the old man anyway? Hadn't he been the cause of her getting shut up in here in the first place?

Several girls wandered past, talking and giggling with each other. As Sue stared scornfully at them, her angry scowl centred on one child in particular, a dainty, pretty girl with long flaxen curls. 'That stuck-up Lily Davies, I'll give her a bashing,' muttered Sue. And without warning, she pounced, grabbing those silken tresses and viciously punching the other child. The two girls rolled over and over on the green lawn scratching and biting between shrill screaming. Other children ran quickly to the house. 'Miss! Miss!' they called. 'Come quick, Sue's hurting Lily Davies again.'

A few minutes later, Sue stood defiantly before the shocked matron. And as Miss Woodcote's car left the drive, Sue was marched off for punishment.

At the age of thirteen, Sue was still living at Barham House. The head girl in a posh private school could not hold more sway than did Sue in this house for under-privileged children. After the departure of Miss Woodcote and the affair of Lily Davies, the sweet but firm matron, whose pink-and-white complexion could get extremely mottled in agitation, spoke kindly to this confused child and seemed to inspire her confidence. 'Promise me, dear,' she begged, 'you will never eavesdrop again. If there is anything that you want to know, come to me and we will discuss it together.'

Untouched, Sue had weighed her up. She was soft this one, she reflected. It wouldn't be hard to kid her. And with this thought, she appeared to give in gracefully.

Matron was sadly understaffed at the home. Sue was a strong girl, so it made good sense to give her some responsibility which would keep her occupied and out of trouble. 'I'll make you a monitor, Sue,' coaxed Matron. 'But you must promise that you will never again be violent as you were to Lily Davies.'

'Never liked her,' Sue replied flatly, sucking on the boiled sweet that Matron had given her.

'Well, Lily's gone home now, so that's the end of that,' sighed Matron, 'but please try and control your temper, Sue, or it will be the undoing of you.'

At night, Sue was dormitory monitor, mornings, she was baby

14

minder and in between she was Matron's pet. Naughty children were smacked or fussed as required. With her dark eyes always on the alert, Sue kept order and made herself very useful. She grew big and strong and very capable. That last year at Barham House proved to be the happiest of her youth. In spite of the monotony, the dreary, unchanging meals and long prayers, the baby washing and ironing, it had become part of her life. At last, Sue was completely institutionalized.

One sunny afternoon, as Sue sat in a window-seat munching an apple and gazing towards the main gate, the ramshackle taxi from the station pulled up in the drive. There was something vaguely familiar about the man who got out. He walked slowly as if in pain, and grasped a walking-stick to support him. Behind him emerged a plump peroxide blonde.

As she ate her apple, Sue surveyed them dreamily. She was quite unconcerned. They are probably some kid's parents coming to take her home, she decided, and she dismissed them from her mind.

Not long after, Matron hurried down the corridor with a flushed and anxious face. 'Sue!' she called, 'I'd like to talk to you.'

Casually, Sue got up from her seat and went into Matron's office. Just inside the door the cripple who had arrived in the taxi came towards her, hands outstretched. 'Sue! My dear little Sue!' he cried.

Sue looked down in horror at this shrivelled little man whom she recognized now as her own father. But he was not the tall good-looking father she had always remembered; instead, he was an aged and wrinkled wreck of a man. Matron put a steady arm about her as she backed away. 'These are your parents, Sue,' she explained gently. 'They've come to visit you.'

'We ain't come on no visit,' the blonde woman's loud grating voice broke in. 'We've come to take 'er 'ome.'

'Take me home?' gasped Sue. 'I live *here*. Anyway,' she added, giving an aggressive stare at the woman, 'who's she?'

'She's your new mother, Sue,' her father wheezed.

'I'm not going,' she declared obstinately, tossing back her head. 'I'm all right here.'

'But we've made a nice comfortable 'ome for yer,' her father begged. 'I want to make up for all the years you've 'ad to spend in this place.'

15

Matron had become slightly annoyed. She straightened her back even more than usual. 'I hope you have the necessary papers to take her away,' she said tersely. 'I will not let Sue go without the correct authorization.'

'Let's get it over,' said Sue's new stepmother, Lil, briskly. 'Here are the papers.' She thrust them in front of Matron. 'We can't afford to make this journey twice.'

In a flash, Sue made for the door. Matron did not try to stop her. She wanted time to try and reason with this dogmatic woman and her sick-looking husband. But it was hopeless. They were determined. 'Sue's a big girl, her father is sick and needs her,' insisted Lil. 'We'll take her home today. Get her things ready. We'll wait.'

Unable to do more, Matron packed Sue's few belongings in a plastic bag, consoling the girl with promises that she would do her best to get her back. Matron then accompanied them to the station to say goodbye. There were tears in her eyes. She had come to love this wayward child, and so the parting between them was not easy.

Wearing a long tweed coat, and a red ribbon in her hair, Sue sat in the corner of the train compartment scowling at her stepmother who nagged continuously. 'Think yourself lucky, my girl,' she said. 'There's plenty in that place would like to have a good home.'

Her father spoke seldom, but his face twisted constantly in pain. Sue sat motionless, her dark eyes gleaming such hatred that Lil began to get worried. She had not minded taking on an invalid husband, but she had not bargained for his difficult daughter as well. As the two surveyed each other, Sue wondered what had induced this cold, common woman to marry the hunched-up shell her father was. No doubt a fair nest-egg – the proceeds of the robbery that had destroyed his home and family – had been the bait.

Lil's home was in Camden Town. It was a small flat in a depressed area where a quarter of the population were immigrants. Sue's first impressions of her new home were lace curtains, paper roses, a plastic mat outside the door and the smell of furniture polish. And the moment she entered she felt depressed. When she met Lil's son, Tommy, a goofy, bespectacled boy of about twelve who stared mockingly at her old-fashioned coat and

16

the red ribbon bow on her hair, she disliked him on sight, and felt even gloomier. How was she going to survive here?

Sue tried desperately hard to acclimatize herself to her new family but she found that she hated Lil and Tommy increasingly each day, particularly since they did not bother to hide their own feelings about her. To her father she was kind and considerate. She took off his shoes for him at night and put them back on in the morning. With his dead weight on her arm, she escorted him to the paper shop every morning and to Mass on Sundays. While in prison, her father had taken up again with his religion, and since the onset of his illness, he had spent many hours on his knees with his rosary beads. Now Sue would kneel stolidly beside him in the church. The stained-glass windows and flickering candles cast golden light on the beautiful statues around them, and the atmosphere was one of peace and tranquillity. But none of this made any impression on Sue. Her mind would tick over as she made plans to escape from the domestic web she was caught in.

At her new school she was a problem. Sue had received very little education at Barham House. All the years of baby-minding and washing, added to the fact that she was word blind, made her unable to compete with children of her own age. So in the overcrowded secondary modern school where she had been sent, she was the tallest girl and the biggest dunce. It was not long before she had earned herself the nickname of 'Soppy Sue' from the other pupils because she was so slow to learn anything. Friendless and bored, Sue would sit at the back of the class casting malevolent glances about her at anyone who dared look at her. The teaching staff also disliked her, for she was always violent and every breaktime there was invariably a fight to break up which involved Soppy Sue.

Life had become a little better at home. Lil worked all day in a factory. Mondays, Wednesdays and Fridays were bingo nights when she would go out straight from work. On Tuesdays she would gather up a big bag of washing and dash out of the flat on the pretext of going down to the launderette. Then she would return after ten o'clock, always smelling of port wine. On Thurdays she did stay at home in the evenings. With her platinum hair-do bound up in a turban and her large frame covered with a spotted nylon overall, she would systematically clean the flat. She swept, dusted and polished every corner and woe betide anyone who got in her way. Red-faced, bad-tempered and perspiring Lil was always to be avoided on Thurdays. On these days, Sue wandered the streets and hung about at the corner of the streets or in the playground. The playground was a concrete square which swarmed with kids of every colour and creed. They all congregated there each evening, fighting to get places on the swings and roundabouts. 'Give us a push, Sue!' the younger children would cry out to her as she watched them from her position by the flower-beds. And because she had nothing else to do, she would obligingly push them high in the swing, ignoring the jeers from the girls of her own age who loudly chanted a street song, 'Look at Soppy Sue'. They stood in groups smoking cigarettes, wearing lipstick and high-heeled shoes as they chatted about sex and dating boys. But whenever Sue approached, all conversation ceased. 'Have to be careful of her,' they would murmur as they drifted off, 'she's not quite the ticket.'

Now nearly fourteen, Sue was a lonely and strangely naive girl, a square peg in a round hole in this working-class community. Her life was not made any easier by the persistent persecution of Tommy, her stepbrother, who, with his gang of mates, would follow her about calling, 'Ol' Soppy Sue! Ol' Soppy Sue!' Sue would turn on them and chase them so that they fled in all directions but she could never catch them. She was nearly always the last to leave the park before it closed because she was searching to get Tommy. With her hands in the pockets of her old-fashioned coat, and her dark hair hanging wildly, she did not make a pretty picture as she hid near the park keeper's hut hoping to pounce on that nasty boy.

The old park keeper had recently been replaced by a younger, ruddy-faced man in his thirties. This particular evening, Sue's dark eyes watched him as he stood in the doorway in his peaked cap and uniform munching a bar of chocolate. Sue was very fond of chocolate; few bars had ever found their way to Barham House. The park keeper noticed her looking hungrily at him. 'Want a piece?' he asked.

'Oh! yes please,' Sue replied, moving towards him. As he halved the bar, his bright blue eyes scrutinized her tight dress and the shape of her bud-like breasts. 'Better cut along home, your ma will be looking for you,' he said.

'I'll be lucky,' she said. 'She doesn't care.'

18

The young man moved closer to her, all sympathy as Sue told him of Barham House. He too had spent his youth locked away, so he knew what it was like. Sue was very happy to be able to talk to somebody else about her problems.

Next evening, the park keeper beckoned her to wait until all the kids had left the park. 'Got a big bar of Milk Tray in my hut,' he said casually.

The thought of this mouth-watering delicacy induced Sue to help him chase all the other kids out of the park, including Tommy, before joining her new-found friend in his little wooden hut.

She sat on the table with her legs wide apart as he shut the door. 'Come on, part up,' she said eagerly. She held out her hand expectantly, unperturbed by the fact that he had taken off his peaked cap, to reveal a semi-bald pate, or that his eyes shone with extraordinary brilliance or that his breathing was short and heavy. All she thought about was that much-fancied bar of chocolate. He approached her, holding the packet up high. 'Here you are, Sue, see if you can reach it,' he said coaxingly. And as she leaned back, reaching out for that prize, he pressed himself close to her.

Eagerly she grabbed the sweet, tearing off the tin-foil wrapping, and biting into the soft brown bar. 'Want some?' she asked, her mouth full.

'No,' he said. His voice was thick and muffled as he fiddled with his clothes. 'Shall I tickle you, Sue?' he muttered as his hand crept up her skirt. Sue hardly heard him as she munched her feast of chocolate. 'Like this . . .' he gasped, his hand fondling her soft flesh.

'Scrumptious,' nodded Sue, relishing the sweet flavour of the bar. She had now realized that he was lying almost on top of her and was quite agitated but she was not sure that she minded or was bothered. 'Come on, Sue,' he urged. 'Lift up your skirt. You show me and I'll show you.' He exposed himself to her and, for a few moments, she gazed dispassionately at this display of hair and flesh.

Suddenly, over the top of the door, Tommy's grubby face appeared. 'Yah!' he yelled. 'I can see yer.' Then he dropped out of sight and fled.

Immediately, the keeper leapt back and grabbed his trousers.

'Get out of here, you little slut!' he yelled at Sue. 'Get out!'

'Don't do your nut,' returned Sue calmly, and, cool as cucumber, she slid off the table.

'Get out of here!' he screeched, 'and if you tell anyone, I'll slit your throat, you dirty bitch!' Nonchalantly, Sue drifted out the door, licking the final traces of chocolate from her lips. She took her time walking home, and was surprised to be met by an irate band of local residents led by Lil who was brandishing a poker.

'You ain't 'alf gonna cop it,' yelled Tommy as he dashed past.

Lil caught Sue firmly by the arm. 'Come on, my girl, we'll deal with that dirty bugger first, and then I'll settle with you.'

The angry crowd moved on down to the park where the keeper was duly beaten up and only saved from a worse fate by being arrested by the police. Sue herself was soon placed under the care and protection of the state once more.

There followed the trial in the magistrate's court during which the nice young probation officer had described those sordid moments in the hut in such a nice manner. Sue had almost laughed aloud to hear the words, uttered so precisely: 'He said that if she would show her private parts he would show his private parts . . .'

The old magistrate had stared at the prisoner in disgust.

'The defendant is suffering from diminished responsibility,' pleaded his counsel. 'He has been in the care of the state for many years. This child is very precocious, and she clearly encouraged him.'

So it went on, like a game of tennis, with volley after volley of disgusting evidence. And Sue did not strengthen her case by telling the court that she did not mind being tickled.

At the end of it all, the park keeper was sent to a mental institution for treatment, and Sue, whose interests were taken up by the Roman Catholic priest who argued that an approved school would do her more harm than good, was to be sent to the convent where a watchful eye would be kept on her until she reached a more sensible age.

Thus our erring young delinquent was to find herself at St Augustine's Convent. When Sister Agnes came to collect her, her mild manner and sweet gentle face had not the slightest effect on Sue. The harassed nun had not relished the task of separating a young girl from her family and had been expecting a scene. She was surprised. With a white face and hard eyes Sue stood by the door waiting for her. She was still wearing the old tweed coat that Barham House had furnished her with, and a small suitcase lay at her feet. 'Come on, Sister, let's get it over with,' Sue said abruptly as the nun arrived. 'I'm ready.'

The gentle sister looked for signs of tears, but the dark, inscrutable eyes stared back at her with no display of emotion at all. In the armchair by the fire, her father wept copious tears of self-pity, while behind him, with arms akimbo, his large spouse waited for Sue to leave. 'Sexy bitch,' she had declared earlier. 'Never will be any good, and I've my Tommy to think of.'

'Goodbye, Susan,' she now said firmly and with no warmth in her voice.

'Why don't you say what you mean?' sneered Sue. 'Good riddance would be more like it.'

As Lil paled and Tommy sniggered, the sister hurriedly drew her cloak about her. 'Come along, my dear,' she said kindly and ushered Sue away.

Even from the beginning, the convent was a let-down to Sue. She had eagerly left the unsympathetic atmosphere of Lil's poky flat, dreaming of warmth and affection, and the green fields and good, if dreary, food of Barham House. The convent, she thought, would be like that. But as they entered the iron gates of St Augustine's, her heart gave a leap and she had an almost over-powering desire to turn and run out again. It was too late. The gates closed with an ominous clang which made her shudder. But she kept on walking, keeping in step with the sprightly Sister Agnes in her long flowing robes.

She followed the nun through long cold corridors, past dark alcoves from which small statues peered, and the huge pictures of the blood-streaked face of Our Lord, which adorned the walls. They meant nothing to her; the disturbed mind of this child was not to find the peace and sanctity that the other inhabitants shared within these pious walls.

They entered the great dining hall as tea was being eaten. Sue was sat on a bench where she gulped down weak tea and ate bread and jam while she surveyed those around her who were to be her companions for the next two years. They were mostly Mongol children whom no one had wanted, and who had now grown old. With their little short bodies and fuzzy heads, they were unwanted humans, pushed out of sight by families who were ashamed of them.

Sue looked fearfully at them as they stared inquisitively at her. Her tall, well-proportioned body, seemed completely out of place amid this flotsam and jetsam of humanity who acted still as if they were little children. Sue recoiled in horror at the sight around her; it was almost too much to bear. But Sister Agnes placed a cool hand in hers. 'Come now, Sue, come and meet our girls. And don't look like that. They're not monsters, you know. You will find them all intelligent, warm and very loving.'

But Sue could not move. She remained rooted to the spot, staring still in shock, so the kind nun left her alone and went off laughing with her little people as they left the dining hall.

Sue sat on a seat in the empty hall, feeling very alone and very forlorn and wondering how she might escape this terrible place.

It was at that moment that Gladys appeared. Very self-important, she came into the hall pushing along a large bath chair which contained a pale, shrivelled shape of a fair young girl. Gladys stopped directly level with Sue. 'Brought any goodies in with you?' she enquired.

'If you mean sweets, no, I did not,' replied Sue with open hostility.

'All right,' said Gladys, 'keep your shirt on, I only asked. It's not so bad in here, you know,' she said conversationally. Sue did not reply.

'Oh,' said Gladys wisely, 'I know what you're thinking, but I'll tell you, we ain't all as potty as we look.'

This comical remark suddenly made Sue relax. She laughed and Gladys laughed, so they both laughed until tears ran down their faces. And so began the precious, life-long friendship between Gladys and Sue.

Chapter Two

Convent Girls

Slowly but surely the convent disciplined Sue as no place had ever been able to do before. At first there were periods of disobedience and the aftermath of punishment. A wet towel was bound over her face to prevent her blaspheming; she was subjected to a solitary cell and a diet of bread and water for refusing to complete her chores; and she spent many hours of penance, kneeling beside stout Sister Winifred until her knees were stiff and sore. But she was young and hardy, and she survived, especially since she had her new friend Gladys there to share her sorrow or joy.

It did not take long for Sue and Gladys to become a team; they were hand in glove in all the little conspiracies that took place in the convent. For although Gladys always managed to keep out of trouble, craftily and steadfastly, she had broken every rule in that tightly run establishment. They shared a dormitory with several epileptic girls who occasionally brought added excitement to the nights by throwing fits, as did two little midget sisters who constantly fought each other tooth and nail. Gladys and Sue would urge them on to fight and then sit back to watch them struggling with each other stripped to the waist, their dried-up breasts swinging from their brown-skinned bodies. The sisters would wrestle and fight, kicking each other with little bandy legs, until they had become so excited that Sue and Gladys would smother them with pillows and sit on them until they had cooled down again. After a morning filled with prayer and schooling, and an afternoon spent studying in the steaming laundry washing clothes, this macabre fun provided relief for the girls. And so they managed to create a fairly reasonable existence for themselves.

Time rolled by, and soon Sue was sixteen. She had a tall and upright figure and in a loud and vibrant voice, she bullied her less capable inmates into shape. As in the children's home, Sue had established herself in a position of trust. The nuns had soon discovered that she was willing and very hard working, but part of her popularity came from her strong, pure singing voice. Sue could not read a word of Latin – it was unintelligible language to her – but the words she learnt by ear came from her long white throat in sweet, clear notes that were greatly appreciated by the nuns and priests of St Augustine's.

Every morning at nine o'clock, Sue marshalled her squad of inmates, all dressed in striped cotton frocks, into the front row of the church. The children who attended the day school would laugh at the sight, and sit whispering and giggling at this queer assortment of females, whose heads were too large, and whose bodies were warped and misshapen. Some would not sit still, some twisted and turned uncontrollably, some rolled their eyes to Heaven. But on the first note of the organ their silver voices were raised up in praise of the Lord and rang through the church. All who heard them were spellbound. The Silly Girls Choir, as the congregation called it, had become the most magnificent in the district. They received invitations to sing in other places of worship, and once they even went to perform in Westminster Cathedral. As leader of the choir, Sue enjoyed this notoriety and the extra luxuries it brought – sweets and fruit, occasionally even cinema tickets.

That Sue was very capable there was no doubt. And some were misled by her apparent good behaviour. 'You can never tell,' remarked Mother Theresa to Sister Winifred, 'Sue may even get a vocation to stay within the Church before she is eighteen.'

Slightly more worldly, Sister Winifred only sniffed and ran her beads through her fingers as she muttered a prayer.

'Yes, Sue has settled in nicely,' continued Mother Superior. 'And no one seems to want her. I heard from Father Paul that her father has entered the hospital for the dying, poor man. Yes, I shall definitely ask for Sue to stay on. I'll write to her probation officer today . . .'

As her future was being discussed, Sue had other things on her mind. She was in the hot, steamy laundry with her pal Gladys, sorting through a basket of old clothes the nuns had collected. Everything in it had to be repaired, washed and ironed, and then distributed to charity. With her head bent, she whispered down to the sphinx-like Gladys beside her, 'I'm going to get myself a fella,' she said in a mysterious tone.

Unmoved, Gladys held up an old dress for inspection. 'How're

24

you going to manage that?' she whispered in reply.

'On Saturday, when we go to the pictures,' returned Sue. 'I've seen one I fancy.'

Now Gladys looked slightly astonished but went on rummaging through the clothes basket. If Sue said something was so, it was no use arguing.

Every Saturday afternoon, Sister Agnes escorted a small party of girls to the corner of the road where the cinema was situated. Sue was in charge of this favoured group and, of course, it always included her friend Gladys and various inmates who happened to be in her good books that week. The local people out shopping often stopped to stare as they passed by. They did make quite a sight, with Sue striding along in front, her long, shapeless cotton dress billowing out behind her like a ship in full sail, followed by the crippled ones who were helped on by Gladys. 'She looks sane enough,' people would remark, looking at Sue. 'But she would not be in there if she was all right, I suppose,' they would add. And Sue would pass them by after giving them a long, enigmatic look from those compelling dark eyes that were reminiscent of the Mona Lisa.

Three doors from the cinema was a musical instrument shop. Highly coloured posters and odd instruments adorned the windows but outside the door, always in the same spot, lounged a young man. He wore a dull red shirt and had long flowing hair. Tiny wisps stuck out on his cheeks as he tried in vain to grow a beard. He would puff surreptitiously on a strangely shaped cigarette, holding it behind his back as people passed by, and stare nonchalantly at the Saturday shopping throng in the street. He never noticed the convent girls go by because his mind was on another plan.

'That's me fella,' whispered Sue to Gladys. 'Ain't he smashing?'

Gladys squinted in his direction but said nothing. She seldom agreed or disagreed with Sue.

'Once we get in the cinema, I'm bunking out again,' Sue continued. 'I'll leave you in charge and I'll bring you back a comic,' she promised.

Gladys' deep-set eyes gleamed. 'Make it a horror comic – *Spiderman* or *Batman*,' she said excitedly. If there was one dark obsession in her life, it was for horror comics. Gladys could not read but she would sit staring wide-eyed at the lurid pictures, usually in the privacy of the toilet.

'Right, then,' said Sue, 'I'll pretend to go to the lav. Don't make no fuss, and I'll meet you outside if I can't get back in.'

Once the girls were settled down and engrossed in the film, Sue sneaked out. But once she was outside, all alone in the bright sunlight, her boldness momentarily left her. Pulling herself up sharply she plucked up her courage and walked with her hips swinging to where the young man stood propped up against the doorway. Although she was trembling a little, as she got near, she gave him a provocative smile.

The young man did not seem to notice her. He continued to stare at the passing traffic as though she were not there. She turned and came back, trying the same approach once more with a sweet smile on her lips. But still there was no response. Finally, she stopped right next to him and pretended to look in the shop window, and in a last desperate effort, she smiled right into his face.

The effect was startling. 'Scram, floozie!' he snarled. 'Get going!'

When Sue did not move, he rushed inside the shop and slammed the door.

With tear-filled eyes, Sue wandered off down the street and went in through the glazed swing doors of Woolworths. There she went slowly around the counters, admiring all the pretty things on display. And before she left, she managed to purloin a brightly coloured slide for her hair and a very horrid comic for Gladys.

After taking a good look at herself in a full-length mirror as she came out of the shop, she returned forlornly to the cinema.

It was not until the girls had all rejoined Sister Agnes on the corner and were returning to the convent that Gladys hung behind to talk to Sue. 'How did you get on?' she asked anxiously.

Sue shook her head sadly. 'He wouldn't even look at me,' she said. Gladys' dark, parchment-like face screwed up in grief. 'It's all right, I got your comic, if that is what's bothering you,' Sue retorted angrily. She deftly passed the stolen comic to her pal who immediately shoved it down her neck. 'He is so lovely,' sighed Sue. 'I'm mad about him, but have you seen what we look like in these frumpy old dresses? I can't blame him not talking to me, a

26

smart fella like that. I look about forty in this outfit. I'm going to get myself some good gear from somewhere – he might fancy me then.'

Gladys squeezed Sue's hand sympathetically. 'Hope you get a fella, Sue,' she said.

After that disappointing adventure out into the world, Sue was determined to try once more. She had to get herself a fella at all cost. Had she not boasted to the other girls that she would? The following evening she sat up in bed chewing her fingernails. All day she had been moody, and overwhelmed by a kind of melancholy that often obsessed her. She had viciously pinched the arm of one of the midgets until it was black and blue, and she had even struck out at Gladys, who fortunately seemed to be made of wood and was never hurt by blows. Besides, she was too intent at goggling at her comic under the bedclothes, while the little midget cuddled up to her, whimpering pathetically and cried herself to sleep.

Immune from all this, Sue leaned against her pillow, carefully planning how to obtain a wardrobe of with-it gear – a bright, tight jumper and a mini skirt. 'I've got it!' she suddenly yelled. 'I'll pinch some of the clothes from the stuff Sister Agnes collects on her scrounging afternoons.'

'But that's all so old-fashioned,' declared Gladys momentarily looking up from her comic.

'That don't matter,' replied Sue, leaping to her feet. 'We'll alter them. The midgets can sew.'

A long plaid skirt was quickly filched from the jumble basket and soon much shortened by the midgets whose keen eyes and nimble fingers could do wonders with a needle and thread. And then the sleeves were removed from a white silk jumper that Sue had also pinched from the laundry. At last, on Friday night, Sue paraded up and down the dormitory wearing her new outfit. No high-class Parisian model had ever moved more gracefully than she nor delighted her audience more. And what a sight she was, with a tall, willowy figure, dark hair to her waist, long slim legs that tapered from the short, tight skirt, and her two pointed breasts sticking out stiffly from under the skimpy white jumper. The midgets, Tilly and Milly, jumped up and down with glee but Gladys looked slightly sceptical.

'What's up with you? Don't you like it?' demanded Sue.

27

Gladys looked down critically at the white ankle socks the convent had provided and the baggy washed-out bloomers that hung two inches below the skirt. 'It's all right, Sue,' she replied timidly, 'but I don't like them drawers hanging down and you ain't got no stockings.'

Tears of mortification filled Sue's eyes. Gladys was right. You can't wear a mini skirt with baggy bloomers.

'Cut them short,' suggested Milly, eager to help in spite of the way Sue bullied them all.

'I got a piece of lace to sew on them,' cried Tilly.

So the bags were cut short and trimmed with lace, and the decision was made not to wear socks. 'You've got such lovely legs, Sue,' the midget said looking up admiringly from their four feet height to Sue's five feet ten. At last next Saturday's going-out attire was complete. And although the bloomers did not fit exactly underneath, Sue was not worried as long as they did not show.

Saturday was a hot, sunny day. As the convent girls lined up ready for their outing to the cinema, Sister Agnes' face was hot and flushed. It was hard work assembling these afflicted young women, for the least bit of excitement triggered off fits and bursts of disobedience. And Sue, who was usually so dependable, seemed preoccupied today. Tucked into the girl's bodice was a paper parcel and over her arm she carried a raincoat. 'That raincoat won't be needed, Sue,' the harassed sister told her.

'It might rain,' Sue muttered sullenly.

'Nonsense, with all God's beautiful sunshine out there? Take the coat back!' urged the nun. But Sue stuck out her chin in her obstinate manner. Sister Agnes sighed. It was hopeless to argue with Sue. At last she gave the sign for the procession to move out.

Soon the girls were all seated in the second row of the flicks, having left Sister Agnes at the bus-stop, from where she went about her charity work until they came out of the cinema. Sue retired to the Ladies to dress up in her new clothes, and then walked out of the front entrance towards the busy shopping centre. As she approached the music shop, her heart missed a beat. He was not there! Her lovely young man with the red shirt and curly side whiskers had disappeared. Tears came into her eyes. She was so disappointed; all this finery was wasted.

Slowly she trailed down the road in the direction of

Woolworths, admiring herself in the shop windows as she passed. Once inside the store, she went from counter to counter, turning over the merchandise. It was the make-up that attracted her most, for she felt a deep envy towards all those teenagers who wore owl-like expressions on their faces, their eyes weighed down with false eyelashes, shadow and mascara. To use make-up was her next ambition. Swiftly, she picked up a small box of eye make-up and slipped it into the pocket of the raincoat she carried over her arm. Then she leaned forward to examine more closely the long sticks of eye-liner. Her tall shape bent like a tree in the wind, exposing long bare legs and pink baggy bloomers.

A young man was wandering nonchalantly around the store, his hands in the pockets of stained jeans, a grubby red shirt open at the neck. When he was level with Sue he suddenly stopped and stared with horror at the long bare legs and baggy pants before him. And then the sleepy eyes showed an added glimmer of interest as Sue expertly passed the long stick of eye-liner into the raincoat pocket to join the other articles she had pinched. He shuffled up close to her. 'Hi, droopy drawers,' he hissed. 'I saw you nick that.'

Sue stiffened in fear but did not panic. Drawing herself up to her full height she turned to face him. 'What are you going to do about it?' she demanded. As the words left her mouth, she saw that confronting her was the lovely young man who usually held up the music shop window. She swallowed hard and her breath came in little gasps as she looked down at him.

The youth stared back at her and grinned appreciatively at the pointed breasts sticking out so defiantly from under the jumper. After a moment of tension, he winked and nudged her with his elbow. 'Come on, kid,' he said casually, 'walk about a bit, yer never know who's watching.'

Obediently, she stepped out beside him and they walked round the store. He was called Roger, he told her, and he seemed to be in a chatty mood this afternoon. 'Cripes,' he said, 'you don't 'alf look quaint with those bags hanging down.'

'Don't be so cheeky,' replied Sue, blushing scarlet with shame.

'Better go over there and nick a pair of tights,' he suggested. 'Might make yer look a bit more presentable.'

Sue stared back at him in astonishment, dumbfounded by this immoral young man who not only made rude comments about her mode of dress but also encouraged her to steal. Whatever would Sister Agnes think of him? But having acquired a fella at last, she was not going to argue with him. 'Will a pair of stockings do just as well?' she asked timidly.

'Gawd, gel!' he scoffed. 'Where have you been? None of the birds wear stockings now. It's all tights.'

Sue remained silent. No one was going to know that she came from that crummy convent. Swiftly she pocketed some black silk tights.

'Got me own group,' boasted Roger. Then he added, 'Come round to me pad and I'll help you put on them tights.' He raised his eyebrows and sniggered but Sue did not notice. So she went with him like a lamb to the slaughter. Having worked so hard to acquire him, this smart young lad, she did not want to upset him.

Roger's pad proved to be rather like himself – dingy and slightly mucky. It was a small dusty room over a shop and contained an old piano and a battered camp bed. Records littered the floor and lurid pop posters adorned the wall.

Sue and Roger sat side by side on the sagging bed. Each time they moved, the smell of stale body odour rose from the bedclothes. Sue sniffed and rubbed her nose disdainfully but kept her mind fixed on pasty-faced Roger who was now lolling back on the bed smoking one of those long cigarettes. 'Got to have a couple of puffs to get me going,' he explained.

Knowing nothing of the intricacies of pot smoking, Sue did not know what he was talking about. All she wanted was to kiss and cuddle this gorgeous young man, which she then proceeded to do.

Roger was astounded at the warmth and ardour of her embrace. 'Here, cool it,' he protested. 'Wait till I've finished me joint.' But Sue pressed him down tight, put hot lips on his and held him down with the weight of her strong body. What happened next was to be expected, but in the middle of it Sue suddenly caught a glimpse of his watch. In horror, she leaped off the bed and charged towards the door clutching those precious tights, still unopened, in her hand. 'I've gotta go,' she yelled, and then she disappeared, leaving Roger lying on the bed with his trousers down and his mouth wide open.

Back at the cinema, Sue just managed to get into the Ladies to change her clothes and emerge as the bewildered Gladys came out into the foyer with the other convent girls. Gladys was looking worried. 'Oh, Sue! There you are. I was getting scared,' she gasped with relief.

'What of?' shrugged Sue with a prodigious wink. 'I was only in the lav.'

And Gladys knew that Sue had at last got a fella. But later that night in the dorm, she sat in bed and howled because in all the excitement Sue had forgotten to bring her a comic. However, she was soon consoled by hearing the long and vivid story of Sue's romance with Roger. With her eyes goggling with pleasure she listened to all the lurid details. 'Didn't ought to have done that, Sue,' she said. 'If you get a baby they won't keep you here.'

'Oh, well,' retorted Sue defiantly, 'that's one way of getting out of this gloomy hole.'

Chapter Three

The Pedlar

All the next week, although the cold grey walls of the convent school closed her in, in her heart Sue was free. She felt as light as air and bounded about the place like a young deer. She was in such an obliging mood and was so unusually pleasant to the other inmates that Sister Winifred watched her with the utmost suspicion. And there was a moment during choir practice, when Sister Agnes' neat eyebrows shot up in astonishment as Sue's loud sweet voice trilled high during a litany. Instead of three *Ave Marias*, the words that came from Sue's throat as she sang solo, were: 'I love you, I love you dear Roger.'

Soon Saturday came round again and the little crocodile of girls wended its way past the music shop. Not wanting Roger to see her with this bunch of idiots, Sue hung her head and turned away. But from the corner of her eye, she saw that he seemed preoccupied, his face pale and twitching, as he stood biting his fingers, and she wondered what was wrong.

It was not long before Sue emerged again from the Ladies in the cinema all dressed up in her short plaid skirt and very becoming black silk tights. Her dark hair, shining with brilliantine, hung free down her back, pulled away behind her ear by a little slide. Her eyes were enhanced by shadow and mascara and a line of lipstick coloured her lips. There was little now to link Sue with the convent. She just looked like a typical teenager out on a Saturday afternoon spree. Only her long strides and awkward boyish gait were likely to betray her.

'Buzz off!' snarled Roger as she approached.

Sue frowned in puzzlement. 'But, Roger, darling, I'm your girlfriend,' she pleaded.

'Some girlfriend,' he sneered, 'running off and leaving me like that.'

But Sue moved closer and put her arms about him. 'I'm sorry about that,' she lied. 'But I had to get back to work.'

'Work? What work?' Roger stared suspiciously at her.

'I'm up at the hospital,' she continued in a very convincing tone. 'They're very strict if you go late on duty.' She had acquired this information from a novice nun who had once been a nurse, and it seemed to satisfy Roger.

They walked to Roger's place in silence; he still seemed to be a trifle on edge. And something about his pad was different this week, Sue noticed: suitcases and musical instruments lay all around.

'The boys are back from Spain,' explained Roger.

Sue had removed her precious tights and was now looking up at him amorously.

'Turn it up,' he said. 'We ain't got time now. I've got to go out.' But Sue's kisses overwhelmed him. 'Okay,' he sighed. 'I'll do you a favour if you do me one. You let me down last week,' he grumbled. 'You said you had had a lot of fellas – I didn't know you was a rooky. I mighta got you in the club.'

But Sue was not even listening. 'Love me, Roger,' she whispered romantically, and in a passive sort of manner, he obliged.

'Hurry up,' he said afterwards as she slowly replaced her tights. 'I told you I gotta go out, didn't I?' From the end of the bed he had taken a bag. It had a long leather strap and was trimmed with a fringe. 'Come on, doll, move!' he said in an exasperated fashion, 'the boys will be back in a minute.'

'All right,' Sue replied sullenly, 'but I ain't got to go to work yet for another hour.'

Roger bit his lip and looked at her thoughtfully with half-shut eyes. 'You can come with me if you like,' he said finally. 'Up London on the tube.'

'Will it take long?' she asked with much interest. She had never been to the West End or on a tube.

'Twenty minutes, that's all,' replied Roger.

And so, an eager Sue went with Roger on that exciting ride up town on the tube with dodgy Roger, the drug pusher.

At the end of the cinema programme, Gladys came out of the cinema with the girls in her charge and waited anxiously for Sue. She was determined to get her comic this time and had warned Sue not to forget. As the girls waited outside the cinema, Sister Agnes waited anxiously for them at the bus stop. Soon some of the younger girls became frightened and began to cry. Gladys raved at them impatiently and punched them in the way Sue

33

usually did. Then the manager of the cinema came out to quell the disturbance, and rang Mother Superior, at the convent. Eventually, the little group had been reunited with Sister Agnes and returned to the sanctity of their home once more. Once Sue's absence had been noticed, the police were immediately notified.

While all the commotion went on back at the convent, Sue sat proudly beside her fella in the tube as it sped to the centre of London. Excitedly, she looked all around her – up at the coloured advertisements on the walls, across at the other passengers and down at her long, slim legs. She was having a whale of a time! The recurring dream she had had for so long, of being all dressed up in modern gear and out with a smart young man, was all happening. To hell with the convent! Time was passing on golden wings . . .

Beside her, Roger sat silent and upright, clutching his shoulder bag. He chewed his fingernails nervously and seemed to have little to say. But Sue was too happy to mind.

At Oxford Circus they got off the tube and stepped out into the back streets of Soho. Their first stop was a dimly lit coffee bar where crowds of young people sat about listening to loud pop music. Sue could hardly contain herself; her head spun, it was all so exciting.

They ordered two coffees and sat down. Another young man joined them, and Roger removed a small silver packet from his shoulder bag and passed it under the table. Some crisp bank notes were passed back in exchange. Without a word, the strange young man then left.

Sue sipped the milky coffee and tapped her feet to the rhythm of the music. The transactions going on at the table were incomprehensible to her. Next, they moved outside to meet two women standing on a corner. Each of these took a silver packet, and more pound notes were stuffed into the bag. After a while, Roger seemed to get very edgy. 'Listen, doll,' he said. 'Take this bag and go and sit down in the tube station. Don't move, I'll send some people who will say, "Got the stuff Roger sent me?" '

Sue listened, wide-eyed. 'I ought to go to work,' she murmured.

'Never mind that rotten job,' snapped Roger. 'Help me get rid of this cabbage and we'll have a good time.'

Sue did not want to argue, so she took the bag obediently, went into the station and seated herself down on a platform bench. Soon a thin, weedy-looking man whose face was all twisted on one side, approached her. 'Got the stuff?' he hissed. 'Roger sent me.'

Sue handed him a silver packet, took the fiver he gave her and put it in the bag.

Next came a blonde woman with a hard, haggard face. 'Okay, duck,' she said, 'Roger sent me.'

Sue handed out the last packet to her and put the money in the bag. Then she sat waiting for Roger to appear. There was still no sign of him. Then, just as a train came swishing in to the station, Roger came rushing down the stairs. His face was deathly white as he snatched the shoulder bag from Sue's arm and jumped aboard the train as the doors were closing. 'Scram, you silly cow!' he called to her. 'Old Bill's after us.'

Sue stood on the platform looking puzzled for a moment, and then she let out a heart-broken wail. 'Roger, wait for me!'

As the train started to move out of the station, two broad-shouldered men ran down the stairs and shouted to the guard to stop the train. But it was too late. The guard did not hear, and the train was soon gone.

Sue suddenly felt a cold clammy feeling of fear creep through her. She had never experienced it before, and she shuddered. The police were after her! With a swift movement she turned and dashed into the ladies' cloakroom, her face ashen, her dark eyes wide with fear. Inside she found the hard-faced blonde, who was just rolling down her sleeve and was about to wash her hands. 'Christ, I needed that fix,' the woman said on seeing Sue. 'I was all in.' She stared at Sue for a moment and immediately recognized the look on the girl's face. Without a moment's hesitation, she grabbed Sue by the elbow. 'Keep calm, kid!' she hissed, handing Sue her coat and a flowered scarf. 'Run in the lav, quick, and pop these on. Then walk out of here coolly and calmly. Don't matter what's going on, take no notice. I'll meet you round the back of the station.'

As Sue took the clothes, Elsie turned back to the mirror and slowly put on a layer of scarlet lipstick over the loose-lipped mouth. 'Bet yer life they sent for the blue-bottles. But don't you worry,' she reassured the terrified girl, 'I'll handle them, I'm used to it.'

Inside the toilet, Sue squeezed into the tight coat and tied the scarf over her hair. Her hands were shaking and she could hardly stand up because her knees were trembling so much. She emerged from the cubicle and made for the door. Elsie was still at the mirror and winked as she passed by.

Sue walked out of the cloakroom, along the platform and then slowly up the stairs to freedom.

Two young policewomen ran past without giving her a glance, hurrying to apprehend Dodgy Roger's female accomplice. But they were to be disappointed, finding only a screeching, swearing prostitute in the ladies' cloakroom. 'I'm no bloody pusher,' Elsie shouted at them. 'If you want any information, you'll have to take me in!' The policewomen did not bother to arrest her. Elsie was too well known to them, but she managed to hold their attention until Sue was safely out of the station.

Sue stood shivering in the doorway of the shop that Elsie told her to go to for what seemed ages. Next door to a dingy bookshop there was an antique stall with a display of all sorts of bric-ßa-brac. The fat, sweaty man in charge of the stall stared at her suspiciously, but then he said, 'Waiting for Elsie?' Sue nodded. 'Pop inside, then,' he said, pointing to another doorway under a porch. 'I'll nark out, and tell yer when I see her coming.'

Standing out of sight from the street, Sue looked at the various postcards pinned on the door. One of them informed her that Elsie lived on the third floor and was a model. The first and second floors seemed to be inhabited by models, one of whom was French. Sue surveyed the notices with interest. It must be nice to be a model, she reflected . . .

At last Elsie came tripping along with a sheepish-looking young man. 'Thanks, Sam,' she said to the stallkeeper when she saw Sue waiting in the porch. 'Come on, love, let's go up.'

They climbed the stairs to the third floor, and Sue was thrilled to see Elsie's cosy flat with its pink divan and frilly curtains. She had never seen anything so beautiful.

'Pop in there and make a cup of tea, love,' said Elsie pointing to a small kitchen. 'I won't be long.' She unzipped her dress as she spoke. 'Won't be a tick,' she said pleasantly, closing the bedroom door on herself and her melancholy manfriend.

In the neat tiny kitchen, Sue began to make the tea. The kettle had just boiled and tea leaves were in the pot when Elsie

36

reappeared from the bedroom, now wearing a long housecoat. Sue heard the front door slam as the visitor left.

'That was a bit of luck,' remarked Elsie, slipping a pound note into the top of her bra. 'Now, let's have a cuppa.'

Sue sat silently sipping her hot mug of tea and watching Elsie deftly butter the bread, put thin slices of luncheon meat between them and cut them into neat triangles. Elsie's square white hands were loaded with cheap rings which hovered like butterflies as she arranged the sandwiches on to a plate. She chattered all the time. 'I'm on the game, love,' she said, 'but I expect you've already sussed that.' She gave Sue a cheeky grin from her lopsided mouth.

Sue stared at her and thought vaguely that Elsie was not such a bad-looking woman. With her brassy blonde hair and neat shape, it did not seem possible that she was a street woman – one that took money for sex. She knew about that sort of thing; she had often talked it over with Gladys.

Elsie screwed up her eyes and peered straight into Sue's face. 'You all right, love?' she asked. 'On the stuff, are you?'

'No I'm all right,' said Sue quickly, without understanding what Elsie had said. 'I was just thinking about Roger.'

'Oh, Dodgy Roger,' Elsie laughed. 'Well, don't love, because he'll soon forget you, I can tell you that now. He only used you, you know. I've seen plenty of his girlfriends come and go, I have.' She passed the plate. 'Here you are, love. Have a sandwich.'

As Sue took a sandwich and nibbled at it greedily, Elsie's shrewd gaze surveyed her. 'In spite of your size, you seem very green,' she commented. 'Where did Roger find you?'

'From the convent,' replied Sue without thinking, relishing her sandwich.

'Oh, dear,' giggled Elsie. 'You must be joking . . . Fancy getting mixed up with that little swine.'

Sue frowned at her, offended. 'He's my boyfriend,' she insisted. 'I'm very much in love with him.'

This last remark seemed to annoy Elsie who suddenly became extremely aggressive. Banging her plate down hard on the table, she shouted, 'Don't give me that! I'm a whore and I know exactly how much a man is prepared to pay for it and how bloody easy they get over it.'

Sue's sandwich stopped half-way to her mouth and she looked at her, horrified. Elsie stamped her feet and yelled, pointing to the scar on her face, 'Look at me! See my bloody face? Chivved me, he did. Me own old man did that. Oh, yes, I could tell you a thing or two, ducky.' Then suddenly, Elsie put her head down on the table and wept noisily.

Sue moved over to her and touched her arm. 'I'm sorry I upset you,' she said gently. 'I'll go now.'

But Elsie caught hold of her hand. 'No, don't go, love, it's me, not you. I'm a bleeding junkie, and that stuff don't seem to do much good lately. It wears off too quick.' She pointed to the cupboard. 'There's a bottle of gin over there, love, get it and we'll have a drink.'

And so, for a solid hour, Sue, who had never drunk or smoked before, imbibed gin and tonics and puffed cheap fags with Elsie the prostitute who, with hardly a pause, related the trials and errors of her life.

Sue was feeling very woozy and her head was nodding drowsily when Elsie finally said, 'Well, I'd better take a bath and get off. Got to get on me rounds. There's a camp bed in the cupboard,' she said. 'Get it out and kip down in the kitchen. The coppers might be around in this area looking for you tomorrow, and I'll be busy all night.'

It did not take long for Sue to stretch her long weary body on the camp bed. She slept like a log and did not hear a single sound as Elsie's customers went up and down the stairs all night.

Chapter Four

A Street in Soho

When Sue woke up the next morning, she sat up and looked around her. The surroundings were strange and unfamiliar. There was no fat nun ringing the bell to wake everybody up, no narrow white bed beside her with Gladys snoring like an old badger. No, she was in a modern, well-equipped kitchen and her feet were sticking out at the bottom of a small camp bed. She lay there for a while thinking over the events of the previous day, and then got up, found the tiny bathroom, washed and dressed and then returned to the kitchen where she made coffee. Carrying a cup to Elsie's bedroom, she tapped on the door.

'Who's that?' came a muffled voice from inside.

'It's me, Sue, I've brought you some coffee.'

'Come on in, love,' called Elsie. Sue entered the room which was dark because the curtains were still drawn. The air smelt of alcohol and stale cigarette smoke, and Elsie lay back on her large bed looking extremely dishevelled. 'Just what I could do with,' she sighed gratefully as she sipped the coffee. 'But I don't get up very early, love, so amuse yourself as you like. But be careful if you go out,' she warned. 'The cops are still looking for you.' She giggled. 'I expect they're digging up Epping Forest by now. They probably think you must have been done in.'

When Sue looked disturbed by her words, Elsie grinned. 'Don't worry, kid,' she said, 'they'll pick you up in the end so you might as well have a few days of freedom. Done a stretch in Holloway meself, I have – ain't got the heart to turn anyone in.' She handed Sue the empty coffee cup and turned over to sleep again. 'There's money in the kitchen cabinet,' she grunted. 'Get some fresh rolls. The other girls might want some jobs done, too. Keep busy, love, and give us a call about half two.'

Used to obeying commands, Sue washed the cups in the kitchen sink and found the silver coins hidden in an old teacup in the cabinet. Then she went downstairs, still undecided about whether to stay put or get the tube back to the convent.

The deserted early morning streets of Soho were heaven on earth to Sue, who had known so little freedom – even to walk about on her own. Clean morning air, sunshine and leisure. What else did anyone want? There was no fat nun to chase her down to the hot steamy laundry, no stinking kids to wash, no dirty jumble to sort out . . .

It was bliss. With Elsie's old-fashioned basket on her arm, she strolled slowly along the street. In her hand she clutched a big red purse that belonged to the Anglo-Indian prostitute who lived in the flat on the first floor. She was called Ida and had been very pleased when Sue offered to do some shopping for her, giving her a list and some money and instructing her to keep the change. Then there was money for whisky from Fat Florrie upstairs. 'Enjoy yourself,' she had declared. 'And don't hurry back, we like a good kip in the mornings.'

Sue strolled nonchalantly from baker shop to off-licence, eating a bar of chocolate here, a cream cake there. Then she bought a packet of her favourite chewing gum, her large red mouth now moved rhythmically as she chewed steadily and watched the streets filling up with life. Office workers dashed briskly from the tube station to disappear into the maze of back streets; flower stalls and newspaper stands appeared, their owners chatting noisily to each other on the street corners. Sue's dark eyes caught every detail, she was interested in everything as she dawdled along. Once, two women constables eyed her suspiciously causing a little tremor of fear to go through her as she thought of being hooked back to that gloomy convent. But to her relief, nothing happened.

After a few hours, she returned safely to the doorway of Elsie's building. The antique stall was now open with all the bric-à-brac laid out for inspection. Sam recognized her from the day before. He nodded his ugly mottled face and unsmilingly grunted a good morning to her as he polished a heavy Victorian vase. In the shop behind the stall, a shrivelled hook-nosed old crone pottered about. She wore a woolly hat and a long, rusty coloured cape. 'Hey!' she called to Sue, who hesitated in the doorway. 'You there, new gel. Mind you clean those bloody stairs – filthy they are!' she grumbled. Sue took one look at the witch-like creature and fled up the stairs to safety.

The women all were fast asleep but there was a plastic bag full of dirty washing outside Fat Florrie's door. Pinned to the bag was a note telling Sue to leave the whisky and fags there and asking her to take the washing to the launderette when she had time. Sue sniffed. 'Can't ever seem to get away from bloody dirty washing,' she grumbled to herself.

The weeks passed quickly as Sue shopped and fetched and carried for the ladies of the house. She scrubbed the rickety old stairs and polished the knocker and bell push until they shone like glass. And she was quite content to open and close for customers who came and went. The ladies had bought her a new green pinafore dress which made her feel very smart. Fat Florrie had also given her a whole caseful of jumpers that had got too small for her, and Ida had provided her with plenty of frilly underwear. Sue felt very pleased with herself. Even gruff old Sam and his grotesque mother had been kind to her – some old fashioned beads and a copper bracelet had come her way for little favours she did them. She would buy thick cough linctus from a special chemist for the old crone who was addicted to the stuff, or give an eye to the stall while Joe went off to put a bet on. All these tasks, Sue did with a willing obedience. 'She ain't saucy,' growled Sam approvingly to his old mother. 'Don't argue, neither, not like some of those bleeding kids we've had here.'

Institutional life had certainly made Sue disciplined, but a crafty shrewdness, probably inherited from her Cockney father, enabled her to agree with them all and take everything they offered her. For Sue had that inborn gift of being well able to feather her own nest.

The establishment did not always run smoothly. There was often trouble and then the East End boys who decorated the street corner had to be called in to sort it out. They were known as Sam's Boys and spent their days playing cards in the pub or cafe, or lolling on the street corner. But they were always handy. And thus this little community of vice somehow survived, progressed and lived comfortably.

It was not usually until about three o'clock that the first meal of the day was eaten. Elsie always emerged from her bed decidedly jaded and ill-tempered, but once she had had her fix and sipped a hot cup of tea, she would recover and entertain Sue with lively gossip about the night life of swinging London Town whose streets she roamed until dawn. 'The heat's off,' she declared one day to Sue. 'Been nothing about you this week in the paper or on the telly. They've put you down as missing. Forget all about you now, they will.'

Sue stopped pouring tea and looked surprised. 'Do you mean the police?' she asked hesitantly. 'That the police are no longer looking for me?'

'Oh, they're still looking for you all right,' replied Elsie, 'but they probably think you've been done in and are just waiting for your body to turn up.'

Sue was puzzled, and not at all sure that she liked the idea of being murdered. 'Does that mean I can go where I wish?' she asked.

'Well, I expect it'll be quite safe to move about a bit more, Sue,' said Elsie. 'But don't go too far, just down Oxford Street. And be wary, always remain stum, my love,' she placed her finger to the side of her nose.

With a long slim finger, Sue repeated the gesture, 'Stum,' she said, 'that's the word.'

The faded, sickly looking Elsie giggled and began to roll up her sleeve ready to inject the needle to give herself that ever-necessary fix. As always, Sue looked on in amazement. 'Run out now, I have,' Elsie said despondently as she withdrew the needle. 'I'll have to get some more from somewhere soon. It's a great pity that Dodgy Roger got nicked.'

'Can I go and get it for you?' asked Sue, anxious to help her friend.

'No, ducky,' replied Elsie. 'You got yourself in enough trouble getting mixed up with that bloody dope pedlar. You stay out of it now. Only wish I could meself,' she muttered gloomily.

That night Elsie was not her usual amiable self at all, and she fought and screamed with a drunken man she brought home, who called her a dirty whore and blacked her eye. Then Sam's Boys were quickly called. Sue got up from her camp bed in the kitchen to watch the rough and tumble on the stairs – three men rolling down them, swearing and fighting, while the women looked on screeching foul oaths. Sue watched it all dispassionately as if it were on a television screen.

Soon order had been restored. The man had been ejected into the street, Sam's Boys had returned to their haunts, and Elsie lay sobbing on her pink divan. Fat Florrie hovered over her, telling her in no uncertain terms of what she thought. 'If you don't lay off that bloody junk,' she castigated her, 'you'll land us all in Holloway . . .'

Long before dawn, Elsie pulled herself together and was out on the prowl again. She returned to the flat in the morning, jubilant and starry-eyed having managed to obtain a fix. 'Got a new contact,' she told Sue. 'Pity it's down in dockland, as I like to stay in me own district, now I ain't got Alfie to protect me.'

'Who's Alfie?' Sue enquired.

'He's me fella, used to live with him I did,' said Elsie with pride.

'Where did he go?' Sue persisted.

'Got his collar felt, poor Alfie,' Elsie replied mournfully.

Sue's pencilled brows shot up in surprise. 'Got what?' she laughed.

'Got collared, nicked, you silly cow!' cried Elsie irritably. 'Christ, you're proper green as bloody grass, you are, Sue. Don't know Stork from butter,' she grumbled.

Sue was anxious not to fall out with Elsie, so for once she backed down. 'I'm sorry,' she apologized. 'I only asked.'

'All right, love, take no notice of me,' said Elsie. 'I've got a lot on my mind just worrying about getting the stuff. Can't get on without it.'

'I'll come with you,' volunteered Sue. 'I'll protect you – look how strong I am.' She flexed her arm muscles.

Elsie hugged her kindly. 'You're a great kid,' she said. 'You never make a fuss and are afraid of no one. I'm getting real fond of you. Tell you what, we'll take a chance tonight. You can come down the Isle of Dogs with me.'

Sue was delighted. 'Oh, thanks, Elsie,' she cried. If she had been offered a free trip to the Riviera she could not have been more grateful – it was all one to her. The South of France or a dreary East End tavern, it made no difference, she had seen so little of the world outside.

Towards evening that day, Elsie seemed to become more agitated, and she wandered about the flat smoking incessantly. Her eyes had sunk into her head and the floppy white puffs of skin underneath them stood out more prominently than usual. Quietly observing Elsie's anguish, Sue wondered how old she was. She only confessed to being twenty-five but without make-up she looked at least thirty-five. In fact, Elsie's real age was twenty-eight but the hard drugs and corrupt life had already begun to take their toll.

Without comment, Sue continued with her chores in her calm efficient way. She ran a bubble bath for the distracted Elsie, and plied her with hot sweet tea.

'Crikey!' ejaculated Elsie as she sat in her bathrobe, her hands trembling as they clung to the mug of hot tea. 'I ain't 'alf got the shakes. Hope the fella turns up with the stuff tonight, otherwise I'm lumbered.'

Sue shrugged impatiently. 'Why do you have to take drugs!' she asked. 'Why can't you stop now?' Her darks eyes surveyed Elsie with a kind of sympathetic scorn.

'Oh, my God,' wailed Elsie. 'I wish I could kick it, Sue, but while I'm on the game it's impossible.'

'Sit still,' Sue told her contemptuously. 'I'll make up your eyes for you and do your hair.' She set at her tasks in a very skilled manner. Her cool firm hands held Elsie by the scraggy chin while she put on the bright eye-shadow, painted long black lines and applied false eyelashes. Then she took out the hair rollers and brushed the stiff pale-gold hair into position. Stepping back to survey her handiwork, she remarked, 'Ah, that's better. You look more like a human being now.'

'You're a smashing kid.' Elsie clutched Sue's hands impulsively but Sue pulled away quickly. Unused to such affection, it embarrassed her.

'I'll get myself ready now,' she said quickly. 'I managed to nick a smart skirt from that boutique up the road yesterday, and I'll wear that Lurex jumper that Fat Florrie gave me. Like my new shoes? I got them from one of Sam's Boys for ten bob – wasn't that cheap?'

Elsie heaved a deep sigh.

'You ought to be more careful, Sue,' she warned. 'Lifting gear from shops and buying stolen property, that's going to get you in a lot of trouble if you get caught.'

'They've got to catch me first,' jeered Sue.

Elsie resumed her worried expression and lay back in her chair puffing at her fag while Sue adorned herself in her new finery. She wore a white, pleated mini-skirt and a black silk jumper with silver thread in the material. The jumper fitted tightly over her full bust and had a deep, heart-shaped neckline. It was old-fashioned because it had belonged to Fat Florrie but it suited Sue, accentuating her broad shoulders and showing up her white skin to perfection. Her long legs were clad in black silk tights and on her feet she wore very smart high-wedged shoes. Her long dark hair, gleaming from constant brushing, hung smoothly down her back, and her face made up to perfection – she had on eye-shadow, liner, lashes, the lot, all acquired surreptitiously on her trips around the big stores. 'How do I look?' she finally demanded of Elsie.

Elsie had closed her weary eyes but now opened them wide in astonishment as she gazed at Sue. 'Well, I'll be blowed!' she exclaimed. 'You look about twenty, Sue.'

'But do I look all right.' Sue's voice quivered for a moment and there was uncertainty in her tone.

'You look lovely,' cried Elsie. 'Why, all the blokes will fancy you tonight. I'll lose all me customers.'

Sue made no comment. This business of Elsie's with men bored her. All she cared about was looking modern and smart after years of faded cotton dresses and clumsy shoes.

Chapter Five

The Prostitute

Travelling in a cab through the moonlit streets towards the seamier side of London – the notorious docklands – Sue's heart beat quickly with sudden excitement. At long last, she was entering the glamorous night life of this famous swinging city. She had gleaned so much information about it from the highly coloured paperbacks that were so disapproved of at the convent. At last, she was going to see the real thing!

A strange feeling came over her as she realized that they had just passed the mean slum street where she had been born. She made no comment then, but a forlorn look came into her eyes as she saw the small park where she used to take the twins for their constitutional, the ride in the battered old pram. Instantly, one traumatic thought flashed through her mind: how had they fared? Did they still remember her?

The sound of Elsie's cracked voice brought her down to earth. 'Taking his blinking time,' she said, referring to the cab driver. 'Ain't satisfied till they get the last lousy penny out of you,' she groused.

Soon the taxi was swinging in and out of the heavy traffic, and then suddenly left it all behind as they carried on down a narrow lane with high walls either side.

'The docks are over there,' said Elsie, pointing over to the right. 'Used to be pretty lively down here, but most of the Cockneys got bombed out in the Blitz.'

The cab had pulled up outside a brightly lit bar. Posters of half-nude women decorated the window. 'At last, we made it,' said Elsie.

'Three quid,' said the cabby holding out a podgy hand.

'Robbery, with bloody violence,' protested Elsie with disgust. But she reluctantly handed over the fare. The cabby stared insolently at her. 'Ain't going to do a lot of good down here, Ma,' he cackled. 'Like them young down here.'

'Balls!' called Elsie after him as he drove off with a silly grin.

'Now, love,' she said, patting her curls and nervously grasping Sue's hand in a clammy grip. 'When we go in, stand up at the bar like you are used to it. Don't talk. I'll do that in case there's trouble.'

Sue was amazed that everything was so complicated, but she was quite happy to do as Elsie told her. As they entered the bar, the noise and bright lights confused her for a moment, but she stood very upright, with a calm, collected expression on her face. Many eyes turned to look at her, but then, catching sight of her companion, turned away. One young Australian sailor gazed on in ardent admiration. 'That's nice,' he remarked to his friend, nodding in Sue's direction.

'No good, mate,' the more knowledgeable one informed him. 'She's just sex bait. The young one pulls 'em in and you end up with the old brass.'

'I can't believe that,' said the green young man unable to take his eyes off the tall willowy girl standing by the bar.

Sue was basking in the warmth of those dark blue eyes like a pussy cat in front of a fire. 'Keep your eyes skinned,' croaked Elsie as she twitched and fidgeted beside her, searching frantically around the room for a sight of that dope pedlar. 'He's a big fella,' she whispered. 'West Indian. He wears those mod specs. Nudge me with your elbow if you spot him first.' As Elsie carried on in her most agitated manner, Sue ignored her. Her head was spinning with joy. Here was life, music and male adoration – all the things she had been deprived of in her life. Elsie's problems were her own business. Warm and confident, Sue sipped gin and tonic and stared superciliously about the crowded bar. She looked enviously at the young girls in their mini-skirts laughing gaily with their companions; and she looked in fascination at the heavily made-up middle-aged women with their long dangling ear-rings and high hair-do's. It was all new to her but one thing was for sure – so much living time had been wasted in that crummy convent.

On the ornate steps, the musicians blew, strummed and thumped with ferocity. A rotund woman in a short cerise dress and hideous wig was the star turn. To Sue the woman looked like mutton done up as lamb and her lewd antics sickened her.

'Stay put, Sue,' whispered Elsie as she spied her contact at last. 'I'll be back.' She trotted off quickly, leaving Sue sitting up at the bar.

The excited and admiring young man was now only two feet away from her, caressing her with his gaze. The moment Elsie had vanished into the crowd, he was beside Sue. 'Where's your ma?' he joked. 'Gone home to bed?' Sue did not reply. She turned her head gracefully and showed her neat white teeth in a welcoming grin.

'What's your poison?' he asked eagerly. 'Gin?' Sue nodded. 'Come on,' he said. 'Let's go sit somewhere quiet.'

So in a dimly lit corner they sat together. The man cuddled her and whispered words of love in her ear. 'Where have you been hiding, beautiful?' he murmured.

Sue did not say a word. Elsie had instructed her to remain stum and she had every intention of doing so. She flicked back her false eyelashes and stared inscrutably at him.

'Wow!' he cried, all the more excited. 'Just like the old Mona Lisa. Come on, baby, put me out of my misery. Just tell me your name.' He grasped her hand.

The corners of her mouth twitched but she did not smile this time. 'I'm called Sue,' she said softly. The man jumped to his feet and began to pull her up. 'Come, Sue, let's leave this hell hole and go somewhere and have a meal.'

'No,' replied Sue, pulling away. 'I must wait for Elsie.'

'What, that old floozie?' he exclaimed in disgust. 'Whatever for?'

But again Sue remained dumb and refused to budge. The man sat down again and began swallowing his pints of beer in a sulky manner. He was nice, Sue thought, and she liked that excited feeling inside her. When he pressed close to her and his hand fondled her knee, little tremors shot up her thighs.

It was not long before Elsie had returned, bright and starry-eyed again having got her fix and found a new supplier of the drugs she needed. She looked appreciatively at Sue's companion but he stared back at her with hostility.

'She's not on the game,' Elsie informed him, 'but I'll give you a good time for a tenner.' She winked knowingly and her lopsided mouth pouted in an absurd manner as she plied the wiles of her trade.

The man had leaped to his feet and was backing away. 'Christ!' he cried. 'I don't want to buy it. I only want to hire it for the night. And I want the kid, not you. You're too old for me.'

Elsie ignored the insult. 'What about a drink?' she asked pleasantly.

The Australian produced a wallet stuffed with notes and swayed to the counter to order drinks. Elsie's eyes gleamed greedily. 'Hang on to him, Sue,' she whispered. 'He's loaded.' Then she added, 'That black git rooked me for that fix,' she complained bitterly.

Sue scarcely heard her. Her head began to spin and she had to get outside in the smoke-free air. She got up and went out. Once outside, she breathed in the clean air that blew up the Thames and immediately felt revived. Her young admirer had followed her out and still clung to her, saying he wanted to dawdle awhile and look at the river. Elsie also came out and became very domineering and business-like. Within minutes she had called a taxi. In the taxi, Sue enjoyed the passionate kisses of that drunken youth, while Elsie sat watching them with a pale, angry face.

They arrived back at Elsie's flat and climbed the rickety wooden stairs. The man, blind drunk, was escorted into Elsie's bedroom. Elsie gave Sue a determined push. 'Get to bed!' she cried. 'I don't like whore robbers. And lock the bloody door!'

For the first time since they had met, Sue stood up to Elsie. Drawing herself up to her full height, she sneered at her. 'I won't,' she said. 'He's mine. I found him.'

The change in Elsie was remarkable. Showing her teeth like a mad dog and with eyes blazing, she flew at Sue, caught her by the hair and dragged her into the kitchen. Caught off guard, Sue was too surprised to defend herself and Elsie pushed her inside and locked her in. 'You can get back to that bleeding convent if you defy me,' she yelled through the keyhole.

Sue stretched out on her narrow bed and wept tears of frustration. Her young man was so nice. How she would have enjoyed making love to that sun-tanned body! What a spiteful bitch that Elsie was. Seething with resentment at that old junkie, she eventually fell asleep, but only to be aroused later by a shocking shindy.

The young man had woken from his drunken stupor to find himself in bed with Elsie. Furious, he yelled at the top of his voice. 'God darn you, bloody old strumpet! Where's that young bird I paid you twenty quid for?'

With her ear to the door, Sue listened feeling very shocked.

Had Elsie actually sold her to this man and then swindled him out of her? Getting down on her knees, she peered through the keyhole to be met by a strange sight of the young man prowling about the hallway of the flat dressed only in a short shirt. An odd tent erection stuck out of it. Then Elsie dashed out of the bedroom, struggling and screaming and yelling for Sam's Boys to come to her aid. Within minutes, they had come bounding up the stairs but the sailor was a powerful lad with a flaming temper, and he put up quite a fight. The struggle went on for some time until he was eventually overwhelmed, and dragged, unconscious, down the stairs. Screaming filthy words at him, Elsie threw his jacket and trousers after him.

Sue watched all this with fascination, and then quietly crept back to bed. A strange thrill ran through her, and she felt as though she had just watched an exciting television play. Feeling no sympathy whatsoever for the unfortunate youth, that violent scene had excited her. She had actually enjoyed the spectacle. She lay awake on her narrow bed for a long time afterwards, pondering on what she had just seen. Feeling so keyed-up with emotion, she hugged herself tight under the blankets until at last she fell asleep again.

At ten o'clock the next morning, as Sue made her usual pot of tea and the ladies of the house were still snoring, she heard an unusually heavy tread upon the stairs. For a moment, she froze, standing wide-eyed and scared, the hot teapot still in her hand. But then she breathed a deep sigh of relief at the sight of Sam's grizzled head. Sam rarely climbed the stairs to the flats above, but did ss this morning puffing and blowing. His rugged face was almost blue from the exertion.

'Where's Elsie?' he growled.

'In bed, Sam,' replied Sue. 'What's up?'

'Never you mind. Get her up!' he snapped.

Elsie looked very dishevelled and rather worried as she let Sam into her bedroom. The moment the bedroom door had closed, Sue pressed her ear to it and listened to the conversation going on in that room. 'Been and done it this time, Elsie,' Sam growled.

'Why? What's wrong?' asked the anxious Elsie.

'Wrong?' he uttered in disgust. 'My life, it's all gone wrong. You're likely to get us all nicked, bringing that kid in here. And that ain't all, the boys croaked that geezer last night and lifted his wallet. He had close to a hundred quid on him – he'd just been paid off his ship.'

'You mean they killed him?' Elsie croaked.

'No, but they knocked him abaht. The point is, he sung like a dickie bird, he did, when he came round in the hospital. That this should happen to me,' wailed Sam. 'Been in good friend to you gels, I have.'

'Oh, my gawd,' said Elsie in disbelief, 'but he was as drunk as a fiddler's bitch when I brought him home. How'd he remembered anything?'

'Well, he knows your name and the kid's. It's all on the news. They've connected that girl with the one who escaped from the convent. They're going to comb the back streets of Soho, they said.'

'Oh, dear!' gasped Elsie. 'I warned her not to talk. She must have told him.'

'Well, it's done now,' said Sam. 'Bet your life they'll be here soon. I'm hopping off down the country with the old gal till it blows over, but you mind what you are about,' he threatened. 'Likely to get the other side of your face shived if the boys get done.'

These last words really upset Elsie and she began to weep very loudly. 'I ain't frightened of them,' she squalled. 'I'll be glad when my Alfie gets out. Clumsy lot of sods your boys are.'

'That may be,' growled Sam. 'But don't say I didn't warn yer, and don't let them get hold of that kid – sing like a bleeding canary, she will.' Having said his piece Sam lumbered through the flat and disappeared down the stairs.

Within seconds, Fat Florrie arrived on the scene followed by Ida and her coloured boyfriend. They talked excitedly, all at once and the din was deafening. Florrie's deep voice boomed out above all the rest. 'Better hide the kid,' she said. 'She knows too much.'

Sue glided in amongst them. 'Hide me? What for? I haven't done anything!'

'No, ducks,' said Ida gently. With her bronze skin and short hair, she was the most attractive of the prostitutes. 'But we can't afford to let them catch you. Come with me! Old Bill will be here soon.' With a firm hand she grabbed Sue by the arm and guided her down the back stairs, leading through Sam's shop into the back yard which was overgrown with weeds. At the back, by the wall, a thick creeper covered a small door. 'Here we are,' said Ida. 'Hop in there and lock yourself in. It's Sam's old toilet. It don't get used now. Not many know it's there.'

Sue stood looking at the dirty, unused lavatory but Ida gave her a sharp shove. 'Don't make a sound or come out till we call you,' she ordered.

So Sue sat on the edge of that evil-smelling seat for a long time. She felt miserable. Cobwebs massed the walls and the stench in the tiny room was unbearable. But Sue did not dare move. Soon she could hear muffled voices, the wail of the police sirens and the tramping of feet as the police searched the premises. Cold, sick and unhappy, she sat and waited for four hours until Ida came to fetch her. Once the all-clear signal had been given, they all sat in Elsie's kitchen, the prostitutes were laughing and giggling over a bottle of wine, and feeling very pleased that they had fooled old Bill.

But Sue did not smile. She felt disturbed and somewhat queasy. 'I feel sick,' she moaned.

'It must have been that dirty lavatory,' said fat Florrie. 'Cheer up, we've saved your bacon.'

'Give her a glass of wine,' urged Ida.

Elsie took a wad of notes from her bra and waved them about in the air. 'That's a bit they never found,' she cried jubilantly. 'Took that Aussie for thirty quid, and then he never got nothing.'

They all began to laugh uproariously, but Sue found little to laugh about. She got to her feet and ran to the bathroom just in time.

'I've been thinking,' said Elsie the next day, 'that fella probably gave a good description of you. They might still be watching outside for you.'

Sue did not reply. She still felt off-colour. Elsie eyed her in a speculative manner. 'No reason why you can't come out with me,' she said. 'The blokes seem to like you, and I've got to work hard the next few weeks to pay that swine for my grass.'

Sue took no notice. She just sat staring out of the window. She had something on her mind and an awful sick feeling at the pit of her stomach.

Elsie rummaged in the kitchen drawer. 'I've got a home perm in here, and an auburn rinse. Let's change your image – short hair makes a world of difference.'

52

'Cut off my hair?' Sue gasped in horror. 'Oh, no, Elsie, I couldn't. My long hair is the best thing I've got.'

'Well, it's up to you,' snapped Elsie. 'Old Bill's still prowling about out there. You might have to stay cooped up a long time. If you change your appearance you can come out with me. But it's up to you.' Sue pondered for a while. 'Might get a job in a club if you look older,' continued Elsie. 'Ten pounds a night, they get.'

The idea of working in a night-club interested Sue. That world of neon lights and vice sounded very inviting. 'All right,' she said finally. 'Get the shears, Elsie.' Bending her head, she threw her lovely long tresses forward ready for the scissors.

Elsie made short work of Sue's hair. In no time at all, the long silken lengths fell to the floor. Then came the tedious and unpleasant application of the home perm. Twice during the long procedure, Sue pulled away and escaped to the bathroom. 'It's the smell of that stuff that's making me feel sick,' she complained.

Elsie had begun to look shrewdly at her as she brushed out the frizzy auburn mop which gave Sue a strangely erotic appearance. 'Your hair will be all right when it settles down,' she muttered, frantically trying to brush it into shape.

But Sue took one look at herself in the mirror, uttered a loud cry, and dashed off to the bathroom once more.

Listening to Sue sobbing and occasionally retching, Elsie began to feel worried about the kid. She made some coffee and at last persuaded Sue to come out of the bathroom. Sue looked ghastly. With that odd frizzy head and her weeping red eyes, she was certainly no longer a beauty. The short hair emphasized the strong jaw line, and her neck looked longer and her shoulders broader than usual. In fact, she looked longer and lankier than ever.

Elsie's lips twitched in a smile as she looked at her. 'Come on, Sue,' she cajoled. 'Your hair will look smart when it's set. Your mother would never recognize you then.'

Very much the worse for wear, Sue sank into the armchair and gratefully sipped the hot coffee.

'Been here about six weeks, haven't you, love?' ruminated Elsie.

'I think so,' replied Sue.

'I heard you being sick in the bathroom,' continued Elsie. 'So I was wondering if you're overdue. You did tell me that Dodgy Roger took advantage of you.'

'I know,' wept Sue. 'That's why I'm getting so worried.'

'Poor little cow,' said Elsie kindly. 'Must have clicked first go.'

'Do you think I'm in the family way?' Sue almost screamed out the words in terror.

'No good kicking up a fuss,' said Elsie calmly. 'But you've certainly queered your pitch. I'll get some pills and if they don't work, you'll have to start earning. It's a hundred and fifty quid for a quick abortion.'

Chapter Six

Approved School

The news that the kid had clicked travelled fast among the ladies of the house.

'Damned shame,' said Ida, who had paid for Sue to go to a local hairdresser to have her woolly auburn frizz cut, trimmed and set into a smart shape. Despite her earlier misgivings, the new boyish look suited Sue.

Fat Florrie kept producing concoctions that were supposed to 'bring it orf', as she told Sue, but they only had the effect of confining Sue to the lavatory and were a sheer waste of time.

Elsie was more helpful and practical. She got Sue two nights' work a week in a seedy club. 'It's hostessing,' she told Sue. 'You don't have to do anything you don't want to, but if you do they pay for a hotel and you get extra. I'll save the money up for you and before you're three months, you can get an abortion.'

Everything was decided for her so Sue cheered up a little. A few days later, she set out for Oxford Street. Again it was her kleptomaniac habits that trapped her. She had decided that she needed lighter make-up to go with her auburn hair. She was due to start her new job that night and she wanted to look the part for it. Wandering into a large department store, she picked up and examined various tubes of lipstick, before surreptitiously slipping one into her pocket. Then she moved on to the perfume counter. After an hour, she had quite a nice little haul. Then she suddenly spied a jewellery tray full of rings. They looked very nice – large and ornate and very modern. She carefully tried them on one by one, visualizing her slim hands loaded with posh rings. She spotted another tray with more expensive rings in a glass cabinet nearby. She swiftly put her hand over the counter, picked one of the rings and slipped it on her finger. Shoving her hand in her pocket, she nonchalantly walked towards the exit. She had only got as far as the swing doors when a rough hand grabbed her from behind. 'Pardon me, madam,' a stern voice boomed at her, 'but I believe you have goods that have not been paid for. I'm afraid that you cannot leave the store.'

Wide-eyed with terror, Sue spun round to stare into the cold face of the store detective. Without a moment's hesitation, she jerked her arm away and dashed through the shop to another exit, only to be confronted by a stalwart woman constable. As the policewoman lunged at her, Sue fought and screamed and fell to the floor kicking out her legs in all directions. Some shop staff ran to the aid of the policewoman and the store detective and in no time at all, Sue had been bundled into a Black Maria, where she sat handcuffed and very sullen.

And so, once more Sue was held in custody behind confining walls. The walls of Holloway Prison closed about her just as the convent walls had done. Elsie's words rang in her head: 'Don't talk, Sue. Never tell the cops anything, they only come down harder on you if you do.' So she remained stum. As a result, the prison authorities were unable to find out where Sue had been in the last two months, but it did not take them long to discover that she was six weeks pregnant.

Sue spent three weeks on remand in the prison while her future was decided upon. Sue soon learned that she was still a juvenile and would be dealt with accordingly, but by the end of the year, after her child had been born, she would be seventeen and out of their jurisdiction.

'Thank God for that,' declared the visiting welfare officer who had spent a particularly exhausting morning trying to get on the right side of Sue. 'Honestly, I think she has a mental kink somewhere,' she informed her colleagues. 'She doesn't show the slightest sign of any remorse, and her one ambition seems to be to get free and become a prostitute.' She wiped her brow with a dainty handkerchief. 'It's like hitting your head against a brick wall, trying to get through to that girl.'

But the tall, robust matron of the remand centre was not so easily rattled. She had handled and conquered many an erring young woman. 'A few weeks here of hard work and discipline, and she'll soon come round to a saner way of thinking,' declared the Captain, as she liked to be called. It was a name that this white-haired virago had kept since her youth when she had been a Girl Guide captain. 'I'll put the girl under the care of the consultant psychiatrist,' she continued firmly. 'If we can find any hereditary mental disorders, the child might not have to be born.'

'It's a pity,' said the young welfare officer, 'she never seems to have had a chance in life. She's been in institutions, on and off, since she was nine years old. And Lord only knows what happened to her while she was adrift in London for two months.' She sighed. 'I give up. Do things your way, Captain, it might have the desired effect.'

So the Captain took over and Sue was hooked out of her cell to work in the laundry where the wardress was given instructions to keep a strict watch over her. Immediately Sue's temper improved, for she was back in her old element in that hot, steamy washroom. She worked hard and willingly and seemed extraordinarily content to do work that others resented.

The Captain was slightly nonplussed to see how well Sue was behaving. She had been expecting her to react differently. She thought she would lose her temper and become so violent that it would have been the Captain's duty to recommend a mental institution, and a quick abortion. In her eyes, it would have been the right decision. Bad blood produced inferior stock, she reasoned, so why put another problem child on an already overburdened welfare state? Had Sue been a vicious dog or cat about to have kittens, the Captain would have given the creatures the greatest care, and understanding. But Sue was a dirty-minded, uneducated human being and the Captain despised such creatures. Now her steely blue eyes surveyed Sue who was marching nonchalantly along the corridor carrying a huge basket of dirty linen from the staff room to the laundry. 'Susan Ward,' she called sharply.

Sue stopped immediately, her dark eyes wary. She was as tall as the Captain and stood facing her now, quite unafraid.

'Carry that basket in a proper manner,' the Captain ordered. 'I don't want linen littered all over the corridor.'

'Aye, aye, Captain.' With an insolent grin on her face, Sue gave her an insolent salute.

The Captain only just stopped herself from hitting the girl, but she gave Sue a paralysing look and marched away.

'That took the mike out of the old cow,' Sue proudly told her laundry companions afterwards. One of these was a faded alcoholic, called Jilly, loaned from the women's prison, and the other was a good-looking Maltese girl called Carmen who had knifed her lover. Carmen's English was somewhat limited but she had spent some time on the East End streets where she had learned a fine list of swear words with which she liberally peppered her conversation. Any that she was short of were quickly supplied by Jilly, so Sue learned plenty of new words which she used loudly and freely.

Eventually Sue came up before the juvenile court where it was decided that she should be treated leniently. The psychiatrist's report had recommended this action, pointing out that too much responsibility had been placed on her at too early an age. The girl needed gentle handling; time and a lot of care, it was believed, would effect a cure.

First Sue was to be put in a training centre until six weeks before her baby was due, and then she would be put in an unmarried mother's home, possibly with further training until she was eighteen.

With a pale face and hard eyes, Sue said goodbye to Carmen and Jilly, and was once more bound for an institution far up north, as far away from London as she could possibly be put. The Captain watched her leave with a big sigh of relief.

Out of the train windows, Sue looked at the fast-disappearing buildings of London and wondered how Elsie was and if she knew what had happened to her. Elsie had been a good friend to her for those weeks they spent together. She would miss her and the other ladies, she thought wistfully. And then she wondered with dread what this new institution she was going to would be like.

The new school, in fact, turned out to be a pleasant surprise for her. Situated high on a hill and surrounded by green parklands, it made a nice change from that old remand centre which had smelled of damp walls and carbolic soap. Surely the head one here would not be such an old cow as that Captain.

'I don't know about me being potty,' said Sue scornfully to the young social worker who had travelled up from London with her. 'She was a nut case if ever I saw one.'

'You'll like it up here, Sue,' the young lady informed her. 'Most of the girls do.'

'We'll wait and see,' scowled Sue.

'It's like a big boarding school with properly qualified teachers. If you want to learn to type or do dressmaking, or anything like that, you'll be given plenty of opportunity to do so.'

'I expect I'll end up in the bloody laundry,' said Sue, 'like I always do.'

Her introduction to the training school was nice and informal. The petite blonde matron who had previously worked as a ward sister was clean and neat, smiling and alert. She had taken the trouble to find out about Sue and was determined to make the girl happy.

Sue was introduced to the other girls and, after a tasty high tea, they had games and watched television. There was not a lot of discipline in the school and the atmosphere was free and easy. Sue should have been grateful for all this but she was not. Within three weeks she had been nicknamed Surly Sue and had been in plenty of trouble for bullying the other girls or dodging classes.

The young, enthusiastic teachers spent many hours trying to coax Sue to read, knit or sew, but it was hopeless. She did not have the slightest interest in anything they suggested. She did, however, develop a very healthy appetite for food and spent most of her time lazing about.

The evenings were spent in the dormitory where the girls would tell each other rude jokes or have pillow fights.

There were several gymslip mums waiting their turn to go to the unmarried mother's home. They would constantly swap stories of how they went to all-night parties and got raped, or of their addiction to pep pills and how they never had a clue what happened to them on that particular Saturday night.

Sue decided that the whole lot of them were a silly bunch of nits and that it would serve them all right if they ended up in Holloway. 'Silly lot of cows,' she would mutter loudly. 'I've been on the game, I have,' she would boast. 'No bleedin' man gets me for less than twenty quid.'

Fascinated, the girls would gather about her to listen to her fantastic, lurid tales of her exploits as a Soho prostitute.

'I don't believe you, Sue,' one brave girl protested one night. 'You're not old enough to have done all these things.'

'That's right,' said another, 'and, anyway, how come you got in the family way? Prostitutes are not like us – they know how to prevent it.'

'Now don't you be so bloody cheeky, Irish Peg,' scowled Sue. 'Just because your black boy let you down . . . Me, I've had all kinds and all nationalities.' Her audience listened, enthralled by her lies.

'At least I know who's the father of mine,' flared out Irish Peg.

'She's right, Sue,' said Pauline, a girl with a solemn face and large specs. 'How can you know who the father is if you've had so many in one night?'

'Never you mind!' retorted Sue. 'Experience teaches you that. I know who he is, he's a boy called Roger and at this moment he's in the nick.'

'Sorry, Sue, I don't believe you either,' said little Rosie who was reported to be carrying twins. 'It's possible that your baby is just as likely to be black as Irish Peg's.'

'Oh, nuts!' said Sue. 'Wait till I get back to Soho. I'll get the boys to carve you up if I catch any of you soppy lot hanging around.'

There was a general scramble back to bed, they all began to laugh.

The months ticked by and Sue became very heavy. She was always eating and had become extraordinarily lazy.

'You must pull yourself together, Sue,' the social worker warned her earnestly. 'How are you going to take care of yourself and your baby? You really ought to learn a trade or at least take an interest in baby care.'

But Sue only gazed silently and superciliously at her. What did she want to sit in a stuffy classroom for, watching a lot of giggling girls playing with a doll, washing it and dressing it? They could not teach her anything about babies; she had taken care of enough of them at Barham House.

When the baby classes were in progress, Sue would hide in the greenhouse and roll herself a cigarette with tobacco scrounged from the old gardener. She liked the greenhouse. It was warm and bright with hanging fuchsias and pots of red geraniums. It was also very peaceful in there, away from the screeching teenagers' voices. One morning she leaned against the bench and surveyed her large, swollen belly. To think that a smaller edition of Roger might be in there, she thought, and she had practically forgotten him already. That she could keep this child if she wanted to, she was perfectly aware, but what fun would it be to slave in some factory all day long and cope with a screaming kid all night? No thanks, she told herself, what a life; she had seen what childbearing had done to her mother. No, the baby would have to be adopted and then she would get back to Soho to the cosy flat and the lively chatter of Elsie and her cronies.

Within a few weeks, the four girls whose babies were nearly due, including Sue, were transferred to the unmarried mother's home run by the Salvation Army. Life was harder there: the discipline was much stricter, the food was poor and the Army sister believed very strongly that scrubbing was good for the stomach muscles. As a result, many hours were spent scrubbing the bare boards and large kitchen tables. This was not such hard graft to the institutionalized Sue, but it was for some of the young ones who considered it to be degrading. They often rebelled and wept, and there were many hysterical scenes which Sue ignored. There were some extremely young girls there – aged thirteen and even less. But they seemed a hard lot and more carefree than those from the approved school; they would spend their precious spare time dancing to pop music and holding their wobbly bellies.

On Sundays, worried and adoring parents arrived to bring sweets and flowers for their errant daughters. Small family groups would walk in the gardens laughing and looking happy, but Sue would sit on a bench with her long legs stuck out before her watching them all with a contemptuous smile on her face. No one ever came to visit her.

Whenever one of the girls awoke in the night yelling with their labour pains, it was Sue who hooked her out of bed and walked with her across the park to the hospital ward. She would hang about awhile to hear the girl yelling, getting tremendous sadistic satisfaction that something was hurting her.

Eventually it was her turn, but she gritted her teeth, did not scream and never complained. It was with comparative ease that she gave birth to a baby girl who was the spitting image of Dodgy Roger.

Much to the surprise of the staff and the other girls at the mother's home, the moody, taciturn Sue was very gentle with her baby and even proud of her. In fact, she plagued the other young mothers in the ward by always remarking upon how pretty her little Elaine was and how ugly the rest of the babies in the ward were. 'My goodness, what an ugly little sod,' she usually said as she inspected the latest baby. The teenage mums were incensed to have their babies criticized by Sue, and it reached climax point one day when Sue screwed her nose up at Irish Peg's little piccaninny. 'Monkey face,' Sue called him.

Peg leaped from her bed with her Irish temper blazing, and it took both the sister and nurse to hold her down and prevent her attacking Sue. 'It's not fair!' Peg wept. 'She's a whore, a real prostitute, and look at the lovely baby she got and she don't want it. I want to keep mine,' she wailed, 'and can't because I can't go back home to Ireland if I do.' As poor little Peg sung out her tale of woe Sue just sat on her bed with a smirk on her face and her arms akimbo. She made it obvious that she enjoyed the scene she had created.

'She's beyond me, that Sue,' sighed the ward sister later. 'But I can't have her upsetting the other mothers. We'll put her in a side ward.'

And so Sue was left to recuperate in solitary and her baby was taken to the nursery as soon as it was fed, to prevent Sue from petting and fussing her.

There was one very conscientious nurse on the ward, called Eileen. Deeply religious, she had a pale, freckled face that always looked rather as if all the cares of the world rested on her own shoulders. 'Why don't you try to be good, Sue,' she begged. 'I know you love your baby.'

'What's the use?' sniffed Sue. 'She's going to be adopted anyway.'

'But she doesn't have to be,' urged Eileen.

'I wish they'd take her now and get it over quick,' complained Sue.

'But, Sue,' protested the gentle salvationist, 'you don't have to have your baby adopted – I know plenty of unmarried girls who have kept their babies. A lot of help and care is given to you these days, you know.'

But Sue just scowled at her. 'I got over it before,' she said bitterly. 'I expect I'll get over it again.'

The young woman looked puzzled. 'But you've never had a baby before,' she said gently.

Sue immediately lost her temper. Putting her hands on her hips, she shouted down at the pale, freckled face, in a loud, dogmatic voice. 'What about the twins, then? I wasn't consulted about them and they was like my very own babies!'

Eileen sighed patiently as she realized what Sue was referring to. 'But they were your brother and sister,' she said kindly. 'This baby is your own flesh and blood – there's a lot of difference between them, dear.'

'Shut yer face!' roared Sue. 'Bloody lot of Nosey Parkers, you are! I'm bloody fed up with the lot of you.'

'Hush, dear, don't swear,' begged Eileen. 'Come and help me on my rounds and tell me about it, love.'

To Eileen's surprise and relief, Sue responded to this gentle firmness and calmly followed her to attend to the newborn babies. Eileen was astounded by the girl's capability as Sue fed and changed the squalling babies with swift, cool efficiency. And she listened quietly while Sue told her story, of her much-admired father who had returned home a whining cripple, of her poor mother who had died of TB, and of the baby brother and sister she had been so fond of. She listened in silence as Sue boasted of how she was going to get her own back on all the people who had kept her in care. Of how she was going up the West End to make a pile of money, of how she would show them that they could not do what they liked with her.

Gently Eileen tucked in the sleeping infants into the cribs. 'Why don't you take up child nursing, Sue? I think you've got a vocation for it,' she suggested.

'No thanks,' said Sue dismissively. 'I know exactly what I'm going to do when I get out of here.'

'Oh Sue,' pleaded Eileen tearfully. 'Pray to Jesus to save you, love.'

'Oh don't start all that,' declared Sue impatiently. 'I thought you were my friend.'

'But I am your friend, I always will be, remember that,' cried Eileen. But Sue was unimpressed. 'Don't go much on all that hypocrisy,' she cried. 'Do more harm than bloody good, those do-gooders.'

Knowing that there was no point in pursuing the matter further, Eileen just sighed and went on her way. Putting her small army bonnet on her head, she set off to spend her off-duty hour delivering the *War Cry* to the sinners in the pubs.

Eileen's efforts all proved to have been in vain. Not long after, Sue signed the adoption papers without a moment's hesitation or the sign of a tear. Her little babe of six weeks old had a mop of dark curls and merry blue eyes. Her sunny temperament made her the most loved of all the unwanted babies. Sue kissed and loved her and took excellent care of her but she refused to take an interest in the baby's future.

'Sometimes I think that Sue has a mental kink,' the harassed matron remarked one day. 'And I'm rather worried about what her reaction will be when we take the child tomorrow.'

'Let her go with Miss Jenkins,' suggested the doctor. 'It often helps when they see that the child has a good foster parent.'

Miss Jenkins was tall, untidy and short-sighted but of a very sweet, obliging nature. She was working hard for her exams in order to become a probation officer and did these voluntary assignments with good will. Next morning, Sue, dressed in a neat school uniform and a white blouse accompanied Miss Jenkins into town. In her arms she carried that special little bundle of love, her own beautiful baby. The staff had expected a dramatic scene but there had been none. Sue's face was set like a cold white mask and she said very little as she cuddled her little one close.

At the local council offices they met a fresh-faced young woman in her thirties who was to foster the baby until an appropriate time had passed before legal adoption. Standing red-faced and hesitant in the doorway, she looked sympathetically at the young girl who still held the child in her arms. Suddenly Sue thrust the child at the woman and walked out of the room without a word. There was no sign of emotion on her face but tears poured down poor Miss Jenkins' face. She took off her spectacles to wipe her eyes. 'It's all for the best, Sue,' she ventured timidly.

Sue stared hard at her. 'Got a fag?' she demanded.

Miss Jenkins looked slightly shocked. 'You can't smoke going along the street, Sue,' she said. 'Let's go and have a cup of tea. I've got some cigarettes in my bag.'

They walked a little way down the main street to a self-service teashop. As soon as they had found a window table, Miss Jenkins handed Sue the packet of cigarettes and then went to the counter to get some tea.

The cups were filled and on the tray and just as she paid the cashier, she glanced back at the table. Sue was gone. The seat by the window was empty. Miss Jenkins let out a cry, plonked the tray down on the side and rushed out into the street where she stared short-sightedly up and down.

But Sue was already half-way down the underpath that led to the motorway, her long legs carrying her swiftly to freedom.

Chapter Seven

Return to Soho

High in the Yorkshire moors, the motorway winds towards the South. Sue walked rapidly along the hard shoulder feeling rather confused as a long line of traffic tore past her. The noise was deafening as lorries and heavy tankers roared past, side by side, striving to out-race each other. It was desolate and wild on the moors, a strange, lonely world up there beside the motorway.

She heard the siren of a police car and, scenting danger, quickly ducked behind a clump of blackberry bushes to hide. She lay very still, even though the blackberry bushes pricked her legs. Only the wild life around her stirred. A rabbit hopped out from behind another bush and a blackbird perched in the small tree above her head and sang his song of love. In a few minutes she was fast asleep, exhausted from her flight.

When she awoke, a cold mist had begun to rise. Stiff and damp, Sue began to wonder if her escape had been such a good idea. It might be a hundred miles to London and she was not even sure which direction it was. Feeling rather depressed, she sat hugging her knees as she peered through the bushes at the traffic that still rumbled past. Lights had begun to twinkle on the cars and the road looked damp and shiny. She had no money, she thought gloomily, and not even a warm coat. Perhaps she ought to go back the way she had come . . .

She got up stiffly, looked back down the road, and then, with a determined shrug, continued along the hard shoulder. 'Must lead somewhere,' she muttered. 'And the further away I get from that rotten school, the better I shall like it.'

Darkness had now fallen. Headlights shed a cold glare on to the road. At last, a bridge spanned the shadowy space and an illuminated sign read: London. It was straight ahead. Sue shivered and put her hands into her blazer pockets. 'At least I know I'm going in the right direction,' she said optimistically.

At a turnoff, there was a well-lit cafe and a fleet of lorries parked outside. Immediately Sue cheered up and headed for it.

65

Finding the toilet, she tidied her hair. It was now a short bob with the auburn rinse fading. Her own coal-black hair was starting to show through once more. 'Look a mess, don't I,' she muttered to herself as she stared in the mirror. 'And I'm hungry.'

She followed the smell of cooking to the cafe window where she stood looking at folk eating inside. Then she wandered over to where the huge lorries were parked.

A short stout man was examining the ropes of his heavy load making sure that it was all secure before getting his supper. On the side of this lorry were painted the words: Ferry Road, London. Without hesitation, Sue went straight up and stood beside the man. He was busy inspecting the tyres of his lorry and did not look up when she came up and stood there waiting.

'Will you give me a lift to London?' she asked sweetly.

The man looked up with a red face. Surprise registered in his mild blue eyes when he saw how young she was.

'Well, will you?' Sue asked again as he said nothing.

'Well, it depends,' he replied slowly, rubbing his oily hands together and shrewdly surveying the busty figure under the school uniform. 'You're on the run, ain't you, chum?' he asked suddenly.

Sue nodded. 'That's right,' she said. 'From an approved school.'

His attitude suddenly seemed to change. 'I bet you're hungry,' he said. 'Come on, kid, let's get some grub.'

Sausage, egg and chips, had never never tasted so good before as Sue gobbled them down hungrily. And Bill was jolly company in spite of the fact that his eyes were tired and red-veined and his chin was bristly for want of a shave.

'They'll cop you,' he informed her. 'They always do. Many times I hopped off when I was a lad at the naughty boys' home.' He chuckled and rammed huge lumps of sausage into his mouth at the same time. Sue was too tired to answer. She ate her meal slowly and allowed the warmth of the cafe to soak into her cold wet body.

'Ended up in Borstal, I did,' boasted Bill. 'But I used to enjoy those few days on the run.'

'I've got a friend in London,' Sue said through mouthfuls. 'They won't get me again.'

'Okay, kid,' said Bill. 'I'll take you there but I have to put you

66

down at Walthamstow. You can nip down the tube there. I can't take you right in, 'cos the cops might be on the look out and I can't afford no trouble. I've been going straight since I got spliced. You're only a bit of a kid, it's a bloody shame. But I'll do what I can and no strings attached.' He gave another fruity chuckle.

And so soon Sue sat up in the cab beside Bill wrapped up warm and cosy in an old overcoat that smelled of diesel oil. As they sped down the M1, Bill sometimes whistled a cheery song or just chatted about his adventurous youth in reform schools. Sue dozed and lightly listened to the drone of his voice as they rode through the night. 'Got to keep whistling or singing,' he explained. 'Gets monotonous on this part of the motorway. I'm likely to doze off and have a crack-up. I often pick up a passenger just for company but not always a nice girl like you. Some of them travellers make me feel cootey. Still, that's me, muggins, can't never say no to anyone in trouble.' He gave another deep chuckle. But Sue was sound asleep. She had lost any fear she might have had, and felt safe and comfortable with Bill, the long-distance driver.

It was a cold, dark, misty morning as they entered the outskirts of London. At Walthamstow tube, Bill pulled up his lorry. 'Here's five bob, luv, I can't spare no more. Pop down the tube and wait for the first train.' He winked. 'And good luck,' he added. With a friendly wave and his tail lights flicking a farewell, Bill went on his way.

It was seven o'clock in the morning when Sue rang the bell of Elsie's flat. At first there was no reply, so she pressed the bell once more. Perhaps Elsie had gone to bed after a hard night, she thought. But then a frightened voice called out, 'Who's there?'

'It's me, Elsie,' Sue called back.

'Crikey!' exclaimed Elsie's cracked voice. 'Open the door, Alfie, it's only Sue.'

The door was opened by a big fat man with wide shoulders, an enormous belly and a thin straggly moustache that wandered over his upper lip. His hair was long at the sides, which gave him an odd sort of appearance, Sue thought. Two hard, brown eyes now surveyed her in a very hostile manner.

'Come in, Sue,' called Elsie. 'Meet Alfie, he's me fella. I told you about him, didn't I?'

Sue nodded and looked about the little flat. It was a mess. With her hair all awry, Elsie kept running about the room stuffing clothes into a suitcase and wrapping up all her little knick-knacks from the shelves. 'Did they let you out, Sue? Or are you on the run?' she asked, still busily packing.

'I'm on the run,' replied Sue flatly.

'Oh, dear!' sighed Elsie. 'Did not ought to have come here, Sue. Got enough troubles of me own. We're hopping it, me and Alfie. Bleeding bookie's boys are after us. Just getting on all right I was, too.' Her voice broke into a wail. 'Been making a bomb, I have, since Alfie came out. And now this . . .' She sniffed and cuffed her eyes with her hand. 'I warned him not to gamble, but he can't help it, he can't.'

While Elsie nagged, her ponce sat stolid on the settee with his hands resting on his fat tummy. His dark, almost black, eyes assessed her, making her feel very uncomfortable, and giving her a prickly feeling at the back of her neck, as if they could bore right through her.

Frantically, Elsie rammed her belongings into the suitcase, moaning all the while. 'Me, I flog meself to death for a few quid and he gives it all to the bookies. Now he's grassed on them and they're out to get him. I've been shived before, and I ain't staying here to get done up again.'

Without a word, Sue stepped forward and closed the suitcase and locked it for the distraught Elsie. She zipped up her dress for her, then began to pick up the odds and ends that lay strewn about the floor.

'You ready?' grunted Alfie, taking hold of the luggage opening the door. Elsie took one last look around her cosy flat and her eyes flooded with tears. 'Oh, dear, Sue,' she wailed. 'What's going to become of us all?'

'Cheer up,' said Sue casually. 'You'll be all right.' She did not hesitate to say what was on her mind. 'Can I stay here?'

'It's twenty quid a week,' replied Elsie. 'But it's paid until the end of the month so you might as well park here, I suppose. You ain't got nowhere else, I don't expect. Ta-ta, love.' Giving Sue a friendly peck on the cheek she dashed out after Alfie who was already climbing down the stairs.

With a deep sigh of satisfaction, Sue stretched out on the pink divan and looked around. Well, she thought, at least I have got a place to rest in. I don't suppose they'll find me yet.

The fact that she was penniless did not worry her at all. In Elsie's larder she soon found a few tins of soup and packets of food she could eat for at least a week. And it would be two weeks before old Nick the landlord would call to collect the rent. But twenty pounds . . . That was a lot of money. If she was going to stay here she would have to think about how to start earning it. Still, she thought, there's no sense in crossing my bridges till I come to them. She decided that she would have a good sleep and then go down and see Ida. Being so well versed in the art of prostitution, Ida could teach her the ropes. It never occurred to her that there might be easier ways of making a living; she was just determined to follow in Elsie's footsteps.

Stripping down to her bra and panties, she washed herself in the little bathroom and then lay full-length on the pink divan, delighted not to have to sleep on that narrow camp bed in the kitchen any more. As drowsiness crept over her, her mind drifted to an image of her baby's little soft head snuggling so close. For a fleeting moment, her face assumed a melancholy expression which she quickly changed. 'Pull yourself together!' she scolded herself, reaching out for the small dog-end that Elsie had left in the ashtray. I must find out from Ida about those pills, she thought. Can't afford to get in the family way again. Finally, as she began to be a little more relaxed, she dropped off to sleep.

When she awoke, the room was in darkness. Switching on a lamp, she realized that she had slept away the whole day. She also realized that there was someone at the door. That was why she had woken. The door knob was rattling and someone was pushing against the door from the other side in a most alarming manner. Then she heard masculine voices. 'Open up, Elsie. We know you're in there.'

Sue leapt from the bed and frantically began to search for her skirt. A moment later, the door latch gave way and the door flew open to reveal three very belligerent young men.

With one leg in her skirt and trying desperately to pull it up, Sue stared at them with terror. It had to be a police raid, she thought. The men came lumbering across the room towards her as, terrified, she backed against the wall. The first was flat-nosed and hefty; the second, tall and red-cheeked, and behind them, she saw to her great relief, the small scrawny shape of Freddie the Sly.

Sue's sense of relief almost overwhelmed her. She laughed. 'Blimey, you didn't half scare me,' she exclaimed, rapidly zipping up her skirt. 'I thought it was the cops.'

Freddie the Sly, his greasy blond hair hanging untidily over his shoulders, looked sheepishly at her. He had been one of Sam's Boys, and had been sweet on Sue. It had been he who had acquired those high-wedge shoes for her first night out. 'What the hell did you want to come busting in like that for?' Sue asked as her courage returned to her. Freddie said nothing, standing with his mouth open as he goggled at her exposed white shoulder and her tight-fitting bra straining across her breasts.

The man with the broken nose leered at her in a greedy fashion, while the red-cheeked man demanded, in a gruff voice, 'What's all this? Where's that bleeding ponce, Alfie?'

He stuck out his chin in a most aggressive way and Sue became annoyed. 'Hop it!' she cried. 'He's gone and so has Elsie. This is my flat now.'

'What's the game?' the first man snarled, bringing his hand down heavy on her shoulder. 'Don't try kidding me or you'll be sorry.'

Sue wrenched her shoulder from his grasp and delivered him a swift punch on the nose. The blow was so unexpected that he almost laughed. 'So we want to spar up, do we?' he challenged. Instantly, his big fist shot out and hit her full in the stomach. The blow winded her and caused her to double up just in time to catch another on the end of her chin. This time she could see stars. 'Freddie!' she screamed. 'Why don't you help me?'

'Sorry, Sue,' said Freddie apologetically. 'I don't work for Sam now, I'm with Apples.'

'Had enough?' roared her attacker, dumping her on to the divan.

'She's only the skivvy,' muttered Freddie feebly. 'I don't think it's worth roughing her up.'

'Mind your own business,' said his boss, 'and get on and search this place. Might find out where Alfie hopped off to.'

Systematically, Freddie and the other man searched the flat, opening drawers and tossing everything out on to the floor. Meanwhile, Apples plonked himself heavily down beside the breathless and indignant Sue. 'Have a fag,' he said offering her the packet. She took a cigarette, and he lit it for her staring right into her face. 'Not grizzling, are you?' he queried. 'Mmm,' he nodded approvingly, 'tough little baby, ain't you?' His teeth showed pure white as he grinned at her.

Despite the bruises he had given her, Sue felt curiously drawn to this tough hoodlum. His eyes were grey-blue, long, and deep-set. When he smiled, laugh lines appeared about them and it was as if his whole rugged countenance lit up. She rubbed her shoulder ruefully. 'I'm all bruised,' she said.

'Teach you not to interfere in what's none of your business,' Apples replied unsympathetically.

Sue noticed that Freddie was prowling about pocketing bits of brass, while the other searched all the shelves. 'Don't make such a bloody mess,' she shouted at them. 'This is my flat now.'

This seemed to amuse Apples who burst into roars of laughter. 'Hear what the lady said?' he chuckled. 'Beat it!' he insisted. 'Get off down the café.'

Once alone with Sue, that bombastic manner disappeared as Apples seemed to become shy. Sue got up from the divan and slipped on her blouse. 'What are you going to beat Elsie up for?' she inquired.

'It's not that old brass we want,' replied Apples. 'It's that fat Alfie. Welshed on us, he did.'

'Well, I'm taking over this flat,' she informed him once more.

'You don't need to keep telling me. I heard you the first time,' he said rudely. 'All I hope is that you got that twenty quid when old Nick calls. My boys are gentlemen compared with the Greekoes he's got working for him.'

'You mean they'll come after me if I don't pay the rent?' She stared at him in disbelief.

'Come after you,' jeered Apples, 'with a razor, gel, and ready and willing to use it on yer pretty face.'

Sue went pale. Her mouth opened but no words came. Apples reached out towards her and drew her gently on to his knee. 'Come here, doll,' he said quietly. 'Don't look so scared. Apples won't let no one hurt you.'

By some natural instinct, Sue snuggled close and his mouth covered hers in a long kiss. It was the most wonderful thing that ever happened to her. It was a beautiful kiss, so sweet and gentle.

'Listen, doll,' said Apples as he stroked her hair. 'Don't tell me that you're a prostitute, because I'll never believe it.'

71

'No, not yet,' said Sue very seriously. 'But I intend to start soon.'

Apples moved away warily. 'Well, you ain't starting on me,' he said. 'I never did like whores and I ain't lumbering myself with one now.'

Sue's eyes showed their disappointment. 'Oh, I'm sorry, Apples, but how else will I live?' she asked.

Now Apples looked annoyed. 'Live? You work, gel, that's what. Not on the game, like Elsie, shagging her arse off every night to keep a fat ponce like Alfie. What sort of life is that?'

'I know,' she said woefully, getting closer to him, her hand caressing his face. 'But I'm on the run from an approved school, so I can't get a regular job.'

'There's plenty of ways to get a living,' said Apples, 'legally or otherwise. But all that filthy sex and porn, I got no time for it.' Slowly her arms went round his neck and they closed together. A timid knock at the door made them start, and then Freddie's thin voice called for Apples.

'Fluff off,' cried his boss. 'And tell the old lady I'll be home in the morning.' Turning his attention back to Sue, he said, 'That's me mum.'

Sue nodded as his kisses rained down on her passionately. Her heart was racing with excitement as she began her first real love affair. That she was shy and inexperienced he was about to discover, but that they appealed to each other, there was no denying.

Chapter Eight

Roast Beef on Sunday

After several days and nights of lovemaking, Apples decided that he had better go home to his mum. 'She's nearly eighty, you know, I'm still really scared of her,' he confessed. 'Every time I go home she gives me hell.'

'Don't try and tell me a ruffian like you is still a mummy's boy,' Sue mocked.

Apples' face flamed, as he blushed almost scarlet. 'Turn it up, Sue,' he begged. 'It's just that I'm the last one left at home, and there used to be nine of us. What's more, all the five years I was in the nick, the old lady stuck by me, fought to get me a parole and never missed a visit. It's my duty to return her favour now that she's old and lonely. But I do admit she bullies me.'

Sue had a rare smile on her lips as she pushed back a lock of brown hair from his brow and planted a soft kiss there. For some reason she was feeling good this morning. 'It must be nice to have someone who really cares about you,' she said wistfully. 'It's a luxury I've never had.'

Apples looked down at her with a gentle expression on his face. 'I'm a real villain, Sue,' he said, 'a damned muscleman. But I make a good living, and enough to take care of you if you'll let me. Please give me a chance to take care of you,' he pleaded.

Sue could not believe her ears. 'You mean live with me?' she asked incredulously.

'Give me the opportunity, Sue. Don't let me lose you. I'll pay the rent here, but that means you play straight with me. I want no more talk about going on the game.'

'You're kidding me,' she replied. 'I'll probably never even see you again.' Life had made her wary.

Apples' big hands grasped her wrists so hard he was nearly crushing her bones.

'Don't!' she cried. 'You're hurting me.'

'I'll hurt you much more if you let me down,' he threatened. 'It's not often I take a fancy to a bird, so listen, dolly, be mine. Be mine and never, never let me down.'

Sue had never had so much excitement and fun as she did for those first three months living as Apples' woman. There was the thrill in her blood whenever he arrived at the flat bringing lovely presents for her – gold rings to wear in her ears, bangles and beads for her slim wrists, and real diamond rings for her fingers. No longer an unwanted burden, under Apples' care and protection, Sue blossomed into womanhood like a peach tree in spring. She felt comfortable and happy, and had a sense of security at last. She no longer roamed the streets dodging every copper she saw. There were elegant clothes in the wardrobe and smart shoes in the cupboard. Everything had been bought and paid for; nothing was stolen.

'Look here, doll,' Apples would say, as he sat playing endless games of cards with his pals. 'Go get something nice to wear. And bring me back the receipt. I don't want you lifting anything. No bird of mine is going to end up in Holloway,' he warned.

Although Sue would laugh at him, she did not disobey. She had learned her lesson during their first few weeks together when she had openly boasted of her exploits in the stores. One day, after she had restocked the larder from the supermarket, he had caught hold of her by the hair and banged her head hard against the wall. 'Get it in your stupid noodle,' he had yelled, 'I'll have no petty thieving in my establishment.'

'Look who's talking!' she had screeched back at him.

'Listen, doll,' he replied grimly, still holding her hair tight. 'I'm a crook, a real hoodlum, but I like my woman respectable. Stop this thieving or I'll personally cut your bleeding fingers off.' And Sue knew that he meant it. And so, after half a dozen social workers, welfare officers and salvationists had failed to make her go straight, it was Apples who succeeded. He was her man. She really and truly loved him. And it was mutual. No one could separate them – not even that old mother he was so fond of. Sue obeyed him totally. She cooked him meals and washed his shirts and found supreme happiness.

Most days Apples just hung about the flat chatting to his pals who were always dropping in, often looking very tired and seedy. 'Put the kettle on, doll,' Apples would say to her. 'Make some toast. Run and get some fags.'

Always willing, Sue obeyed these commands and was very

popular with the boys. And she would sit listening quietly as they planned various jobs. No one had any doubts about Sue's trustworthiness. 'Not like the majority of birds,' Apples would boast. 'She can keep her trap shut.'

Under his care, Sue grew better looking, she lost her hard expression and became more soft and alluring. And she always took good care of her appearance. When she and Apples went out together at night – either to the dogs or on a pub crawl – he was proud of his beautiful doll, and she felt happy and carefree with him. But there were some nights when he would come back at dawn, and creep shivering into bed beside her. Then she would cuddle him tight, knowing that it had been a bad night and some job had gone wrong. They never spoke about his activities, but when his working clothes – dark shirt and rubber plimsolls – were laid out in readiness, Sue knew that he would be going out without her that evening. And on successful occasions Apples would sit and celebrate with his mates the next day, drinking the hours away while they shared out the loot. Sue would go down to the bakers and buy hot rolls for them and make black coffee. She fitted into this dangerous existence perfectly.

During Sue's first month living in Elsie's flat, Ida had visited her one morning. She did not look as smart and sophisticated as she usually did, her coffee-coloured skin looked rather sallow and there were dark rings under her lovely Asian eyes. 'Oh, it *is* you, Sue,' she exclaimed. 'I wasn't sure. And when I saw those boys on the stairs, I knew they were after Alfie, so I lay low.'

'Come in, Ida,' Sue welcomed her.

'I must say you're looking extremely well,' said Ida, looking her up and down. Sue was wearing the scarlet lounge suit that Apples had bought her. It fitted very well and suited her white skin and emphasized her dark hair. Sue laid out a couple of tea cups.

'How did you manage to get away from that school?' asked Ida.

'It wasn't hard,' said Sue loftily. She poured the tea dreamily. 'And I got myself a regular fella,' she announced.

Ida did not look impressed. 'What's the difference? They all do the dirty on you in the end,' she said bitterly.

'No, not this one,' Sue assured her. 'My Apples loves me.'

75

Ida looked incredulous. 'You ain't got one of those tearaways have you? Crikey, Sue! You're a bigger mug than I thought.'

'Do you mind,' sniffed Sue, offended. 'He wants to marry me.'

'A lot of water will have gone under the bridge by then,' muttered Ida. But then, seeing that Sue was rather crestfallen at her cynical response to her love affair, Ida felt a little ashamed. 'Sorry, ducks,' she apologized. 'I'm being a little bitchy. It's not been the same since Johnny hopped it with all me dough.'

'You mean your lover ran off?' asked Sue, scandalized. Everyone knew how much Ida had loved her coloured protector.

'Yes,' Ida said sadly, 'it's changed plenty since you got picked up, Sue. Fat Florrie snuffed it – was found dead in bed, and now Elsie's gone.' She assumed a mournful expression as if pining for the good old days. Sue sipped her tea and listened quietly to Ida's gossip. So fat Florrie was dead, she pondered, so no more four-lettered words would come roaring down the stairs.

'Got a couple of queer boys up there now,' continued Ida. 'They make blue films for a living. Old Sam moved down to the seaside when it got too hot for him around here. He sold the shop to a bookseller, and crumbs! What books he sells! It's pornography in the raw.' She giggled as if the thought of the dirty books cheered her up.

'It seems very quiet downstairs,' said Sue. 'Have you been working, Ida?'

'I'm not doing much,' said Ida, woefully. 'As a matter of fact, I'm considering quitting and going to Tiger Bay. It really threw me when Johnny ditched me.'

'I'm sorry,' murmured Sue.

'Stripped me of every cent, the bastard,' continued Ida, 'so I got a job flogging fags at Wing Wong's Club to try to put a bit back in the kitty.'

'So you're not on the game now . . .' Sue could not hide the note of disappointment in her voice. To her mind, there was still a lot of glamour attached to the profession.

'Not entirely, Sue,' replied Ida. 'I just hang on to those kinky old devils on afternoon sessions because they pay so well.'

'Kinky old devils?' Sue repeated the phrase as if she failed to understand.

'Christ!' exclaimed Ida. 'They wear me out, but as long as they

76

part up, I can take it. Do you know they actually enjoy being whipped, and one silly old fool likes stinging nettles up his bum.' Back to her own merry self, Ida began to laugh heartily.

It was contagious; Sue joined in. 'It's not true,' she choked, 'you're kidding me.'

'No, I'm not,' laughed Ida, 'I'm afraid you've got a good deal to learn . . .' And she proceeded to go into more intimate details of her profession.

Eyes gleaming with interest, Sue lapped it all up. 'I just find it beyond belief,' she kept gasping.

'It's all true, honey, I can assure you,' worldly Ida replied. 'Why, some old geezers actually call out for their mummy . . .'

That was the first of several intimate gossips Sue and Ida had in the flat until one day Apples arrived home early and caught Ida there. He was not at all pleased. 'Get that tart out of here!' he ordered. 'And keep her out.' So Ida and Sue's education in the ways of the world stopped for a while.

These were happy and contented days for Sue. The house was quiet as Ida slept most of the day and worked in Wing Wong's Club all night. The effeminate youths from upstairs crept furtively past her door every night. They had long, bleached hair and shoulder bags she noticed, but they did not bother her at all. She noticed that not so many old pals congregated at the flat nowadays.

'Where are all your mates?' she asked one day. She missed the jokes and friendly patter of the East End boys.

'All in the nick,' said Apples despondently. 'I suppose I can be grateful to you because if I had not been out with you celebrating your birthday last month, I'd have probably got me collar felt, too.'

Thinking back to that night, Sue was reminded of something else. They had had a good meal in a restaurant and got back very drunk. They had started to make love as soon as they got home, and though her alcoholic haze she had remembered the pills that Ida had obtained for her. Stumbling and groping her way to the bathroom, she had swallowed the first pill she found and fell back into bed beside her man. It was only in the morning that she had realized that she had taken an aspirin by mistake. She had been very disconcerted, but Apples had just roared with laughter

77

and then consoled her in that warm affectionate way he had. But a month had passed. Now, with a worried expression on her face, she told her lover of her fears.

'Don't worry, doll,' Apples said confidently. 'I've got a big job coming off soon. We're a little short on cash at the moment but this time I'm going to make it big so we can leave this bloody brothel, and buy a little pub in the country.'

'I wouldn't go through all that again,' she told him, 'I still dream of little Elaine, my baby they took from me.'

Apples cuddled her close. 'Now, Sue,' he said gently. 'Don't look back. Look only forward to happiness. This kid is mine and he'll want for nothing as long as I can provide it.'

She snuggled close, happy and content to hear these words. Everything would be all right this time . . . It was almost too good to be true.

'When this big job is over,' he said, 'we might even get married, that is, if I can get my sister to take the old lady,' he muttered rather doubtfully. He stuck out his chest. 'That's it, Sue, we'll get hitched, that'll surprise 'em.'

'It must be nice to belong to a big family,' said Sue.

'I've got three brothers and four sisters, and they've all done well in life, except me. I'm the black sheep. Take after me father, I suppose,' he added.

Every Sunday, Apples spent the day with his mother. 'I can't get out of it,' he complained to Sue. 'She cooks a joint of beef on Sundays and nags for weeks if I miss one dinner.' Apples tried to explain his attachment to his domineering mother. 'She's used to having a family to cook for and simply can't break the habit on Sundays.'

It did not bother Sue too much because she had the day to herself. She would stay late in bed, then wash her hair. Later, she would go down to the launderette to listen to the local gossip spread by the skivvies, the dreary old women who open and close doors for the prostitutes. But for Apples, Sundays became more and more frustrating. In the morning he would go down the Lane to buy a piece of china or a plant in a pot, 'for muvver' and then go on to see her in his old home. In that small, bright living-room there was a fantastic array of pots all over the window sills, and shelves. Indoor plants trailed and climbed everywhere; glass and china bric-à-brac lined the mantelshelf; family photographs lined the walls. 'Blimey, Muvver,' Apples would always say, 'why don't you get rid of some of this junk, it's like King's Road market in here.'

His mother's wiry little figure would stiffen in wrath. 'If you don't like it here, you can go where you've been all the week,' she would declare. Her wrinkled face would be screwed up in anger, and her rosy cheeks would stand out.

'Don't know why you live in this dump,' Apples remarked this particular Sunday. 'Why don't you go and live with Lilly up in Epping?'

This suggestion really incensed her. She began to stamp about her kitchen. 'Want to get rid of me, eh? Don't worry, I won't bother you much longer. I'll go, but in a box. Fifty years I've been in this house and no one is going to drive me out now.'

'All right, Mum, don't get upset.' Apples tried to calm her. 'But I was thinking, suppose I got married?'

'Married!' his mother shouted in disgust. 'Who's going to marry a layabout like you?'

With a frustrated sigh Apples got up. 'Give over, old lady. I ain't going anywhere,' he said, 'unless it is over the pub to have a drink.' A few minutes later he stood in the bar across the road and drained his pint to the dregs. Through the window he could see that tiny house with its starched lace curtains the hearth-stoned doorsteps in a perfect circle. He could almost smell the aroma of roast beef as Muvver basted the joint in the oven. How pleased he had been when he had finished that long prison sentence and come home to Muvver and the roast beef on Sunday. But since he had met Sue it had lost its appeal. Also, the old lady was just getting even more awkward . . .

That evening, he discussed the matter with Sue but she was non-committal about his mother. 'How can I advise you?' she said. 'I never cared tuppence about anyone until I met you.'

Apples hugged her. 'Honest to God,' he murmured, 'I never ever thought of going straight before, but now I want our kid to have a good life, a posh home and birthday parties.'

Sue sat on the bed, nonchalantly varnishing her nails a bright purple. 'What's for us we'll get,' she said philosophically. 'At least I've learned that much,' she said.

'I guess you're right, Sue, it's the luck of the draw.'

'That's it, lover, let's live for today,' she replied. 'Where are we going tonight?'

'It's your choice, Sue,' offered Apples. 'Say where you like.'

So, like brilliant moths about a candle, they fluttered around the bright lights of London from pub to club, until the early hours. At midday the next day, they were still sleeping it off, lying close together. Suddenly, they were woken by a pounding on the door. Sue opened it to see the small Chinese boy who worked at Wing Wong's standing there. 'Got a message for . . .' he announced to the sleepy-eyed Sue.

'Well, what is it?' she asked, very irritated at being roused.

But the boy shook his head. 'Me onny to hem,' he said defiantly. Apples had heard and was getting out of bed and pulling on his pants. 'All right, Lu, I got the message,' he called. And the boy scooted away.

'What on earth was all that about?' Sue asked as she poured the coffee.

'It's a big job,' he replied, 'the signal I've been waiting for.' Swiftly, he packed his dark shirt, plimsolls and his shaving gear.

'Be gone long?' asked Sue placidly.

'I hope not, but don't try to contact me. Whatever happens, just go on as always. That'll keep you out of it. If it's impossible to come back here, someone will bring you a message.'

Her dark eyes surveyed him in a deep sombre gaze, causing him to grab hold of her close to his heart. 'Oh, my lovely Sue, you are the best thing that ever happened to me.' He picked up his bags. 'I'll be back and loaded. Then you'll have the best that this damned world can give.'

The door closed and he was gone. An air of gloom slowly descended on the flat as she heard his footsteps down the stairs until there was silence. He was gone, never to return to that little love nest in the heart of Soho.

Chapter Nine

No Return

It took a while before Sue realized that something had happened. The first few days after Apples had gone, she lazed around the flat thinking about him and paying great attention to her looks. She would carefully make up her face, re-set her hair and gave a lot of thought to what she should wear. In the evenings, she would go out to eat in Wing Wong's expensive restaurant. There she would take her time over a good meal and ponder on her life before she had met her lover. One evening her thoughts drifted to Gladys, that little mongol who had been her only close friend, she wondered if she was still living in the convent. When I'm married and settled down, I'll go and get her, Sue decided. She'll be a great help if I have a big house. Thus she wallowed in pipe dreams while savouring the warmth and comfort of the restaurant where she received special attention from the staff who knew her man was a big spender.

After her meal she would cross the road to Wing Wong's Club. It was there that Ida sold cigarettes and other things from a tray. She would always be dressed in a very short skirt from which her slim coffee-coloured legs tapered and which had a very low neck-line. It was so low that her bosom peeped out of the dress and almost rested on the tray of wares she carried about her neck. She always gave Sue a wink as she tripped by.

Sue would sit at a table and take in that revolting floor show and observe how the hostesses wiggled their hips provocatively as they persuaded the customers to buy more drinks. Wing Wong, the proprietor, was a very suave young man whose only Chinese features were those narrow slit eyes. In all other respects, he was almost a Cockney. He certainly sounded like one, having imbibed the language from the East End rogues he associated with. He always treated Sue very courteously and warded off any ardent males who wanted to get to know the lovely young woman who sat all alone perched on the bar stool night after night. After a while, Sue realized that no one ever mentioned her man, or even asked after him, and she began to have a feeling that down here in this dreary club that they knew a lot more about Apples than she did. And there was a feeling in the air of watching and waiting; it worried her.

After two weeks the money Apples had left her had dwindled to almost nothing and Sue felt very despondent. There was still no sign of her lover. On Sunday she went to the launderette. She liked going. It was bright and light in there, and people chatted to her and happily included her in their conversations. So when she entered that steamy atmosphere, clutching her plastic bag of smalls, ready to listen to the gossip of the turban-headed woman, she was quite unprepared for what she heard. Two middle-aged women greeted Sue pleasantly, and then returned to their perusal of the Sunday paper.

'They caught that bloke,' one remarked. Sue stuffed her washing into the machine.

'What, that bloke that shot the copper?' asked another.

'Yes, up North.' She pointed to the article in the paper. 'It says here. They've been trailing him for days. Never got a light from that bullion hold-up. Some say the coppers were tipped off.'

'You don't say,' whispered another.

'I know him well. Comes from around here, he does,' said the reader of the paper.

Sue looked anxiously over her shoulder to look at the newspaper. There she saw a large photograph of a man with a coat over his head being escorted by two policemen. Only his two large feet were exposed to view, and Sue gave a cry of dismay. Those familiar legs were bent at the knees as if the weight of that tired body could not be supported by them. The caption confirmed her fear. It read: 'Capture of Billy Rafferty, the armed bandit.' Leaving her washing in the machine, Sue turned and ran out of the launderette. Billy Rafferty was Apples' real name. Tears poured down her face as she ran desperately back to her little flat, where she threw herself down on the pink divan and gave vent to her grief. For a long time she cried and sobbed herself almost into hysterics, until Ida's gentle hands soothed her brow and fortified her with hot sweet tea.

'What's wrong with me, Ida?' she cried. 'Why did I not try to stop him?'

Ida eyed Sue scornfully. 'It's not your fault, love,' she said.

'You're as green as grass, you know very little about this stinking world we live in.'

'You may be right, Ida, but I'm beginning to learn,' she replied. 'I love him, and I'll fight to keep him.'

'Sue, darling,' sighed Ida, 'Apples plugged a copper. You have to resign yourself to the fact that he will go away for a long time.'

'I must see him,' wept Sue. 'How can I find out where he is?'

'That won't be hard,' replied Ida, in a softer tone. 'I'll find out tonight, at Wing Wong's. That Chinese bastard is up to his eyes in it.'

Ida's good-looking face looked more wan and sallow than ever when she returned from her night's work the next morning. Sue had been sitting by the window chain-smoking anxiously as she watched Ida cross the road and come wearily down the narrow street. As she heard the prostitute's footsteps on the stairs, she sprang eagerly to her feet. Ida was bringing news of her lover. 'Heard anything?' she gasped excitedly as Ida came in.

'I did, Sue,' she replied seriously, 'and the message is that on no account are you to visit him.'

Wide-eyed with disbelief, Sue stared back at her. 'Why not, Ida,' she said with a puzzled look on her face. 'Please, for God's sake, what did he say?' She was panic-stricken at the thought he did not want her.

Ida looked depressed and shrugged her shoulders. 'He's right, Sue,' she said. 'Once those newspaper hounds get a wheeze of you, they'll be here like bees round a honey pot, not to mention the cops that will come with them.'

Sue stood by the window with her hands clasped in front of her. 'How will I know? What shall I do?' she cried plaintively.

'He's going to smuggle out a letter later on,' Ida assured her, 'so relax, darling. Come on, let's go down to the pub. A stiff drink will buck you up.'

A couple of weeks later, a crumpled badly spelled letter arrived home with Ida one morning. In agonized silence Sue read this battered missive from her lover who wrote that he truly loved her, but that she was not to think of waiting for him. Having messed up his own life, he said, he did not want to ruin hers, too. 'They are going to do me, doll, good and proper this time. Get rid of that teapot lid. I won't feel so bad about us then. Don't come near the court and don't write to me. They read all the mail,' he warned.

83

Sue sat for a while in a daze, letter in hand. So it was the end of a wonderful dream. It was easy for him to tell her to get rid of their baby. Her fairy castle now lay in ruins. Fate had decided for her. She would probably end up like Ida, now, flogging fags at Wing Wong's . . .

After that there was a long period with no news. The days seemed long and endless as she waited to hear more. Wing Wong had discreetly disappeared and the staff at the Club were not so polite now to her anymore. Money had become a big problem, and she sold a piece of jewellery to make ends meet. A dark-skinned evil-looking character called for the rent and after that had been paid, there were only a few pounds left for food.

Ida was losing her patience. 'Got to do something about that baby soon,' she informed Sue. 'Can't leave it too late.'

'I'll wait till he's sentenced,' declared Sue. 'If he gets a light sentence I might go on and have it.

'God in heaven,' wailed Ida. 'Wake up, will you? He's already done five for grievous bodily harm. He'll get ten at least.'

Sue shivered. 'Please don't say that, Ida. Oh, whatever shall I do?'

'Same as others do,' replied Ida. 'Keep going. But personally, I would not raise a kid whose old man was in the nick.'

'Oh, I know you're wise and probably right, Ida,' wept Sue. 'But I honestly haven't a clue how to go about it.'

'Just get the lolly, and I'll make all the arrangements,' replied the resourceful prostitute. 'Harry the cabby does all the business. He takes you there and brings you home. But it's for a price, a big price. Makes a good living, does Harry.'

As Ida chattered on, Sue remained quiet. There was wild terror inside her at the thought of killing this life. It belonged to her and her true love, her true love who was shut up behind high walls, just as she had been not so long ago. Suddenly her mind was made up. 'I must see him,' she cried. 'I want him to tell me to my face that he doesn't want our baby.'

'Christ!' declared Ida. 'Don't make an issue of it, Sue, it will only make it harder.'

'No, I'm determined to hear it from his own lips.' Sue's mouth assumed an obstinate line as she spoke.

'Well,' shrugged Ida, who could see that Sue meant what she said, 'I'll see what can be done. He'll be brought up to London for the sessions. He'll be in Brixton, no doubt.'

'Thanks, Ida,' Sue said gratefully, and in a rare show of affection, she put her arms about Ida's neck and kissed her.

'Don't know why I stick my bloody neck out for you,' said Ida brusquely, but there was a hint of tears in the eyes of this battle-scarred prostitute to whom sentiment was a real luxury.

The next few weeks were very dreary, spent drinking with Ida in the saloon bar at the local. Each day Sue sat with her to pass the time away consuming many gin and tonics before going home in a befuddled state to sleep the night away. Then, at last, the long-awaited visiting order arrived after Apples had finally relented. How thrilled she was at the idea of seeing him once more. She could hardly wait for the day . . .

A week later, tall and majestic, and very solemn, she walked into that gloomy building. Her heart was beating fast, as she saw him behind a square window of wire and glass. For a moment she had an impulse to turn and run as a claustrophobic feeling gripped her but bravely, she resisted it and looked into the tired face of her man. Apples was smiling, and showing those fine teeth and those little creases about his eyes. She noticed faint blue bruises on his face and there was a fresh scar at the side of his mouth. 'How are you, dear?' she whispered.

'Oh, I'm bloody fine. Don't I look it?' he grinned.

Sue relaxed, they had made contact once more.

'I warned you not to come here,' he grumbled.

'But I had missed you so terribly,' she muttered pathetically.

'Now look here, doll.' His voice was low and tense. 'I'm telling you to forget me. It'll be a long time before I get free.'

'I'll wait for you,' she said earnestly. 'I'll work hard and look after our baby,' she pleaded.

His hands clenched till the knuckles showed white. 'Do as I say, doll,' he commanded. 'I'll write later on, but at the moment old Bill is listening to every word.' As he looked away, she saw tears in those grey-blue eyes but then he turned back and hissed viciously, 'Now scarper, doll, be a good girl and do as I say. Get going quick before anyone recognizes you.'

Sue got up and left as slowly and majestically as she came. Although her cold, pale face showed no emotion, inside it felt as though her heart was breaking. Not a sound from the dense London traffic penetrated her ears; it was as if a cold melancholic silence had swept over her. She went straight back to Soho and joined Ida at the local pub where she downed a series of straight gins. Gradually the noise of the other customers in the bar ebbed through her stunned brain. The lunchtime crowd was noisy with its laughter and merry chatter. Slowly her mood turned into vicious, violent temper. With a sneering gaze and her mouth turned downwards she surveyed those smug, well-cared-for office workers out for a lunchtime drink with the boss. They all looked safe and comfortable, and middle class. Her fingers tightened round the stem of the glass, as she had an impulse to smash it into the face of the nearest respectable female, and then tear out her hair, and rip off her nice dress. Her dark eyes glowed with hatred, and her face stood out fierce and white as she looked for someone to attack.

Ida instantly scented danger. Leaving her escort's side, she gently took the glass from Sue's hand and placed it on the bar counter. 'Come on, kid,' she said. 'Let's go home.'

Once inside the flat, Sue burst into a shrill scream that echoed through the house, then she pulled all the bric-ßa-brac off the shelf and flung it to the floor. Sobbing and crying out, she trampled it all into the carpet. Next came the cups from the dresser. One by one they smashed as she aimed them against the wall.

Ida sat quietly outside on the stairs, watching through the open door. 'That's it, kid,' she commented cheerfully. 'Let off steam.' She nodded her appreciation as each piece of china smashed. 'It's only a lot of bloody junk that Elsie collected, anyway,' she said.

Chapter Ten

The Street Walker

On a sunny morning in the sleepy back streets of Soho, life began to emerge. News vendors put up their stands; flower sellers arranged their wares; crowds tumbled out of the tubes to invade the office blocks. And the vice girls turned over in their tumbled beds – it was much too early for them to rise. Up in her flat, Sue wallowed in a luxurious bubble bath. The hot, scented water was so refreshing to her after a very sleepless night. She had been unable to sleep because there was so much on her mind. This was the last day of Apples' trial which she had followed diligently on the news and in the newspapers. But today she was determined to be at court to see and hear him for the last time.

All the arrangements for going to the abortion clinic had been finalized. Harry the cabby would pick her up at six o'clock that evening. The money had been raised by selling almost everything she possessed. And when it was all over, she would forget him just as he had advised her. She would make a living in some way – perhaps on the game – who cared? Passing the sponge over her body, she surveyed her tummy with its small hard lump. There was no feeling there yet. That small life that was part of them both was going to be disposed of, flushed down the toilet, like so much filth. She began to think of Elaine, that beautiful babe she had cuddled so close. She would be ten months old now . . . It was strange how prolific she was, she thought. She must take after her own mother. Her thoughts wandered back to a traumatic picture of a faded woman retching into a chamber pot each morning. Her face yellow with fatigue, and the room reeked of baby nappies and body smells. If Sue had been able to live a normal, happy life she would probably have raised a big family – at least she would have known how to care for them and keep them clean. That, at least, was something her life had taught her. But one thing was certain now, she thought, splashing water over her legs: she would never lead a life like that of her mother, who was sick and defeated at thirty, and died leaving a brood of children to the care of the state. She squeezed the water from the sponge with vicious intent. 'They won't beat me,' she muttered. 'To hell with them! I'll live a life of my own.' And she leaped from the bath and carefully prepared herself for the final visit to the courtroom to hear the father of her child being sentenced.

Inside, the court house was quiet. Newspapermen huddled expectantly at the door, pencils poised. In the front row sat a long line of Apples' friends and relations. Sue, sitting half way down the room and next to Ida, could see their sober faces, and observe the mixed variety of hats and tammies, and thinning heads and lone hair-dos. Her gaze travelled along the line with interest. His family seemed to be there in full force, she thought. Although she had never been introduced to any members of this much-talked-of family, she was infinitely curious about them. That must be his mum, she thought, looking at a wizened old woman who bore a funeral-black turban on her silver hair and sat bolt upright, her sharp eyes darting about the room. From the family likeness, Sue could count the nine brothers and sisters and God knows how many grandchildren. For a fleeting moment she thought about rushing up to the front to tell them her secret. After all, one more little one added to that great brood would surely not make any difference. She did not, of course, and she felt her chest harden with bitterness. If they wanted her, they would have included her, she thought. Her road was already washed with bitter tears; she could not go back.

Suddenly the court clerk rose to his feet and called for everyone to be 'upstanding'. Then, from a door behind the bench, the great judge appeared and marched solemnly to the throne. Sue gave a gasp as she saw that the judge was a woman.

'That's Ena Rosenberg, the woman High Court judge,' whispered Ida beside her.

'Then she'll probably be merciful,' Sue whispered back.

'Not on your nelly,' retorted Ida. 'She's a hard cold bitch.'

Now her man was standing in the dock, Sue tried hard to will his gaze in her direction but it did not work. Apples stood upright with a far-away expression on his face, as if to say, 'let's get it over with'.

The summing-up went on for hours, with long speeches from the lawyers from both sides, and the slow court procedure. At times it was very boring, and Sue lulled herself into complete oblivion with her gaze fixed on the judge. It was she, the expressionless, middle-aged woman in large spectacles and a grotesque wig, who held Sue's own life in bondage. Could it possibly help if she jumped to her feet and cried out: 'Oh, don't take him from me, he's the father of my unborn child.' But Sue knew that it would be useless; a woman like that had little compassion for the working classes.

At last it was time to pass judgement. Fixing the prisoner with an icy stare, Judge Rosenberg began. 'You are a most fortunate young man,' she said, 'that the constable you attacked received only a minor injury. But you have continuously defied and broken the law and this last time was with the use of a firearm. Therefore, I find it necessary to impose the maximum penalty. You will go to prison for fifteen years.'

A murmur of dissent swept through the court room. There was a shrill scream and the sound of much sobbing. The prisoner himself covered his face with his hands as he was led away.

As everyone else left the room, Sue stayed put, dazed and numbed, with hardly any feeling at all.

Harry the cabby was very punctual. At ten minutes to six his fruity Cockney voice called upstairs: 'Ida, is yer mate ready?'

Sue was having that last cuppa with Ida in the flat. Her suitcase, packed, was beside her. Her face looked pale and scared. 'Oh, Ida,' she whispered suddenly panicking. 'I'd sooner have the kid than go through with this.'

Slick and smart in a tailored suit and stiff white shirt, Ida laughed loudly. 'Do me a favour, Sue, it's nothing. You'll be back tomorrow.'

And so, screwing up her courage, Sue allowed Ida to take her suitcase and escort her to the waiting taxi. Harry greeted them as he squeezed his enormous bulk into the driving seat. 'Come on, girls,' he shouted. 'Anchors away!'

Moments later, the taxi pulled out leaving Ida waving a cheerful goodbye to Sue, the very doleful figure in the back seat.

The journey to the nursing home was uneventful, except that during a traffic jam, they were stopped for some minutes right outside the convent where Sue had spent many of her teenage years. Peering out of the taxi's dark windows, she stared at the grey turrets, and tiny barred windows and at the blue plaque on the gatepost that informed passers-by that the Bishop of Westminister had once lived there. There was not a sign of life from the huge dwelling. It was six-thirty, so all the girls would probably be at prayers before going to bed. She thought of the little mongol, Gladys, and wondered what had become of her.

Soon they were driving along leafy lanes and then turned down the drive of an exclusive nursing home tucked away on the borders of Epping Forest. After a few discreet words with the receptionist, a bright little nurse conducted her up the wide oak stairway to the cold clinical atmosphere of the abortion clinic. Harry the cabby shouted after her, 'Collect yer same time tomorrow. Good luck!'

Sue remembered very little about the next twenty-four hours, although she did recall a dark-skinned doctor with gold in his teeth and a grim-faced theatre sister. She remembered, too, waking from the anaesthetic feeling deeply depressed and unhappy. Now there was nothing left of that all-consuming love affair and nothing but emptiness in the cold dark world outside.

She heard Harry's gruff voice in the corridor, earlier than she had expected. He had brought in another customer and had arrived at four o'clock instead of six. But Sue was quite ready to get out of that place as quickly as possible. 'Just as well you came early,' she complained, 'or I might have jumped out of the window.'

'Got rid of yer bleedin' bundle, didn't yer,' shouted Harry. 'What are yer grousing abaht?'

Sitting in the back of the taxi, Sue had nothing to say, but Harry had plenty. 'Christ!' he ejaculated. 'A hundred and fifty nicker! Making a bleeding fortune. Wish I knew the ropes, I'd do it me bleeding self, I would.'

Sue sneered, 'You get your cut, you fat old ponce. What are you complaining about?'

'Well now, that's nice I must say,' retorted Harry with a throaty chuckle, as if she had paid him a compliment. But suddenly Sue's attention was elsewhere as her gaze caught sight of a little group of girls outside the cinema. There was Gladys, as small and tough as ever, marshalling her squad of convent girls who still wore those short white socks and their hair in long plaits with bows tied on the ends. Still the same little crippled ones were helped along by the hideous ones, and they were still all in the charge of Gladys, who pushed and punched them into position. Sue opened the window. 'Gladys!' she called, but the cab shot across the lights and passed them quickly. 'Stop, Harry!' she cried. 'I just saw someone I know.'

'Sorry love,' replied Harry. 'My instructions are to take you back to where I picked you up. From then on, it's your pigeon.'

Tears pricked her eyes, and Sue felt even more depressed. Seeing Gladys had brought back forgotten memories. I'll go back and see her once I've rested up, she promised herself as the taxi pulled up in her Soho street.

Ida came down to welcome her. 'Come on, honey, have a nice drop of hot gin and then it's beddy-byes,' she said.

Sue was grateful to Ida for her kindness. She felt she needed some care and attention because she felt a peculiar kind of light-headedness. The weeks following the abortion were strange and hazy. Sue frequently felt faint and far away, and for the best part of the day, she would doze fitfully in a chair, only rising in the evening to go with Ida to the cafe for a meal. Gone were the days of expensive Chinese suppers and visits to the Club bar. Money was now very short. The last piece of jewellery had gone to pay the clinic, so she knew it was to be a hand-to-mouth existence until she found some means of supporting herself. Ida was very kind and always as generous as she could be. It was she who paid for those meagre meals of sausage, egg and chips at the Italian café. Tonight, over coffee, they discussed the future.

'Can't afford to go mad now,' said Ida, thoughtfully, picking the food from her good teeth. 'I've got used to living easy, but that Wing Wong's a mean old git. Don't exactly overpay me.'

Sue stared desolately at her friend with cow-like eyes. 'I'll pay for the meal today,' she said firmly. 'I'm going to start work tomorrow.'

'Work, Sue?' exclaimed her startled companion. 'But where?'

'On the street,' Sue replied flatly. 'How else?'

Ida frowned. 'Be careful, Sue,' she warned, 'there's a lot to learn. It's no picnic, you know – why do you think I'm wanting to quit?'

'Don't worry, Ida, I'm big enough and ugly enough to take care of myself,' replied Sue with a trace of the old grin.

'Pity you still got that charge hanging over your head. You could get a nice shop job if you could acquire some National Insurance cards.'

'Give over, Ida,' scoffed Sue. 'You're clucking and fussing like some old hen.'

Ida shook her head. 'I'm fond of you, kid, but I suppose we all have to learn the hard way.' Then she changed the subject with a nonchalant shrug.

The next evening, after Ida had gone to work, Sue left the flat wearing long, black silk tights and a short leather skirt. Swinging her handbag to and fro, she walked to the corner of the street with a provocative swing to her hips. Then she hesitated. For on each of the four corners, stood the pimps. As the slant eyes surveyed her with knowing winks, sallow faces exchanged evil grins. She knew exactly what those men were thinking: 'Here comes a rooky. Better watch it. Don't want her pinching our girls' clients.' Gathering up her courage, she crossed the main road, walked the length of Oxford Street, and once around Picadilly Circus. Every time a solitary man hurried past her, she would give him a meaningful look, but nothing happened. By now her legs had begun to ache and she was feeling thoroughly unhappy. Making her weary way back to Soho, she dived into the little bar where she and Ida often had a lunchtime drink. Ordering a gin and tonic, she sank, exhausted, into a red plush seat. Young couples cuddled in dim corners. Virile young men lined the brightly lit bar. But not once did a head turn in her direction. Sipping her drink, she pondered over the strange fact that men had fallen over themselves to flirt with her while she was with her lover, but now that she was on her own, they were not interested in her. However did one start? What were the magic words once spoke to differentiate oneself from a girl out on the town to a paid prostitute? She sighed and looked in her purse. She had four shillings left - just enought for another gin. She went to the bar, ordered her drink and put the money down, but a firm hand pushed it away and a voice said, 'Make it a double.'

Her heart leaped. She had made it at last! She had clicked, as Elsie used to say. The man was tall, fair and young – probably about twenty. His bright blue eyes were sleepy and streaked red by alcohol, and it was on slightly unsteady legs that he carried the drinks over to a quiet corner where they sat down.

'Cheers,' he said raising his glass. 'Drink up and cheer up,' he said.

Sue smiled wanly. The warm liquid flowed down her throat

and helped to restore her confidence. Soon she was able to chat with her pick-up, who said his name was Terry. He kissed her cheek, put his arm about her and in a very maudlin way told her of how his sweetheart had gone off with his best friend in his home town in the Midlands.

Sue was scarcely listening. As he came out with his sorry tale, she was busily working out what to charge him and how best to approach the subject. He had told her that he was a student, so he might be broke. If this was the case, she would have to tactfully back out of this situation. Then the tipsy young lad gazed wistfully at her. 'Let me come home with you Sue,' he whispered.

She fixed him with her hard, dark eyes and was about to say, 'Only if you pay me,' but he rattled the loose change in his trouser pocket and then, reaching inside his jacket, took a five pound note from his wallet. 'That's all I've got, Sue,' he said, 'but you're welcome to it. I need the company tonight.'

With a swift movement, Sue took the note. 'Come on, lad, let's go then,' she said in the professional tone she had heard Elsie use. Terry looked a trifle surprised, but he took her arm and they walked to the flat.

Terry's lovemaking was rather like his person – clean, warm, sweet and generous. But at one time during the night he wept on her bosom, and cried, 'Don't leave me, Sylvia.' She suddenly felt very ashamed, and cuddled him close. Terry finally fell asleep but Sue lay awake for some time. This lovesick boy's ineffectual passion had stirred that animal desire in Sue, and she longed even more for her lovely strong man who was now shut up behind bars.

By the time dawn came, she had fallen asleep very heavily. She woke at nine o'clock to find that her customer had fled. On the mirror in the bathroom he had written in lipstick: 'Bye Sue.' Picking up a tissue, she wiped the lipstick away. That had been an easily earned fiver, she thought, but she wondered if it would always be so. At the thought of that crumpled fiver, she panicked. Dashing back to the bedroom, she looked in her handbag. It was still there, safely tucked into the corner where she had placed it the night before.

Contrary to Sue's expectations, Ida was not very impressed by her first exploit as a prostitute. When Sue visited her that afternoon, she was sitting cross-legged on her divan, clad only in a brief black bra and panties. She looked very tired. 'Thought I'd never get through that session,' she declared having just disposed of one of her kinky regulars.

'I did it!' Sue informed her jubilantly, and proceeded to tell Ida all about it.

But Ida was quite scornful. 'It's no good, Sue,' she said. 'A soft guy like that is likely to come back for more and without any dough. He'll pester the life out of you. And I know, I've been through it all.'

'Not him, he's too nice a boy,' Sue defended her youthful client.

'Get us a drink, Sue,' said Ida. 'I'm all in. Might take a holiday. Would you like to carry on here?' she asked.

Sue looked nervously at the formidable array of whips and dog leashes hanging up in the half-opened cupboard by the wall. 'Oh, no,' she gasped. 'I couldn't. I'd be terrified.'

'No more terrifying than being beaten up or getting a dose,' said Ida bluntly. 'And that's what is likely to happen to you, Sue, unless you find a protector. Not only that, but the cops are likely to run you in if they catch you prowling the streets.'

'I don't care,' cried Sue defiantly. 'I don't want no ponce to run my life for me. I'll go it alone.'

'Please yourself,' replied Ida. 'But don't say I didn't warn you.'

Without any heed to her friend's warning, Sue obstinately went out again on to the streets that night. It was a wet night. A cold wind drove clouds of fine rain along the damp, shiny pavements as the theatre crowds hurried home. With a provocative strut, she prowled the streets for several hours – up and down the road, and round and round the square. But her luck was out. Soon she was tired and fed up. Her shoes let in water and her grandly lacquered hair-do had collapsed into an untidy mess. Desperately, she stepped out in front of a gentleman wearing a white belted raincoat. 'Would you like some love to warm you up this cold night?' she asked coyly.

The man looked astonished at first and then he smirked. 'Not tonight, darlin',' he replied before hurrying across the road. Sue crept into a shop doorway out of the wind, and stood there thinking for a while. Then she saw that same man talking to a traffic cop at the junction where the lights flickered from red to yellow. As the red light flashed, Ida's warning went through her brain, and she knew that he was telling the police that she had accosted him. With her heart pounding against her ribs, she darted quickly through the back alleys, running, fleeing from that fear of the grey prison walls, of being caged like a wild bird . . . . A police car went whizzing by, blue lights flashing and siren screaming. Wet and shivering, she pressed her body back into the dark recess of a doorway until she could hear the siren no longer. Suddenly she realized she had company. In the opposite corner of the doorway, she now made out a shadowy shape who was distinguishable only by the light of a cigarette. She gasped fearfully.

'Who's old Bill after?' a thin, bitter voice asked. 'Done a bunk or just soliciting?' As her eyes became more accustomed to the darkness, she could see a youngish man with long hair that flowed down to his shoulders. He was wearing a bright plaid shirt and old jeans. He came over to her side. 'Christ!' he exclaimed. 'You look all in. Have a fag.' He passed her the packet and lit one for her. She puffed gratefully with shaking hands.

'What the cops after you for?' he asked, putting his hands in his pockets and eyeing her speculatively. 'A brass ain't yer?' he decided. 'Must be new at it – they don't often freak out like that.'

'That's right,' she answered. She could feel her courage returning; for some reason, this impudent young man irritated her.

'Got a pad, have you?' he asked.

'I've got my own flat, if that's what you mean,' she replied airily.

'Good,' he said, 'then what are we waiting for?'

But as he took hold of her arm, she pulled away. 'I'm not for free,' she snapped. 'It's my living.'

'Okay, I'll pay,' he replied. 'But don't get so shirty – it's bleeding cold out here.'

With the long-haired youth slouching beside her, Sue returned home. While she was removing her wet clothes, he had found a can of beer in the fridge and was guzzling it. Silently he surveyed the room with mean eyes. Spotting the biscuit tin, he opened it and grabbed a handful, munching the biscuits and spilling crumbs all over the carpet. In the bathroom, Sue rubbed her hair vigorously. For some reason, she was feeling very apprehensive about this wild-looking, grubby man. He definitely smelled of

B.O., there was some other, sweet, sickly smell that she could not recognize. The house was very quiet, and she wished Ida were home. Still, she told herself, she had chosen this way of life and had to take the rough with the smooth, as Elsie had frequently commented.

Emerging from the bathroom, wearing only a dressing gown, and with her hair hanging loose, she saw that he was leaning against the door with the beer can in his hand and a sneer on his face. She glanced at his long, dirty fingernails and was disgusted. 'Well, let's get it over,' she said sharply. 'Money first.' She held out her hand.

The man threw the beer can down on to the floor and lunged at her. He grasped her wrist so swiftly she was thrown off balance and went down on the floor with a crash. What followed was the most revolting experience of her life. The man straddled her and placed his filthy hand across her mouth. Sue was a strong girl but she did not stand a chance against this maniac who had the strength of ten men. For what seemed like hours, she fought like a tiger while he stuffed parts of his filthy body into her, tearing at her breasts with his teeth slobbering and grunting like an animal. At one time he held her down and beat her on the head with the empty beer can, until she was practically unconscious. But not so unconscious that she could not then see him standing over her and sending a stream of filthy smelling liquid into her face as he urinated over her. Then she passed out.

When Ida returned at dawn she was surprised to find the front door wide open, and running up the stairs, she found Sue, a weeping, pathetic mess on the floor. Ida gently bathed the filth from Sue's young body and tried hard to comfort her, but she nagged her, too. 'Oh, Sue, you little fool. I warned you. It's lucky he never done you in. Some damned junkie, I expect. Better come round to the quack's tomorrow. God only knows what condition his body was in. Oh, Sue, silly little Sue,' she wailed. 'Just give it up, love, you're too soft for all this.'

Sue lay on the bed, too bruised to move. Her eyes were blackened and her lips were swollen. Each time she moved at all, she cried out in pain. 'Men! I hate them!' she muttered.

'He was an animal, Sue, not a man,' said Ida. 'But it doesn't do any harm to hate, not in our profession.'

It was nearly a month before Sue had recovered. She had had

to get medical treatment and the doctor was bound to send in a big bill. Ida was very kind but Sue had begun to feel obligated to her. Also, she looked so tired and Sue knew that she was not making life any easier for her. Ida had settled the month's rent and Sue had no funds for the next month. She just could not impose on Ida's generous nature any longer. Something had to be done. Staring out of the window, she would shiver at the idea of walking the streets again. She could not face it, her confidence had gone. No, she would have to leave Soho, she knew that, but where could she go? She could return to the convent and throw herself on the mercy of the nuns, but she shivered at the thought. And then suddenly, a brilliant idea flashed in her mind. Her old friend from the convent, that capable, strong, aggressive Gladys would be the ideal protector. If she had Gladys, perhaps she could stay in Soho . . .

Next Saturday, she crept quietly from the flat. Wearing a long mac, with her hair covered by a scarf and with her face devoid of make-up, she looked more like a maid on her day off than a prostitute from Soho. The bus deposited her outside the cinema where Sue waited patiently.

Punctually, at three o'clock the little procession from the convent arrived. There were the two bathchairs containing little twisted bodies – one pushed by Gladys and the other by stout Sister Winifred. Behind them trooped seven or eight girls. Sue recognized Milly and Tilly, walking hand in hand, as always. They seemed shorter than ever, and they laughed and giggled as they went by. For a moment Sue felt very sad. How dull and grey their lives were, yet these unwanted human beings retained so much humour and affection for others. They were so brave.

Sue waited while Sister Winifred had bought the tickets, and shepherded them all inside. From then on, the group was in the charge of Gladys because the sister went off to spend the afternoon shopping. Swiftly, Sue got her ticket and in no time she was seated behind Gladys and her squad. Gladys' charges whispered and rattled sweet bags noisily, thoroughly enjoying their Saturday treat. Sue did not make her presence known until the interval when she tapped Gladys on the shoulder. 'It's Sue,' she whispered in a low voice. 'Don't turn around yet, Gladys.' Gladys' large head turned slightly, and her small hand came out and gripped Sue tightly. 'Come out, in the toilet,' she whispered. 'Don't let anyone see you.'

In that small compartment between the sink and mirror, the two women met once more. Gladys flung her arms about Sue's neck, 'Oh, Sue, I thought you'd been murdered,' she cried.

'Don't be daft,' joked Sue. 'Who's going to do me in?' But she was as close to tears as Gladys from the emotion that their reunion had brought forth. 'I'm doing fine,' she told her friend. 'And I've got my own flat. Want to come and live with me?'

Gladys looked shocked. 'You mean, run away?' she whispered in awe. She had been in the convent since her teens. Now turned thirty, it seemed a terrible thing to even think about running away.

'Well, you will have to make up your mind quickly,' Sue told her brutally. 'I can't hang about here in case Sister Winifred recognizes me.'

Gladys' parchment face was screwed up in emotion as she stared up at Sue's tall figure. 'Will I live with you forever?' she asked eventually.

'Of course, darling,' replied Sue, 'you're my best friend.' Sue went gently down on one knee and cuddled her.

'All right,' decided Gladys, 'but let's go now.

Out of the cinema, they ran hand in hand across the busy Saturday afternoon street where they boarded a bus back to Soho. Sue had found a protector.

Over ten years, under the dogged protection of Gladys, Sue flourished in her chosen trade. One satisfied client would pay her well and recommend her services to a friend. And so her business grew until she was an established prostitute in Soho with regular clients, a large bank account, and a notice on the front door which read: 'Sue, model. Knock twice'. Sometimes she was depressed, especially when the occasional letter arrived for her from Apples in prison, and sometimes she drank too heavily and became aggressive but overall, Sue was happy with her life and her contentment showed in her glowing features and healthy body. Most of all, her happiness stemmed from her friendship with Gladys, the little mongol, the only person in the world who had always loved her and remained loyal. Although she would never admit it, Sue valued her funny-looking friend more than any of the comforts she had earned herself through her success. And Gladys, as always, was devoted to Sue.

Chapter Eleven

An Old Client

The last few years had not been unkind to Sue. Hers was a hard life and as always she was quite prepared to take the rough with the smooth. She got drunk very often, smoked incessantly and swore like a trooper, yet still her figure was perfect – her waist was slim and her limbs were well-shaped. Her velvety-brown eyes had hardened but the nonchalant expression with which she stared out into the world was no different from that she had had as a teenager. Now nearly thirty, she no longer prowled the streets looking for customers, nor did she sit in the night bars watching furtively for some man to look in her direction. She did not need to. She was well known and had the reputation of giving a fair deal. She was the tops of her profession. In fact, other ponces would often recommend her to particularly well-set-up young men looking for a good time. These were mostly young business-men with expense accounts who would not touch the ponces' own tribe of doped-up young whores. And so, Sue made a good living, with little inconvenience. Best of all, she could pick and choose her clients and take time off, if she felt so inclined.

Gladys was still firmly entrenched in her position as Sue's protector and friend. She did not seem to have aged at all. Her flat brown face, with its sallow skin and slanted eyes, looked the same as ever. And she still clung to Sue with a passionate devo-tion for the person who had snatched her from a dreary convent. Her small squat shape could often be seen walking beside the tall, willowy Sue as they walked along Oxford Street on shopping trips. The two made a familiar sight, with a smartly dressed Sue swinging her hips sexily, while Gladys plodded alongside, a grim expression on her rugged features. And she was always dressed in a rusty brown dress and battered straw hat.

'Why do you have to wear that horrible brown shade?' Sue would frequently ask. 'It only makes you look more sallow.' Sue herself was always very careful about her appearance.

Then Gladys would look up at her with an irritated look and

say gruffly, 'I likes brown.' Indeed, when she bought a new dress, it was always the same shape and colour.

From under her veil of false eyelashes, Sue would stare disdainfully down at Gladys' well-scrubbed face. 'God knows why I put up with you,' she would often remark.

Little Gladys would laugh out aloud but it was obvious that she was irritated. 'I knows why,' she would reply, 'because yer don't want no dirty ponce bashin' yer abaht, that's why. Because of me, yer makes good money and I don't take 'alf of it orf yer.'

For a few moments Sue would stare coldly at Gladys and then start to laugh. And Gladys would dash forward like a little child and put her arms about Sue's slim waist. 'Oh don't let us have a row, Sue,' she would beg.

Sue would stroke that fuzzy head and say, 'All right, love. You're right, I know I couldn't get by without you.'

Then peace would be restored for a while.

Elsie's old flat had now been modernized and two more rooms had been added. The landlord – the son of her old landlord, old Nick the Greek – had doubled the rent. But Sue did not mind since she was well able to pay. She had made a lot of money these past five years.

The majority of Sue's customers came regularly on business trips and left behind a hundred pounds or more. They always took her out to expensive dinners and were not ashamed at all to be seen escorting this tall, well-disposed model. Certainly the word 'whore' was never used.

One bright day, as Sue and Gladys strolled along Oxford Street on a shopping trip, they met an old friend. It was Gladys who spotted him first. 'Don't look now, Sue,' she muttered, 'but here comes one of those old kinky sods – you know, one of Ida's leftovers.'

Sue was wearing dark glasses under a wide-brimmed straw hat, but taking off her specs, she looked in the direction that Gladys had indicated. 'Why,' she exclaimed, 'it's old Claud. He looks a bit weatherbeaten. I wonder where he's been these last two years.'

Gladys pulled a long face at her. 'Come on, Sue,' she said. 'Don't stop. It don't look like he got a lot, so why bother with him?'

But Sue stood still and smiled directly into the old man's face.

100

Claud walked with the aid of a stick and wore heavy tweeds. He had a red face and a bushy white walrus moustache. 'Hello Claud,' cried Sue. 'Long time no see.'

As he realized who was calling to him, Claud's face lit up with a smile which displayed large white false teeth and humorous blue eyes. 'Well, I'll be jiggered!' he cried. 'It's Sue.' He held out his hand to her. 'How's tricks, old gel?' he asked, poking Gladys playfully with his stick. 'Ah, little donkey, still going strong, I see.'

Gladys gave him an evil scowl as she recalled one of his kinky sessions when he had insisted on riding stark naked on Gladys' back and singing the 'Donkey's Serenade'. Sue had rolled about on the bed with hysterical laughter at the expression on poor Gladys' face. Gladys had not been at all amused.

'Well now, what about a drink, gels?' Claud suggested, and hailed a cab.

The three of them went off to 'The Duke', Claud's favourite pub in Soho. Sue was pleased to meet him again, for she had always had a soft spot for old Claud. She had inherited him from Ida, who had given up the game and gone home to Tiger Bay. Claud had not been around for a couple of years. His tastes were kinky but usually paid her well and he was no trouble. In fact, she had had many good laughs with old Claud.

Now they sat drinking gin-and-tonics and discussing old times. Gladys sat in the corner looking like a statue of Buddha, stolid and silent with disapproval written all over her face.

'I don't get up to town much these days,' explained Claud. 'Lost me wife, you know, and had a bit of a stroke last year. Ain't up to the old antics.'

'Well, it's nice to see you again, Claud,' said Sue pleasantly. 'I often wondered what happened to you.'

When Claud was in his prime his special act was to tie a blown-up balloon to his penis, chase Sue all over the flat and toss the balloon up in the air until it burst. Sometimes when it really got out of hand, he had chased Gladys as well. She had never forgiven him for that. Sue was always grateful to Claud, for he had given her a few good laughs, which not many of her clients did.

'I've packed it up now, old gel,' admitted Claud. 'Got too old for all that.'

'Well, never mind, love,' said Sue kindly. 'But we did have fun, didn't we?'

'We sure did, Sue,' Claud looked her up and down. 'I must say you look well and prosperous.'

A smile crossed Sue's face. 'Things aren't bad, Claud. Made a few quid and don't have to slog now.'

'Good, good, now look after it, there's a good gel. Put a bit of money away for that rainy day.' He produced a card from his waistcoat pocket. 'If you're interested – it's holiday flatlets, a new idea in self-catering holiday flats. Plenty of money in it, too. I'm on the board of directors.' He handed her the card. 'My address is on the back. Got a small hotel in Devon, in East Bay. You might like to come down there for a holiday. It'd do you the world of good.'

'I'll think about it,' said Sue. 'You coming home for a coffee, Claud?'

Claud shook his head regretfully. 'No, lovey, got to catch a train. Only up for the day. Don't forget, give me a ring and I'll be at the station to meet you. It's been lovely seeing you again. Good luck, old gel. Take care.' And off he went to the station.

Back home, Sue took a bath and got ready for her next client. He was a young business executive she had not met before who was coming over from Holland that evening and staying for a few days. He would probably be very young and expect a lot of sex. And no doubt his conversation would be unintelligible and extremely boring. She lay in the perfumed water thinking. She could not complain, she told herself, the money was always very handy. And they did not bother her, these soft, stupid young men; she could eat them for breakfast. Her thoughts settled on her old lover, Apples, or Billy, as he was really called, locked up in jail. Now, he had been a *real* man. If she had kept him she would never have wanted to bed another man.

Rising languidly from her bath, she put on a gown and went over to her wardrobe and took out an old cash box. In it were all the souvenirs of her time with Billy. There was the little turquoise ring, the first he had ever given her. She had had to pawn that to pay for her abortion years ago but she had got it back the moment she had some money. It meant a lot to her. Then there were the two letters, both on blue, official notepaper and marked 'O.H.M.S. – Prison Service'. The first letter had been sent when Billy was on remand and had ordered her to get rid of the teapot lid – the baby she had been expecting. The second letter was

102

posted only last year, when he was in an open prison up north, and it said that he might get parole in a year. He had explained that he was sending the letter to the old address hoping that someone would forward it to her. 'I'm sure that you've left Soho behind,' he had written. This, to Sue seemed like a veiled threat, for Billy detested whores. He had been a violent criminal but he hated loose women. So she had decided not to answer that letter but she put it with the other one and kept them both safe. They were very special to her and always brought back vivid memories of her true lover, Billy Rafferty, known to the underworld as Apples. Now he was about to end his long prison sentence. Sue longed to visit him or write to him, but much water had passed under the bridge since then, and if Apples found out about the life she lived he would certainly cut her throat without any qualms. Next to the letters in the cash box was a stack of bank notes, all earned the hard way, and some letters from clients making appointments or thanking her for a good time. Thoughtfully she examined them and then put them back. Searching in her handbag, she found the card that Claud had given her that very day. In big black letters it read: Maritime Investments, High Holborn. Perhaps she should put some money away for a rainy day, as Claud had advised. Then, if it paid up good dividends, she would give up prostitution and become a respectable citizen with a good residential address. Who would ever know how she had obtained her money? She was still in good health at the moment, but she might not always be so lucky. 'Yes, that's it,' she muttered to herself. 'I'll kick the game and be there to meet Billy when he comes out.' Her heart beat excitedly at the thought of seeing him again.

With a knowing smile she closed the box with a bang and put it back into the wardrobe. Then she heard three sharp rings on the front door bell. 'Gladys!' she yelled. 'That's that bloody cheesehead. Let him in!' And so business began again.

Chapter Twelve

A New Way of Life

A week later, on a bright sunny morning, Sue prepared to leave the flat on her own. Seeing Gladys' expression, she said, 'I'm going out alone. Tidy up a bit. I don't want any more callers today. I've some business to attend to.'

Gladys screwed up her face in dismay. During the day, she went most places with Sue.

'No, you can't come with me,' shouted Sue, slipping on her smart, tailored jacket. But seeing how unhappy Gladys was, she softened. 'You can go to the launderette if you like,' she added.

A trip to the launderette was always a special treat for Gladys, particularly these days when she was not allowed to go there very often. It was at the launderette that she gathered up all the local gossip from the other maids who took care of the tomcats of Soho. For a long time it had been her main source of social life. But then over the years the Soho scene had changed dramatically. The Chinese had moved on and Commonwealth immigrants had moved in. Gladys was an aggressive racist and disliked them all. 'Bloody niggers,' she would say loudly. 'Slimy Pakkies, I hate the sodding lot of them.' And, of course, her loud remarks in the launderette often landed her in trouble. There was one fight in particular which landed her in the local police station where Sue had to go to collect her and promise to keep her out of trouble in the future. After that, Gladys was barred from the local launderette but occasionally, as a special treat, Sue would allow her to go to the big new washerette on the main road, but with a stern warning: 'I'll let you go but you behave yourself.'

Having appeased Gladys with this olive branch, Sue strolled out into the street shortly after nine o'clock. The streets were almost deserted and quite silent – so different from what they were like at night. As usual, she was struck by how different the area was from what it was like when she first moved in. Wing Wong's Club was now a hamburger bar and a souvenir shop combined. Wong himself had left in a hurry for Hong Kong a few years back. Now the surrounding streets made up a hive of beer cellars, strip joints, blue film shows and porn shops, which only seemed to exist when their blazing neon lights were turned on after six o'clock. Now in the cold light of day Soho had a dreary face. A few junkies were hanging about on the corners, coming down to a shivering miserable existence after a night on drugs. Ignoring them, Sue recalled bright sunny days before she was even on the game, when she had gone shopping for the prostitutes, Fat Florrie, Ida and poor Elsie. The wide boys had stood on the corners then and given her shrill wolf whistles as she passed. She could remember the lovely smell of freshly baked bread that wafted from the small delicatessen and the fat man laying the checked table-cloths on the little tables outside. In those days, strings of onions hung in the shop windows and the shelves were laden with the bottles of foreign wines. It was all gone now, that small Continental community. The modern world of vice and violence had driven it out.

Still in a nostalgic mood, Sue boarded the bus to the City. Perhaps it was time she opted out of this world, she thought. Next year if Billy came looking for her, it would be a disaster if he discovered she was on the game.

Getting off the bus at Holborn, she wandered past the tall finance buildings until she reached her destination – the offices of Maritime Holdings. She went up in the lift, and, as Claud had instructed her, requested to see a certain Mr Henderson. After several minutes waiting, she was ushered into a large office and was soon sitting opposite the managing director, who was a bright young executive and typical of her business expense customers.

'I came here on the recommendation of Mr Claud Ames,' she said, handing the young man the card Claud had given her. 'I want you to explain to me how to make an investment in this Maritime Holdings.'

The managing director was very pleased to explain it to her. 'We have holiday homes all along the coast and now we're about to expand to the Continent. It's a new venture in self-catering chalets. We let them and keep them in good repair and there is a good dividend each year. Many professional people have found it a very good way to invest profitably. I can also assure you it is completely honest and above board, as your Mr Ames has probably told you.'

Sue sat very still in her chair. Her long legs clad in sheer nylon stockings, were crossed and she looked very cool and calm in her neat black suit and white blouse.

Surveying her, the managing director wondered who she was. She was certainly rather attractive. 'Is there a sum you had in mind that you wish to invest?' he asked.

'Yes,' Sue replied coolly. 'Five hundred pounds.'

His eyebrows shot up over his specs in surprise. 'Well, that's a good sum,' he said. 'If you will kindly sign these documents, I'll expect your cheque in about a week's time.'

'I've brought the money with me,' said Sue, opening her hand-bag and handing him a bundle of notes.

This sight gave the clever young man another rude shock. The pen was quivering in his hand as he wrote down her name and address. His eyes furtively glanced at her long legs. The address she gave was a shady one and he thought it had a familiar ring about it.

'Is Mr Ames an old friend of yours?' he asked casually.

'No,' said Sue without blinking. 'Just an old customer.'

The man saw her out of his office and very politely said, 'Read those papers carefully. They'll give you all the information you need.' Once Sue had gone, he darted back into the office to inform his secretary. 'Guess what,' he said proudly. 'I've just signed up a prostitute from Soho. Five hundred pounds in notes she brought with her.'

'Don't know what I am wasting my time at this bloody type-writer for,' the secretary returned acidly.

When Sue returned to the flat, she wrote a letter to Claud in Devon telling him of her investment. Within a couple of days she received a letter from him in return. 'Great guns, old gel,' he wrote. 'Now take a holiday. I shall be expecting you. Come now while the weather is still fine.'

So it was that in September Sue cancelled all her engagements and went on a holiday. It was something she had never done before.

Gladys did not like the idea of a holiday at all. 'Why,' she exclaimed, 'you've got some regulars due this month, and good payers they are too.'

'Let 'em sweat,' announced Sue breezily. 'I've always longed to go to the seaside. All my life I've wanted to, so I'm going now.'

She had been thinking a lot lately about her poverty-stricken childhood and was quite determined. 'Down our street they all used to go hop-picking about this time of year,' she said. 'I used to watch them put everything except the kitchen sink into an old van, then load it with the kids, aunties, dads and even grannies, and off they'd go to the Kent hop fields. I always thought it was the seaside they were going to, and I'd feel very deprived.'

Gladys did not reply, and just gave a disapproving grunt. Her childhood and youth had been spent in that dreary convent. She had never seen the sea and had no desire to do so now.

'Now, pack up the glad rags, Gladys, and we'll "gang awaw",' Sue said cheerfully, using a phrase she'd picked up from a Scottish client.

Gladys did as she was told but very ungraciously, slamming doors and crashing open wardrobes to show her disapproval of Susan's latest folly.

The following Monday morning, they travelled from Waterloo Station, first class. Sue looked particularly smart in a well-cut cotton suit and a white blouse. Her dark hair was plaited and bound around her head, and small pearl earrings dangled from her dainty ears. She looked, smelled and felt very expensive.

Leaving Gladys to take care of the luggage, Sue lunched in the dining-car where some of the comfortable-looking gentlemen at other tables gave her admiring glances. She ignored them all. She was going to have a break from that world of sex and vice, she told herself. She was now just a well-dressed lady travelling with her maid.

As they passed Southampton Waters she peered out of the window to stare at the long silver strip of the Solent as it flowed out to sea, and the huge liner in the docks. 'That's the sea, Gladys,' she whispered. 'Isn't it exciting?'

Hours later, the train came to a halt at the quiet little station in Devon. As he had promised, Claud was on the platform waiting to greet them and, to Sue's surprise, outside in the car park stood a smart pony and trap he had brought to collect them.

Gladys was very nervous about climbing aboard. 'Mind 'e don't run away,' she cried anxiously. ' 'old 'im.'

Sue made no fuss. She climbed into the trap and sat upright like a queen. Surveying the distant white cliffs and the vast expanse of blue sea, she murmured, 'So much space. It's amazing.' Almost overcome with a strong sense of freedom, she wanted to stretch out her hands towards the sun. But she restrained the impulse, and just sat very still with a secret smile on her face.

Claud was a little boozy but as gracious as ever. He held the reins gently as the little pony trap rattled along the steep cliff road. The strong sea breeze ruffled the pony's mane. 'I like this form of transport,' he said. 'I lost my licence to drive a car last year – had one too many – but this little chap is marvellous, always knows his way home.'

The East Bay Hotel was situated high upon the cliff tops. The only nearby buildings were a few modern bungalows, and the view from the hotel over the bay was stupendous. In awe, Sue gazed down at the sea beating against the huge rocks below. 'Oh, it's just as I thought it would look like,' she cried.

'It's a wild, rocky bay,' replied Claud, 'but I like it. It does get a bit lonely during the winter months, though. It's all right this time of year. Still got a few guests – shark fishermen. Don't go in for a lot of visitors since I lost my wife. Used to at one time, though.'

But Sue was hardly listening, so thrilled was she at the view from the garden. As they entered the small hotel, she noticed that it had a quiet air about it, and the smell of furniture polish and spicy food helped to make her feel at home. Claud showed them their rooms, which were clean and very comfortable. But Gladys, still in a very bad mood, complained about the cold.

'Oh, do shut up complaining!' Sue told her after Claud had left them to settle in. 'I'm here on holiday and that's what I intend to have.'

After dinner, Sue went to the bar and drank with Claud who introduced her to some of the shark fishermen. These were husky, sun-tanned men who went out to sea fishing each day, but at night drank themselves silly and sang songs in raucous voices. Sue enjoyed their company and a good time was had by all.

The next day, she explored the small village and climbed down to the rocky shore where the huge gulls screeched overhead. She felt ecstatically happy. All her life there had been someone making demands on her, using up her energy, dulling her mind. She had always been tormented by a nagging feeling that there was something else to be done. Now this was really freedom! She was as free as those gulls circling overhead . . . In the children's home

108

and the various other institutions where she had lived, the days had been divided into time. Every night in Soho someone needed her body. There had never been time to do all the things she wanted to do. Now, on this wild, rocky shore she was alone and completely free. It was a strange and wonderful feeling. She found herself thinking of Billy and wishing that she could share this moment with him. She wondered if he would appreciate it as much as she did.

Gladys would never go very far from the hotel. She would occasionally go out into the garden but never for long. The sight of the high cliffs and the narrow path down to the sea really scared her. And there was too much expanse of blue sky and sea.

'No, fanks,' she said when Sue first asked her to accompany her. 'One false step and you could break your neck. I'll sit in the garden.'

Sue spent her days alone, feeling free and completely captivated by this rocky cove on the Devon shore and she began to entertain thoughts about leaving London and settling down in this peaceful haven. But when she mentioned this idea to Gladys, her poor friend immediately became very alarmed.

'Sue,' she cried. 'Have you gone raving mad? This 'ere place will be deserted in the winter. It'll be a wild and windy place, and with that terrible rough sea, and nuffing else to look at.'

This was a long speech from Gladys, but she was outraged that Sue could even consider giving up her way of life in Soho.

'Don't worry, Gladys,' Sue tried to appease her. 'You'll still be taken care of. You know you have a home with me as long as you need it.'

'It wouldn't be the same, Sue, if you came 'ere,' Gladys tearfully explained. 'You wouldn't be independent no more.'

But now Sue lost her temper. Flying into one of her terrible rages, she slapped Gladys across the face and shouted and raved at her. 'Don't be so bloody stupid! Who's independent? I let some bastard do anything he likes with my body just because he pays me a few quid. So how independent is that?'

Afraid of Sue's temper and unable to stand up to her, Gladys wept and then went into a sulky silence.

Feeling very angry, Sue went down into the bar and, for the first time since her holiday had begun, had too much to drink.

After a while Claud joined her and then they retired to Sue's

109

bedroom. But Claud was well past sex nowadays and his efforts to achieve it made Sue want to vomit. 'Better tie a bloody balloon on it, like you used to,' she said nastily. 'That's the only way it's going to rise up.'

Claud was sitting on the edge of the bed completely naked. He had a sad look of dejection on his face, but his old wrinkled body and his wispy grey hair repulsed her.

'Sorry, Sue,' he apologized. 'I wanted to try and please you. I'm fond of you, you know that, but with me it's all over – there's no use in me trying any more. But if you want to come down here, why don't you come and share the business with me. I've no children to take over from me. My next of kin is a distant relative.'

With her dark hair hanging loose over her bare shoulders, Sue looked sideways at him in a speculative way. 'You've given me an idea, Claud,' she said slowly. 'I'll sleep on it. That might solve a few of my problems.'

'Good night, Sue.' Claud bent down and kissed her. 'I'm not such a bad old sort, you know, once you get to know me.'

Chapter Thirteen

A Crooked Friend from the Past

After two idyllic weeks, the holiday came to an end. Tears had filled Sue's eyes as she said goodbye to old Claud at the station. Confident that they would meet again soon, Claud had been more cheerful. 'Think about my suggestion, Sue,' he had said. 'I'm sure you'd be happy here, and it might be a good proposition for you. The life you lead now will beat you in the end.'

'Well, Gladys,' said Sue as they sat in the train, 'it's back to the old grindstone.'

Gladys sniffed. 'Never felt warm the whole time I was there,' she grumbled.

Sue grinned. 'You're getting old, Gladys,' she said. 'Can't take the fresh air no more.'

'Aren't we all?' replied Gladys disagreeably. 'Hasn't done your looks any good, all that sunbaving. Yer got bags under yer eyes now.'

'I guess I'll just have to get a facial,' returned Sue, good-naturedly patting her face. 'I certainly don't want to go home, I loved it and felt so free.'

'Free's the right word and all,' sneered Gladys. 'I didn't see no men there who wanted to part wiv an 'undred quid. They would all want it free.'

'Oh, you're a depressing old bugger,' snapped Sue. After that exchange, she fell silent and sat looking out of the window. As usual, her thoughts went back to Billy. He had had practically no freedom; he was just locked up in a cage. She wondered if he had ever seen the seaside. It was very likely that he hadn't, having also been reared in a back street of the East End. He used to tell her about how, in his youth, he and his mates would go scrounging along the Thames shore at low tide finding rings and coins, anything to raise money. Seeing him now in her mind's eye – his rosy cheeks and his strong, fair body – she wondered if they would ever get together again. If she married old Claud and lived respectably, she would write to Billy but then he could never be her lover again. So that was not the way. But the present way was not right, either. He hated prostitutes. 'Get them whores out of my house,' he used to yell whenever Ida or Fat Florrie came visiting.

She sighed deeply. She really was between the devil and the deep blue sea. There was no end to her problem. Still, she decided that it was better not to think about it. She would not cross her bridges until the year was out.

Having made this decision, she returned to Soho, she plastered on her make-up and lounged on the pink divan draped in her lovely negligee awaiting her customers. And life went on as usual.

Back in the flat, Gladys was in her element. She always kept the place perfectly clean, cooked appetizing dishes for Sue, and opened the door each evening to the eager clients. In her hard manner, Sue coped with it as always, but now she pushed all thoughts of Billy from her mind and refused to recall the smell of the salt sea or the warmth of that cosy hotel on the Devon cliffs. Business always livened up in the winter because many more conferences were held in the big hotels and more businessmen were in town. The money rolled in for Sue from her work, and then, in the New Year, she received her first dividend from the Maritime Holdings. It was a very substantial sum.

The night life of the swinging city continued. The vice, the violence and the criminal activity increased. More and more foreign immigrants poured into London, and groups of teenagers on hard drugs sat around the statue of Eros in Piccadilly. The pushers and the pedlars invaded the coffee bars and loud reggae music blasted out into the streets so loudly that it could be heard over the noise of the traffic.

'It's becoming such a bloody noisy town,' commented Sue one night.

'Better than being bored out of yer mind at some old seaside,' retorted Gladys.

Deep in her heart Sue longed for the peace and beauty that she had had for those two weeks in Devon but stoically she plodded on. She was taken out most nights by her clients to posh restaurants or business parties. And deep in her heart she hated the muscular young men who used her body night after night. Slowly she began to allow herself to think again of the future and she would jubilantly turn over the idea that as soon as spring came she was going to escape from this sordid life.

112

Coming home early one morning with one of her clients, a big blond West German called Jurgen, she saw a shadowy shape in the porch. She hesitated. There were so many dangers at night now in Soho – muggers and pickpockets who waited for the prostitutes and their escorts going in late at night. The German's hold tightened on her arm as a gruff voice said, 'Is that you, Sue? It's Freddie, that old gel won't let me in.'

Now she could just see his features. The shadowy figure was Freddie the Sly, the wide boy from the past. Another lad from the slums, he had been one of Sam's Boys and a companion of Billy's. Immediately she thought he might have news of Billy.

She released her arm from the young German's grip. 'Just a moment,' she said, 'it's a friend. I must speak to him. You go inside. Gladys will open the door for you.'

With some reluctance, the client did as he was told and Sue took Freddie to one side. 'Hullo, Freddie. This is a surprise.'

'I can see that you're busy,' sneered Freddie.

'Oh, just an acquaintance,' lied Sue. 'He won't be staying.' She took in Freddie's seedy appearance. He was just out of nick, by the look of him, she thought. Slipping him a fiver, she said, 'Go down the road to the all-night café and get a meal. I'll see you back here in about an hour.'

Freddie grabbed the note and slid off. He did not return for two hours by which time he was a little drunk and somewhat belligerent. By this time, Sue had managed to get rid of the young German and now sat on the settee freshly bathed and dressed in her very best dressing-gown as she waited anxiously for news of Billy.

Freddie was not particularly helpful. He told her that he had seen Billy when he was on remand up north. It was only for one night, though, and they did not get much chance to communicate. But Freddie told her, Billy had looked well and was about to go to the open prison to finish his sentence. Freddie looked nosily around the room. 'This is old Elsie's flat, ain't it, Sue?' he said. 'How do you manage to keep it? Must be doing well.'

Sue's heart missed a beat. Freddie did not know that she had turned professional. Could she trust him?

Gladys stood in the corner with a very sour look on her face as she stared aggressively at Freddie. She was tense and ready to turn him out forcibly, if Sue required.

113

'I'm only out on bail,' Freddie informed her. 'I'm going down on a long stretch this time. I got mixed up in the hijack of a lorry full of gin.'

Sue gave him a sympathetic grin but her mind was working hard to think of a way to fool Freddie. She could not trust him, she decided. He must not find out the truth. 'I work in a hotel,' she finally said. 'Not much else doing around here. Wing Wong's Club is closed.'

'So you're not on the game, then?' Freddie seemed a little surprised.

Sue looked shocked. 'Me? On the game? Of course not, for Christ's sake. Billy would jump the wall and slit my throat if I was.'

Freddie nodded knowingly. 'Oh, so you're still a goner for him. Then what's with the German guy?' he asked slyly.

'Just a fellow escorting me home from work,' Sue replied blithely. 'Going to have a drink, that's all.'

Freddie shrugged. 'Well, I should have thought you would do all right here, Sue. It's a nice little flat, this. I remember poor old Elsie – what a junkie! You never heard from her, I suppose.'

'No, Freddie,' said Sue. 'I keep the flat on because it's handy but I'm perfectly straight, I can assure you.'

'It's your business, Sue,' said Freddie. 'Can I kip down here till tomorrow?'

'If you want to,' relieved that he had stopped asking questions. 'Get him a blanket, Gladys. I'd better get some kip myself. It'll soon be daylight.'

Muttering loudly under her breath, Gladys threw a blanket at Freddie.

'Who's the dragon, Sue?' Freddie asked as he made up a bed for himself on the sofa.

'That's Gladys, my maid and she's okay, Freddie, as long as you don't upset her.'

Soon they had all settled down for the night – Sue in her bedroom, Gladys in hers, and Freddie on the sofa. Sue was very tired and she slept heavily, waking up very briefly only once when she thought she heard a movement in her room. But then she sleepily dismissed it and dozed off again.

She was awakened at daylight by a series of loud thumps and Gladys' voice calling her. Staggering out of bed, she opened the door to the sitting room and groaned. There was no sign of Freddie, and the room was in a total upheaval. Drawers were open, the carpet was ripped up and cupboards had had all their contents spilled out onto the floor.

'Oh, dear!' cried Sue. 'The slimy bastard!'

Gladys had been locked in her room and was hammering loudly on the door. When Sue unlocked the door, it was as if she were releasing a wild animal. Gladys charged out and ran back and forth across the room, picking up an article here and there. 'I knew it!' she exclaimed. 'Should never have let him in, Sue. He had the look of a crook written all over him.'

But Sue had gone very quiet. Stepping quickly back into her bedroom, she looked into the wardrobe and there, staring at her, was the precious cashbox lying upside down and empty. 'Oh no! he's pinched everything!' she cried. 'All my letters! And Billy's ring – whatever am I going to do?'

'Inform the police,' said Gladys. 'Put 'im where 'e belongs.'

'No,' said Sue, 'he can have the money and I'll try and get my letters back. But, oh, I feel so lost without my Billy's little ring. It was the first one he ever gave me.'

'All that damned 'ard work for nuffing,' complained Gladys.

Sue threw the blanket which had covered Freddie onto the floor and lay languidly on the sofa. 'Right,' she said. 'My mind is made up. I'm quitting in the spring. I've really had enough. Put the kettle on, Gladys.'

The next day, Sue visited all the shady bars and low-class cafés in the area looking for Freddie, but did not find him. Later that night she got news that Freddie had been put away for five years. A young newspaper reporter told her. He had been at court that morning.

'Well, that's that, then,' said Sue. 'He might have torn up the letters. I'll probably never get them now so it's no use worrying.'

But she could not help worrying a little. Some of those letters were pretty sharp and were from old customers who had put pen to paper. Some were not very nice and some just thanked her for her services . . .

Her determination to start a new life remained with her. 'I'm bloody well going to kick this game,' she said. 'I'll give it up. I want to be clean and free.' Each day the desire became stronger. Increasingly she longed to escape, to get away from this stinking

115

web of vice. She loathed the crime and the evil that clung tenaciously on to her way of life like a big maggot eating into a fresh cabbage. It all revolted her and she thought it strange that she had not thought of it like this before. It was the big fleas living off little fleas. Her attitude to her life had been changed by that holiday by the sea. Soho had not been so bad a few years ago – of course, the ponces had beaten up their girls if the girls did not hand over the money, but that was an accepted thing. Nowadays they stripped the girls naked, manhandled them and then dumped them onto a rubbish tip. Sue often read the *News of the World* on Sunday mornings and reading about all the vice sickened her. Afterwards she would lie on her divan resting and dreaming of the blue skies and stretches of golden sands. How she had loved those rocky coves where the huge waves dashed themselves against the rocks, and where the high winds seemed cool! The whole shore had had a peaceful air. She often thought about those large herring gulls screeching overhead and fighting persistently with each other on the beach for scraps. The big ones were so beautiful – smooth and white with grey wings, but the smaller ones had been grey and very ugly.

'They are the squeakers,' Claud had informed her. 'They remain that dirty grey colour until they're adult, just like young swans.'

Sue had been amazed by all the new wonders that Claud had shown to her during those two weeks. Now she lay thinking about them in her little flat in the centre of London amid the roar of the traffic which sounded loud through the window. Although it was still just a dream, she knew that she had to go back to East Bay. She was not ready yet, since Sly Freddie had stolen all her spare cash. She had to save up a fair bit again. It was just as well she had put that five hundred pounds away, she told herself, otherwise he would have had the lot. It was the loss of the letters that bothered her most now, but she hoped that Freddie's conscience might prick him after he had read the letters. He might, she hoped, send them back to her. So, forcing herself to be optimistic, she concentrated on her work, satisfying the desires of an endless procession of stupid, drunken men as well as her regular clients. She had to take on the extra work to earn back what she had lost.

Finally, in February, she put an advertisement in the paper: 'Flat fully furnished for sale.'

Gladys was horrified. 'Oh, Sue! You can't do that. Don't burn your boats yet, it would be a disaster.'

'Shut your face,' snarled Sue. 'I don't need the furniture so I might as well have the money for it.'

'But, Sue,' wailed Gladys, 'you'll never be able to find another flat in London.'

'I don't want one in London. I'm not coming back,' Sue announced firmly.

'But what about your business?' cried Gladys. 'You can't afford to lose those regular clients.'

Sue grasped Gladys firmly by the back of the neck and shook her till that frizzy head with its golden earloops rattled. 'Get it into your thick head,' she yelled, 'that once and for all times, I'm quitting this lousy game while I'm still in good health. I don't want to end up like those whining, grizzling whores scrounging drinks at The Duke.'

Gladys' slant eyes looked for a moment as if they might produce tears but they remained dry. She just sat on the sofa looking crestfallen and very sorry for herself.

'Don't just sit there,' raved Sue. 'Get up and start packing!'

Gladys got up and did as she was bid. Instant obedience had been instilled in her by the convent.

'Don't know why you're complaining,' continued Sue. 'You're retiring to a nice rest home by the sea.'

Sue had a whale of a time, smashing up the rest of Elsie's knick-knacks, tearing up old negligées and fancy underwear, and stuffing shoes and dresses into a plastic bag. 'I'm not taking any of this rubbish,' she declared. 'You can phone Oxfam and tell them to come and collect it.'

Gladys did not answer but watched with mournful eyes as the sequinned dresses, low-necked blouses and many other lovely things disappeared into the bag.

'I'll buy some sober kind of dresses,' declared Sue, 'and have a new start. We'll both have a new start.'

Chapter Fourteen

East Bay

The journey down to Devon that spring was an exciting one for Sue. She had accomplished her task and saved a lot of cash and, at last, left Soho behind for good. She had no regrets at all and was determined to begin a new kind of life.

As Sue expected, Gladys was very depressed, but Sue had been firm with her. 'If you really don't want to come to Devon with me,' she told her, 'I suppose you can go back to the bloody convent.'

'No, Sue,' Gladys had pleaded sadly. 'Never that. I'd sooner stay here and get a job somewhere else.'

'You want to desert me after all this time?' Sue had stared at Gladys in astonishment.

At this accusation, the wizened little face had crumpled up in grief. 'Not unless you don't want me,' Gladys had wailed.

Immediately, Sue had repented. 'Don't be silly,' she said, cuddling Gladys tightly. 'Of course I want you. Why, we'll have the time of our lives down there at the seaside – you should think yourself lucky.' Gladys had then smiled and cheered up slightly.

Now as they sat in the train, Gladys said quietly, 'No one ever wanted me but you, Sue. My parents gave me to that rotten convent when I was born. I was too ugly and unsightly, they thought, to be owned by them.'

'Didn't you even know who they were?' asked Sue gently.

'I did hear that they had plenty of money and gave to the Church. That's why the convent took me. Once I heard Sister Winifred remark, "Conceived in drink, God save us", and I think she meant me.'

'Oh, don't think back, Gladys. Let's look forward now,' said Sue. She smiled. 'I must say, you look very smart today. That beige suit is nice – much better than that drab old brown.'

Gladys' mouth twisted into a little smile and her tiny rough hands reached up to adjust the new straw hat that matched the suit. 'Do I, Sue?' she said anxiously.

Claud was at the station to meet them. Sitting in his little pony cart, he did not look well. His old face seemed more lined and was pallid and drawn.

'Had a bad dose of flu in the winter,' he explained. 'Haven't quite got over it yet.' He gave Sue a hug. 'It's great to see you, love. There'll be plenty for you to do down here when the season starts. Why, hullo little donkey . . .' He gave Gladys a friendly pat. 'Going to put you out to grass – how's that?'

Gladys was not at all amused, and she pulled away from him with an angry scowl on her face.

As the pony cart rattled along the cliff road, Sue thought that East Bay looked magnificent on this fine spring day. There again was the lovely view across the bay, and the long line of cliffs stretching round the cove glowed white and green in the brilliant sunshine. The air was so fresh and clean and smelled of the sea. There was not a soul down there on the little patch of sand, for it was still too early for the holiday-makers. But her old friends, the herring gulls, gracefully circled the bay, their cries echoing over the land. 'It's all so clean and bright,' Sue said. 'It's as if everything has just been newly washed – even the houses look scrubbed.'

'I expect the winter gales have cleaned them up a bit,' remarked Claud. 'It's been a long, cold winter. We had some very heavy storms in December – we lost a couple of fishing boats, with all the crew aboard.'

But Sue was not listening as they drove up the steep slope to the hotel for her heart was pounding with excitement as she saw the huge waves crashing against the rocky shore. This was to be her home now, she thought. And it felt like home, as no other place ever had before. That made her very happy.

It did not take long for them to settle in. And even Gladys was content once she realized how much she was needed to keep the huge, rather neglected hotel in order. She became her old self once more, and even acknowledged Claud's jovial banter with a sly grin. Her convent training made her such an asset to the hotel. The old brass coal-scuttles and wall-plates were all grimy and black from neglect. Claud was not fit enough to do them and the domestics who came in every day were not reliable enough to see that the brasswork was done. But Gladys burnished and polished them all until everything was bright and shiny. And she kept it up, vigorously polishing everything each morning until it all shone brilliantly. Gladys would stand back and smile proudly at the sight.

'My word,' Claud would declare to Sue, 'what a worker that little one is. Those horse brasses around the fireplace haven't looked like that since my wife died. Now she was a stickler for cleanliness.'

'Gladys will be all right as long as she's needed,' Sue told him. 'She's hard as nails and will work like the donkey you're always calling her.'

Sue learned to serve drinks in the bar and had a way with all the customers, whether they were in the public bar or the hotel. She also loved to pick flowers from the garden and arrange them in vases. Since it was spring, the hotel was scented throughout by pink and mauve hyacinths, and large clumps of yellow daffodils brightened up the gloomy hallways.

Claud was very pleased. 'They've done wonders,' he would inform his customers. 'Can't think how I managed without them.'

During the day, in a smart tailored dress, Sue would look after the reception desk and see that the guests were booked in and out. Tall, elegant and bursting with energy, Sue was everything that Claud needed to keep his business and his home going. 'Made no mistake there, old son,' he would tell himself repeatedly.

What Sue enjoyed most was the early morning, when she went down to the small harbour to watch the fishing boats come in. On the quayside she would wander between the huge baskets full of shining mackerel which could be bought for a few shillings, or freshly caught crabs and lobsters struggling to climb out. It all fascinated Sue, and in her chatty manner she got to know the various boats and the fishermen, who greatly appreciated her smart slacks and tight jersey. She liked them all; they were her own kind of men – solid, earthy types she was always at ease with. She could sit on the harbour wall laughing and talking with them for hours.

When summer finally arrived, Sue would spend her leisure hours lying on the beach clad in a brief swimming suit and wishing she could swim. Sue had never learned to swim, for there had not been the time or the opportunity in her cramped youth. Now she would look on enviously as the holiday-makers romped confidently in the waves. She would often imagine herself and Billy floating out there on a calm sea. She knew that Billy could swim, for he had learned the hard way by playing on the muddy banks of the Thames and falling in.

She smiled to herself now as she thought about him. How he would love it down here! Billy would be just finishing his sentence, now, she thought, in that open prison. She still remembered his prison number – it was stamped on her heart. Suddenly she leaped to her feet, scattering sand everywhere. She knew what she had to do . . . She would go home and write to Billy. She would write him the first letter in years to find out if he still loved her. She now had a respectable address for his letters to come to, so it could not do any harm.

The hotel bar in mid-season was busy, so it was long after midnight before Sue finally sat down in her room to compose a love letter to her man on Claud's headed notepaper. East Bay Hotel, Devon: it looked nice and sounded very respectable, she thought with pleasure.

Dear Billy,
    After all this time I felt I must write to you. I expect you will be going home soon. I am working down in Devon in an hotel. It is very nice here. Do hope you have not forgotten me. I have never forgotten you and my love for you is as strong as ever. So if you will drop me a line perhaps we can keep in touch once you are out.
                                                        Love Susan.

Sue read the letter through and sighed. It was not much of a love letter but then she had always found it difficult to put words on paper. But at least her handwriting was strong and clear.

On her way to the beach the next morning, she posted the letter and stood by the letter box with fingers crossed. 'Oh, please, Billy, please still love me,' she whispered.

Billy's reply came two weeks later. Claud picked up the mail and gazed curiously at this particular letter addressed to Sue. The blue envelope was marked 'O.H.M.S., Strangeways Prison'.

'Is this yours, Sue?' he asked.

Sue quickly snatched the letter from him. 'It's from my brother,' she explained. 'I wrote to him. He's in trouble but we correspond.' With that, she dashed off to her room to read it.

121

Billy's handwriting had improved quite a lot since the last letters he had written. A feeling of happiness washed over her as she read his words.

Dear Sue,

So pleased to hear from you, Sue. Also so glad that you have left London and are now working. I often used to worry over you but now you have given me hope that we can begin again, my love. I lost my old Mum since I was inside so I have only you to care for now. I've still got three months to do but it will soon pass. In the meantime, keep writing. You don't know how good it made me feel. All my love,

Billy

Sue wept and kissed the letter. After that she kept it in her pocket and every free moment she would take it out and read it over and over again.

Gladys did not think much of this. 'Don't tell me you're still mooning over that bloke who got put away?' she sniffed.

'Mind your own bloody business!' snapped Sue. 'And keep your mouth shut.'

'Who cares? It's your pigeon,' retorted Gladys, going off in a huff.

Throughout that beautiful and bright summer, Sue got a letter every month from Billy. She in turn wrote to him every week without fail to tell him of her plans to get him to come down to Devon. She had saved quite a bit of money, she told him, and would get a little beach cottage for them to live in. Inwardly, she was concerned about Claud and what his reaction would be to this plan of hers. Claud always gave her Billy's letters with a sort of questioning look on his kind face. But Sue adamantly refused to discuss anything with him which concerned her plans.

As autumn approached, the early morning mists lay over the sea and a sharp breeze blew in from the east. The hotel began to empty as the holiday-makers went home. There was much less to do in the hotel now and Sue would often sit with the others in the dining-room around a log fire. Claud and Sue would chat while Gladys sat crocheting, a hobby she had recently taken up. She had become very good at it and had started to make things, like lace doilies and pretty tablecloths. Once she even gave Sue a present of a pretty open lace-work jumper she had made. Gladys had settled down at the hotel and become as contented as a sleek old cat.

'Would you like to go up to London with me for a week, Sue?' Claud asked one evening. 'Do a bit of shopping and visit old places. The hotel's done very well this year, thanks to you, and I'd like to repay you, Sue.'

Sue hesitated and then said, 'No, you go, Claud. I'll look after things here.'

She knew that Claud was disappointed that she had turned down his offer, but Billy would be arriving any day and she was determined not to miss him.

So Claud went off to London on his own one misty November day. 'I'll see about our investments while I am in town,' he told Sue. 'We should get an extra dividend this year.'

As soon as he had gone, Sue called Gladys. 'Come on,' she said, 'help me get the best suite ready. We're going to have a very important visitor.'

'I ain't never 'eard of no important visitor,' complained Gladys. 'I thought the 'otel part was shut for the winter.'

'Well, it's not,' Sue informed her. 'I've got a very special guest coming.'

Gladys' eyes gleamed. 'A man, Sue?'

'Oh yes!' replied Sue with a coy smile. 'A real male, a he-man, my lover, Billy.'

Gladys gasped. 'Oh, no, Sue, you can't do that to Claud!' she cried. Now that she had got to know Claud better, she was steadfastly loyal to him.

'Who says I can't?' Sue challenged her. And the determination in her eyes made Gladys retreat. She knew her wilful mistress very well, and there was no point in trying to change her mind.

When Sue went to meet Billy at the station, she wore her fur coat and a little beret. He had a week's parole to adjust himself to life outside the prison walls before his official release. At first she did not recognize him as he stood there on the station platform. He wore a cheap, ill-fitting suit and had lost a lot of weight. His hair line had receded and his high polished forehead made him look much older. But Billy knew her instantly and swept her into his arms. Regardless of who saw them, they stood locked together on the little station in a close embrace for several minutes. Then, hand in hand, they walked up the High Street with smiles on their faces. 'Quaint little spot,' said Billy. 'How did you find it, Sue?'

'The job was advertised in the paper,' lied Sue. 'The boss has gone off on a holiday and left me in charge. I'm going to smuggle you in there. Is that all right with you, Billy?' She stared lovingly at him.

'I have to be very careful, Sue. I'm only out on parole and I can't afford to get into any trouble.'

'There won't be any trouble, darling,' she assured him. 'It's all laid on. Just trust me. The only thing is that I've told the two servants that you're my brother. There are no other guests. The hotel is closed for the winter and only the bars are open.'

Sue called a taxi and soon they were at the hotel where Billy was booked in as an unofficial guest, and Sue's brother. The cook and the lounge barman, the only staff retained for the winter, accepted this as the sort of thing that happened when the boss was away.

Billy stared around the huge bedroom and at the bathroom next door. 'Blimey, Sue,' he exclaimed. 'What's this? The honeymoon suite?'

'Yes, darling,' said Sue, already removing her dress.

It was early afternoon when they went to bed and made passionate love. Billy was a little shy at first but Sue, experienced in these matters, soon made him lose his fears. She had never been so happy. This was her man, her true mate. Not since she was a teenager and had fancied Dodgy Roger had she been so eager for love. They made love over and over again, and did not emerge from the guest room until the next morning.

Chapter Fifteen

Poor Old Claud

It was a sad moment for Sue when the week was up and Billy had to return to the nick. Their brief honeymoon had been a great success. Billy had lost his prison pallor and had even put on a couple of pounds in weight. But best of all, they had taken the opportunity to get to know each other again and neither had been disappointed. Sue loved Billy's rough, possessive ways which made her no longer feel like an aggressive woman with a chip on her shoulder. She felt that she had put her past life well behind her and was most decidedly a reformed character; indeed, it showed in the subdued way she dressed and the nice upright way she walked.

'Sue, my love,' said Billy, as they lay in bed together on that last day, 'you've certainly grown into a very nice, mature woman. I'd be proud to have you as my wife, if you still want me . . .'

'Oh, Billy!' cried Sue ecstatically, flinging her arms about his neck. 'I love you so much, I can't bear the thought of you leaving me.'

'I'll be back, darling,' replied Billy. 'But remember that I haven't got a job, and I've never held on to a regular job. I've always been a tearaway, you know that.'

'That doesn't matter,' she cried, holding on to him fiercely. 'Billy, darling, if you desert me I don't know what I will do now that I've had you back with me for a short while. But we'll get by, I've got some money saved. I'll quit the hotel and find us a little cottage, or something. There are a lot of things we can do together.'

'Well, I ain't no bleeding gigolo,' announced Billy, 'so don't count on it, Sue. It's fine down here for a holiday but whether I'd get a living is another matter.'

'But you could get a boat and go fishing – a lot of the men do that down here.'

'There's no money in fishing, Sue,' said Billy, shaking his head. 'I like it here, the sea fascinates me, but we've got to eat.'

Sue hugged him tight. 'I've told you that there's no need to worry. I've got money saved up for us.'

'We could get spliced when I come out and then go back to London,' he told her. 'Me brother-in-law is in the transport business and might give me a job.'

'Oh, Billy, Billy, darling,' she cried. 'Please be quiet. Don't spoil our last day together.'

He kissed her hard on the lips. 'Don't worry, I won't,' he said with a smile. 'And I promise you that I'll go straight once I'm out. I've had enough of the bloody nick.'

'Good, good, darling,' Sue cried, covering his face with kisses. 'Now, love me so I will have so much to remember . . .'

Sue's eyes were still red with crying when Claud returned from his London trip. For Billy had gone back to his cage and would not be out again for several months. Claud looked at her strangely when he first arrived home, but it did not take long for him to find out at least some of what had been going on in his absence. The cook was the first to let on. 'We had a guest in the best suite all the week,' she informed him.

'A honeymoon couple?' Claud enquired.

'Well, it could be,' the cook said with a shrug. 'It was supposed to be Sue's brother but she spent most of her time with him up there.'

Claud looked annoyed but was reluctant to jump to conclusions. 'Ah well,' he said, 'Sue was in charge and it was up to her what she did.'

That evening it was a very subdued Sue who served behind the bar. It was Saturday and, as usual, the locals came in force to the public bar.

The women all huddled together on a long seat swallowing their stout, and whispering and gossiping while the men played darts and shove ha'penny or simply lounged against the bar. It was a nice homely scene and usually Sue felt very much at home there; she liked the locals and they in turn were fond of her. But tonight she was feeling a little shifty about her behaviour the week before. She had come down to the bar on Saturday evening with Billy and, unfortunately, they had had a few drinks too many. Without thinking, Sue had lolled all over him, fussing and petting him, and practically raping him with her dark, passionate eyes. The locals had been shocked at this display.

'Ah, ee's no brother,' Dora had said in her Bristol accent.

126

'Oi ain't never bin *that* fond o' me brother,' said her daughter Bess, who was sitting beside her.

Regardless of the locals' sharp scrutiny, Sue had continued to love and fondle her man.

'Blimey,' remarked Bess, 'she's even turning me on.' Bess' husband, who was playing darts across the room, was a Cockney and known to everyone as Titch.

The gossip zipped around the bar like a forest fire, and there was a series of nudges and winks as Sue kissed her man and fondled his knees. Billy had begun to look very embarrassed as his penis stiffened and showed through his tight jeans.

Then the men passed coarse remarks among themselves and laughed loudly.

'Who is he?' demanded Dora. 'I've never seen him afore.'

'He's a Londoner,' said Titch. 'Spoke to him down on the quay. A nice chap.'

'Never seen Sue act like that before,' announced Bess looking very concerned. 'I thought she was old Claud's woman. He's certainly very fond of her.'

'The cat's away and the mice will play,' said Dora's friend Marie. 'He's nice,' she added. 'I could fancy him myself.'

'Tut, tut!' declared Dora. 'What a disgraceful thing for an old woman like you to say.'

'Oh, who cares?' replied Marie. 'My old man can't supply me any more, and there's no harm in wishing.'

And so the conversation in the bar continued until Wendy, the part-time barmaid, rang the bell for time. 'Come on,' she called. 'Let's get home, it's past time.'

The locals began to leave, but Sue and her man had already disappeared – back to bed. Then, as always, Jim the butcher came to the bar. This was his Saturday routine: always at eleven o'clock he would come in for a drink and also catch the last few customers going home who might have forgotten their Sunday joint. After he had had a drink, Jim would supply anyone from his mobile van. Tonight he had to needs listen to all the goings-on in the bar with Sue and her so-called brother.

'What? We having incest now?' he joked. 'That makes a bloody change down here. It would cause a bit of excitement in the local paper, that would.'

'He's not 'er brother,' decided Dora.

'No,' agreed Bess, 'I think they know each other, if you know what I mean.' She was always very precise, was young Bess.

'Ah well, Jim,' said Titch, 'got a nice bit o'steak, have you? I better get going – all that sex talk has turned me on.'

'All as I hope,' said Dora's husband, Alfred, who was a very quiet man, 'is that old Claud don't get a wheeze of it. It'll upset him a lot, it will.'

But old Claud had quickly got the wheeze of it when he got back from London. In fact, he was fed up to the teeth by the number of people who wished to talk to him of Sue's misdemeanours. He only had to walk the dog down to the village post office to be stopped several times by people who 'thought he ought to know . . .' He returned to the hotel feeling despondent. His shoulders were slightly bowed and he felt he had little to say to Sue.

So now Saturday night had come round again and Sue had to face the consequences of last week's behaviour. 'I wonder what the gossips will have to say tonight,' she muttered somewhat anxiously to Gladys, who was drying glasses.

'Well, you were a bit naughty, Sue. The cook heard all sorts of things about your goings-on with that Billy.'

'Oh, sod them!' declared Sue. 'If old Claud asks me, I'll just tell him the truth.'

'Just as well,' said Gladys. 'Then perhaps we can go home.'

'Go home?' yelled Sue. 'You are home!'

'Back home to Soho, I meant – that's home to me.'

'Oh, Gladys,' sighed Sue, 'will you never change your ways?'

When Claud came in with the dog, he slowly put his stick into the umbrella stand and wearily wiped his feet on the mat.

From her position in the bar, Sue watched him. He looked pale and his features were drawn and tired-looking.

'Feeling tired?' she asked brightly. 'I expect you've walked too far.'

'Not far enough, Sue,' replied Claud. 'Can't get away from the buggers all keen to tell me about your goings-on.'

Sue blushed but she decided to take the bull by the horns. 'Well, that's how it is, Claud. Do you want me to tell you the truth?'

Claud nodded. 'I'd be much obliged if you would, Sue.'

Sue took a deep breath. 'Okay, then,' she began, 'the man they

128

are all talking about is Billy Rafferty. He's just out on parole after seven years inside.'

Claud nodded as if he was not surprised. 'But surely you could have gone to stay in town with him,' he said. 'Why poop on your own doorstep?'

Claud's attitude suddenly made Sue become extremely angry. Why should she make excuses? After all, she was still a free agent. 'If you mean shit why don't you say shit?' she snapped irritably.

Claud drew back and looked offended. He was, in all circumstances, always a gentleman. 'The folks down here have learned to respect you, Sue. It'd be a pity to spoil it for yourself.'

Sue tossed back her hair. 'Oh, they can go to Hell,' she declared, 'because I don't care any more. When Billy comes out in a few months' time, we're going to be married.'

Claud paled a little. 'Well, that's your prerogative, Sue, but I had hoped that you'd settled down. If you marry an ex-convict now, you'll be back on the game in no time.'

Two scarlet patches appeared on her cheeks as one of her terrible rages overwhelmed her. 'Is that what you think?' she screamed. 'Well, my Billy hates whores. He was my man before I went on the game. I said I'd keep straight and I am going to.'

'All right, all right,' said Claud, trying to calm her. 'That's all up to you, but give me time to replace you. You've been a great asset to me here and I'll miss you. You know I'm not as fit as I was.' As he spoke, his old hand trembled and he grabbed the back of the chair to steady himself.

Instantly Sue was at his side. She put her arms about his neck. 'Oh, I'm so sorry,' she said. 'Sit down now, and don't let me upset you, please, Claud.'

'It's all right, pet.' Claud patted her shoulder; his voice was choked. 'I suppose I've got fond of you but it's possible I expected too much of you.' He sat down in the chair as Sue went to the sideboard and poured him a glass of brandy. She gave him the drink and sat down beside him.

'Let me explain, darling,' she said. 'I'll never stop being grateful to you for what you've done for Gladys and me, but I love this man, you have to understand that. He fathered my second child and because he was sent to prison I had it aborted. Please understand, Claud, I have this dream of living a clean and full life once more. Am I a fool for wanting that? You tell me.'

Claud shook his head and patted her hand. 'No, Sue, you're probably right, and I'm just an old fool, so let's not cross our bridges till we come to them, shall we?'

She kissed him on the brow. 'Now you sit there. I'll go and open the bar. I'm quite ready for those gossiping old women, so don't you worry.'

After a few weekends the whispering and the chuckling in the public bar had died away and Sue was once more a well-loved figure there, part of the community again, rather than apart from it. Life settled down once more and Sue was quite content. Poor Claud's health, however, deteriorated over that winter, and he began to rely on Sue more than ever.

Meanwhile, Sue wrote regularly to Billy outlining her plans for their future, and she visited a local house agent to investigate the possibility of renting or buying a small cottage.

In January, there were some terrible gales. The sea roared angrily and ceaselessly up over the front and the lifeboat had to be called out several times. On these occasions, distress rockets whizzed up into the night sky, and the villagers huddled together on the cliffs in little groups to watch the rescue. This was an element of the coast that Sue had never known before – the wild wind and dangerous deserted shore made her shiver with fear at times. In this appalling weather, the little fishing boats were lying at anchor in the bay while their owners spent their days in the public bar. That nice world Sue had known had temporarily come to a halt. But despite the stormy scenes, she still had her inner peace and every day she marked off the calendar another day towards Billy's release.

Poor old Claud's health was getting worse. He coughed repeatedly all through the night and often spent the day in bed. One very cold night, he crept into Sue's room and asked pathetically, 'Can I get in bed with you, Sue? It's just to keep me warm. I feel so cold I can't get to sleep.'

Sue sighed and moved over to make room for his bony old body next to hers. The smell of the embrocation which he used to rub on his chest was disgusting, but big-hearted Sue cuddled the old man up to her warm smooth body and Claud, sighing like a contented child, finally went to sleep.

130

After that, Claud often came to be warmed by Sue's voluptuous body. But one night, after Claud had gone to sleep in her arms, Sue woke up, to find her arm trapped uncomfortably under Claud's head. She pushed him over in order to try to dislodge it, and switched on the bedside light with her free arm. 'Gosh, Claud,' she said, 'you are heavy. Move over, love.'

Awkwardly, she managed to sit up. Claud had still not moved. His mouth was wide open but no sound came from it and he had a strange pallor on his face. Sue gave him another push but his head was very heavy and did not budge. Suddenly, in panic, she wrenched her arm away. Now his old head lolled to one side and Sue knew immediately that he was dead. Her screams made Gladys dash in wearing her nightgown. Her head was a mass of curlers. Gladys took one look at Claud and then rushed to Sue. 'Don't look, love,' she said. 'He's snuffed it.'

Sue howled with horror and then passed out.

Claud's death badly affected Sue. She had always dealt with the living before and had an inner horror of illness or death. She recalled how shocked she had been to see her father return from prison as a bent-up cripple, and now poor Claud was gone. It was with great sadness that she remembered his sky-blue eyes which always had such a lovely humorous twinkle . . . But now he was no more. She shuddered every time she thought of his cold stiff body lying in her arms all night. The memory made her want to vomit.

An inquest was held and the nosey crowd from the village attended. The verdict was simple: death from natural causes. And Sue discovered that Claud was a good few years older than he had ever admitted to being.

In the village churchyard they laid him to rest beside his wife, who had been a local woman. The mourners included many friends and neighbours. Sue served them all drinks and sandwiches in the hotel bar. Only one close relative turned up – he was a nephew on Claud's wife's side. He was a big fat fellow who stayed to enjoy the free drinks. In fact, he had started to drink as soon as he arrived.

Later that afternoon, the will was read in the sitting-room. In a solemn voice the lawyer read Claud's will. '. . . I bequeath the hotel and all money in my bank to Susan as long as she will continue to run the hotel in the same way as my wife, Nadia, had always done.' There followed a few bequests of his guns and his collection of coins to old friends. The big fat nephew was left a mere five hundred pounds, which probably only covered the expenses he must have incurred attending the funeral. All other monies owed to his estate were to be forgotten. At the end of the reading, the nephew got up and marched out of the room. 'I'll contest it,' he muttered. 'Who is she anyway? Just a mistress.'

Sue was astonished by the contents of the will. She really had not expected anything. Dumb, she sat trying to comprehend this generous and wonderful gift. Finally, she turned to the lawyer and said, 'If that is what old Claud wanted of me – to take care of the business – then that's what I'll do.' Inwardly she could not believe her luck. This was a nice little hotel and it had dropped right into her lap. What more could she and Billy want? The fact that the villagers were a little suspicious of Claud's sudden death did not bother Sue. In that respect her conscience was completely clear.

The gossips started on the following Saturday night. 'Ah, he took to the bottle those last few weeks,' cried Dora in a loud voice.

'Had a bit of a shock,' agreed Albert. 'That were what triggered him off.'

But Sue just cast cold glances in their direction and, knowing that it would upset them, had them all out of the bar dead on time.

'Gladys,' said Sue, 'in a couple of weeks, when all this is settled, you and I will have a very comfortable home here for the rest of our lives.'

Little Gladys' face wrinkled suddenly with grief. 'Poor old Claud,' she said. 'He wasn't so bad, was he? God rest his soul.' Then she made the sign of the cross.

Sue stared at her in amazement. 'Why, you don't still keep up that old hocus-pocus they taught us in the convent, do you, Gladys?'

'Oh, yes I do,' replied Gladys defiantly. 'And it would do you good to say a little prayer now. He has taken good care of you.'

Sue looked slightly alarmed and gazed towards the bed where Claud had died. 'You know, I think I'll move out of this room to that nice big double down the corridor. Come on, let's get cracking, we'll move everything tonight.'

132

Gladys stared at her and mumbled, 'Don't know why you should be frightened of that poor old man. He was very fond of you.'

Sue stalked angrily past her. 'I am not afraid, but illness and death give me the creeps.'

As always, Sue got her way and moved her bedroom. Then she began to prepare it for Billy's return. She bought colourful new curtains and covers, installed hi-fi equipment and a bookcase full of paperback books. Her Billy was not going to be deprived of anything any more, not like he had these last years spent in prison.

Chapter Sixteen

The Boss

The first thing Sue had to do when she took over the hotel was talk to the staff. She was determined to show them her authority and gain their confidence. There was Frannie, the big, moon-faced cook; Tommy the tall, thin old gardener; small, robust Mary who combined the duties of chambermaid and below-stairs helper and was a sort of tweeny, and finally, the tall bright barmaid. They all lived outside the hotel and off-season, they worked a rota system between them. Most of them lived in the village and had held down these jobs for years. They were all good and Sue did not wish to lose any of them.

They were all assembled in the large kitchen downstairs, and they looked rather anxious. 'There's tea and cakes there,' indicated Sue. She smiled at them. 'No need to look so scared,' she reassured them, 'I'm not going to sack anyone. But I do want to know if I have your cooperation to help run this place. I'm a relative newcomer to the hotel business and you all know more about it than I. So I'd like to establish a good working relationship between us all. I shall be getting married soon so you'll have a new boss. Meanwhile, I'd like to think that we can all work together in harmony. I know you all tittle-tattled to poor old Claud about me but I hold no grudges. I'd like you to state now if you wish to stay and work with me because I'll have no whining or complaining behind my back. If you do stay, I hope you'll always come to me with your complaints and I will always do my best to put them right. But I would like loyalty and trust from you.'

Gladys looked amazed, for this was a long speech for Sue whose normal conversation was fairly limited. Yet here she was making a speech in a clear and precise voice, looking them all straight in the eye.

When Sue had finished, the staff started to fidget. Then Wendy, the barmaid, said 'I'd love to stay with you, Sue, but I'd already told Claud that I'm booked to go and work in

Switzerland for the summer. I thought I'd get out of this deadend place. Might find a rich husband out there . . .' She grinned at Sue.

Sue nodded. 'That's it, Wendy, see the world while you're young. And thanks for being straight with me. Is there anyone else quitting?' she asked, looking at the others.

'Oh no, Sue,' they all protested in unison. 'We're quite happy at our work.'

'Good,' said Sue, most satisfied with the outcome of this meeting. 'Get stuck into the cakes, now. We all know where we stand, don't we?'

But there was no reply, only the nodding of heads as they stuffed the cakes into their mouths.

From then on, life in the hotel went more or less smoothly. The season began again and the holiday-makers arrived as the front brightened up with vendors' kiosks, Punch and Judy stands and cockle stalls. Sue liked to stroll down to the harbour every morning to buy fresh fish and chat with the seamen and she loved to see all the colourful signs of the new season. She longed to share these sights with Billy when he finally returned to her.

The week before Wendy left, Sue advertised for a new young barmaid. She wanted a girl who would live in so that she could train her the way she wanted her to work. There were plenty of applicants and Sue spent many hours interviewing, but so far she had not seen anyone who was quite suitable for the position.

One day, a young couple arrived on a motor cycle. They parked outside the hotel and the young man took off his crash helmet and sat on the grass while he waited for his girlfriend. The girl came in while Sue was getting the morning bar ready. The sun was behind her and Sue was struck by her fair beauty as a shaft of sunlight shone on her silvery gold hair. As she approached Sue could see how neat she was – tall and slim and dressed in a tight-fitting summer dress.

'Ah coom aboot the joab.' The girl spoke slowly and politely.

'Come in, love. Sit down. I'll be with you in a minute,' said Sue. Grabbing her book and pencil, she sat down to interview this young girl who was from the big town of Bristol, quite a way from East Bay. She spoke slowly and so quietly it had a fascinating lilt; she seemed somehow to swallow her words.

'Bristol's a long way,' commented Sue.

'Ah noa,' replied the girl, 'me boyfriend broaght me on his boike. But a'd loike to live in, ef et's possible.'

'Well, that's what I am looking for,' said Sue. 'Are you experienced in hotel work?'

The girl shook her golden head. 'Noa I worked in the bacon factree. Am saving ooop to get married and me young man goes to sea. A'd like to work away from home so ah can save more money. Ad doan't like the factree an ah ain't niver bin away from Bristol afore.'

Sue looked her over. She was pretty dim but nice and clean with a clear white skin, and her shoulder-length silvery golden hair was very attractive. 'I'll take you on a month's trial. Is that all right?' asked Sue.

'Ah yeh! that'll be fine,' replied the girl, giving her a sweet smile.

'By the way, what's your name?' Sue asked. She had been so taken with this nice girl that she had forgotten to find out her name.

'It's Mandy,' she said with her slow drawl.

'How about your young man, Mandy? Will he mind you only getting one day off a week and not much time off at weekends, especially at the height of the season?'

'Ah knows,' smiled Mandy. 'Andy says it will be good for us to be apart for a while afore ee haas me.' Sue wanted to laugh at her words. Mandy was nearly eighteen, and Sue thought about herself at eighteen: a lot of men had had her by then. She had learned quite a lot. Mandy seemed so sweet, naïve and innocent, it hardly seemed possible that she was that age.

Naïve or not, Mandy seemed to adapt very well to life at the hotel and everyone liked her. She was open and friendly, and if she got a tip from a customer she would put it in a little box towards her wedding dress.

Sue quickly became so fond of Mandy that Gladys became jealous. Every time she got near Mandy, she would give her a vicious jab in the back with her elbow. But mild Mandy would only open her wide blue eyes and say, 'What be the matter, leetle Gladees? Oim big enough to see, eren't I?' She certainly never lost her temper.

On her day off, Mandy's boyfriend would arrive from Bristol on his motorbike and they would spend the day on the cliffs together.

'You can bring your young man in here,' Sue said to her one day, 'and spend a little time in your room if you want to, I won't mind.'

'Oh, he wouldn't do that,' asserted Mandy.

136

'How long have you been courting?' asked Sue.

'We bin engaged six months,' Mandy replied proudly.

Sue stared hard at her in disbelief. 'You mean to say you never got to know each other yet, not once?'

Mandy blushed and hung her fair hair. 'Ah noa,' she murmured. 'Andy wants me to be very pure when he haas me. So we are going to wait till we marry.'

'Oh, crikey!' exclaimed Sue. 'What sort of a nut is that boyfriend of yours, Mandy?'

'Ee be very nice,' said Mandy stiffly. 'Oi loves eem.'

'All right, darling, forget what I said.' Sue suddenly felt ashamed, and stopped herself from making any more comments. She liked Mandy and did not want to hurt her.

Although the atmosphere in the hotel was generally pleasant, it was inevitable that the gossip would start up again at some point. 'Where's this fella she was going to marry then,' remarked Dora. 'And is it the same one she cut all those capers with last year?'

'I think so,' replied Bess. 'I believe he works abroad in Saudi Arabia, or some such place like that.'

'Never! Not on your Nelly,' piped up Marie. 'Why, he was as white as an 'addack. Ain't seen a lot of the sun for years.'

'What are you getting at, Marie?' demanded Dora who liked to be top dog.

'I'm not saying,' Marie replied haughtily. 'It's not going to be me that said anything.'

Bess leaned over and whispered in her Mum's ear. 'I know what she's getting at – he's been in prison.'

'Well, if that's the case, I'm sorry for the poor devil,' said Albert, who heard his daughter's whisper. 'And I for one will make him welcome.'

Dora sniffed. 'It depends what he's done,' she muttered.

'Now, if I was you I'd mind me own business,' said Marie. 'You know what Sue's like in a temper . . .'

So they all agreed and waited anxiously for the arrival of Billy Rafferty.

Sue kept very busy and was extremely happy. She seemed to blossom like an over-blown rose, her eyes shone and her cheeks were pink. Bursting with energy, she worked from early morning to late at night to keep the hotel in order and running smoothly.

Soon the season was over. A cool wind blew across the pier and the boys who fished from it put on their big woolly jerseys. The hotel emptied, and Sue was glad to have a few weeks' respite before Billy came to claim her for his bride. They had already decided to make it a secret wedding. They planned to go into the small, nearby town of Bideford to get a special licence, stay overnight in a small guest-house, and return to East Bay the following day as legal man and wife.

'I think it's a good idea, don't you, Gladys?' asked Sue. Gladys was the only one she told of her plan.

'I think it's a very silly idea,' grumbled Gladys. 'One man isn't going to be enough for you, Sue, and he's the kind that'll murder you if he ever does find you with another man.'

'Gladys!' yelled Sue. 'Don't you ever let me hear you saying things like that again! As far as we are concerned, the past is well gone.'

'Please yourself,' snorted Gladys.

It was a misty September morning when Sue crept out of the hotel by a side door and got into a waiting taxi. She looked extremely smart in her tan suit and pink accessories, and her heart was thumping with joy as she sat in the back of the taxi as it ferried her to the main station to meet her Billy.

The train was late but contentedly she waited on the platform until it arrived at last. Eagerly, she jumped up and, as Billy finally appeared, his tall figure stepping off the train, she flung herself at him.

Billy looked very smart in a light-grey, tailored suit and his hair was neat and short. In his right hand he carried a small suitcase.

'Oh, Billy, you look fine!' cried Sue as she held on to him.

'You like the whistle and flute?' he asked, turning around to show off his suit. 'My sister got all the family to chip in and they bought it for me. She's a champ.'

Sue immediately felt a pang of disappointment and jealousy. He had gone back to the East End to see his family before he came to her on their wedding day. How could he?

'I didn't tell them I was getting spliced,' continued Billy. 'Still, I'll take you up to see them one day,' he promised.

Sue ignored what he had just told her. 'We've got to be at the registry office at three o'clock,' she said. 'We'd better get some lunch.'

'As soon as that?' Billy exclaimed a little nervously.

138

'Yes,' said Sue with a laugh. 'You're not getting away from me so easily this time.'

Billy bent down and kissed her lips. 'I'm quite sure that I'll never want to,' he said.

Sue's happiness knew no bounds. The wedding was a short ceremony and two witnesses were provided by the registrar. Afterwards, as the newly-wed couple, they walked to the small guest-house without uttering a word. Their happiness and contentment was too great. At last Sue had captured her Billy and now wore a beautiful gold wedding ring like any other self-respecting woman.

Billy clutched her hand tight as they walked up the red-carpeted stairs of the guest-house. 'Want a drink Sue?' he asked.

She shook her head. Little tremors of passion ran through her body and all she could think about were Billy's strong arms encircling her.

'I'd carry you over the threshold but I might rupture myself,' jested Billy, and Sue began to giggle.

Once inside their room they closed the door on the world outside and made love tenderly and closely for hours. Sue had never been so happy in her life. At last her life was complete.

Of course news of the secret wedding had leaked to the East Bay Hotel so when Sue and Billy returned the following evening, a special dinner had been laid on for them in the dining-room. Cook had baked a cake with silver trimmings and 'Congratulations to Billy and Sue' written on it with pink icing. Sue ordered champagne to be brought out from Claud's secret hoard down in the cellar and the toasts were made with real bubbly. The staff then presented the newly-weds with a silver tray, and there was more drinking while the cake was eaten. It was a jolly party and a good time was had by all.

With their arms linked, Sue and Billy watched everyone finally depart on unsteady legs. 'It seems impossible that I can be so happy,' Sue murmured. 'I'm afraid to think about it.'

Always spontaneous in his affections Billy kissed her gently. 'You've earned it, Sue. They all seem to like you down here, and this is a swell place.'

As they finally settled down for the night, a few doors away, Gladys sat hunched up on her bed with her mouth in a tight grim line. She was feeling very unhappy and sadly neglected, having lost her Sue who had been everything to her in her uneventful life.

The next morning Billy got up very early and put on some old jeans and a warm woolly.

'Oh, Billy,' moaned Sue, looking at the clock, 'it's only five o'clock.'

'Sorry, Sue,' he explained, 'but I'm used to rising early and I must get out for a bit of exercise. I'm going to take a trot down to the harbour and watch the fishing boats come in.'

'Good,' said Sue from the depths of the blankets, 'you'll like that, Billy, I always do.'

Later that morning, after Billy had returned looking very refreshed and sounding very interested in the boats, he helped Sue with her chores and then they discussed the future.

'I see no reason why we can't be happy here, Billy,' said Sue. 'We can work together and improve this place – make it a bit more modern.'

'All I am hoping, Sue, is that I don't let you down. I'm a pretty restless guy, as you know, and I've been cooped up a long time. I might find it hard to stay put.'

'No, you won't,' insisted Sue. 'We can work hard in the summer and go abroad in the winter. That's what most of the hotel keepers do in these parts.'

'Yes, but that takes a lot of lolly,' replied Billy.

'That's not a problem, Billy,' Sue continued. 'Claud left me this hotel, lock, stock and barrel. And I've certain little investments of my own if we can't make it pay.'

Billy looked worried. 'Why did that old boy leave all this to you, Sue? What was there between you?'

Sue looked annoyed. 'Oh, there you go, Billy, starting to get jealous. I worked for him, that's all, and he needed me. We were just very good friends.'

Billy poured himself a pint of beer and sat down to drink it. 'Well, it's good to be able to get a pint like that. Where I've been that was only a dream.'

Sue sat in his lap and kissed him. 'I know, darling, and I'm going to make it up to you,' she said gently.

'Oh, well,' said Billy philosophically, 'perhaps I'll enjoy being a kept man.'

140

Sue laughed. 'Oh, no, you won't. You'll work the same as I do. Come on, now, it's time to open up.'

So Billy became mine host at the hotel and made a very pleasant landlord, mixing well with both the lounge and public bars. He played cards with the older guests and learned to play golf and go fishing with the younger ones. And he never stood any nonsense in the bars. One gesture of Billy's big fist and all argument ceased. He also became very popular down at the quayside with the fishermen. The shimmering sea seemed to fascinate him, he would often go out in all weathers with his new friends and come back full of beans and with a great yearning to own his own boat.

'We'll see how we've done at the end of the season and then I'll buy you one,' Sue promised.

After his time at the hotel, Billy was now looking very healthy and sun-tanned. He always wore a skipper's cap jauntily on the back of his head and talked of fishing and boats with the rest of the skippers down on the quay. Watching him, Sue would think that there was little trace of the old Cockney tearaway left in him, and this made her exceedingly happy.

But still Gladys was full of gloom and had little to say to Billy, who ignored her anyway, and certainly never allowed her into the bedroom while he was there. So poor Gladys were left to her own devices quite a lot, which she resented.

One day she and Sue were sitting out on the balcony overlooking the sea. 'Oh, Gladys,' sighed Sue. 'Who would think we could be so happy and comfortable?' She was dressed in a cool summer dress and stretched out her legs in a leisurely manner, as she used to do on Elsie's pink divan.

Gladys was busy with her crochet hook, her hunched figure bent over her work. 'I shouldn't court the bleeding devil if I was you,' she snapped.

'Oh, you're getting to be a miserable old bugger,' said Sue, getting up and stalking inside.

Gladys looked up to watch her disappear and a wry grin appeared on her wrinkled face.

Chapter Seventeen

The Return of Freddie

The atmosphere in the lounge bar on Saturday night was warm, comfortable and congenial. Dressed in their light summer clothes, the relaxed customers drank, chatted and laughed gaily. The bar was looking very attractive with large tanks of exotic tropical fish swimming peacefully amid the coloured lights, graceful plants climbing up the walls and tubs of bright flowers in every corner. The large window offered a wonderful view across the bay. It was still not completely dark outside so it was still possible to see the shadowy line of the cliffs above the bright lights of the funfair which was in full swing down on the front. The gay music from the carousels drifted across the village.

Tall, slim and exceedingly graceful, Sue served behind the bar. With an enigmatic *Mona Lisa* smile on her face, she kept a weather eye on Billy who was chatting to the fishermen in the next bar. Just looking at him now made her heart swell with pride. Billy was wearing his white yachting cap at a jaunty angle on his head, and his blue eyes were shining with excitement and the effects of the booze. His broad, strong shoulders bulged out of his white roll-necked sweater, and, watching the muscles flex in his arms, she thought that he was such a fine specimen of a man.

Sue served those thirsty Saturday night revellers with great skill, and she was assisted by Mandy, the young girl from Bristol. Fair as a lily, even when she was harassed with the rush of customers, Mandy looked fresh, sweet and still very young. The days in the sun had given her skin a mass of golden freckles and tonight she wore a pretty, low-cut pink dress. Looking round the bar, Sue reflected on how lucky she had been since old Claud had died. She had both a very prosperous business and Billy who, much to her relief, had settled down to a life of leisure by the sea. She had no regrets whatever. And if Billy got restless in the winter they could, she was quite sure, take a nice long holiday in the Bahamas or Spain, where it was pleasant and warm. How happy she felt, so warm and mellow – life could not be better, she thought.

It was then she noticed that Billy had moved into the centre of the bar and was heartily slapping a newcomer on the back. This person was short and thin with a shock of lank sandy hair; his face was pallid and he had a long pointed chin and deep-set eyes. It was none other than Freddie the Sly, who met Sue's startled gaze with a sneering smile. Sue only just stopped herself crying out aloud and she nearly dropped a glass as she heard Billy giving his old friend an overwhelming welcome.

'Well, I'll be blowed!' exclaimed Billy, 'if it ain't me old mate, Freddie. What are you doing down here, old son?'

Sue felt quite faint as she watched Billy get Freddie a bar stool to sit on and order him a pint. Billy then stood beside Freddie, waving and gesticulating in a very excited manner, and talking about old times and new. Her head was swimming as she tried to go about her chores, and the voices in the bar around her grew louder, adding to her confusion. Freddie the Sly spelt trouble, she knew that. What did he want? He was just out of the nick, by the look of him. And however did he find her?

After time was called, a well-boozed Billy brought Freddie over to meet her. 'Remember Freddie?' he asked. 'He was one of old Sam's Boys,' he told her.

Sue stared at Freddie with burning hostility in her eyes, but she murmured coolly, 'How are you, Freddie?'

'Walked in out of the blue,' said Billy, looking very pleased with himself.

Freddie seemed a little sheepish. 'Got a nice place here, Sue,' he muttered. 'Was on me way home. Just off the island, you know, so I thought I'd have a little holiday. Was astounded when I walked in, seeing Billy all poshed up like that, and he tells me he's the landlord.'

Sue's gaze did not flinch. 'Amazing,' she murmured, her voice loaded with sarcasm.

'Nice to meet up with old pals,' continued Freddie, with a semi-concealed sneer on his lips.

Sue just stared back at him wide-eyed with fear. Freddie was not going to go away easily, she told herself, not without a rip-off of some kind. She knew him well enough to be quite sure of that.

'Hand us a bottle of Scotch, Sue,' Billy called to her. 'We'll go into the dining-room and talk over old times.'

With fear and hatred in her eyes, Sue watched them go. Asking

Mandy to clear up for her, she ran upstairs to find Gladys who was in her room, watching a horror film on her portable television.

'Oh, Gladys!' Sue cried breathlessly. 'That devil Freddie has just walked into the bar.'

At first Gladys turned her wizened face towards Sue impassively, but then noticing how distressed her friend was, she turned off the television set and looked concerned. She was needed once more.

'Oh, dear, what am I going to do?' wailed Sue.

'Billy seen him yet?' asked Gladys.

'He's with him now. They are both getting drunk in the dining-room.'

'Well, Sue,' said Gladys, 'looks like you are going to have to face the music. But don't worry, I'll stick by you.' Her funny looking face wrinkled in a smile.

Sue sat down and chewed her nails in agitation. She had completely lost her cool. 'I don't trust that little swine,' she muttered. 'Supposing he's still got those letters?'

'Well, if he has he'll want a price for them,' said Gladys shrewdly. 'But he won't show his hand yet. Now, don't lose your head, Sue, he might even push off if we butter him up a bit.'

'Let's hope so, but he's such a vindictive little swine,' replied Sue, in a hard voice, but then, as she thought about the threat he represented, she wailed. 'Oh Gladys, after all we've been through, some dirty little crook is going to spoil the happiness we've found here. It makes me so furious!'

'Go to bed, love,' said Gladys turning on the television once more. 'Nothing will be gained by worrying.'

In bed, Sue pulled the sheets up over her head and tried to shut out the drunken sounds coming from the dining-room as Billy and Freddie sang bawdy street songs. She clutched her hands nervously. She had to get rid of Freddie at all costs, she told herself. She had to. Inside she felt desolate and empty. At one point she even toyed with the idea of murdering him. She just wished she could do something to get him away from there. For she was quite convinced that he would bring her nothing but trouble.

In the middle of the night, Billy crawled into bed fully dressed and very drunk. Lying on his back he fell asleep immediately and snored loudly. Sue crept out of the room to rout out Freddie, but he was lying on the dining-room floor absolutely out. Although Sue gave him a sharp kick in the ribs with her pointed slipper, he did not stir. How easy it would be to hit him on the head with something hard and get rid of him, she thought angrily. But she instantly checked herself. How could she seriously think such murderous thoughts? That was not any solution at all . . .

She went into the kitchen and made herself a cup of coffee, and then returned to bed. Perhaps she could face it better in the morning.

The next morning, she woke up to the sound of Billy singing in the shower next door. Her head felt like a pumpkin and she felt terrible. Yet morning was here, and she knew that she had better face the music.

Billy blustered in, rubbing himself briskly with a towel. 'Going out in the boat, Sue,' he yelled. 'I've put Freddie in one of the rooms. Poor old sod ain't fit for nothing this morning.'

Pretending to be asleep, Sue did not stir. Thank God, she thought, as Billy left, now she had the chance to tackle Freddie and find out just what he was up to.

At eight o'clock, she took a tray of tea up to Freddie. She locked the door before she roused him.

'Christ!' said Freddie, sitting up in bed. His long lank hair hung down over his eyes. 'Phew!' he groaned, 'what a bloody hangover!'

She poured him a cup of tea and sat on the end of the bed. Her teeth showed in a fixed smile.

Freddie drank his tea and as soon as he finished she snatched the cup back. 'Now Freddie,' she hissed, 'tell me what you're doing here.'

'Me? Nuffink. Why, I only came here by accident. Got the shock of me life when I saw old Billy all ponced up in his yachting cap.'

Sue stared at him with narrowed eyes. 'Don't give me that,' she snarled. 'How did you find us?'

'I swear I never knew where you were, Sue. I've been on the island a year. I just wanted a break from the smoke, that's all.'

Sue sighed. How she wanted to believe him! She got to her feet and looked down at him threateningly. 'Well, then, you can come up with me bleeding letters,' she declared reverting to her Cockney dialect.

'I ain't got 'em, Sue,' whined Freddie. 'Sorry I pinched yer money but I got on the booze and some tricky bastard dipped me wallet.'

'I'd like to believe you, Freddie,' said Sue, 'but I don't. So get your arse out of here before Billy gets back.'

'Oh don't be like that, Sue, I can keep me mouth shut. I know what Billy's like, slice yer head off if he knew about your Soho capers.' He let out a little snigger.

Sue instantly lost her temper and struck out at him with her fist. But Freddie dodged out of the way and in seconds he was pointing a flick knife at her. 'Cool it, Sue,' his thin mean voice said. 'I'm still very handy with the old flicker here.'

'You bastard!' yelled Sue backing away. 'Get out of my hotel! I'll not let you mess up my life with Billy.'

Freddie grinned slyly. 'I don't want to, Sue, honestly I don't,' he whined.

As Sue let herself out of Freddie's room, the tears were falling fast.

Gladys was waiting for her outside. 'Don't let him upset you, Sue,' she comforted her. 'Where there's a will there's a way, as we learned in Soho. Come on, love, have a nice cool wash and forget him for a while.'

Sue took her advice and went down to help with the breakfasts in the kitchen where she snapped and snarled at everyone.

'She's got out of bed the wrong side, ain't she?' remarked the cook.

There was no way in which Sue could dislodge Freddie from the hotel. He stuck there like glue and stayed close to Billy. Every time he passed Sue in the corridor, he would give her an oily smile.

Gladys pushed her luck with him one day and stood in front of him. 'Why don't you piss off?' she muttered.

But Freddie just smiled, spun her round by the shoulders and gave her a sudden kick in the rump that sent her reeling. After that, she avoided him.

'How long is Freddie staying?' Sue asked Billy.

'He's just done a stretch. I thought you, of all people, would have a bit of understanding.'

Sue looked forlorn. 'It's not like it used to be with him around all the time.' She put her arms around his neck. 'We don't seem as close to each other as we were.'

146

'The bleeding honeymoon can't go on forever, Sue,' he said impatiently and pulled away from her.

A hard lump came to her throat and seemed to go on down to her heart. Boiling rage and hatred churned inside her for Freddie whom she knew was her enemy.

Chapter Eighteen

Mandy's Dilemma

Now that Billy and Sue were at loggerheads over Freddie the Sly, Gladys had come into her own again. Freddie also seemed to wallow in the fact that he had come between them and still did not show the slightest inclination to leave East Bay Hotel. He swaggered around in Billy's wake with a sneering smile on his face.

This situation made Sue sad, very depressed and extremely bad tempered. And she vented her feelings on the staff in a relentlessly vicious manner, day and night.

Even her favourite, sweet Mandy, commented, 'Eeh, what's oop wi't'missus? 'Er be loike a bear wi' a sore head.'

'It's that slimy git Freddie,' the cook informed her.

'Why! eeh be a very nice boy,' Mandy said with her blue eyes wide open. For Freddie was exceedingly charming to Mandy and she, in turn, chatted to Freddie about her boyfriend, Andy, and her forthcoming wedding at the end of September. With a twisted smile, Freddie would listen affably to her and Mandy would give an extra flick of the wrist whenever she poured him his drinks.

When Freddie was not lounging at the bar talking to Mandy, he was out in the boat with Billy. A cold atmosphere had built up between Sue and her Billy. He now kept as far away from her as possible, and there was a sulky expression on his face when they met at meals or in their room.

'I don't think that I can stand much more,' Sue confided to Gladys. 'I feel as if I am living on the edge of a volcano. Something's going to blow any minute.'

'We'll both attack Freddie and beat him up,' suggested Gladys. 'Then he'll go.'

Sue sighed and shook her head. 'No, Gladys, that's not the answer. Freddie's very vicious with that flick knife. I know, because I've seen him in action. But we're not going to let the grass grow under our feet, I can assure you. The next time he goes out with Billy, we'll search his room systematically. If he's still got those letters we had better find them.

So the next day, once Freddie had gone out in the boat with Billy, Sue and Gladys searched every nook and cranny of his room. They looked everywhere – all the pockets of his clothes, all the articles packed in the battered old suitcase he had brought with him, under the bed, inside the wardrobe – but they found nothing of interest. Defeated, they sat on Freddie's bed wondering what to do next. Suddenly they heard footsteps echoing along the corridor and before they could move, Mandy walked in. In her hand she was carrying a glossy magazine. 'What be you doing in Freddie's room?' she asked innocently.

'Cleaning it up,' complained Gladys. 'It's a bleeding pigsty.'

'Look!' cried Mandy holding out the magazine. 'Isn't that lovely, that long wedding dress? It's just what I want. "Mandy", oi said to meself, "that's the dress for you", and now I've got enough money in me box to buy it. Wait a minute, I'll show you.' She dashed off and returned moments later holding the cash box that she saved all her tips in.

Sue and Gladys exchanged glances of amusement.

'Nearly twenty pounds oi got in there,' said Mandy, proudly. 'It's enough to buy that dress – isn't that exciting?'

'That's nice, dear,' said Sue kindly. 'Now you go and put your little box in a safe place.'

With the box clutched under her arm and still admiring the dress in the magazine, Mandy went off down to the kitchen to talk to the cook about it.

When she had gone Sue and Gladys still sat gloomily on the bed, returned to their problem.

'The fact is,' said Sue, 'we could knock him off but sure as eggs is eggs we'd get caught and end up behind closed doors again. It's just not worth the risk.'

And Gladys regretfully agreed.

Meanwhile, Freddie was out in the bay with Billy in his boat. The sun was shining, the sky was blue and in the hold there were several crates of beer. Billy pointed to the shoals of mackerel dashing past the boat, darting here and there like slivers of silver. 'There'll be a porpoise chasing them,' said Billy, 'driving them inland. Watch for him. You see, I've learnt a few good tricks from the local fishermen,' he added proudly as he threw out his nets with great skill.

The two men laughed and chatted about the old days. 'The

fellas would larf their 'eads orf if they saw us now,' commented Freddie.

'Oh well, it's certainly a great life,' said Billy. 'I'd never turn back.'

'Did you know that Sue resents me, Billy?' asked Freddie, cautiously sounding out Billy.

'She's a little jealous, I suppose,' replied Billy. 'Not to worry, old son. I'm still the guv'nor.'

'Yes,' sneered Freddie. 'You've both come a long way since she was a kid skivvying for the old prostitutes in Soho.'

Billy shot Freddie an angry look. 'We never look back,' he said sharply. 'Sue and I live for each day.' He pointed to the silver glint of the mackerel shoal to the right. 'Come on, lad!' yelled Billy. 'Get your finger out! Here they come!'

At mid-afternoon Billy slopped into the hotel kitchen and began hauling off dripping oilskins and heavy rubber boots. He was jubilant. 'Fifty mackerel in one haul,' he boasted.

Sue cast him a side-long look and then went forward to pull off his boots as she used to when they were more friendly. She knelt down and looked up at him whereupon Billy bent forward and kissed her full on the lips. 'Oh, Sue, don't let's quarrel,' he pleaded.

With a wonderful sense of relief, Sue put her arms around his neck and immediately they were clenched in a passionate embrace.

'Help me out of me gear,' Billy whispered, 'and let's go to bed.'

Sue gasped, pretending to be shocked. 'In the afternoon, Billy?' she asked.

'Who cares?' said Billy, his big rough hands fondling her breasts.

And so they disappeared into their bedroom where they spent the rest of that hot afternoon making love to each other, oblivious to everything except themselves.

'Seen the missus?' everyone asked, but no one needed to answer.

Like an old watchdog, Gladys prowled up and down the corridor outside the bedroom while Sue slept a deep sleep of exhaustion and did not emerge till the morning. As she patrolled, Gladys passed Mandy and Freddie chatting to each other, but she did not hear the conversation between them.

'Andy be away in the deep sea,' Mandy was telling Freddie. 'And when he come back in three weeks' time, then oi will go home to be wed.'

'Good for you,' remarked Freddie, looking very interested.

'Oi be going to buy this nice wedding dress,' she waved her magazine at him. 'Look at that!'

But Freddie's mean, narrow eyes missed the page and focused on her neck and soft bosoms. Reaching out with his finger, he touched the tight pink jumper stretched over them. 'Got a nice lot of tit in there,' he said cockily.

'What a naughty boy you are, Freddie,' replied Mandy, drawing away and blushing.

But Freddie just sniggered and ignored her. 'What about a date, then, Mandy?'

'I told you,' replied Mandy, 'I've got a boyfriend.' She walked away hurriedly, her bottom waggling in her tight skirt.

'Okay,' Freddie called after her, 'so yer said.'

The next morning, after he had dressed, Billy kissed Sue again with great passion. 'You were right, Sue,' he said. 'At the end of the season we should close up this part of the hotel and go off to Spain for a holiday. That's when I'll give Freddie the elbow.'

Sue was overjoyed. 'Do you really mean it, Billy?' she asked.

Billy nodded. 'But for the time being, leave Freddie alone. He's useful and gives me a hand with the nets when I'm out in the boat.'

It was a very radiant Sue that agreed.

That evening, Sue sailed into the lounge and took over the bar looking more like her old self than she had for days. She wore a nice tailored black dress and some pretty jewellery to liven it up.

She noticed that Mandy seemed a bit overexcited, and kept doing everything wrong.

'What's wrong with you, Mandy?' asked Sue sharply, after she had smashed a second glass.

'Oi doan't feel well,' cried Mandy, with tears welling up in her blue eyes.

'All right, take an early night,' said Sue kindly, 'you're getting too worked up about this wedding.'

As Mandy gratefully went off duty, she passed Freddie playing darts in the public bar. He looked furtively at her as she hurried past. Noticing this, Sue reminded herself to keep an eye on them, since she knew how easily Freddie could corrupt innocent little Mandy, who was obviously missing her boyfriend.

Early the next morning, everyone was woken up by such a to-do. A distraught Mandy was running about the place weeping madly. Someone had rifled her money box and taken the nineteen pound notes but left behind the coins.

'That slimy bastard, Freddie, is at it again,' declared Sue to Gladys.

Mandy was almost hysterical. 'Now oi can't buy me nice wedding dress,' she wailed, wringing her hands in distress.

'Now, pull yourself together, Mandy,' begged Sue. 'I'll replace the money so you can still buy the dress. I've always warned you to lock your bedroom door. I'll give the money to you on Friday when you get your month's pay. Then on Saturday you can go into town and take out a Post Office Savings book. You can let the money stay there until you go home at the end of the month.'

'Thank you, Sue,' said Mandy, wiping her eyes.

'Now, go and get dressed and start work. And forget about it,' Sue told her kindly. When the girl had gone, she sighed to herself. 'I for one shall be very pleased when Mandy is finally wed,' she murmured to herself.

'He's after her,' Gladys announced later.

'Who's after who?' asked Sue.

'That Freddie, dirty little sod,' declared Gladys. 'I saw him talking to her in the passage upstairs, yesterday evening.'

Sue looked alarmed. 'Surely Mandy wouldn't be so foolish,' she said.

'She's hot,' cackled Gladys, 'only waiting to be laid.'

'Now don't be so coarse,' said Sue. 'I certainly shall be relieved when she finally goes at the end of the month.'

On Saturday morning Mandy caught the bus into town. She was looking very pretty, with her hair freshly curled and wearing a plain white summer dress and carrying a big white handbag. In the bag she had all the money that Sue had so kindly given her.

When she arrived in town and had been to the post office, to her astonishment, she met Freddie. It was such a coincidence, she told herself, but she wasn't displeased to see him.

'Wot abaht a cuppa?' asked Freddie, piloting her into a posh teashop. She was happy to be with Freddie and enjoyed sitting at the table and pouring tea from a silver-plated teapot. 'Oi must remember the time the bus goes,' she said. 'Oi promised Sue I'd be back by one o'clock.'

'Well, that's it,' grinned Freddie, pointing out of the window. 'It's going up the road.'

'Oh dear,' cried Mandy in dismay, 'I've missed it.'

'Not to worry,' Freddie reassured her, 'there'll be another along in two hours. How about a trip to the funfair in the meantime? Would yer like a ride on the bumper cars, eh, Mandy?'

His suggestion sounded very exciting, particularly since she had to hang around for a couple of hours. 'If you like, Freddie,' she replied sweetly.

'Right, then,' said Freddie, swaggering to the cash desk to pay the bill with one of the many pound notes he had stuffed into his pockets.

They walked along side by side down the streets. Mandy was shyly silent but Freddie walked with his hands in his pockets, whistling a tune. At the funfair they had a ride on the bumper cars. Freddie behaved very badly, bashing violently into the other cars, and yelling and swearing at their drivers.

'Oh, dear,' cried Mandy. 'I feel sick, Freddie, let's get off, please.'

'Nice bit of fresh air will do you good,' said Freddie leering at her. 'Come on, then, let's go up the cliffs.'

He pulled her up the steep path and they sat right on the edge of the cliff in the long grass. Quite unexpectedly, Freddie grabbed hold of her knee.

Mandy pushed him away. 'Now, Freddie,' she said mildly, 'doan't ee be so rude.'

But Freddie ignored her. 'Come on,' he urged. 'Give us a kiss.' With that, he pushed her back down into the long grass.

But Mandy was big and strong and she fought like a tigress to get free.

Seeing that she was going to be so much trouble, Freddie jumped up at last. 'Mingy cow,' he sneered.

Mandy got to her feet and, from her greater height, looked down at Freddie with an air of superiority. 'You know I have a boyfriend,' she said, 'so you behave yourself. I'm going to wait for the bus at the bus station, now.'

'Please yerself,' shrugged Freddie. 'I'm going to get meself a bloody drink. Thought you'd be a bit sporty,' he taunted her. 'Don't see why you're hanging on to it.' With that, he swaggered off.

Mandy carefully climbed down the steep slope and sat in the bus station to wait for her bus. At last it came but it was just pulling out of the bus depot, when Freddie, looking a little worse for drink, shuffled out of the pub opposite and jumped aboard. He plonked himself behind Mandy, giving her an occasional poke in the ribs and offering her a cigarette.

'No, thank you, I don't smoke, Freddie,' she said in response.

'Why can't yer be a bit bleeding sociable?' demanded Freddie aggressively.

Mandy blushed and decided not to speak to him any more. But when they got off the bus at the end of the road that led up to East Bay Hotel, Freddie ambled along beside her. Mandy did not protest because she had always been a little afraid of the lonely winding cliff road, as though somebody might jump out at her from behind a bush. So she did not complain when Freddie shuffled along beside her, particularly since he seemed to be in a better frame of mind.

'This bloke of yours, what's he do for a living?' Freddie asked quite sociably.

'He be a sailor,' replied Mandy proudly.

''Ow long since yer seen 'im?' continued Freddie.

'Well, tiz now three weeks,' said Mandy innocently, 'an' in another two weeks I go home and we be wed.'

'Well, you must be getting bleeding hungry,' returned Freddie with a change of tone.

'Oi don't know what you be getting at, Freddie,' Mandy replied mildly.

'Git orf it,' Freddie said, 'mean ter say that yer don't fancy a bit of the uvver?'

As she realized what he meant, Mandy stopped and stared at Freddie looking very shocked. But with a quick shove of his shoulder Freddie sent her spinning towards a dark spot where the cliff dipped into a deep cavern.

'Stop it, Freddie!' Mandy screamed out with fear, but his fist landed her a blow to the chin. Her handbag flew out of her hands and she fell on her knees.

He was on her in a flash and had her spread-eagled on the ground. His knees held her legs apart as he tore at her dress. Mandy bit and scratched and fought, but when she tried to scream again he shoved his hand over her mouth.

'Shut up, you silly bitch!' he hissed. 'Because I am going to fuck you whether you like it or not.'

154

So Freddie stole Mandy's virginity in a very brutal manner, that precious thing she had hung onto with such tenacity for the sailor boy she loved.

When Freddie finally released her, Mandy got up and ran blindly up the cliff path towards the comforting sight of the lights of East Bay Hotel. She did not even notice that she had lost one shoe and her big white handbag, which Freddie immediately rifled – taking her purse and the Post Office Savings book – before throwing it in the sea. Freddie then ambled quickly back down the road to lie low until things had blown over.

When Mandy burst into the hotel kitchen, Sue was refilling an ice bucket for the counter. 'Oh, Christ!' cried Sue when she saw the state of Mandy, she rushed forwards to the young girl. Mandy's dress was torn to ribbons and there was blood running down her face. 'Whatever's happened to you? Oh Mandy, Mandy.' Sue held her tight.

'That Freddie, he done it to me,' sobbed Mandy.

'Gladys, come down here!' yelled Sue. Whereupon Gladys left her television and came to the aid of the distressed little Mandy.

They took the girl upstairs and bathed her gently. They gave her a hot toddy and then put her to bed. Throughout this time, Sue was white-lipped with rage. 'The bastard,' she muttered, 'the slimy git, he's done it this time. Stay with her, Gladys, and lock the door. I've got to go back to the bar.'

White-faced with rage, she stalked into the bar.

'What's up, Sue?' asked Billy.

'Where's that bloody mate of yours?' she hissed.

'Who? Freddie? He's gone to town. Why, what's the matter? What's he done?'

'Never mind,' replied Sue, her face set hard with hate.

'I'll go and get ready now, Sue,' Billy said. He always went out with the local fishermen on Saturday nights but Sue hardly heard him, her rage was so great.

When the bar finally closed and Mandy lay in bed sleeping, Sue called to Gladys. 'Come out now, Gladys. Lock her door and we'll wait for him. He's bound to sneak in the back door. Lock all the other doors and we'll wait for him here.'

The two women then waited in the wine cellar next to the pantry until at last they heard a well-boozed Freddie come whistling up the garden path to the back door. He breezed into the lavatory. While he was busy in there, Sue took off her high stiletto shoe and, as Freddie came out, she made a mad dash at him waving the shoe and crying out, 'You bastard! You slimy bastard!' She struck him on the head and about the face with the sharp heel of the shoe.

Freddie was taken completely by surprise and instinctively backed away, but from behind him another sturdy figure jumped on his back and pulled him down on the concrete floor where his head struck the floor with a decided thump. Gladys then grabbed his long hair and proceeded to bang his head on the floor while Sue hammered at him with her shoe, and kicked and jumped on him like a maniac.

Freddie's eyes rolled in terror and he gave a loud gasp as he passed out.

'Oh, Gladys,' cried Sue, suddenly backing away. 'I think we've killed him.'

'No such luck,' said Gladys giving him an extra kick in the ribs. 'Let's drag him along and aim him out of the back door,' she suggested.

So they dragged him down the passage and pushed him out of the back door down a steep flight of steps so that he lay on the path in an unconscious heap.

'Now, lock the doors, Gladys. Billy won't be home till the morning. Then get Freddie's belongings and throw them out on top of him in case he gets any ideas about coming back in. I'm going to have a stiff drink.'

Gladys took the old suitcase and all Freddie's clothes and threw them out onto the grass.

Sitting in the bar, Sue sipped a big brandy. 'Well, I feel much better,' she said with satisfaction, 'we have really done it now, Gladys.'

'Good job, too,' announced Gladys, looking quite invigorated. 'I enjoyed that.'

It was a rosy morning over the harbour when Billy came ashore. He spent a while with the other fishermen sorting out the catch and hanging out the nets to dry. In the old boat shed, he joined the locals in a hot cuppa liberally spiked with rum. He always found it strange that he, a London lad, had this affinity with the deep-sea fishermen. He liked nothing more than being out there, battling with those huge Atlantic waves. He had his own little runabout, a motor boat, but that could not compare with those trips out in the trawlers. He never missed the Saturday night trips, if he could help it.

Sue lay in bed restlessly looking out at the grey sky lit with the pink and gold of the dawn, and wondering where Billy was by now. The huge gannets screeched and swirled around the chimney pots as she morbidly imagined Billy coming up the cliff path and seeing Freddie's lifeless body lying there. Or worse, imagining that Freddie had recovered and was now down at the harbour waiting for Billy, to enlighten him of Sue's secret life in Soho. Her body shook with terror and sweat came to her brow, for she was still very afraid of Billy's violent temper. Unable to stand the anxiety any longer, she shot quickly out of bed and ran to the window. From where she stood, she could just see the back steps where Freddie had lain, but there was not a sight or sound of him, and no suitcase or clothes littered the lawn. She drew a deep breath of relief and ran quickly along the corridor to look out of the back window. It was clear. There was no reminder of last night's horror scene.

'Gladys! Gladys!' she called softly, 'come out here.'

Gladys' squat form arrived, clad in a balloon-like nightie, and a crochet shawl around her shoulders. She scratched her woolly head irritably.

'He's gone!' gasped Sue, pointing towards the steps. 'Look for yourself.'

'I know,' replied Gladys. 'I watched him pick up his things and go about half an hour after you was in bed.'

'Wonder where he's gone?' pondered Sue.

'He looked very sorry for himself,' said Gladys with much satisfaction. 'Bunged his clothes back in the case, swearing all the time. I put two fingers up at him, I did,' she declared.

'Oh, Gladys, you never!' cried Sue, but she chuckled at the thought.

'Now, if you don't mind, I'd like to catch up on my sleep,' said Gladys wandering back to bed.

Sue stood looking out of the window out to sea at the white choppy waves rolling line after line towards the shore. The sea always fascinated her, and Billy, too, since he had come here. He had adapted himself to the life in this little seafaring community so well, it would be a pity if it were all over. She could only hope

157

that it was not. Creeping back to bed, she waited for Billy to return. At last she heard him dump his fishing tackle in the hall and take off his sea boots. Minutes later, he entered the bedroom. 'Don't get up yet, Sue,' he said. 'I'm cold, let's have a cuddle.'

She moved over to make room for him, sighing a deep sigh of relief. All was well. Billy was home safe and Freddie had gone away. She put her arms about him. 'Oh Billy, Billy, I love you so much,' she whispered sleepily.

'Gor blimey!' exclaimed Billy with a laugh, 'wait for it, let me get in the bed . . .'

A week passed and there was still no news from Freddie. Billy was very annoyed. 'There's a bastard for you,' he said. 'I've been a good mate to that Freddie and he's pissed off without a word.'

Sue made no comment but she knew Freddie. He was an animal, he would stay somewhere and lick his wounds and would eventually come back to his prey.

Mandy, looking very pale and subdued was up and about again.

'Would you like to go home a little early, Mandy?' asked Sue one morning.

Mandy's lip trembled. 'Do ee want to get rid of me?' she cried.

Sue shook her head and smiled kindly. 'No, no, nothing like that,' she said. 'I'll pay your wages in advance and that will help with the wedding. You'll need it since you've lost your Post Office Savings book. I'm closing the residential part of the hotel early this year, and Billy and I are going to take a holiday, so you can go home and be nice to Andy and get this wedding over at last.'

Mandy's lip continued to tremble and her blue eyes filled with tears. 'Oi doan't know, Andy might not marry me now.'

But Sue grabbed her by the shoulders and shook her hard. 'For God's sake, Mandy, don't be such a little fool! He'll never know if you use your head. All this talk of virginity is an old wives' tale, I can assure you. If you really love each other, it don't matter.'

Mandy stared dolefully at Sue. 'I believes you, Sue,' she said. 'So if Andy haas me it won't matter what Freddie did.'

'That's the idea.' Sue was relieved to find that Mandy had some sense in her. 'Now come on, let's get you packed up and on your way and you'll be there when Andy comes home from sea.'

158

Mandy was given a little farewell party and packed off on a train the next day. Sue watched as the girl waved from the train window, her lovely blonde hair shining in the sun. 'Oh, dear Mandy, I hope all goes well with you,' she said with a sigh.

Chapter Nineteen

Peace Before the Storm

Even by mid-September it was clear that a very bad winter was on its way. Already there were gale force winds tearing at the rocky coves, howling like banshees and keeping the residents of East Bay awake at night. Massive waves bounded over the sea wall, washing over the empty promenade where all the small kiosks were closed and boarded up, well protected against nature's wild elements. Throughout the little fishing village, anticipation was felt as the residents awaited the long stormy period ahead.

High up on the cliffs, at East Bay Hotel the atmosphere had already become extraordinarily peaceful. Most of the holiday-makers had gone home and now the only guests were a couple of old men taking a late vacation.

Sue herself was kept busy getting the rooms prepared for the winter season during which they would not be in use. She covered the furniture with dust sheets and stripped all the beds; this was how it would all remain until the early spring. She was still determined that she and Billy would take a holiday in Spain during November and get away from the hotel completely. She wanted to take Billy away on a second honeymoon and also to get him away for a while in case Freddie came creeping back into their lives.

'It's strange,' Sue remarked to Gladys, 'that Freddie just disappeared like that.'

'Gone back to his own rotten sty,' said Gladys with a vicious tone in her voice.

'I'd feel so much more relieved if I could be sure,' replied Sue. 'Anyway, I'll be glad to get away at the end of the month, what with the weather and that damned villain on my mind.'

'Don't worry, love,' Gladys assured her. 'I'll be here if he comes back and he'll get another good clobbering.'

Sue looked at her little protector with affection. Where in all the wide world would she ever find anyone as loyal and affectionate as sturdy little Gladys?

Billy had quickly forgotten about Freddie disappearing without a word and went back to his seafaring friends. He had recently become very interested in the lads of the lifeboat crew whom he met socially in the bar once a week. Billy had put on quite a lot of weight over the past few months, his face had become red and weatherbeaten, and he had developed a rolling gait. He deliberately seemed to assume the air of an old sea salt and talked of nothing that was not connected with the sea. And now when the lifeboat went out training on Sunday mornings his strong muscular arms willingly pulled at the oars. The lifeboat was housed on the beach not far from the hotel, and when Billy was nominated for the second stand-by crew of the East Bay lifeboat, he was completely over the moon about it all. 'Don't be so silly, Sue,' he said when she mentioned going to Spain. 'How can I go off to Spain? They need more men for the lifeboat in the winter. Why, someone else might volunteer and I'd lose me place on the crew.'

Sue was quite upset by this development. 'Billy, all this will be here when we get back, and anyway, the weather might improve.'

'Do me a favour, Sue,' replied Billy, 'you go to Spain. Take old Gladys with you. I'd sooner stay here.'

'Oh, Billy,' Sue wailed again. 'I was so looking forward to this holiday for both of us, to get away from this stormy sea and the continuous howling wind. Out in Spain at this time of year the sun will still be shining.'

But Billy just kicked off his sea boots and lay back in his chair. 'You still don't understand, do you? When I was in London I was a nonentity scrambling for a few quid the best I could. Here, I'm accepted without any questions. It means a lot to me, it does.'

'Well,' snapped Sue, 'not only is what you do bloody dangerous but your popularity only boils down to all the free beer you give everyone to drink in the bar.'

'You still don't see it, do you?' declared Billy. 'When I'm out in me little boat and the wind is whistling by, I get great excitement. I ride the waves. I'm like a king in a world of me own. I'm not afraid of the sea, and I've never been so happy and so free.'

'Now, Billy,' replied Sue severely, 'this is Sue you're talking to, who knows you and knows that you never saw the sea till you came down here. So don't get carried away.'

Billy looked gloomy. 'Oh well,' he said, 'I've found what I was

161

looking for and getting on the lifeboat crew has really pleased me. Do you know that they have saved hundreds of lives in the last few years.'

'Yes, and lost a few, no doubt,' retorted Sue with irony.

'The lads like and respect me, so I'll not let them down. And that's final, Sue.' He suddenly lost his temper and stalked out of the room in his sock-clad feet.

'Oh well,' Sue sighed sadly, 'I'll have to spend the winter here, then, I suppose.'

October slowly advanced into November, dark storm clouds chased over the choppy sea. The air was frosty and the winter sun blood red like a ball of fire.

Sue had dismissed all thoughts of the holiday from her mind, and settled down to making improvements to the hotel. She even began to feel pleased that she had left Billy to his own peculiar pleasures, for he seemed very happy and it pleased her to see him so. He occasionally spent a night on stand-by down in the lifeboat hut and drank and played darts with his pals in the bar at other times. He still went out fishing in his own boat and on these occasions, would come home in the early hours of the morning. Sue would listen to him thumping across the room in his heavy boots, his frame coming into the bedroom looked so burly in his dark blue sweater and smelling, as he drew near, of fish and the fresh salt of the sea. Sue would always sit up in bed and hold out her arms to him.

'Now Sue,' Billy would laugh, 'pack it up.'

But Sue would nestle close and kiss his rough whiskery face. 'Come on, Billy, get your things off,' she would whisper enticingly. 'Sue wants to make love to you.' And in spite of Billy's protests, she would have her own way. Their two strong bodies locked together making passionate love in the early dawn. Then afterwards, Sue would lie contentedly in his arms, smoothing her hands over his perfect body. 'Oh, Billy, my love, I could never lose you now; it would kill me,' she would whisper.

In December there was snow on the cliff tops and the thatched Dorset cottages looked very picturesque with their roofs snow-capped and their gardens covered in a blanket of virginal white.

'This is the first white Christmas I have ever seen here,' remarked Gladys as they decorated the hall and rooms with Christmas garlands and wreathed the pictures on the wall with holly.

'Put a big bunch of mistletoe out in the hall, Gladys,' Sue told

162

her. 'I've been lucky, really,' Sue said. 'We've got some guests coming for Christmas – Americans who have a family in the village but they're sleeping here. I think I'll have a Christmas Eve party. Billy would like that, and he could invite all his sea-going pals.'

Gladys could not help having gloomy thoughts. 'It will be just our luck if that bleeding Freddie turns up.'

It was as if a dark shadow crossed Sue's path. She scowled. 'Oh, shut up, Gladys! Don't remind me. I just hope that we've seen the last of him. Now, hand me that paperchain . . .'

The next morning, wearing navy blue slacks and bright blue jumper, Sue took a brisk walk down to the harbour to look at the little boats now all covered with snow. Large gannets, uttering shrill cries, perched on top of the masts, as the boats rocked gently from side to side at their moorings. These were holiday boats which would not be back in action until the spring.

Noticing that the door of the small fisherman's church was open, and acting on some impulse, Sue walked inside. It was cold inside but smelled of pine wood because the altar was decorated for Christmas with huge pine branches taken from the woods. It was not at all like her own church, yet she suddenly had a weak-kneed feeling that frightened her. She sat on the edge of the polished pew but she did not pray; she had forgotten how to. But the peace and serenity that pervaded the building soothed her. Looking up, she noticed the board of remembrance on the wall, containing the long list of sailors' names and the ships that they had gone down with. Alongside that was a big brass plaque commemorating the very first East Bay lifeboat that had been lost with all aboard her. Sadness crept over her – imagine, twenty men from a small place like this. How terrible. There must have been so many widows, so many orphans. She gazed about her. A shaft of pale wintry sunshine glanced through the stained-glass window which depicted Christ walking on the water. The vivid blue, greens and golds of the glass entranced her. 'Oh, dear God . . .' The words came from her lips involuntarily, and almost unconsciously, she began to pray. 'Do not let that terrible sea get my Billy,' she whispered. When she left the church, her cheeks were wet with tears. She did feel a little depressed but she also had a sort of inner peace. She went and sat on the sea wall for a while, to listen to the relentless waves pounding the shore.

Gladys had come down to meet her, well wrapped up in heavy coat, scarf, gloves and big woolly hat. She looked just like a little gnome. 'I've brought you a coat, Sue,' she said. 'Fancy going out like that! You're perishing with the cold.'

'I'm not cold,' insisted Sue. 'In fact, I'm quite warm inside.'

The Christmas Eve party went with a bang. All the locals turned up in a very festive mood, and all the staff joined in. Sue gave free drinks after time and served a good supper of turkey sandwiches, mince pies and the usual traditional fare.

The American family were most impressed by all the celebrations. They let themselves go and danced and sang 'Knees up Mother Brown'.

'Who is this Mother Brown?' the wife frequently asked, but no one seemed to know or care.

The snow continued to fall, deep white and silent, and for a while, the roaring sea abated. At midnight the party goers gathered outside on the terrace and threw snowballs at each other, singing 'Good King Wenceslas' around the lamp posts.

At last, everyone went rolling home singing in inebriated harmony, 'By the light of the silvery moon', and Sue was able to relax at last. Putting her long legs up over the arm of the chair, she sipped her last drink.

Billy was quite flaked out and fast asleep on the settee. After she had watched him for a few minutes, Sue went over and smoothed back his unruly hair. She kissed his brow and covered him with a rug. Gladys had long gone to bed and the whole place seemed full of memories as the dawn light came across the sea. This had been the best Christmas Eve she could ever remember. Last year old Claud had still been alive but he was never one to entertain and before that, well, she had been in Soho where she had worked half the night. She shuddered and tried not to think about it. But the bad memories still persisted, pushing aside the good ones, so she slept thinking about how the men were very drunk and then often violent and little Gladys had fought with them and pinched their money. It all seemed so unspeakable to her now. She could not bear to think about any of those days in Soho and she knew that it was because if Billy ever found out, he would never forgive her.

The sea seemed to get rough once more, and the howling of the wind was tremendous as the tide came in. Sue shivered a little and kissed Billy once more. 'Happy Christmas, darling,' she whispered. 'May we be together for the rest of our lives. I'll ask for nothing more.' Then, as tiredness overcame her, she went off to bed.

On Christmas morning a strong north wind had risen and sleet viciously lashed at the window panes. She turned restlessly in her sleep as Billy's big hand thumped her on the shoulder.

'What is it?' she mumbled sleepily.

'Hear that?' he asked. 'It's distress rockets being fired out in the bay. There's a ship in trouble. I'm off down to the lifeboat shed – I might be needed.' He was sitting on the bed struggling into his big woolly sweater and pulling on his long boots.

'Oh, Billy,' murmured Sue in protest, 'you can't go out in this weather.'

'Don't be daft, Sue. Wake up! It means I might get a bit of action. So long.' He kissed the top of her head and strode out. Moments later she heard the front door bang shut, and she managed to rouse herself enough to sit up and listen to the roaring sea and the strange swishing sound of the rockets going up. Then she flopped back and snuggled down under the blankets. There was not much point in her getting up; she would not be needed.

At ten o'clock Gladys woke her by bringing in a tray of tea. 'Mean to say you slept through all that excitement?' she cried.

'What excitement?' Sue was still half asleep.

'Been a ship on the rocks. Six men been rescued – all foreigners,' said Gladys.

Then Sue remembered Billy. 'Where's Billy?' she cried, with a touch of panic in her voice.

'Need you ask?' sneered Gladys in disgust. 'Downstairs getting drunk, of course. Thinks he's a bleeding hero.'

Sue jumped out of bed. Dressing hurriedly, she was downstairs like a shot. Although it was so early in the morning and the bar not yet officially opened, it was full. Everyone was talking at once, and oilskins dripped all over the carpet. Behind the bar, Billy was serving drinks hand over fist. His red face wore an ecstatic expression and in a booming voice he called out to his mates and recounted to others the story of the six men being rescued from their sinking ship.

The ship had been a Dutch tramp steamer that had been swept

onto those vicious rocks by the heavy storm. Four of the crew had been taken to the hospital in town. The remainder of the crew, the captain and first mate were in the bar. They were big, whiskery men who looked very jaded and depressed.

Billy gave them free drinks and they seemed to cheer up a little. Sue noticed that in the lap of one young man sat a big ginger cat. She rubbed the top of its damp head and the cat purred in satisfaction. 'How did you manage to rescue the cat?' she asked.

'We couldn't leave the poor sod on board,' replied Billy, explaining how he and one of the crew had scrambled up to the crow's nest to get the cat. Everyone laughed and talked. It was a good start to Christmas Day.

'So, now we've got a cat,' said Sue, delighted, picking up the ginger bundle and cuddling him to her.

The captain and his mate stayed for Christmas dinner and afterwards Billy took them into town to visit their pals in the hospital. All this was carried on with great enthusiasm by Billy; he was having a great time. Sue was very pleased for him and even her anxiety about Freddie began to wane.

'Billy has settled down so nicely here,' Sue said to Gladys.

But Gladys screwed up her mouth and muttered, 'Well, he's got it made, ain't he?' She still had very little affection for Billy and was eaten up inside with jealousy of him.

On Boxing Day it had stopped snowing at last but the sea was still like a raging tornado. The bravest of the locals went up on the cliffs to look at the tramp steamer breaking up on the rocks. Among these was Billy who, because of his big hangover, went up with the American couple to get a breath of fresh air.

Sue could see the small knot of people standing in the cold as she looked out of the window.

'They want a bloody job,' said Gladys. 'Must be freezing out there.'

Sue agreed. 'Well, you know Billy, he can't stay away from the sea for long.'

As Billy stood on the cliff top, a small bedraggled figure in a long mackintosh and a large cloth cap edged up close to him. 'Hallo, 'ow are yer, mate?' a thin voice piped out.

Looking down, Billy recognized Freddie the Sly. 'Well, I'll be blowed,' he exclaimed. 'What hole did you crawl out of?'

'Well, that's nice,' whined Freddie. 'What a way to greet an old pal.'

'Sorry, cock,' said Billy giving him a thump on the back. 'But you sodded off without a word. Where did you go?'

'Only went up to London. Had a bit of business up there but the coppers pulled me in because I'd not reported. I was only on parole so they done me and made me finish me time. I just got out.'

'Oh, you poor sod,' said Billy sympathetically. 'What about a drink, then?'

To Billy's astonishment, instead of jumping at this suggestion, Freddie sidled furtively away from him a little and said, 'Not now, mate,' and looked quickly from side to side like some trapped animal.

'Come on,' declared Billy. 'Let's go up to the hotel and see Sue.'

At this remark Freddie behaved even more oddly. He hunched his shoulders and turned away. 'No,' he said, 'she won't want me up there. I'll see you tonight when it's a bit dark.'

'Now, what have you been up to, you sly sod?' growled Billy.

'Nuffink,' said Freddie, shaking his head. 'Just got a little business to do, somefing what might interest you. I'll meet yer six o'clock by the boathouse.' And after these enigmatic remarks, Freddie slid off into the mist.

Billy strode back to the hotel wondering what Freddie was up to. 'Can't trust him,' he muttered to himself. 'I ain't going to get involved in nothing shady, not now that I've settled down here.'

So when Billy returned home to lunch he did not mention Freddie to Sue, knowing that she would start to nag him. Sue was in a lazy, languid mood and after lunch she sat with her feet up on the settee reading a love story in a woman's magazine. The log fire blazed brightly, their new ginger cat lay in front on the sheepskin rug. Bowls of Christmas fare were strewn about the sideboard – oranges, apples, nuts and tasty mince pies.

The warm, cosy atmosphere made Billy feel nostalgic. 'Looks nice in here,' he said. 'This room's got a nice warm feeling. I feel like I used to when I got home to me muvver after a long spell in the nick.'

Sue looked up from her book and shook her head. 'Now don't start thinking about your old lady just because it's Christmas,' she said.

Billy grinned. 'She'd laugh her head off if she could see me now,' he said. 'Never had a day out of London in all her long life, and never wanted to neither.'

Billy's stomach was full after their big lunch and he was soon dozing peacefully in the deep armchair by the fire. And Sue, unaware that her fate was in the balance, continued to read her magazine.

At five-thirty, Billy was woken by Gladys who grudgingly handed him a mug of tea. He yawned and stretched, drank his tea and then got up. 'I might take a walk down to the beach,' he said casually. 'Won't be long, Sue.' Pulling a big woollen cap over his ears and then his sou'wester and oilskins, he went off into the cold air to meet Freddie.

'I'll bung Freddie a tenner,' he told himself as he walked down the hill. 'Need to get rid of the sod. Don't want him hanging about down here.'

Sleet was falling again, driven by a heavy wind. He saw Freddie huddled next to Billy's boathouse which nestled under the cliff. Billy had built it earlier in the year to protect his boat, the *Saucy Sue*, from the winter tides and heavy gales. 'Come in, mate,' Billy said, unlocking the wooden doors, 'there's a bottle of rum in the locker.'

'Bleedin' rotten weather,' whined Freddie, as Billy lit the hurricane lamp. 'Dunno how you stick it down 'ere.'

'It's great,' said Billy, pouring the rum into two enamel mugs he had pulled down from the cupboard. 'You'll never get me back in London.'

Freddie swallowed the rum very quickly and the two men sat on a plank beside the boat.

'Well,' said Billy, 'what's all this you are going to talk to me about? If it's dodgy, I don't want to know. I am going straight down here.'

'No, it's nuffink like that,' muttered Freddie. 'I just wanted yer to read this.' Putting his hand into his pocket he pulled out a letter that was addressed to Sue.

Billy stared at it suspiciously. 'It's addressed to Sue,' he said. 'What are you doing with Sue's letter? You pinched it, didn't you, you sly bugger?'

'Read it!' snivelled Freddie. 'Read the bleeding thing, then you might have something to get mad about.'

With a puzzled frown on his face, Billy opened up the letter. It was just one page long and written in a big printed hand. In very plain language, the writer of the letter thanked Sue for a hectic and enjoyable weekend and suggested that they did it more often. As he read through this, Billy's face first went white and then scarlet. With a snarl, he screwed up the letter and threw it on the floor. 'Dirty rotten sod, you are,' he said to Freddie, 'prying into other people's business.'

'She was on the game in Soho an' was a bloody old tomcat,' sneered Freddie, standing up for himself. 'And I got more letters to prove it.'

Billy was on him in a flash. Swiftly, Freddie tried to wriggle away from Billy's grasp but Billy had grabbed his tie and pulled it tight. Freddie's eyes seemed nearly to pop out of his head as Billy half strangled him.

'You blackmailing bastard!' he shouted, shaking Freddie about like a captured rat. 'Where are the letters? By Christ, I'll do for you if you try to upset Sue and me.'

'All right, all right, I only wanted a stake,' gasped Freddie. 'Let go and I'll give them to you.'

Billy let go and Freddie dropped to the floor gasping for breath. The moment he got to his feet, he tried to run for the door, but Billy's big arm barred his way.

'I'm yer mate!' wailed Freddie. 'I thought yer ought ter know. That's how she came down here with that kinky old bastard who left her the hotel. Just give me a hundred quid and I'll part up with the rest of the letters. I've got them at me lodgings.'

Billy had grabbed the bottle of rum and was drinking from the bottle. His face was red and angry-looking and his eyes had a murderous glint in them. 'I'll make you eat those words, you git,' he hissed. 'Come on, we'll go up and talk with Sue. I'm going to get the bloody truth, I can assure you.' He pulled open the door and Freddie quickly pulled away from him with a jerk and fled out into the night. 'Come back here, you blackmailing cow son!' roared Billy out into the dark night but only the crashing of the waves and the whistling of the wind were his answers. Freddie had disappeared.

With a grunt, Billy sat down and finished the bottle of rum. There was a deep frown on his face and the drunker he became, the more the veins on his forehead bulged. Almost purple with rage, he got up, kicked the wall and banged his fist against the

169

door. Then he stumbled out into the night and ran all the way back to the hotel.

Sue was in the kitchen making some coffee. After all the festivities they had decided to give the staff a night off, so there was no bar that night. Suddenly Billy dashed in from outside, rushed across the room and grabbed her by the throat. Pushing her viciously against the wall, he held her tight and glared at her with his wild, drunken eyes.

Sue was stunned. 'Billy, Billy, whatever's wrong?' she gasped.

'Tell me that you are not a whore,' he growled, 'and that I've not been living off your immoral earnings. What sort of a ponce am I, for Christ's sake? Now, tell me about the flat in Soho when I was in the nick. I want the truth, Sue, or I swear it's the last word you'll ever utter.' To show her what he meant, he squeezed her neck with brutal strength.

'Let go, Billy!' The pain was excruciating. Sue tried to push his hands away but he was much too strong and she felt weak with fear. Freddie had obviously been in contact with him.

Billy then loosened his grip and Sue put her arms about his neck. 'Oh Billy, Billy,' she cried. 'It's your Sue. Don't hurt me,' she begged.

'Talk then,' he said, swinging off to the other side of the room and pouring himself a mug of coffee.

'I suppose you've seen Freddie the Sly,' said Sue dolefully.

'Yes, I bloody well have,' returned Billy, 'and I read a filthy letter addressed to you. He says he's got lots more that he wants paying for.'

Sue felt as though her heart had almost stopped beating. Her worst fears had been realized. How was she to get out of this? Billy certainly meant what he said about killing her. 'It's not true, Billy,' she whispered. 'Or only some of it is.'

'Bloody hell!' swore Billy, slamming down his mug on the table. 'So I *did* marry a whore, and God only knows who you have mucked about with.' He seemed to pull himself up to twice his normal height and rushed at her again. He took a swipe at her and missed. Picking up his mug, he hurled it at the wall with such violence that it crashed into the shelf which was neatly stacked with glasses. There was a loud crack and the glasses flew in all directions. As a large piece of glass hit Sue in her face, she screamed and instinctively brought up her hands to protect her

170

eyes. Blood poured through her fingers all over her clothes and on to the tiled floor.

Billy looked in horror at the sight of Sue bleeding, then he dashed to her, crying, 'Oh Sue! Sue!' He was too late to stop her falling to the floor as she fainted, and he groaned in anguish when he saw the huge gash on her face which ran from her eye to her mouth. Overwrought and panic-stricken, he pulled her tightly into his arms. 'Gladys! Gladys!' he yelled.

But Gladys was already there, having been listening to the rumpus from outside. Rushing forward, she pushed Billy away and held a clean white towel to the terrible wound. 'Go and get the doctor,' she whispered between sobs, 'unless you want her to bleed to death.'

Without a word, Billy rushed to the telephone.

Chapter Twenty

The Cruel Sea

The next day, an atmosphere of gloom hung over the hotel as the news spread that the missus had had an accident. It seemed she had tripped on a rug carrying a big glass in her hand and had cut her face very badly. It had happened the night before.

Sue was a very popular employer and everyone sent their condolences and flowers. Now she lay upstairs in bed, heavily sedated after the village doctor had stitched up her face. Beside her Gladys sat with her eyes red from weeping.

'It's a deep wound,' the doctor had told Gladys. 'She really ought to go to the hospital but she's losing so much blood, I'd better do the stitching here.'

While Sue was in bed upstairs, Billy served in the bar downstairs. He had been completely devastated by what had happened, and kept crying like a baby. Now he just filled himself with drink. It never occurred to anyone that Billy might have been responsible for his wife's injury. Everyone knew that Sue and Billy were a devoted couple, and nobody knew, except Gladys.

Gladys had cleaned up the mess in the kitchen before the doctor had arrived, for she knew that Sue would not want anybody to know what really happened. She was glad to do that for Sue but she hated Billy more than ever and stared at him malevolently whenever he crept into Sue's bedroom to kneel beside the bed. 'Oh, Sue,' he would weep, 'I'm so sorry.'

Over and over again Gladys would listen to Billy's deep, racking sobs and miserable apologies, and she sighed disapprovingly when Sue on one occasion reached out her hand to him and whispered sleepily, 'Don't worry, darling, Sue has forgiven you.'

And on another occasion, Gladys had snarled at him, 'Sling yer bloody hook and leave her alone. Ain't you done enough damage?'

Late that night, Billy staggered out of the bedroom, ran downstairs and went out into the dark night. 'I'll find him,' he muttered to himself. 'I'll get the bastard.' He lurched along the beach, fighting the fierce wind until at last, exhausted, he reached the little boathouse and slept all night there.

Early the next morning he set off on his quest for Freddie once more. Going down into the village, he asked his friends down at the harbour. 'Has anyone seen a stranger in a long mackintosh?' But he had no luck there. Shaking his head, Billy went on through the village to the town, searching in all the sleazy bars and lodgings, and looking in the hotel registers. Still there was no trace of Freddie. He had completely disappeared.

At the end of the long day, Billy returned home to Sue and sat beside her bed. She seemed more alert and he tried to persuade her to take some nourishment and to cheer her up.

'It hurts me to smile,' she said. 'I hope I'm not going to have a big scar on my face.'

'I'll never forgive myself for hurting you, Sue,' Billy said gently. 'I don't care about anything else any more.'

'It's not all your fault, darling,' said Sue. 'It's that swine Freddie.'

'I swear I'll get him,' vowed Billy. 'He won't ever bother you again once I've finished with him.'

Sue shook her head but winced at the pain. 'No, Billy,' she said, 'let's forget about him. You and I are happy here. We've learned our lesson the hard way. Let's live and love each other – that is all I ask.'

Unable to hold back his emotion, Billy put his big unruly head down on the bed and wept like a child.

For a week or ten days peace was restored, and the East Bay Hotel business carried on as before even though Sue was still recovering in bed and Billy spent most of his time at her side. The staff had volunteered to do extra work to keep things running smoothly for the time being.

Gladys continued to sit in the corner of the bedroom, crocheting a long scarf and casting evil looks in Billy's direction as if he were likely to attack Sue again. She would never forget or forgive what he had done.

The day the dressings on Sue's wound were to be removed, the doctor took Gladys aside. 'She's going to have a very nasty scar on her face and it's not going to be very pleasant,' he said. 'When

173

I remove the bandages, I don't want you to react in any way. It's going to be a great shock to her so it's best for us to be as calm as possible.'

Gladys nodded in agreement and was glad that Billy was absent. He had gone out fishing that morning.

When the doctor removed the dressing and Gladys saw the beautiful face of her mistress so badly disfigured, she wanted to cry out. Instead, she looked away.

'How does it look, Gladys?' Sue asked anxiously.

'It's fine,' replied Gladys turning back. 'Can hardly see it.' But the bright red angry scar went from Sue's eye to her lip and made her mouth appear distorted.

'Let's me see,' said Sue. 'Hand me the mirror.' She reached out towards the hand mirror on the dressing table.

The doctor coughed nervously. 'Now, Mrs Rafferty,' he said, 'remember that it's going to get better and better with time. It looks a bit red now but the colour will gradually fade until it's quite pale.' He picked up the mirror to hand it to her but hesitated again. 'And of course, if necessary we can later talk about cosmetic surgery – they can do marvellous things nowadays . . .'

Instead of allaying Sue's fears as the doctor had hoped, his words only alerted her. 'Hand me that mirror!' she shouted. 'Let me see!'

The screams that came from Sue's throat as she looked at herself in the mirror rang throughout the hotel. Over and over again she screamed, holding her hands to her face in horror, screaming as if she would never stop.

As the doctor stood immobile and speechless, Gladys gave him a great shove out of the room and rushed to Sue's bedside.

'Oh God! Oh God!' sobbed Sue. 'Have you seen my face? It's horrible, it's dreadful. Oh, Gladys, why didn't you warn me?'

But Gladys just cuddled her tight. 'It'll be all right, dear,' she said reassuringly. 'The scar has not healed yet. You'll be as right as rain.'

Sue was quite hysterical by now and continued to scream.

Moments later, Billy, who had just returned from fishing, came dashing upstairs to find out what was wrong. He was shocked to find that his sweet, gentle Sue had disappeared, and in her place was a screeching cursing virago who hurled angry, bitter words at him.

'You bastard!' she yelled. 'Get out! Get out of here and don't come near me!' She picked up the breakfast tray and hurled it at him

174

across the room. 'Get out! Don't come in here!' she yelled hysterically. 'Just look what you've done to me!'

Billy held out his arms to her, and tried to plead with her. But Sue began to hurl everything in sight at him; toilet brushes and pillows flew across the room until finally, with an ear-splitting wail, she threw herself back on the bed and continued to scream loudly, kicking her legs in the air.

'Go and get the doctor!' Gladys said to Billy. 'Get out of here! You're only upsetting her more with your presence.'

As white as death, Billy ran down the road to catch the doctor whom he had passed on his way in, and then he went down to the harbour wall where he sat dejectedly looking out to sea.

And old man puffing his pipe joined him and made a number of comments about the weather but Billy was so down in the dumps that he hardly heard a word he said.

'Heard you was looking for that Cockney git who used to hang about here,' remarked the old man.

This Billy did hear. He raised his head and looked at the old man.

'Yesterday,' the old man continued, 'I took a trip round the cove to Medport and I think I saw him there. There's some sort of hostel in the town there. Lots of slimy ex-convicts staying there. Supposed to be rehabilitating them, they say. Bloody cheek if you asks me, all us tax payers' money down the drain.'

Billy leaped off the wall. 'Are you sure?' he asked, alert and ready to go. 'How do I get to Medport?'

'Well, I sailed me boat o'er there. Wanted to get some repairs done to 'er. I came back by train. But if you go in the boat, it's a long haul and very rocky, it be. You have to know the tides.'

'Right!' said Billy determinedly. 'I think I'll make it. The tide's full now. Give us the bearings, and I'll go pull out me boat.'

'I shouldn't go alone if I was you,' warned the old man. 'The sea's fair choppy, there's a storm not far out.'

But Billy was not put off by these words and soon he had the *Saucy Sue* out of the boathouse and on the runway. The old fellow gave him a hand to push her out.

With a final wave, Billy sailed away into the mist, heading for the shore on the other side of the bay. His raging thoughts were focused on one thing: vengeance on Freddie.

It was evening by the time he arrived at Medport. The harbour lights were winking and the waves rocked his boat and drove it quickly inshore. Billy was cold and hungry but he did not care. All he wanted was to find Freddie. Once he had anchored his boat in the small harbour, he trudged along the pebble beach towards the lights of the town. Medport was a fair-sized town with rows of seaside bungalows, caravan parks and a long winding main street with bars and other tourist attractions. At the bus depot he asked an old man sweeping the floor about the rehabilitation centre. The man stopped sweeping and glared at him suspiciously but then pointed to the end of the street.

Billy soon found the place. It was a large Victorian house standing apart from the other houses in the street. A dim lantern hung in the porch and just inside, in the lobby, several young men were lounging about.

'Anyone seen Freddie Hicks?' asked Billy boldly. No one answered. The young men just surveyed him in stony silence. Having been inside himself, Billy knew the drill. He took out a packet of cigarettes and offered them around. The men accepted eagerly. Then as they lit up, Billy held the match quite close to the face of one long thin lad and muttered, 'It's all right, I'm his mate. We done a bit of bird together.'

The man's narrow eyes flickered, and he took a long drag on the cigarette. Then, slowly, he looked over the road towards a sleazy bar where music was drifting out into the street.

Not a word needed to be said. 'Thanks, mate,' said Billy.

As Billy entered the bar, the bright lights dazzled him for a moment, but it only took a few seconds for his eyes to adjust. He spotted Freddie over in a remote corner playing shove ha'penny with another man. Freddie's sandy lank hair hung over his eyes and, judging by his obviously deep concentration, he had a good wager on this old rural game.

Billy bought himself a pint of beer and slowly edged his way over to Freddie's corner. He was very careful not to let Freddie see him first, for he knew that the crafty blighter would spring like a rat from a trap if he did.

Eventually Billy stood beside him. 'Hullo, pal,' he murmured.

Freddie turned swiftly, tensed up as if to run, but Billy grabbed him by the elbow in a hard, brutal grip.

'Don't start nuffink in 'ere,' whispered Freddie. 'I ain't supposed to be in 'ere.'

'Right, then!' said Billy. 'Let's go outside. I only came to settle up that unfinished business, so there's no need to get the wind up, mate.'

Hearing this, Freddie relaxed. Sweeping his long hair back off his forehead, he said, 'Come on then, let's go.'

As they walked up the main street, Billy said, 'I don't bear any grudge, Freddie, and I'm quite willing to give you fifty quid for those other letters.'

Freddie's little eyes gleamed. 'I won't tattle, mate.' He gesticulated with his hands in his plausible manner. 'But you can see how I'm placed, on the bleedin' rocks, stuck in that old gloomy 'ostel. I ain't even got the price of a packet of fags in me pocket.'

Billy handed him a packet of Players. 'Come down to the harbour,' he said. 'I came over in me boat. We can talk there.'

'You've got a lot of bottle,' grinned Freddie, 'sailing round in weather like this. Just wait a tick, I've got the letters in me suitcase at the 'ostel. Yer got the money with yer?' he asked anxiously.

Billy opened his wallet so that Freddie could see it was well stuffed with notes. 'Right, mate,' said Freddie. 'Won't be long.' He sidled off like a fox.

As Billy lounged against a brick wall waiting for Freddie's return, Freddie crept up to the hostel dormitory, and pulled the pile of letters from his suitcase. Then he slipped out into the overgrown garden at the back and dug under a bush to find his old friend, the sharp stiletto knife. It was well-wrapped up and well hidden. No weapons like that were allowed in the hostel. 'Just in case,' he muttered to himself pushing the blade down the inside of his boot. Then, with a satisifed smile on his face, he went to meet Billy.

The two men walked together down to the harbour to the *Saucy Sue*. The boat rocked and rolled at her moorings as the heavy swell of the sea tossed her around.

'Bit dangerous, ain't it?' said Freddie, hesitating on the ladder from the shore.

Billy gave him a quick shove. 'Get aboard, yeller belly,' he said. His voice had suddenly become much harder.

Without further argument, Freddie jumped aboard and went into the small cabin.

Billy watched him disappear into the cabin, and then quickly unhitched the mooring rope. As he jumped down on to the deck, his heavy figure caused the small boat to leave the harbour wall.

'Some booze in there,' said Billy pointing to a small locker.

Freddie went eagerly forward to grab a bottle of rum. Through the porthole, Billy watched the harbour receding fast, then he sat on the bunk to survey Freddie, with a wry hard gleam in his eyes.

Freddie took several long swigs from the bottle. He held it out to Billy. ' 'ere yer are mate,' he said.

Billy shook his head. 'Well, got the letters?' he asked.

'Yes, mate, 'ere they are,' said Freddie diving into his pocket with one hand and holding on to the bottle with the other. The next moment, the boat lurched and he staggered and fell over. 'Cor blimey!' he exclaimed. 'The boat's adrift.'

But Billy just picked up the bottle, replaced its cap and put it back in the locker. Reaching over, he grabbed the packet of letters from Freddie's grasp.

'Christ!' muttered Freddie, struggling to rise, 'the bloody boat's moving out to sea.'

'I know,' said Billy quietly.

''Ow am I goin' to get back?' yelled Freddie. 'I 'ave to be in by 'alf past nine.'

'Don't worry so much, son,' said Billy counting out fifty pounds. He placed it on the bunk. 'Here's your blood money. Count it, son!' He turned and went outside to start up the outboard motor. The *Saucy Sue* rocked and rode high on the waves. She was now out in the stormy bay and was heading for the open sea.

Freddie grabbed the money but dropped it again, scattering the notes everywhere. As the boat rocked precariously, he fell down again and banged his head on the floor. 'For Christ's sake, Billy,' he hollered. 'Get this bleedin' boat back to the 'arbour. It's murder out there.'

Billy stood by the motor as the huge waves crashed over the sides. Deaf to Freddie's pleas, he forced the little boat further and further out to sea, bravely mounting the great Atlantic rollers, occasionally laughing at Freddie's cries for help.

Freddie crawled out of the cabin and held on to the mast, gasping for breath. 'Turn around, you barmy bugger!' he cried.

Billy laughed cruelly. 'Why? Are you afraid to die? Too bad,' he continued, 'because tonight you will, one way or another, you

178

evil scum. I nearly killed my Sue because of you.' But his words were lost in the wailing of the wind.

Freddie prepared to attack and pulled the knife from his boot. Then he flung himself at Billy, who let go of the wheel and struggled with him in an effort to loosen Freddie's hold on the knife. But with a sudden thrust, the knife entered his side. Billy let out a howl of pain.

'You asked for it,' screamed Freddie. 'You bastard! Now tell me how to get this boat back to Medport.'

Although in pain, Billy's strength had not gone. Reaching out with his great arm, he grabbed Freddie's long hair and cracked his head on the deck. Freddie immediately collapsed and lay limp and bedraggled in the hold, motionless as the waves washed over him.

Still holding his wounded side, Billy valiantly tried to reach the wheel, which was spinning around, to tie it in position for the duration of the storm. But as he staggered towards it, a huge wave that looked like a galloping white horse, swept over him and picked him up as if he were a rag doll. Carrying him high on its foaming crest, it roared off again into the great Atlantic, taking Billy with it.

In the morning when the storm had dropped and the tide had receded, the *Saucy Sue* was found stuck fast on some jagged rocks. Freddie's dead body was quickly found.

Later that day, the local radio station reported that a small motor boat had hit the rocks in the storm, and an unidentified body had been found inside. Gladys heard this and, knowing that Billy had not returned home the night before, guessed immediately what had happened. 'Silly fool,' she muttered to herself, 'I knew he'd do it in the end.' She went upstairs and sat beside Sue who was sleeping peacefully. The doctor had sedated her to control her hysteria.

At midday Sue awoke and sat up. Gladys fed her with hot chicken soup as she would a child. Sue asked what time Billy had come in. 'I was having such a terrible dream about him,' she said. 'He was hanging on to something and crying for help and his cries were drowned out by the sound of that hymn, 'Rock of Ages'. I was unkind to him, wasn't I, Gladys?'

'I suppose so,' muttered Gladys.

'After all,' continued Sue, 'it was an accident. He never did it deliberately, did he?'

Two little tears fell out of Gladys' eyes into the soup bowl. 'Oh well, I'd better get on,' she said, getting up and hurrying out of the room. Her heart was almost breaking at the thought of Sue's great sorrow to come.

Downstairs, the police inspector and the coast guard captain had already arrived to see Sue. Gladys' heart sank. The traumatic moment had come. But according to the police, it was not Billy in the boat at all. The lifeboat captain had apparently identified the man in the boat as Freddie Hicks, an old pal of Billy's. It had, however, definitely been the *Saucy Sue* that had been wrecked in the storm. Everyone was in a quandary about whether to break the news to Sue or wait for Billy, or his body, to turn up.

'By six o'clock the air patrol will hand in their report,' the police inspector informed Gladys. 'They are at the moment searching the area for signs of a body, so I think we might as well hang on for a bit longer.'

Later that afternoon, Sue got up and dressed and sat looking out of the window with a very pensive expression on her pale face. A chiffon scarf was wound around her head and draped over her face at one side to cover the scar. She called Gladys. 'Has Billy come home yet?' she asked. 'I haven't heard him at all and it sounds very quiet downstairs.'

Gladys murmured and muttered but did not give any clear answer. But she watched in horror as Sue then suddenly reached over and turned on the radio. It was already too late to do anything; the voice of the announcer came over the air very clearly: 'A search has been going on all day off the coast of Devon for a missing yachtsman. A small boat was wrecked on the rocks in last night's storm. One man was found dead on board but an air sea rescue is still searching for another man who, it is understood, owned the boat.'

Sue stood in shock. 'Billy!' she called, 'it's Billy! Oh Gladys, why did you keep this from me?'

Her little companion rushed to her and put her arms about Sue's waist, hugging her gently as she always did. 'Sue, Sue don't panic, dear. It was Freddie the Sly they found in the boat. Billy might yet turn up.'

Sue sat down again and turned to look out of the window again. 'My Billy's gone,' she said calmly. 'The terrible cruel sea has taken him from me.'

The winter sun floated on the horizon like a huge orange ball and the grey, now calm sea washed quietly over the rocks. Sue sat very still and quiet just staring out across the water.

And that was how she stayed for many days. Many people came up to her room to offer their condolences but she never seemed to notice any of them. She just sat watching the sea with her big dark eyes in a bewildered manner. And not one tear did she shed.

Down in the bar the locals wept for her and the extrovert Cockney, Billy, who had been their host and companion.

'I wonder what he was doing so far out in the bay,' one of them said, 'in a bad storm, too.'

Old John, who usually sat down on the harbour wall, sucked his pipe. 'Saw him, I did. Helped him get the *Saucy Sue* out. He was looking for that fellow what got drowned. I told Billy that I'd seen this fellow in Medport, but I warned him. "Don't go alone," I sez, "dangerous tides out there." But he went just the same.'

Upstairs, at last, Gladys had persuaded Sue to undress and get into bed. But Sue seemed to be in a trance. All she would say, as Gladys tucked her in, was 'It's all my fault, Gladys, God has punished me for my sins.'

Spring had come at last and the daffodils were once again in bloom in the garden of the hotel. Clumps of golden blooms that Sue had planted grew under the trees and along the path the primroses and tiny crocuses declared their beautiful presence. This year Sue had no eyes for previously beloved flowers. Still she sat upstairs in her bedroom just staring out of the window with a chiffon scarf round her head and face, or standing alone on the shore.

Billy's body had never been recovered. For a while, Sue had hoped that, having settled his score with Freddie, Billy had disappeared back into the underworld of his youth, but in her innermost heart, she knew that he was gone forever. That cruel sea which he had loved so much had gobbled him up like some enormous monster. And she had finally known this to be true when a memorial service had been given for Billy in the little fisherman's church and his name had been added to the remembrance board in gold ink. She knew for certain then that her big, robust Billy was no more.

Sue had taken to going on her own to the shore every day and would sit beside the breakwater out of the wind and watch the water, always waiting and watching for that grey stormy sea to return her lover to her arms.

When she did this, Gladys would keep an eye on her and go down and persuade her to come home. 'Come on, Sue, you've had enough for one day. It's blowing up cold.'

Sue showed no interest at all in the hotel which she just left in charge of the staff. They were very distressed about her state of mind and felt that their lovely alert Sue seemed to have left them with her Billy.

'Ought to do something about her,' advised Bess. 'She's going to lose her wits if she mopes about much longer. Can't you get her to take a holiday?' she asked Gladys. 'We'll carry on here till she's better.'

Gladys thought it was a good idea but when she broached the subject to Sue, there was no response. Sue just stared at her in a scornful manner and said nothing. So Gladys knew not to pursue it.

One morning, however, Gladys was amazed to find Sue sitting at her desk in the office writing a letter. Gladys did not comment but Sue turned from the desk and said, 'If anything happens to me, this hotel is all yours. Then you'll have an inheritance to last you for your lifetime. I'm writing to the lawyer in London to get it legalized. There are also those Maritime Holdings shares that I have. I've put them in there.' She pointed to a drawer in her desk.

Immediately little Gladys was like an angry bantam hen. Glaring furiously, she strutted up and down the room. 'For Gawd's sake, Sue,' she said, 'give over. I don't want yer bleedin' money. All I ask is for you to pull yourself together and let us leave this bloody gloomy cold place and go back to where we belong.'

Sue just drooped her head and said, 'Don't get awkward, Gladys, where would we go?'

'Back to London!' cried Gladys vehemently. 'I never did like it here and you ain't the same person. We was close friends when we was up in London.' Gladys started to weep.

Sue cuddled her. 'Well, dear, you can go if you want, if you're really unhappy here.'

'Sue,' sobbed Gladys, 'I couldn't get along without you, now, let's get home.'

Sue shook her head. 'I can't leave, Billy,' she said. 'It's no good, I've tried hard but he calls me all the time. Whether I'm asleep or awake, he's out there calling me.'

Gladys threw up her arms in despair. 'Oh, my Gawd! Whatever am I going to do with you?'

'Go and make a cup of tea, Gladys,' said Sue. 'I'm going to take a short walk.'

'But it's getting dark,' cried Gladys.

Sue did not answer. She got up, put a dark-blue chiffon scarf around her head and pulled on her raincoat. Then she gave Gladys a kiss on the top of her grizzled head. 'I'll expect a nice cup of hot tea when I get back. You stay and make it, there's a good girl.' In a slow, majestic way she took a quick look round the room where she had spent her happiest days with Billy then calmly went out into the cool spring air.

It was dusk. The birds twittered as they settled in their nests and a sweet scent of blossom from the May trees was in the air. Sue was oblivious to it all. With a vacant expression on her face, she glanced around her garden and then slowly went off towards the cliff top. There she stood, a slim dark shadow, watching the tide cover the rocks below. 'Billy,' she whispered, 'are you there?'

A gannet gave a shrill cry and the waves battered the cliff.

'I'm coming to you, my Billy, I can't live without you, darling.'

A dark mist began to rise and Sue wavered on the edge of the cliff. 'Billy! Billy, darling,' she pleaded, 'give me the courage to jump.' Then, bending her body forward, she took a final step towards the edge. But as she did so, two strong arms grabbed her from behind. 'Sue! Sue! You mustn't! I thought you were my friend? How could you think of deserting me?' Some kind of telepathic sense had told Gladys to follow Sue outside, and now the two women stood there, poised on the edge of the cliff, mistress and servant clinging to each other like frightened children.

Sue stared down at the funny wizened face as Gladys' words rang in her ears.

'Sue, Sue, it's me, Gladys.' Gladys' stubby fingers gripped her tight. 'I know you've lost your Billy,' she said earnestly. 'And I'm sorry, because I hate to see you so unhappy. But you haven't lost everything, Sue. You've still got me, you've still got me to look after you and love you. You can't end it all just like that and leave me. You know I love you, Sue, and,' she added as tears appeared in her eyes, 'I thought you loved me, too.'

For the past weeks Sue had been shut off from the rest of the world, thinking only of Billy who was no longer with her. But gradually now, seeing the tears pouring down Gladys' imploring face, the words began to penetrate the barrier that had detached her for so long, and a strange sensation seemed to travel from Gladys' strong hold across to her own body.

Slowly Sue began to hear again the crashing of the waves against the rocks below and see the muted colours of the sea grasses around them. She smelled the salt in the air and heard the rustle of the wind in her hair. And there before her was Gladys, her friend, who, with utter devotion and love had brought her back in touch with the world. With a little cry of relief, she hugged her tight. 'You're right, Gladys,' she murmured, 'I've been nothing but selfish. You are my friend and I could never leave you. I've promised you that before, and I'm sorry for all this . . . Billy's gone and I have to accept that.'

Gladys was leading her away from the cliff towards the hotel. 'I'll stop complaining about being here, Sue,' she said. 'I promise I'll stop pining for London. I understand that you would want to stay down here where you were so happy with your Billy.'

There was silence for a few minutes while Sue was deep in thought. Finally she spoke. 'No, Gladys,' she said. 'We're going back to London. Being down here will only remind me constantly of Billy. We have to live in the present, not the past. You have never been happy here and we had some good times in the city. No, I'm going to sell up and buy a comfortable flat in London.' She touched the scar on her face. 'I don't know if I'll ever work again, looking like this, but I could have plastic surgery, as the doctor said. I don't have to decide now. We'll just take it one step at a time.'

And so the two women walked back to the hotel with their arms linked – a tall, willowy figure next to a short, squat shape. Both had resigned and calm looks on their faces as they took their slow, deliberate steps away from the wild, murderous sea towards a fresh start and a new life together. And both knew that despite all their tragedies and losses in the past, so long as they had each other, the future ahead was bright for them . . .

184

Down our Street

This story is dedicated to the slum street where I was brought up. It was called Witham Street, part of a poor area between East and North London, a small street that is no longer there.

I can still see in my mind's eye the shop on the corner run by the rosy-cheeked Mrs Appleby; the coal shed around the corner from where I humped a shopping bag full of coals every other day after school. I can taste the ha'p'orth of cracklings from Coren fish and chip shop in Hyde Road, the pie and mash, pease pudding and faggots – we never went short of food if we had a penny to spend, though that was not very often.

This book is for the little gang of mischievous boys that roamed our street – Dinny, Georgie, Nobby and Tony. One got the George medal for bravery in the Second World War but lost it to Long & Dowty's (the pawn broker) because he was Hearts of Oak. Some were lost in the war but others are still strong fine men who made good lives for themselves.

It's for the girls with whom I played endless games of hopscotch and skipping – Ninny, Eadie, Maudie and the Davis sisters.

We fought and made up, played out till dark in the street, which was the only place left to play as there was no room in our overcrowded houses. We were all poor, no one had many possessions yet our little community survived, until that big bomb razed it to the ground leaving us just with sad and fond memories. So to Witham Street I dedicate this story and I know all of you who write in and tell me of your memories will welcome it.

Lena Kennedy

Chapter One

Hopping

The Flanagans lived in a typical small back street of London's East End and theirs was the biggest family in the street.

'Twelve times Annie Flanagan's been in child bed,' old Gran, the midwife, remarked the last time. 'Annie's no bother. They just pops out on their own by now, they does.'

Indeed, childbearing was no trouble to Annie. After each child was born she would be up the next day and off to her job around the corner in the coal yard after handing the new baby to one of her daughters. Nowadays it was Sheila, who was thirteen and had not yet left school. She would often be seen parading up and down the street with a large cumbersome old pram in which two children sat at one end and the new baby was tucked in at the other. Around Sheila's skirt, several little ones hung on as she walked along the pavement, this tall, thin, ungainly girl who took on her responsibilities without a grumble. It was quite a burden for a girl of her age but she had had to take care of her little brothers and sisters since her elder sister Emily had started work in a blouse factory.

Sheila accepted her role with good will and cheerfulness. And while her daughter took charge of the brood, Annie Flanagan would be hard at work. With her mop of black curly hair swept up in a bun and her face so blackened by coal dust that only her bright blue eyes were visible, Annie would shovel lumps of coal onto a large set of scales to weigh them for her customers. These customers of hers were mostly young chldren. Coal was very necessary but extremely expensive so it was only bought at the yard in small amounts. Annie would dole it out into shopping bags – seven pounds or fourteen pounds at a time – and then it would take all the strength of two skinny little kids to lug it home.

Annie Flanagan was always bright and cheerful as she set about her work, for this was her livelihood and she enjoyed it. Her boss was a man called Jack Davies. He owned the business and was usually out all day with his horse and cart delivering coal to those better-off customers who could afford a whole sackful. He would roam around the streets yelling, 'Coal! Coal!' in a loud voice which echoed around the neighbourhoods. Sitting with him in the cart would be one of the Flanagan boys ready to help with a delivery or hold the horse's head to stop it bolting.

If one Flanagan boy left the job on Jack Davies' cart for a better job elsewhere there was always another Flanagan boy ready to take over. It was much the same with the wood chopping after school. One small Flanagan lad would sit on the cold stone floor of the back yard chopping wood up into thin sticks. After tying the sticks into bundles, he would take them to the local shop to sell for firewood.

When it came to part-time jobs – big or small – the Flanagans had a monopoly. No one else got a look in. And inevitably that caused some resentment in the street and harsh words were often muttered. 'Money-grabbing buggers, those Flanagans,' someone would say, and others would nod their heads in agreement.

But the Flanagans didn't care. Like most big families they clung together and looked after each other. Their small two-roomed house was the same size as all the others in the street and it was a wonder how they all managed to sleep in there, let alone eat. But that was always a secret, for outsiders were not encouraged into Annie's house. Every little Flanagan was up early in the morning and off to some kind of work before school or after school. Each one had his or her part to play; and every year Annie produced another little worker to add to this family workforce of hers.

Her husband, Dan Flanagan, worked at the docks. His was not a regular job but he had good luck as a casual worker and seldom missed a day. Every day the casual labourers went down to the dock and waited in a gang to sign on as the ships came in for unloading. Dan was a big man with a red face and a thick bull neck, and he always managed to push his way past the other fellows when it came to getting a day's work. Then in the evenings he would arrive home to be greeted by his mob of kids. The sides of his coat would bulge out from the loot he had managed to scrounge that day and secrete away in hidden pockets. If anyone had suggested to Dan that he was not honest they would have got a bunch of fives. What he had in his pockets was considered by him to be genuine perks of the job. Bottles of spirits were swapped with the butcher for legs of lamb; the grocer's bill at Appleby's was paid for with a couple of large tins of bully beef and there was always at least one little Flanagan urchin knocking at the neighbours' doors trying to flog some article of clothing or other.

Such was the Flanagans' way of survival. Theirs was a big untidy nest but it was a cosy one too, and kept warm and dry by the business spirit of all the members of the family.

When Annie began to carry her thirteenth child, nobody was surprised. Nor were they amazed that Annie shovelled up and weighed out the coal almost to the last day of her pregnancy, singing in her strong Irish voice or returning the jibes in her humorous way. 'Ah well, 'tis the grace of God,' she'd say. 'I'll hope for another girl this time. Got eight boys, so I might be lucky.'

Once a year when the coal yard was slack, Annie took her whole family for a holiday to the hop fields for three weeks.

'Gives the kids a bit of a holiday,' she always remarked, and some might have whispered that it helped her to save a few pounds as well.

So every August the Flanagan family made a general exodus from our street. They all went, except those who had to work – Dan and the two older boys, Joe and young Dan and, this year, Emily. But Sheila, Nancy, Letty and the other six little brothers all went off early one morning with Annie, wide with her pregnancy. Letty pushed the big pram full of toddlers while Sheila pushed another pram full of luggage and household equipment. The street folk would get up early on these occasions to peer out between the curtains to watch the Flanagans go. Each little child carried a packed bag and they all laughed and chatted and waved goodbye as if they were going on a world cruise. The smiles on their faces showed that they could not have been happier. On they marched, through the pale morning mist, all the way to London Bridge Station to board the train, the 'hopper special' bound for Kent, where the Flanagans had a regular pitch down at the hop fields.

It was a long train journey to Kent, taking five hours from London Bridge, but invariably the Flanagan family would arrive at the little Kentish station in good spirits ready to pile into the farmer's cart which was waiting ready to transport them all off to the hop fields.

Like the rest of the hop pickers they were given an old tin hut to live in for their stay. While the small kids shrieked with wonder and excitement as they ran through the farm's green meadows and pointed and yelled at the cows and sheep, Annie and her older girls would set about making their hut as comfortable as possible. There was an old wood stove in one corner but otherwise no furniture at all. In no time the mattress covers were pulled out of the suitcase and stuffed with sweet-smelling hay collected from the farmer. The old stove was packed with wood and lit so that soon it was hot enough for the kettle to be put on to boil. For their essential privacy, old lace curtains were hung up at the window, and the larder was well stocked with their provisions – tea, sugar and plenty of tinned milk.

After a supper of mackerel brought with them from London, the Flanagans would go to say hello to their neighbours in the other huts around. Every August it was the same. Many people came every year, so there were plenty of old friends to see and memories to recall. Someone lit a camp fire and the adults sat around it sharing bottles of beer while the children played outside until bedtime.

The next morning it was an early start for everyone to get a good pitch to work from sun up to sun down, stripping down the hops from their vines and dropping them into the hop bins. Everyone joined in. Whole families worked together each getting paid for the quota of hops they picked. Whatever the weather in wind, rain, heat or cold they all worked with a will and a lively spirit. Cockney songs passed along the lines of pickers; rude jokes were shared during the midday meal which was eaten hurriedly beside the hop bins. Lavatory facilities were provided at the edge of the field but they were rarely used. Most people went behind the heaps of empty vines so as not to lose precious time from the pulling and the picking of the hops.

The very small children all played together. These little mobs of London kids would go off scrumping apples and picking berries wherever they liked, leaving gates open and tramping over crops and becoming a general nuisance to the farmers. But the kids didn't care; this was their annual holiday from which they returned suntanned, healthy and happy, though occasionally a little lousy, since the washing facilities were not particularly good.

Typically, Annie who had been hopping for the past ten years, had it all well organized. A big tin bath was hidden under the hut. Every Friday night it was pulled out, placed beside the camp fire, and filled with water. In it, protesting loudly, the small kids were washed and scrubbed until their skin shone, and then their hair was denitted with a small-tooth comb. Annie's children were always immaculately clean by the end of it.

On Sundays no one worked. This was the time to wander in the woods and stop and paddle in the cool streams. It was the time to take in the strange countryside that was so different from their usual world, to look at the birds and the deer, the fish in the stream and to listen to the wind as it raced through the trees, rustling the leaves and causing great trunks to sway. Everyone always liked it in Kent but no one was ever sorry to return to the grime of the city they loved. For they felt more at home in London than in the Kent countryside.

Annie Flanagan and her brood were well known to be the hardest workers on the farm and they had always made plenty of money by the time the three weeks were up. When it was time to return to the smoke, Annie was always happy to be going back with her fine healthy brood and the pram packed with huge hopping apples and the toddlers perched on top.

Fond farewells were exchanged amongst the hop pickers. 'See you next year,' they all called to each other. Some seemed a little sad but at least they knew they could look forward to seeing their new and old friends the next summer.

This year Annie was very heavy and her footsteps slow as they walked to the country station. The farmer's cart that had collected them did not take them back to the station.

'Reckon yer'll make it, Annie?' someone asked with great concern.

'Yus,' Annie replied confidently, 'I'll get 'ome in time.'

But back at London Bridge Station she said wearily, 'Come on, girls, let's get the bus. The boys can walk it and push the prams 'ome.'

So with her three daughters, Sheila, Nancy and Letty, Annie boarded the bus and made tracks for their East End home. She sat on the seat moving restlessly, and then she gave a big yell and clutched her belly.

'Stop the bus!' cried someone. 'This woman's having a baby!'

All the other astonished passengers got off to catch another bus and the kids were turfed off while a kind woman who knew what she was doing went to Annie's aid.

The ambulance arrived much too late. By the time it came, Annie was sitting up nursing her baby, but the ambulance men still insisted on taking them both to Bart's Hospital.

Sheila, Nancy and Letty trekked home together. 'Muvver had our baby on the bleedin' bus,' cried Sheila to a neighbour in the street.

'Oh, my Gawd!' the neighbour cried. 'What she have?'

'A girl,' said Letty. 'Goin' to call her Amy, after Amy Johnson.'

'Well, I never,' said the neighbour, and Annie Flanagan giving birth on a bus was the talk of the district for days. The *Star* and the *Standard* newsboys ran around yelling: 'Late night final. Baby born on London bus.' And the Flanagans even made it into the Sunday papers with a picture of the whole family standing outside their small house with Annie seated on a chair with the new baby on her lap. And the baby, Amy, was from then on known as 'our Amy, the one who got herself in the newspapers.'

Later, Annie said to Gran, the old midwife, 'Sorry, gel, I never made it for yer. I was so showed up with all them people looking on. I swear I'll have no more kids. I don't care where old Dan sticks it but it won't be up me.'

And Annie kept her word, for this little girl was the last of her brood. The baby of the family she remained and our Amy was generally spoilt by everyone. Not only had her arrival into the world brought a little notoriety to our street, but she was also a beautiful, pleasant baby with lots of golden curls, so who could not dote on her?

Annie went back to her job in the coal yard and did not fall pregnant again. As her large family grew up extra money was brought into the household. They now had lino in the passage and all the way up the stairs, and a pair of pretty new curtains in the front room. Emily, now courting, would sit in that front room on Sundays, kissing and cuddling with a nice young man, while her little brothers and the other street urchins would peer in through the window giggling and nudging each other as they spied on the young lovers.

And so life went on down our street much as it always had, even when times were hard for most people. The huge Flanagan

192

family weathered the storm of the Depression and survived quite well in comparison to other poor families in the street. Perhaps it was their flair for enterprise and their unity that protected them.

In two years Annie was three times made a grandmother. First, Emily, who was now married and lived just round the corner, gave birth, and her baby was first to inherit Amy's pram. Then Annie's second son, young Dan, who now lived on the south side of London, became a father when his wife had produced one child and then another in quick succession. Nothing disturbed or bothered Annie. The kids left home, married and produced children; it was all in the way of life. No one got a posh wedding and very little time was taken off work for any sort of celebration. In 1938 her eldest son, Joe, joined up for the army.

Annie was quite stout now that she had finished childbearing and would puff out her cheeks as she lifted the huge coal shovel to fill the scales. But on Saturday nights, she scrubbed the coal dust from between the lines on her face, put on a white blouse and went to meet her husband Dan in the pub on the corner. Sometimes they would come home shouting and quarrelling and the whole street would listen. And sometimes they just sang uproariously and in harmony all the cheery Cockney songs, adding to the general belief that the Flanagans were one great big happy family. Perhaps some were aware that war was in the air but none had a clue that it would change the pattern of life down our street and everywhere else, for that matter.

When Joe came home on leave from the army one day, Annie was pleased that he looked very smart and had two stripes. But Joe was not concerned with his appearance.

'Mother,' he said, 'you should think seriously of moving this lot out of London, because when the war comes it will be London that will get it.'

'What bleedin' war?' asked Annie in surprise. 'I never 'eard o' no war.'

Dan said, ' 'Ush yer mouff, boy. Don't come 'ome 'ere scarin' yer muvver and the kids.'

And Joe could see that there was little point in saying more.

Amy was now five and skipped and jumped along beside the pram and played ball in the road with the other kids. There was no problem with parked cars because it was a dead-end street, and so mobs of children played out in the road in perfect safety.

At the other end was the Regent's Canal where the boys swam during the school holidays or fished for tiddlers.

One night big Dan came down the road looking a trifle weary. Half way down the street, he suddenly fell face downwards. All the kids milled around him not knowing what to do, until Charlie, the knock-up man, rushed out of his house and picked Dan up by the arms. Then he supported Dan's head which had lolled forward. Dan's face was bluish.

Little Amy took one look at her dad and then ran crying for Annie.

No one could revive Dan. He was taken to the local hospital in an ambulance but the bad news came back that Dan's heart had just given out. He was forty-five years old.

There followed the sad days of mourning and then the funeral. All the little girls wore homemade black-and-white checked dresses, and the boys wore black ties and had black squares sewn on their jackets. The neighbours were very kind; it was a shame to see this big Flanagan family so subdued. Yet the very next day after the funeral Annie went to the coal yard, and Siddy joined Jack Davies on the coal cart, Billy ran the paper stand, and Wally chopped the wood. So life went on. Annie's brood learned to survive the hard way. Only Amy was fussed and spoilt more than ever before. With her lovely blonde hair and her fat little legs, she would skip, jump and run, gathering compliments wherever she went. She was a charming, lively child, and well-loved by all.

That August the neighbours asked, 'Will you still go 'oppin', Annie?'

'Course I will,' replied Annie who yearned for the smell of the wood smoke and the happy company of the other hop-pickers. And indeed they went down to Kent, but that year they had travelled in style. Billy had learned to drive and had bought an old van which he used to do part-time removal jobs. So this year at the beginning of August they all piled in the van and off they went to the Kent hopfields. Thus Annie, her children and her grand-children headed down to the old familiar hopping hut amid the glories of rural Kent, to the camp fire, the booze, the happy campers and hard work. Annie still wore a black dress but that was the only sign of her widowhood. The lines on her face had deepened but still the bright blue eyes looked out shrewdly onto the world, as amid her brood she began to pick the heavy, sweet-smelling hops at a terrific rate never ceasing to work until the sun went down.

Amy was not one for working hard and she spent most of the day playing with a tiny mongrel puppy that Wally had obtained for her. The dog was black and white and known as Spot because of the black patch over one eye.

No one in the hop field cared about what was going on away from it – that the world was in turmoil, and that Chamberlain was visiting Hitler. No one was bothered. There was always peace and beauty down there in Kent. The huge ripe apples dropped from the trees and the children played in the sweet meadowlands. Life could not have been pleasanter.

But one rather chilly evening just before dark, a light mist rose from the road. A large car came down those country lanes rather too speedily. It was driven by a lady, a member of the local gentry, who had drunk rather too many sherries at a neighbour's drinks party. She was in a hurry to get home before her husband started getting angry. He did not like to attend these social occasions she loved so much and he tolerated his wife's attendance at them on the understanding that his own timetable was never put out. He liked to eat at 7.30 sharp every night.

This lady drove on, deep in thought and not paying attention enough to be able to brake as a little black-and-white dog rushed out from the hedgerow and ran across the road. She put her foot on the brake then but as the car went into a skid, she heard a great thud and saw a small figure, a child, being flung into the air.

The car had hit a tree and stopped. The woman was dazed and sat bewildered in her seat as blurred figures stood around the car, shouting and shaking their fists at her. Above their curses, she thought she could hear a child crying and gasping for help. Then as she was pulled from the car, she realized that the child was trapped between the wheels.

It was only when the fire brigade came that they were able to cut the young girl free. Then little Amy, unconscious, and badly injured, was placed with tender care in the ambulance and with her mother beside her, was taken to the Maidstone Hospital.

Annie sat in that hospital corridor for days, waiting and hoping for good news. On the fourth day she was told that Amy would live but that she had bad injuries and would need a lot of special care.

Annie sank to her knees. 'Oh, dear Lord,' she prayed, 'thank you.'

Amy was in that hospital for six months. Annie visited her twice a week every week. They had shorn off Amy's lovely curls. She had a deep scar on her forehead; her poor little legs had been broken and were in splints. But after the six months Annie brought her home to care for her. And as always, the other members of the family rallied round, taking it in turns to accompany Amy to the London Hospital for therapy as an out-patient.

It was nearly hopping time again before Amy recovered. She was no longer the little sunshine girl everyone had loved. She was often cross and querulous and got thoroughly spoilt.

The lady driver of the car had felt deeply ashamed of what had happened and offered Annie some compensation. But Annie had pride. 'No,' she had retorted. 'Just pay the horspital expenses, that's all I want from you.' She almost spat the words out. For she knew that her daughter would bear those scars for the rest of her life.

Chapter Two

The Blitz

It was the beginning of September 1939. The sun shone down the street and Annie stood in Mrs Appleby's little shop on the corner, her hands folded under the big sacking apron which she usually wore when she went hopping.

Mrs Appleby's moon face was more solemn that usual as she loaded Annie's purchases into the shopping bag for her. 'News ain't so good, is it, Annie?'

'No, it ain't,' replied Annie crossly. 'Bloody farmer don't want us dahn 'oppin' this year. He told Billy that the soldiers is goin' to do it.'

'It means one thing,' replied Mrs Appleby, 'that we definitely will have a war. It's not all propaganda, yer knows.'

'Well,' said Annie, ramming the rest of her packets in the bag, 'I won't be buyin' so much if I ain't goin' dahn 'oppin'. Won't need ter stock up on tea an' sugar.'

'Yer might as well, Annie,' replied Mrs Appleby. ' 'Cos it's all goin' ter be rationed, that's what they say.'

'I'll believe that when I sees it,' grumbled Annie. 'And I'll still save a few bob on yer bills.' With that, Annie stomped out of the dim, dusty shop into the bright sunshine. Standing on the corner of the street she yelled in a loud voice. 'Emily! Emily! Come over for a cuppa, and bring the baby. Want ter tell yer somefink.'

Annie's daughter Emily put her bedraggled head out of her top window and yelled back. 'All right, Muvver. I'll just finish makin' the bed an' I'll be o'er. Put the ke'le on.'

Five minutes later, they were sitting in Annie's untidy cramped kitchen drinking tea. On her lap Emily held a chubby child who gnawed at a huge crust of bread. Emily looked like a younger version of her mother, with the same black hair and wide hips.

'I dunno what the world's a comin' to,' grumbled Annie. 'No 'oppin' this year and that old cow next door 'ad a face like a kike 'cause I didn't stock up on me provisions like I usually does.' Annie's big face was distorted with rage as her wide mouth

197

worked angrily and her odd upper teeth gnawed at her bottom lip.

Emily said, 'We're goin' t'have a war, Muvver, there's more t'worry abaht than yer bleedin' 'oppin'.'

'And that ain't all,' declared Annie. 'Ol' Jack says he ain't openin' up the coal yard next season. Somefink abaht it ain't bein' worff it, and the guvment's takin' 'im over. I can't understand it.' Annie was quite indignant that her little world was being changed in ways and for reasons she couldn't understand. She was very upset.

'All I 'opes is that my Fred don't get called up,' muttered Emily. ' 'E might be, 'cos 'e's bin in the Terrys, yer know, an' they says that they will be the first ter go.'

'Ger away,' cried Annie, 'they got plenty o' soldiers. What abaht all the lads from this street? Only 'ad to ger in a bit o' trouble wiff the law and they was shoved in the army.'

Emily sighed and picked up her baby. 'I'll go 'ome an' listen to the wireless,' she said in a depressed voice.

'Lotter good that'll do yer,' said Annie, who never listened to it. 'It'd be better if yer cleaned up that bleedin' 'ouse o' yours.'

'Oh, shurrup,' cried Emily, her eyes full of tears. It never did any good to argue with her mother.

But Annie put on her cardigan. 'It's gettin' cold. I'll go and get the kids from school,' she muttered to herself. Then off she went down that familiar street towards the big council school to wait for the younger members of her family to come out at four o'clock. She realized how strange she was feeling; she hadn't felt like this since the day poor Dan had collapsed and died. She stared dismally at the spot outside Charlie Nelson's house where Dan had lain and drawn his last breath. She passed the big factory beside the canal where the workers seemed to be working hard at something or other. There were lots of sandbags all piled up; they seemed to be preparing a deep shelter. A shelter was what Annie would be needing before the end of the month, but she was a long way from realizing that. Annie never read newspapers, and seldom listened to the relay wireless that rang out from almost every house in the street except hers. Absorbed in her own world, the world of horror, bloodshed and partings had not become real to her, not yet.

The kids dashed out of school full of the news of the day. 'If there's war, we got to get evacuated,' said Nancy.

'Wot the bleedin' 'ell is that?' demanded Annie.

The little boys hopped up and down and ran around, yelling, 'I'm an airyplane, bang! bang!'

'Oh,' said Annie, ' 'ere yer are, go an' get some chips. I ain't cooking tonight. Might go an' 'ave a glass o' stout. I'm fed up wiff all this bloody talk o' war. C'mon, Amy, my luv, come and wait wiff me.'

Outside, Annie grasped hold of Amy's hand. But Amy, whose scarred forehead and stiff leg made her different from the other children, put out her tongue and snapped, 'No, I ain't! I'm going with Nancy to the chip shop.'

With a deep sigh, Annie let go of Amy's hand and went over to the pub. It was not open yet, and would not be until five. Annie felt quite fed up. It had really been a rotten day, but there were many, many more to come.

It happened on Sunday morning the next week. The relay wireless, which was very loud, was being operated from a shop across the main road. For a small sum each week it was then relayed into the houses. The announcer was saying in a deep voice that the prime minister was about to make a special announcement. Everyone stood around waiting. The boys on the corner gathered round the nearest house and stood listening, caps perched on the back of their heads, chokers around their necks. The kids stopped playing and old folk stood by their front doors. There was a silent air of expectancy throughout the whole street, as if the words of doom were to be spoken.

'We are now at war with Germany,' the prime minister's voice declared with such a feeling of finality.

The silence remained in the air for a second or two, and then there was a loud buzz as everyone began to mill about talking.

One old man muttered, 'Wot's all the fuss? Lived frew two wars, I 'ave, an' wiff enuff brahn ale I'll live frew anuvver.'

But one old lady looked very worried. 'Oh, dear, the poor kids,' she wailed.

It was then that the eerie sound of the siren started up, at exactly eleven o'clock. Everyone looked astounded and then rushed hither and thither for a few moments before moving more quickly towards the new shelter which Annie had seen earlier being built underneath the factory.

Annie gathered her brood together and took them back inside her house. 'Nuffink to be frightened of,' she said. 'It's only practice.'

Ten minutes later the all-clear sounded and Emily came rushing back from the shelter with her children. 'Oh, Muvver,' she gasped, 'why didn't yer take cover?'

'Wot for?' asked Annie calmly. 'Was only a false alarm.'

'Well, it might not 'ave bin,' cried Emily in exasperation. 'I tell yer wot, I ain't stayin' 'ere. I'll get 'vacuated, me and my kids.'

'Please yerself,' returned Annie, 'but I ain't leavin' me house, not for 'alf a dozen bleedin' 'itlers.'

The day the kids came out of school with their notices to be evacuated, Annie was still arguing. 'Wot the bloddy 'ell for? We ain't had no air raid,' she reasoned.

But Emily, who was always very sensible, said, 'Look, Muvver, it's compulsory for the kids, and you can go as well, if you like.'

'No, fanks,' said Annie, 'If I can't go 'oppin', I ain't goin' nowhere else.'

Nancy, however, was very practical. 'Get our fings together, Mum, 'cause we gotter be outside the school in the morning if we are going.'

'Won't it be nice,?' Letty said. 'It'll be real country where we are goin'.'

'Do what yer like,' declared Annie, plonking herself down in an easy chair. 'Yer always bloody well do, but I warns yer, yer will all be glad to get back 'ome again.'

The next morning, well scrubbed and quite tidy, the younger Flanagan children stood ready to go. Labels hung about their necks detailing their names and address; gas masks hung over their shoulders; and sandwich boxes swung by their sides.

Annie looked sulky and folded her arms obstinately. But Nancy kissed her and prepared to marshal the little group out of the front door.

Amy clung to Nancy's hand.

'Oh, not Amy!' cried Annie in despair.

'There's no reason why yer can't come, Muvver,' said Nancy, who was very adult in her way, 'other muvvers are goin'.'

Annie's lips clamped down hard. 'Write to me,' she said. 'I betcher will be 'ome next week,' she added.

200

As Nancy marched the little family out of the house Annie sat in her chair, too upset even to cry.

There was great excitement outside the school that morning. Everyone was saying goodbye. The mums were tearful and the kids were all playing up and enjoying the attention focused on them. It was such a momentous day when the kids were evacuated from our street.

And after they had gone, taken off in a bus to the railway station, an eerie silence hung in the air. The street was abandoned, deserted, the pavements were clean and tidy, and just a few straggly dogs and cats snuffled about searching mournfully for their little owners.

Annie sat in her tiny kitchen feeling quite dejected. Her arms were crossed and her brow knitted in a sullen expression. That is how she looked when Sheila came home from work. Then Billy popped in and Siddy arrived back from his last day working on the coal cart. He was black with dust. 'Muvver,' he said, 'where's the 'ot water? I wanna wash.'

Shelia had sat down very weary as usual. 'Wot we got for tea, Mum?' she asked.

'Get any Woodbines from Appleby's today, Mum?' asked Billy.

Annie shook her big mournful head, let out a sob, and then burst into tears with loud Irish howls. 'The kids 'ave bin 'vacuated and Emily and her kids have gorn wiff 'em too. What'm I goin' ter do?'

Her remaining children rushed to comfort her. Sidney kissed her and hugged her tight leaving a black mark on her blouse. Sheila clung round her neck and wept. 'Cheer up, Mum,' she said, 'I'll go an' get us some fags.'

Annie wiped her eyes and blew her nose. 'Oh, come on,' she said. 'Let's get the supper ready, life has ter go on.'

Soon the fire was burning bright and the kettle singing on the hob. Annie sliced up the big ham she had been keeping for the weekend, while Sheila fried chips. Soon the family, though somewhat reduced in size, was sitting around that great table once more.

Things began to happen very quickly over the next two weeks. First, Joe's wife wrote to say that Joe was in France, and then Emily's husband got called up. Billy volunteered for the Army

Transport and young Dan was going into the Air Force. Annie could hold on to her family no longer. Before Christmas that year, her brood had gradually dispersed, leaving poor Annie feeling very alone and somewhat confused about what was happening.

Sheila clung close. She changed her job to sewing army uniforms and always came home after work each evening to keep Annie company. But when Sheila's boyfriend, Stan, got called up, she was very upset.

Only young Sidney seemed indifferent to what was going on. The war had lost him his job on the coal cart. The horse and cart had been sold and his boss had gone off to the country. Siddy now hung about on the corner with a small group of youths. Only those unfit for the services or too lazy to work were left, for most of the lads in the street had gone. Siddy signed on the dole and hung around all day. He lay in bed in the morning and stayed out half the night.

'Gerrup, you lazy sod!' Annie would charge into the communal bedroom in the mornings and bellow at him. To lie in bed late was a crime.

'Wot's wrong wiff Sidney?' she asked Sheila. 'Why's 'e loafin' around when there's good money to be made on war work?'

Fair, gentle Sheila would try to explain. 'Muvver, he don't believe in it.'

'Don't believe in wot?' Annie would asked querulously.

'In war, Mum. He doesn't fink people should kill each other.'

'Don't fink wot? Why, if 'is Dad were 'ere he'd ger a good 'iding, he would.'

'But, Mum, Siddy is really sincere. He had no intention of fighting in this war. He says it's against his own working class. He has got principles.'

Annie could hardly believe her ears. 'Well! I never 'eard such nonsense! He don't 'ave ter go in the army if he's scared. Why can't 'e work in the factory, or somefink?'

'Oh, Mum, leave him alone,' Sheila begged, eager not to allow any rows to start.

Annie could not understand and was most disgruntled by her son's behaviour. But Siddy did not care. He wore a striped suit and a big wide hat. He spent a lot of time with his many pals and was seldom ever at home.

202

'Now where's that sod?' Annie would demand.

Gentle Sheila, sitting quietly knitting socks for the soldiers, would look at her anxiously. 'Mum, you have driven him out. All I hope is that he don't get into trouble.'

'What trouble?' exclaimed Annie. 'Ain't we all got enough trouble?'

And trouble had indeed begun, for each night it was a general exodus over to the shelter for Annie and Sheila since Hitler had begun his bombing of London. Even Annie realized that it was better to be in the safety of that deep shelter than under the flimsy kitchen table. She and Sheila went over every night and also often in the day when the daylight raids began. Sheila clung close and lovingly to her mum, and wrote long letters to her boyfriend until he went missing at Dunkirk. Then she became even more withdrawn and extremely nervous of the bombs. And so Annie Flanagan with that one last daughter, sat out the early days of the war in London, often wondering if she would ever see the rest of her family again.

Chapter Three

Evacuation

On that September morning in 1939, when the long crowded train pulled slowly out of Victoria Station and puffed its way down south, it had several hundred children aboard. The East End had been emptied of its child population, and these children were now being transported off to rural areas away from the expected forthcoming blitz.

The kids leaned out of the windows waving wildly and shouting goodbye to everyone in great excitement. To most, it was a great adventure. They sang raucous street songs such as, 'Let's all go dahn 'oppin',' with memories of happier days. A few tears were shed but were soon forgotten.

Nancy sat with Amy on her lap and pointed at the cows in the field through the train window.

Amy looked unhappy. 'Why didn't Mum come wiff us, Nancy?' Her voice sounded depressed. 'She will get killed when the bombs drop.'

'Oh, you mustn't say that, darlin',' cried Nancy, hugging her close.

Nancy was not yet fourteen and a very pretty girl. Her auburn hair hung down her back in rippling waves; she had long slim legs, a small waist and sleepy brown eyes. She was already becoming a lovely young woman, and here she was on her way to an unkown destination with a family of little brothers and sisters in her charge. But she was used to minding the children; like her elder sisters, she had done this from a very early age.

An anxious Letty sat facing Nancy, occasionally sniffing or rubbing her nose. She was dark and a little highly strung. Next to her was Lily, who was dark, sturdy and very self-possessed. 'I wonder how the boys are,' Lily said. Boys and girls had been segregated on the train and kept in their original school classes to make it easier when separating them.

'We must try and find them when the train stops,' said Nancy. 'You know how mischievous they are.'

The train rolled on through the English countryside towards the southwest coast, but at a junction just outside a station, the train was split in two. While the first half continued on, the back half went off up to the Midlands, taking Annie Flanagan's little boys with it. They were to disappear for quite a few years.

Nancy was very worried when she realized that the boys had gone but a kind schoolteacher calmed her down and explained that there had been too many children for the small village that they were heading for, so they had sent half in another direction.

It was nightfall when the train finally stopped at a small station on the borders of Devon and Dorset. That first night away from home, the travel-weary children huddled down together under grey army blankets on the floor of the village hall, munching their sandwiches and sipping mugs of steaming cocoa. Some began to cry for their mothers, while others were simply too excited to sleep. The billeting officer, a young woman with a nice smile, spent the whole night going around and consoling them.

In the very early morning when the cock crowed and the Devon shores were lit up by the rising sun, the children were roused and told to stand up straight on the stage.

'We don't leave each other,' whispered Nancy firmly. 'Hold hands tight, Letty and Lily, and I'll hold on to Amy's.' The four girls' faces were white and fearful.

Gradually the hall began to empty as nicely dressed folk came in to look at the children and take them away to their homes. One woman was directed towards the Flanagan girls. She smiled at them and then went out again.

'We are like a lot of bloody monkeys in a cage. I want to go 'ome,' snivelled Letty.

Nancy grimaced. 'Shurrup. I am tryin' to get someone who will 'ave all of us. I've told the obliging lady but she finks it's doubtful.'

Amy sat on the edge of the stage dangling her thin odd legs and each time anyone looked in her direction she put her tongue out at them or sometimes put her thumb to her nose and banged her heels against the stage to make a noise like a big drum.

'Stop it, Amy!' Nancy cried. 'Behave or no one will 'ave us.'

A very nice lady in a nurse's uniform came and stood beside her. 'What's your name?' Her voice was soft and musical. She had a fresh face full of freckles and a lovely smile.

'Nancy,' she replied quietly. 'And these are my sisters,' she added, pointing to Letty, Lily and Amy.

The woman cast an amused glance at the other girls. 'You can come to me if you want,' she said, 'but I can't have the other children, I'm afraid. I have to go out to work.'

'Oh, I'll look after them,' cried Nancy. 'No trouble, I always have done.'

'Well, bring that sister,' she said, indicating Letty, 'but I'm afraid we'll have to find a place nearby for the smaller ones.'

Nancy was at a loss. But because she did not know what else to do, she agreed. 'Be a good girl,' she whispered to Amy. 'I'll see you every day.'

But Amy wasn't having any of it . She started to scream and cry out. 'I want my sister!' she shouted, and began to jump up and down noisily.

As Letty and Nancy disappeared, the billeting officer tried to cope with Amy. 'Now come, dear, you have got your other sister, and you're to go with this nice lady who doesn't live far away.' She pointed to a jolly fat woman who stood by the door waiting for Amy and Lily.

After many tears and much to do, the girls all settled into their various billets. Amy was very crestfallen at having been separated from Nancy and she clung frantically to Lily who was a little bewildered herself. But the jolly fat woman took them home along with some other kids to her cottage, gave them a nice meal of stew and potatoes, and did her best to please Amy.

Nancy and Letty were taken off in a smart pony cart driven by the kind lady who had chosen them. 'I am Mrs Trelawny,' she said, 'but I would like you to call me Miriam.'

The girls were amazed at everything they saw as they drove up a long drive hedged by huge bushes with purple flowers and came within sight of a big house with tall chimneys. A large glistening pond broke up the soft, rolling carpet of lawn.

'This is my home,' announced Miriam with some pride. 'Do you like it?'

Nancy and Letty just stared, open-mouthed and speechless as a motherly, white-haired lady took their coats.

'This is my mother-in-law. My husband is away in the army,' Miriam introduced them. 'I am sure we will all get on so well together. While the men have gone away it will be nice to have you help me take care of this big house. I am sure you will love it here.'

Nancy looked all about her, taking in the lovely fireplace, the shining brass and the gorgeous flower arrangements. Always a lover of beauty, she gasped. 'It's lovely, just like in the films we seen.'

Miriam put an arm about her shoulder. 'You know, you are a lovely young girl,' she said gently. Then seeing Letty standing there looking so forlorn, she put out a hand to her too. 'You darlings will be safe here with me, away from all those nasty bombs.'

That night when the sisters snuggled down into separate soft downy beds, it felt like sheer heaven. They had never had a bed to themselves before, or such a lovely hot bath with all that perfumed water. 'Oh, ain't it grand to be rich?' said Letty.

Nancy agreed. But then her expression became grave. 'I am worried about Amy. God knows what Mother will say about me leaving her.'

'She'll be all right,' replied Letty sleepily. And Nancy nodded as she too drifted off to sleep. They were all safe and well. Everything would be all right.

But all was not well with Amy. In that small cottage in the village Amy was being very naughty and badly behaved. She grizzled, would not eat her food and wet the bed in the night.

Poor Lily got up and tried to rinse the sheet under the tap and dry it before the morning but it blew away in the night and was found in the morning hanging on an apple tree.

'Oh, what naughty children,' cried the fat lady. 'Does your sister always wet the bed?' she asked Lily.

'Only when she's upset,' said Lily.

'All right,' said the lady in a firm voice, 'then she must sleep on this camp bed in between the rest of you. I'll not have my mattress ruined.' She did not look so jolly now.

But Amy would not stay in the camp bed. She screamed and cried, climbing into bed on top of the other kids and punching and kicking them. Throughout the second night pandemonium reigned.

The fat lady smacked Amy's bottom and then took her right back to the billeting officer in the morning. By midday, Amy had been sent on to stay with someone else in another village six miles away.

When Nancy and Letty found Lily wandering around the village weeping, they were horrified. Staging a protest, they sat on the steps of the village hall and refused to move until someone agreed to tell them where their little sister was.

They rang Miriam Trelawny up at the military hospital where she worked, and she came to them at once. When she arrived, she was hot and breathless, having driven the pony cart furiously all the way. After much argument and debating inside the hall, she eventually came out with a triumphant smile on her face. 'Come on, children, let's collect your sister,' she said. 'And Lily, go and get your belongings. You can come too. My first decision was a mistake. I can see that now there will be no peace down here until you Flanagans are all together. And we can remedy this present situation easily enough,' she exclaimed.

Nancy flung her arms around Miriam's neck. 'Oh, Miriam,' she cried, 'you are wonderful! I'll be grateful to you forever.'

Miriam smiled. She was already fond of her young charges. 'I was an only child. It must be nice to have a lot of sisters.'

They rode out to the next door village and collected Amy from a thin anxious woman who had tied Amy's hands up in her pinafore because she had picked her nose at the table, and was making quite an issue of it. The Flanagan sisters hugged each other tight, delighted to be reunited again.

That night they sat around the big log fire in the library; Miriam listened while they talked of their mum and older brothers and sisters and the little brothers who had gone astray, and above all, the street where they had lived.

Miriam took Amy on her lap and pushed back the straggly locks from her brow. 'Now that is a bad scar,' she said. 'Perhaps we can do something to hide it.' With gentle movements she began to brush Amy's hair into a fringe to cover up the red scar. Amy loved all this attention and snuggled up close. At last she had found a friend in this big wilderness so far away from home.

So the girls all settled down to a peaceful existence with Miriam Trelawny in the very big country house that had been in her husband's family for many generations. Soon it was only the five of them because Miriam's mother-in-law returned to her own home.

Nancy and Letty took care of the house so that Miriam could keep her wartime job at the hospital which she seemed to enjoy so much. It was a good arrangement. Letty took the younger girls to the village school, did the shopping and then returned to help Nancy, who loved to clean and polish the nice furniture, and helped get the meal prepared. It wasn't long before Miriam had begun to rely on Nancy, that slim chit of a girl who learned so quickly the ways of the rich folk and kept the house so nice and tidy.

Miriam would cook in the evening and Letty took care of Pedro the pony, Barney the cat, and Mick, the red setter. They would eat their supper together and then each evening they spent together playing games, listening to gramophone records and writing letters to home.

Life was really very pleasant and the months flew past. The war seemed far away. Even when the bombs began to fall on London, no hint of such horrors ever entered Miriam's home.

'Once I am off duty from the hospital I like to think only of nice things,' Miriam often said. Then she would play the piano to them – beautiful classical music that the girls did not understand but Miriam's soothing spirit gave off a happy aura as they lay around listening to the sounds produced by her fingers.

Amy soon became Miriam's pet, and every night she got special treatment. One of her legs was still thinner than the other one, a little wasted, having been in a plastercast for a long time after the accident. Miriam would take this leg up on to her lap as they sat around the fire and she would slowly and affectionately massage the weakened muscles. She cut Amy's hair and gradually trained it into shape so that it covered the nasty red scar.

Amy loved all the attention and began to thrive. She was still boisterous but not so naughty, sliding down the huge banisters, and chasing the cat everywhere, but within weeks there was a noticeable difference in her.

Nancy wrote to her mother: 'We are happy down here and Miriam is a very nice lady. You are welcome to come down and see us, if you like,' she added.

Sheila read this letter out to Annie as she sat enjoying a much-needed cup of tea after having come up from a long night of bombs. They had slept in the damp shelter beside the canal. Annie's face was very red and her hair dishevelled, but her hard eyes brightened with tears as Nancy's words were read out to her. But she held back her feelings. 'Oh, well,' she said casually,

209

'that's four less to worry over. They certainly seem to like it down there.'

Sheila sighed. 'Oh, I miss them all so much,' she said. 'The house is dead without them.'

'Better ger off to work, Shelia,' said Annie, refusing to wallow in sentiment. 'You might mis that bus. They don't run regular to the city now.'

Pale faced, Sheila put on her hat. 'Now mind you stay near the shelter, Mum,' she said, as she kissed her goodbye.

Annie gave her a grudging peck on the cheek. 'Stop worryin',' she said.

After Sheila had left, Annie stood at the small front door and stared out into the street. Some men were on the corner fiddling with a barrage balloon which had come down in the night and all the houses had a gloomy air about them. Old Gran and Grandfather had gone away. Mrs Appleby's shop was closed. There was Emily's house all shuttered and empty and those that still lived in the houses in the street nearly all went out to work. Most of the old neighbours had gone but those houses did not remain empty for long. Young men on leave got married and took them over and their wives got pregnant and now a new generation was growing up. All gone was the comfortable old street full of kids. The fish-and-chip shop and the cooked meat shop had been bombed, and Charlie was no longer knocker-up but instead was an air raid warden.

Annie stood gloomily in the doorway thinking on these things and not knowing how to pass the day away. She was forty-five years old and the family had always kept her going. Now the warmth and the comfort of them all was gone; only poor thin worried Sheila was left. Joe was in the army now as a sergeant, Billy was there too, and young Dan was in the Air Force. God knew where they were. And what about her little boys who had been sent to some God-forsaken farm in the Midlands? She hadn't heard a squeak from them for some time.

'It's just like hopping, Mum,' Wally had written, 'but we don't like it so much because we get cold at night. Please send some sweets because we are hungry.'

Annie had gone up to the town hall to show them that letter, but they had waved it aside. 'Children exaggerate,' she was told. 'They are all together at least. If you want them home, just give

210

the correct notice and we will bring them back to you.'

But Annie had shaken her head. 'No, let 'em be,' she said. 'I don't want 'em back.' As she left the town hall she sighed to herself. 'No use grumbling, I suppose. We're all alive, so that's wot matters. I'll go in an' 'ave a kip. Don't s'pose we'll get much rest down that shelter tonight.' And Annie went indoors and slept the day away.

Sheila came home in the evening, and the two of them had a meal together and then waited for the warning siren. Once it sounded it was off to the shelter for the night, on that cold stone floor on that old mattress, with Sheila tossing and turning fearfully all night while Annie's hip started to throb with that bloody arthritis again.

Such was the picture of our street in 1941. All around them had been laid waste but still the old street survived, even though some doors were missing and most of the houses were windowless.

'It's the old Cut that protects us,' one wise old man said. 'The Germans follows the water and head in towards the docks and the City.'

'Well, it's the only good thing it's done for us,' retorted Annie caustically, 'and it stinks to 'igh 'eaven.'

The next day the air raids started early before Sheila was even home from work in the city. Annie began to get quite worried. The Spitfires and Messerschmitts were having a dog fight over the town and the drone of the incoming bombers throbbed menacingly through the air.

Sheila had got stuck in town when she was unable to get on a bus. The conductor had pushed all the passengers off shouting: 'Take cover! We ain't going through this!'

The docks were ablaze. Acrid smoke filled the air and people ran, white-faced with panic, towards the tube to take shelter.

Sheila was worried about her mum, so she started to run in the direction of home, her thin legs going nineteen to the dozen. She gasped for breath as she ran, sometimes glancing up at the sky where the dog fights were going on. Suddenly she saw a huge flash and heard a loud explosion as a plane came crashing down over the roof tops into the Thames. Sheila stopped in her tracks and watched in horror as the pilot's body whirled out all alight through the air to land entangled on the telegraph wires just in front of her. He was a fair young man – not unlike her brother

211

Dan – and he screamed terrible screams as the flames consumed him.

Sheila fell to the pavement in panic and shock. A burly air raid warden came running to pick her up but by then she was hysterical and fought him off with extreme strength, screaming and shouting at the top of her voice. Eventually poor Sheila had to be tied up before anyone could get her into an ambulance.

All this while, Annie sat in the shelter listening to the screams of the bombs. Through them she knew she could hear the screams of her Sheila.

'Lie down, Annie,' a neighbour said.

'No,' said Annie, 'somefink's happened to Sheila, I knows it. Oh, the only little gel I got left,' she wailed, 'what shall I do?'

Hot tears poured down her cheeks. The neighbours were silent; it was not often that they saw Annie Flanagan cry.

In the morning a policeman came to see her. Annie stared at him like a zombie. What else could happen to her now?

But his news was not what she expected. 'Your daughter Sheila is safe. She just collapsed with hysteria yesterday. They are sending her home in the morning.'

'Oh, fank gawd,' said Annie, in great relief. But the shock had done its damage. From that day Annie's hair began to go grey and she no longer was the lively woman she had been before, leading the community singing down in the shelter carrying her bottle of stout. She became withdrawn and quiet and clung to Sheila who was in an even worse state. Sheila was not fit to go back to work because she was still suffering from that terrible shock. She just sat with her head down shivering and sobbing every night and no one could persuade her to pull herself together.

Danny got compassionate leave and Emily came back from evacuation with her two babies. She had hated being billeted with a middle-class family down in Sussex.

'Oh, blimey, Muvver,' she said, 'it was terrible dahn there. Yer life's not yer own, and those toffee-nosed cows just don't like yer.'

With Emily back in her house and Danny home on leave, Annie's life was brighter, but Sheila still did not improve. She would not stay a moment on her own and followed Annie everywhere like some nervous little puppy dog. The folk down the shelter shook their heads in sorrow. 'Poor Sheila Flanagan,' they would whisper. 'Not quite there, she ain't.'

But between them Emily and Annie took care of Sheila and Emily's babies.

Dan was not happy about them staying in London. 'Go back to the country and take the kids with you,' he said. 'It's not safe here.'

But Annie was as obstinate as ever and clung on to her little house which by now had been badly blasted. They spent the days in their shattered home and went into the shelter at night, Annie keeping Sheila close to her and her grandchildren around her.

Those Londoners who survived the blitz would always remember the bombing of 1942. How short those dark days were! No sooner had everyone finished work than it was off to the deep shelter for an unsettled night of sleep, and then out again in the morning traipsing through the burnt-out streets to work, past the acrid smell of burning flesh, and the tired faces of the firemen and the air raid wardens, who had fought a long night of bombing with no respite. But many still managed to laugh. 'It's a wonder that we are alive to tell the tale,' they would say. And usually, no matter how terrible the circumstances, someone always managed to raise a laugh to cheer the others. Every day long funeral processions would go by, and the rationing caused hours of waiting in queues for the few luxury goods that occasionally came their way, such as an orange or a banana.

A well-known figure Annie was, toddling off down the market in her faded blue cardigan wearing her carpet slippers which had pieces cut out at the sides to allow her huge bunions to have more freedom. As she passed the still-smoking buildings, Annie never gave those tragic heaps a glance. Her mind was riveted on the lastest shop in the market to have been bombed, for it would be having a damaged-goods sale. Then she would come home later with little toys and sweets for Emily's children and damaged dry goods for the larder. She was always in search of little extras. Sometimes she managed to get under-the-counter butter, or a bit of offal that might be going. Such things would be great treats to add to an otherwise dreary diet.

Emily was pregnant again – after her husband's latest leave. She rarely left the house now, in case she had to dash over with the kids to the air-raid shelter next door. She had become quite nervous.

Annie would sit on the long wooden seat in the dirty old shelter, peeling a much cherished orange for her grandchildren. In many ways she still looked as if she never had a care in the world, as if she had a natural resistence to life's knocks. And strangely, not once did she mention her younger children who had been evacuated to the country. She never answered their letters and so eventually they stopped writing to her.

It seemed as if Annie had entered a world of her own and was determined to survive. But even her resilience gave way after that terrible night when a stick of bombs fell right across the poorest parts of London wiping out the small streets and generations of families.

Earlier that month, after a bomb had hit the big shelter in Shoreditch, not far away, there had been plenty of talk down the market of it not being safe even in the shelters any more. But Annie just thought it was panic.

Emily's husband came home one night because he was stationed nearby. Emily decided to stay in the Anderson shelter in their garden with him and the children. 'At least we will all be together,' she said to Annie.

Annie shiffed 'It's up to you, but I'll take Sheila down the deep shelter. She can't stand the noise of the bombs, let alone the guns.'

That night was the roughest London had seen. At ten o'clock at night the air raid wardens began to watch the incendiary bombs raining down. 'It's going to be a rough night,' they muttered to each other.

Annie and Sheila were tucked up together near the door of the shelter, so they were just missed when a huge bomb came whistling down and hit the top end of the shelter. That section disintegrated, and disappeared, with a mass of bodies, legs and arms, into the canal. The lights had gone out and the screams of the injured and dying were terrible. A huge cloud of dust rose up and large bits of timber fell on them. Annie and Sheila lay still, too terrified to move. The people who did rush into the street got caught by the next bomb which hit the end of our street and swept away all those little houses.

After the bombers had left, Annie and Sheila were helped out of the piles of debris. When they emerged coughing and spluttering into the street, what they saw before them was a

214

wasteland. Sheila collapsed in a faint, while Annie stood, just bewildered, looking over the road to where Emily's house had been. Now there was only a pile of rubble.

The air raid wardens were everywhere, carefully picking their way through piles of rubble in their search for survivors. Annie stared, speechless with shock, hardly daring even to hope that her eldest daughter and family were still alive.

But by some miracle, they were. They were pulled from the mangled remains of their Anderson shelter bruised and dusty but otherwise unhurt. Annie ran towards them all and flung her arms around them, 'Thank God,' she murmured, 'Thank God.' Tears poured down her cheeks.

'It's a bloody miracle,' someone said.

Annie stood blubbering. 'Oh, Emily,' she sobbed, 'I can't stand no more. I'm ready to go to the country.'

Through the dawn came a mobile canteen giving out hot drinks. As the dust settled the extent of the damage became clear. It was appalling. Over a hundred people lost their lives that night in one little block of slum streets. Both Emily and Annie had lost their homes; nothing was left.

'Right!' said Emily's husband. 'You must go down to Dorset to join Nancy and the girls. They seem to be all right down there.' And Annie could not wait to be off.

Someone had put an old fur coat around Annie's shoulders and they went straight to Victoria Station in a Fire Service van. All along the way to the station they saw that the East End was not the only place to have been hit. The whole of London was laid waste. A bus had been overturned in the road and a sad silence hung over the great city.

Chapter Four

Village Life

It was a very different scene in the little village of Ashmullen, down on the Dorset moors within sight of the sea. In the spring the marshlands were full of flowers – gold masses of marsh marigolds, tall purple irises, and delicate blue and pink flowers mingling in the long grass bordering the dykes that ran down to the river.

On the higher ground the wild heather bordered the moorland and the tall pines swayed in the sea breeze. Before the war, Ashmullen had been a quiet, sleepy village but now there was a large army camp up on the moors, and huge tanks rattled constantly through the village. The village pub, the Tavern, was always full to bursting every evening with soldiers from every part of the world. For this was a training camp where the young men came to do a specialized course before going into battle. And the cottage hospital was now a military hospital and had doubled in size.

The village inhabitants were not at all pleased by this invasion of their tranquil existence but did at least appreciate the fact that they got a good living working for the army. And they had by now become quite used to the little evacuees from London. At first it had been difficult having them all milling around the place, but soon the shopkeepers had learned how to handle them, and the school teachers likewise. In two years, those children who remained had become quite accepted by the country folk. Certainly the girls up at the Cedars, Miriam Trelawny's house, had settled down very nicely.

Nancy had grown tall and willowy. At almost seventeen years of age, she was quite a young lady. She now ran Miriam's house to perfection and received a weekly wage from Miriam, while Letty was a maid at the family hospital in the camp, coming back home every evening. Lily and Amy were still at school. Lily was a real tomboy and could play football and cricket for the village team better than any boy. But the one who had changed the most in this time was Amy. From that small cheeky guttersnipe with a chip on her shoulder, Amy had emerged from the chrysalis to become a charming little girl. She was tall and bonny with ash blonde hair she kept in pigtails, and she had developed a very posh way of speaking (having imitated Miriam, her heroine, mother and auntie all in one). 'I live up at the Cedars with Auntie Miriam,' she would boast to the kids at the village school.

Miriam found what materials she could and, because Letty was very handy with the sewing machine, the girls all had excellent wardrobes. At Christmas when they had a village party, Letty had taken an old evening dress belonging to Miriam and picked it apart. It was made of beautiful pink satin and was cut in a flowing style with loads of material. Letty made a straight low-necked dress for Nancy and a wide skirt for herself. The bits that were left over made a little dress for Lily, and Miriam bought a nice one for Amy.

All dressed up they went to the village Christmas party and stayed late to attend the dancing which followed the party. Nancy sang in a crooning voice into the microphone. 'Mares eat oats and does eat oats,' and she got everyone jiving. She was a lively girl and very popular with the boys of the services. What fun that Christmas party was! They all talked about it right through to the spring.

Life went on at an even pace. No one talked about the blitz, even though some nights they could hear the bombs dropping in the distance as Southampton and other coastal towns were bombed.

Miriam would hug the girls tight. 'It's all right, darlings, you are quite safe here,' she would comfort them. And so, in the warmth and security of this lovely home, the Flanagan girls grew up into lovely young women.

Miriam Trelawny had a lover. He was a captain named Jack, and he had been injured at Dunkirk and spent some time in the hospital. Now he was quite well, and fit enough to spend weekends with Miriam. Jack was fun and Miriam was very happy with him.

The girls quickly realized what was going on and were surprised.

'What about your husband?' Letty asked cautiously.

Miriam suddenly looked sad. She shrugged. 'We'll cross that

bridge when we come to it,' she said, 'I truly love Jack and no doubt that will happen to you one day.'

'Not me,' said Letty firmly. 'When I get old enough I'm going in the WAAF'S.'

Nancy looked very dreamy. 'Oh, it must be nice to have a lover.'

And Amy began to giggle. 'What about Dick?' she asked with a mischievous look in her eye.

'Be quiet and mind your own business!' Nancy snapped, looking very cross all of a sudden. 'Go off to bed at once!'

Any mention of Dick always made Nancy very angry. Dick was the son of the local fruit farmer whose land adjoined Miriam's. Each day Dick would arrive at the kitchen door bringing the produce for the day. He was a big husky lad with dark auburn hair but was very slow of speech, shy and awkward. The boy had spent his entire life on that fruit farm and now that his father was an invalid, he was responsible for the entire tract of land and those famous apple orchards which provided the special apple for the Devon Cider.

From the very first day Dick had gazed cow-eyed at Nancy as she swept the kitchen floor, her slim hips swaying, the short cotton dress displaying the long slim legs and her bud-like breasts sticking out under the clinging bodice. Dick was devoted; he had never seen anyone so beautiful. In all his twenty years this kind and gentle lad had only ever loved his horses.

Nancy, however, was a little impatient with him and would snatch the basket of farm produce from him saying, 'Mind your muddy feet on my clean kitchen floor,' and would grumble and nag if he brought the wrong sort of vegetables.

Dick loved it and would sit there with a silly smile on his face, which just aggravated this pert Cockney miss all the more.

Dick was a sore subject with Nancy. He offered to take her riding and to the pictures. At this second offer, Nancy had bent a little. They went off one Saturday afternoon to the cinema but came back early. 'Oh, he's such an oaf,' Nancy complained. 'I can't stand him. He tried to put his arm around me in the pictures.'

Soon Dick had become quite a joke among the girls, but Miriam would say, 'Well, he's not such a bad boy and he's got a comfortable future. He's an only child and that's a big property.

I nursed his mother and I visit his father pretty often.'

But Nancy was not going to be persuaded otherwise.

'Sorry, Miriam, but he is so slow, I can't stand him.'

One morning after Captain Jack had left his weekend bag behind, his batman came to the house to collect it. Nancy took one look at him and fell head over heels in love. The batman was small dark and half French, and was called Gene.

Nancy gave him cakes and coffee and smiled right into his face. His dark eyes flashed in admiration. 'You sure are a pretty gel, Nancy,' he said. 'You coming to the camp dance on Saturday night?'

Nancy smiled her lovely smile. 'I'll have to bring my sister Letty,' she said.

'That's all right,' said Gene with a grin. 'I'll soon get her hitched up.'

And so began the romantic times. On Saturday night Nancy and Letty put on Miriam's high-heeled shoes, made up their faces and curled their hair and kept that date at the village hop.

While Nancy danced with her dark admirer, Letty was fobbed off on to a sergeant who ended up very drunk.

Looking very pretty in her pink satin dress, Nancy danced very close to Gene. Their bodies were close, hot and sweaty, and every time the lights were dimmed, their lips met.

On the way home, they lingered down the lane. Letty yelled back 'Come on, Nancy! Don't hang about.' She had got rid of the fat sergeant.

A trifle hot and dishevelled Nancy ran towards her. 'Oh shut up, Letty, don't be such a spoilsport! Gene is so charming.'

'That's not what I would call him,' said Letty. 'Better watch him, if I were you. Don't go out with him any more.'

Letty's words of warning were wasted, for every evening Nancy was out on the heath with Gene, lying in the purple heather lost to the world of lovers with her dark French passionate Gene.

Miriam was not aware of this affair. Not one of her sisters would have betrayed Nancy by telling on her.

The autumn laid a glorious carpet of red-brown leaves in the woodlands when Nancy was in Gene's arms for a last farewell. He was returning to the front with his officer. 'I will write, darling,' he promised. 'We will be married the next time I get some leave.'

'Where are you going?' Nancy asked, her eyes wet with tears.

'I cannot say,' said Gene, 'but I promise I will let you know. I love you, I will never forget you, whatever happens to me.'

Nancy returned to the Cedars and dashed up the stairs crying, her heart felt broken.

Miriam sat beside the fire drinking a glass of wine. Her face was white and sad, for Jack too had just said goodbye. Realizing the situation she went to comfort Nancy. 'Oh, don't get so distressed,' she said gently. 'There will be plenty more boys in your young life. But for me it is truly over. Jack has a wife in Canada.'

The autumn breezes gave way to the frosts of winter. Soft white snow covered the land. They all stayed around the big log fire in the evenings, the huge tree logs sent out a warm glow. 'What would I have done without Dick this winter?' murmured Miriam. 'He got us all those logs, you know.'

Nancy said nothing. She kept her head bent and continued sewing.

'And hay for Pedro,' chimed in Letty, who sat on the rug with her old friend the red setter, who rested his head on her lap.

Lily and Amy were doing their homework. It was a cosy scene as the winds howled over the moors and the snow froze hard. Not many people came this far out of the village in this kind of weather, so it was surprising when they heard the noise of a car engine.

'What's that?' said Miriam when she heard the noise outside. Amy dashed to the window. 'It's the station taxi, and it's coming down the drive,' she cried excitedly.

When the loud sound of the door knocker echoed through the house, Miriam looked a little scared.

'I'll go,' said Lily.

'No, wait for me,' said Miriam, but young Lily had already reached the door and opened it wide.

To everyone's amazement, standing there was a little crowd of wet and decidedly unhappy people. There was Annie all wrapped up in an old fur coat, Emily, heavily pregnant holding on to her two young children, and thin pale Sheila in her old woolly hat.

Nancy ran out into the hall crying. 'Oh, my God, it's our Mum, Sheila and Emily! What are they all doing here?'

Annie let out a big howl of welcome. 'Oh, Nancy, we've got nowhere t'go so we all came to find you.'

Nancy hugged that faded old lady, for Annie's hair was now quite white and her shape sadly deteriorated.

'Come in out of the cold,' cried Miriam, ushering them all into the hall. 'Take your wet things off and come near to the fire. Go and put the kettle on, Nancy.' She gave no sign of any annoyance, she was just concerned for those cold shivering people.

Emily rubbed the little girls' hands and warmed their toes to the fire, while Nancy got hot drinks for them all. Suddenly that cosy sitting room was full of people. 'Sorry to inconvenience you,' said Emily, 'but it got too bad in London and our houses got blitzed and the shelter received a direct hit. Lots of our neighbours were killed, so we packed to go away and this is the only place I could think of.'

'Well, you did right,' said Miriam, patting her hand and looking around her at this motley throng with a look of confused pity on her face.

There was Sheila who just dropped in a chair by the fire and simply stared into space and the little girls lay on the rug with Amy who gave them some of her cherished store of toffees. Annie sat in the middle of the room looking like some mournful cow while Emily sat back with her long untidy hair in a pony tail, no make-up, a tear-stained face, and her stomach very high.

'How long have you got, Emily?' Miriam asked.

'Two weeks,' said Emily. 'I fink I'll 'ave ter go t'the 'orspital.'

'Well, we'll sort it all out,' said Miriam reassuringly. 'In the meantime, you can all stay with me till we find somewhere for you to live. Come with me, Nancy, we'll try to get that spare room into shape just for tonight.'

Nancy went with her upstairs but stopped at the top landing. 'Miriam,' she said, 'if there was ever an angel it must be you. How could they do it? All of them descending on you like that? I feel quite ashamed of them.'

'No, you must not say that, Nancy,' Miriam said, 'For these are desperate times and they need desperate measures.'

Within a couple of hours Annie and her elder daughters were installed in the spare room, and Emily's little girls were in with Amy and Lily in their cosy bedroom. A good time was had by all.

Of course, it did not take long for this big family of the Flanagans to disrupt the tranquillity of the Cedars. Emily's girls played snowballs, built snowmen, ran in and out of Nancy's

221

clean kitchen, and made the floor filthy, and during the night poor Sheila had screaming nightmares waking up everybody.

Then Emily went into labour and they had to get an ambulance to take her to the hospital. Miriam was as calm and smooth as ever, her medical training seemed to carry her serenely through these adverse circumstances.

Annie would insist on sitting in the middle of the kitchen, a bowl in her lap as she slowly peeled the potatoes and dropped bits on the floor. If she had nothing to do then out would come her packet of Woodbines, and the dog ends would be thrown in the clean grate.

Nancy cleaned up after her with dustpan and brush and was getting more and more exasperated every day. Poor Sheila did nothing all day. She just crouched in the same spot on the wide window seat staring out at the snow-covered garden, while Letty was always busy with the pony or the dog and cat when she was off duty from the hospital.

Lily, who often used to help, now larked about all day with the small girls, playing hide-and-seek and rummaging in the big attics; they all had a good time except Nancy, who was very depressed.

When Dick arrived with the vegetables the first time after the family had arrived, he stared in amazement at Annie sitting puffing at her fags. 'You got a big houseful, Nancy,' he said slowly.

'Mind your own business!' she snapped. Then to prevent him making any further comments, she began to go down to the gate to intercept him.

Dick, however, was rather pleased with this arrangement and took it as a compliment. He would hang on to the gate looking at her and prolonging his visits.

But one day Nancy stood with her head against a tree and really wept. Dick put down his basket and put his arms around her, Nancy did not resist. His were warm and comforting arms, and she was feeling so very down-hearted. She had not had one word from her love, Gene, and it was breaking her heart. In addition to having the burden of her family, it was all too much to bear. She was weeping tears for her lost lover, and Dick was concerned. 'Don't 'ee cry, lass,' he said gently. 'I'll find them a cottage and that will make you happy.' Nancy did not pull away. She let Dick wipe her eyes and cuddle her close. She was so hungry to be loved and the sensual sexy Gene had awakened such emotions in her so that she did not know whether she was here or there.

Dick was as good as his word. 'There's a tied cottage down the road to the village,' he announced a few days later. 'The old folk who lived there have died but I'll get it tidied up for your family, Nancy, and maybe they can get work on the farm in the spring.'

When Annie was told about the cottage, she was not at all sure about it. She even went so far as to say that perhaps she ought to go back to London. But, Emily, exhausted from the demands of her newborn baby was quite adamant. 'For Christ sake, grab that cottage for us, Nancy,' she said. 'Why, it's a Godsend; you'd never get me back to the blitz,' she added. 'Got me kids to fink abaht.'

Miriam was delighted and thanked Dick for his help. Dick smiled in his slow way and said, 'I thought it would be better for Nancy, not having so many folks to take care of.'

Nancy smiled at him gratefully and allowed Dick to put his arm around her. And Miriam's eyes gleamed with amusement and pleasure at the sight of them both.

So it was that Annie, Sheila, Emily and Emily's three children moved into that small cottage. It was very old and small and lit by candlelight. But it had charm and was quite comfortable. Miriam had collected bits and pieces of furniture for them and even gave things of her own which she said she did not need. The girls all helped to make the place look nice and everyone was pleased.

Occasionally Annie grumbled about the place, complaining about how quiet it was and how far from the shops, but Emily was quite firm. This was their home and it would stay that way. They were not going back to London, she had had enough.

Even Sheila seemed to improve in the country quiet. She left off her woolly hat as the spring came and spent many hours walking along the woodland paths picking snowdrops and primroses to take home to put in a jar for the windowsill.

Slowly and quietly, Nancy's attachment to Dick grew. It became a common sight to see her walking out with him hand in hand through the woods and now she often went over for tea at the farm where Dick's Aunt Edie kept house and looked after Dick's father who was now crippled with arthritis.

Nancy came home one day looking quite flushed. When she

was alone with Miriam, she told her why. 'Dick wants to marry me,' she said. 'Very soon.'

Miriam smiled nad hugged her tight. 'Congratulations,' she said. 'I'm delighted for you both – but what's the big rush? Don't you want to enjoy your engagement for a while?'

Nancy shrugged and looked away, a sad look in her eyes.

'But why so sad, darling?' asked Miriam. 'You are in love with Dick, aren't you?'

Nancy pulled her to her and tears fell down her cheeks.

'Oh, no Miriam,' she wept, 'but he does love me. Gene never even bothered to write to me.'

Miriam stared keenly at her for a moment and then stroked her hair gently. 'It's all right, darling, I'll see you have a nice wedding. And I won't lose you, you'll be my neighbour when the war is over. And it must end some time.'

The wedding of the pretty young Londoner to the local farmer's son was the talk of Ashmullen for quite a while. Nancy made a lovely bride and Dick, the big husky farmer lad, was very proud of her.

Big brother Joe came all the way from London to give Nancy away and Annie was made to wear a hat, which she did under great protest. It was a big black straw hat which Letty had trimmed with a bunch of artificial cherries, Annie wore it lopsided, her face a beetroot red. She had never worn a hat before and it embarrassed her.

Nancy's four sisters were bridesmaids and Emily the matron of honour. Miriam bought their headdresses and Letty made all the dresses. It was a big community affair and even with rationing they did well with legs of pork and turkey delivered at the back door. Even the village baker managed to bake an enormous fruit cake which he iced for them in elaborate patterns. The excitement was great. It was Easter and sunny. The village church was full of spring flowers. It was such a lovely peaceful scene that no one would have believed that not many miles away the army was secretly preparing for that big invasion of France where much blood would flow and many lives would be lost.

Joe was now a strapping great sergeant and physical training instructor, having served his time at various battle fronts he was now in England with a commando regiment. The Flanagans were all very proud of him and showed him off to the rest of the

224

village. Joe, a happy-go-lucky character, had married a young Irish girl at the very beginning of the war. She had recently returned home with her children for the duration of the war, and it seemed that Joe was looking out for a good time.

When Joe first arrived, he told them the news of the three little brothers who had disappeared in 1939 during the evacuation. While he had been stationed in the Midlands he had tried to find out what had happened to them. When Annie never replied to their letters, the little boys had given up writing. No one had heard from them for years.

Joe had found out quite a bit about them. 'Those buggers played up merry hell in that village, I can tell you,' he informed his mother. 'When I got there they were in an approved school, something like Borstal. I protested right away but it seems they got no reply from you, Muvver, when they wrote.'

Annie shrugged. 'Ain't I got enuff to put up wiff wiffout them buggers playin' up?'

'Well, they are all right now. The twins are at the Duke of York Army school, but I couldn't get Wally in there, he's too young. But he's working on a good farm now and loves the life there.'

'Always was one for bloody animals,' grunted Annie.

'So you don't have to worry about the twins,' continued Joe. 'They'll go straight into the army when they are the right age. But I hope the war's all over by then.'

Although he did not show it, Joe was impatient with his mother. He could not understand her nonchalant attitude to everything, for he was a conscientious man, a hard grafter, and a leader who had made a good career of the army. Joe's only one failing was that he was a womanizer. At Nancy's wedding he got very drunk and made it obvious that he had his eye on Miriam who looked extremely chic that day.

Joe insisted on escorting Miriam, Amy and Lily back to the Cedars, and he did not return to the cottage that night. In fact, he was seen sneaking out of the back door of the house early the next morning.

'He slept in Miriam's bed,' Lily told Amy.

'Don't let on,' replied her sister, 'stay stumm. It pays.'

After Easter, with the long summer days stretching ahead them, Annie, Emily and Sheila got work on the farm picking fruit and helping in the packing sheds. Annie felt in her element. It was

225

just like the good old days down at the hopping, sitting out in the fresh air with Sheila and Emily eating a meal under the hedge and Emily's baby in a carrycot beside them. The weather was good and the extra money they earned helped them live a more comfortable life.

With her face covered with freckles, and her long hair tied up in a bright scarf, Emily looked the picture of health as they picked the sweet strawberries. 'I've 'ad a few ups and dahns in me married life,' she said, 'but this is the 'appiest time I can remember. Here in the fields, it's so peaceful. Yer gets the backache but wot's that ter wot we bin frew in London?'

Annie squatted on a stool deftly putting the ripe strawberries in the wicker baskets. 'Yus, Emily,' she agreed. 'And just look at Sheila, she works wiff a will. I've seen a big change in that girl, I 'ave, since we come dahn 'ere.'

'I can't fank Dick enuff for it, our Nancy's done well for 'erself when she 'ooked 'im,' said Emily.

'Oh, well, she's a lovely gel, an' now got a baby due for Christmas. All the time the family grows, an' some goes,' said Annie. 'Poor Danny,' she added, thinking about her second son who had been killed in the Air Force.

'Now don't start, Muvver,' said Emily. 'Let's all be cheerful while we can. Wot abaht a song, eh?' Emily did a little dance and in her Cockney tone sang, 'Wiff the partin' of the ways, you took all me 'appy days and left me lonely nights.'

Annie and the other field workers joined in.

Amy was now in the fourth form at school. She always studied hard, put on airs and graces to the village kids and spent very little time with her own family, preferring to pretend that she belonged to the more refined air of the Cedars than anywhere else.

Lily, however, was quite different and romped with her small nieces, Emily's children, taking them on long hikes in the woods and rambles over the common. Letty had turned sixteen and announced that she was going to join the forces just as she had always planned. She was now just waiting for her papers to come through.

'It seems that I am going to lose my little family,' Miriam said rather sadly.

'No, you are not, Auntie Miriam,' insisted Amy. 'I'll never leave you, ever.'

Miriam stroked her head where that faint line of the scar still showed.

'Yes you will, darling,' she said. 'It's a big old world out there but I will always love you.

As far as the Flanagans were concerned the war could go on forever. They took little notice of events or news from the Front, and just merged into life of the village. Whenever Joe got a week-end leave he would come down and take them all – including Miriam – to the village pub, and they would sing all the Cockney numbers. The bar would be quite taken over by the Londoners.

Nancy, now a respectable farmer's wife, kept her own counsel but she would come visiting bringing eggs and butter, precious commodities that were rationed. It was all great fun, but as usual life was not going to allow them too much happiness.

When Emily's husband was invalided out of the army, he came down to stay at the cottage. Fred was always a worker but he hated rural life. 'It's fairly quiet up London now, Emily,' he said. 'Why don't you come home?' he begged.

Emily was not impressed, 'I can't leave Mum,' she replied flatly.

So Fred went back to London on his own and went into lodgings. Emily was very fond of him and got depressed when he wrote to tell her he was going to the Midlands where he had been offered a job in a car firm. Now she gave in, 'Find us a house and I'll come to live there,' she promised him in a letter.

So by autumn Emily had gone, taking her children to live in the Midlands. She said goodbye to her happy days, and was never to return.

Letty was the next to say goodbye, all dressed up smart in her WAAF's uniform. Then Lily, who had been working at the hospital as a maid, got a chance to train as a proper nurse and went off to Plymouth to be a probationer nurse in the big hospital. That left only Sheila and Annie in the cottage, and Amy living with Miriam.

Amy loved it at the Cedars. Now she did Nancy's job of looking after the house. As far as she was concerned this was her own lovely home and Miriam her auntie, her much loved auntie.

Joe's outfit was moved on. Billy was still in London and wrote

227

to say he had been allocated a house and that his wife and baby were now back home with him. He said it was a big house with three floors in Gospel Street not far from their old street, and that if they wanted to come home they could live upstairs.

Annie began to pack right away. It was too lonely down in the country for her without Emily. 'You coming home wiff us, Amy?' she asked.

Amy looked aghast. 'No, I'm not – certainly not, I'm staying with Miriam.'

'Please yerself,' said Annie, 'she won't want yer 'anging on forever.'

Chapter Five

Back to the Old Surroundings

With Sheila in tow, Annie returned to her own grass roots. She did not get on with Emmy, Billy's wife, who wisely stayed clear of her. Annie and Sheila occupied the upstairs flat of Billy's house, one of the strong, well-built houses in that street which had survived most of the blitz. The War Damage Authorities had renovated these buildings during a respite in the bombing. The raids tended to be lighter now and mostly on the coastal towns, the Spitfires having deflated Hitler's bombers and 'given them wot for', as the Cockneys expressed it.

Annie wasn't the only one home. The Londoners came back in droves to new accommodation for themselves and their children. They were all a bit older, there were more weddings and more babies. And life went on for a while quite peacefully for the ex-evacuees.

Annie put on her old cardigan and her tatty carpet slippers and toddled off each day down to the market stopping to gossip to the stall holders who remained and the conversation always revolved around the blitz. Everybody knew Annie and most of them liked her as she stood around gathering up the threads of the life she had left behind.

'Nice ter see yer back, Annie,' they said.

'It's good to be 'ome,' replied Annie. 'So yer got frew it, all right. Wat abaht old Barnet?' She pointed to the bombed-out shop that had once been the shoe shop.

'No, mate, he copped it,' said the stall holder.

'Oh, well,' said Annie, 'it's a good job some of us is left. I lost my Danny, I did. First time 'e was in tha aeroplane. And I never wanted him to join the Air Force.'

'Never mind, Annie, you still got Billy and Joe and I see Siddy doing all right for 'eself.'

'Don't talk to me abaht that bleedin' Siddy,' said Annie. 'Never went to war and now 'e's a crook, so they tells me.'

'Oh no! not as bad as that, Annie, just a spiv – has a little fiddle, that's all.'

'Well, he can stay out of my 'ouse,' said Annie flouncing off in a very determined manner.

Always not far away from home was Sheila, who had gone back into her shell since they had come home. She found herself another woolly hat and drooped along behind Annie without a word to say for herself.

'Pull yer bleedin' self togeffer, gel,' Annie would say. 'You was all right when we was 'vacuated, wot's wrong wiff yer now?'

But Sheila's lips would twitch and her eyes would roll.

'Oh, my gawd, she's goin' ter 'ave a fit.' Annie would yell for Billy and he would lie Sheila down and put a spoon in her mouth. For Sheila's delayed shock had developed into epilepsy.

'Take Sheila to the hospital,' Billy would say, 'I am sure that someffink can be done for 'er.'

'Leave 'er be,' said Annie gruffly. 'She's all right wiff me.'

So lovely gentle Sheila, so fair and so sweet, was condemned in her early twenties to a life of misery.

Emily wrote very often to say that Fred had a good job and they had a nice house in the Midlands town, Joe had been posted out in the Far East.

One day Siddy came visiting. He had grown very big and broad shouldered and wore a pin-striped suit and a wide hat. He was carrying a big parcel of food, and when he grinned he revealed a gold tooth in his front teeth. Billy welcomed him in. But Annie refused to allow him up the stairs. 'I don't want that crooked sod up 'ere,' she yelled from the landing. Billy knew his mother too well to press the issue further, but Siddy had brought whisky and chocolate with which he treated Billy, so he was quite happy. 'How yer doin', Sid boy?' he asked.

'Okay,' Siddy said. 'Got a bar dahn Befnal Green Road. It's called a Beer Club, but you know how it works, still plenty of booze to be got under the counter.'

'Good luck t'yer mate,' said Billy. 'Glad some made it. You married?'

'No fanks,' said Siddy, 'but I got a nice little gel who runs the bar for me. You remember Sadie Goldman? Her old man is Yiddish, he used to 'ave a stall dahn the market.'

'Oh, yes,' said Billy, 'clicked all right there, mate. Not to worry abaht 'er,' he indicated upstairs. 'Knowing Muvver, she'll come round in the end.'

'But what happened to Sheila?' asked Siddy. 'She didn't know me. She just ran away when I spoke to 'er.'

'The blitz, mate, sent 'er crackers,' said Billy very noncommital. Sheila was not his problem; she was Annie's.

Placidly Annie settled down to her own old surroundings and to everyone she met she chatted about the good old days before the blitz. But within two months of their return, one of the worst periods of the war began. It came without warning when everyone was settled to sleeping at home, starting as a curious kind of drone from the sky, just one stray plane that looked too small to worry about. Then quite suddenly the drone of the engine ceased and the plane dived down to earth devastating all before it. This was Hitler's new weapon – the dreaded buzz bomb.

Billy had been on fire watch that night and could see these small flying bombs coming down just outside London. 'Looks like a dog fight out there, mate,' he told his companion as with huge flashes the buzz bombs exploded in the air, the rest went down on built-up areas of the town.

In the morning the results were devastating. Hundreds had been killed and wounded but luckily the big house in Gospel Street was still standing. Billy sandbagged the cellar and made it secure for everyone to take cover. 'When the engine stops, dive down into the cellar,' he instructed them.

This had a terrible effect on poor Sheila and Annie, whose arthritic hip made it very difficult to get down there in time. The buzz bombs came by day, hour after hour, but as with most things, the Londoners got used to them. They would listen to them coming down and say, 'Yer number's not on that one, chum,' and go on with the day's work.

After a few days, Annie had had enough of being cramped in that cellar, and she began to go out on her regular trots down the market. 'I can't go runnin' away no more,' she told them. 'If it's me lot, that's it. Can't keep on dodgin' 'em.'

Later on, the rockets came, a bigger version of the buzz bomb but without the noisy little motor. These bigger bombs came with no warning at all and did a lot more damage, but the fighter planes went up and intercepted this latest hazard as they came in across the coast. And the British and Allied Forces stood their ground against Hitler yet again.

The war had been on for four years and Annie's family was

now spread all over the war areas. Joe was out in the Far East, Letty was in Scotland on a gun site. Lily was in a Plymouth hospital and Emily with her little family was in the Midlands. Annie's twins were now in an Army Training School and Wally was a farmer's boy, though no one ever heard from him. Annie would sit and think of her brood of children, spread all over the place. For in her awkward way she was fond of them all except poor Siddy. There was just no way she would entertain Siddy, even though he left little packages of food on her doorstep, good food which she found very acceptable. But for his kindness, she would not acknowledge him.

One day Billy received the terrible news that a rocket had hit Emily's house in Coventry, and that the whole family had gone under – Fred, Emily and the three children. Billy stood in the passage sobbing. 'Who's going to tell Annie?' his wife, Emmy, asked gently.

'Oh God!' cried Billy, 'I can't do it, not yet, I can't.'

Emmy said, 'Well, don't say anything then, give yourself time to get used to it.'

Siddy was told and they all decided to stay stumm, for no one could face telling Annie. She thought so much of Emily her eldest girl and those three little granddaughters.

But of course Emmy told her mum, who in turn told someone down the market who told someone else and, as Annie came toddling down the market street one morning with a cheery smile on her face, a woman came to her side saying, 'Oh, Annie, I'm sorry about Emily and her kids.'

Annie stared back at the woman in amazement. 'She's gorn up to the Midlands. Ain't 'eard a word since before Christmas.'

'D'you mean she never got bombed?' continued the woman without a thought. 'Well now, I 'eard they all went under, 'er 'usband as well.'

Annie opened her big mouth wide as if to speak but not a word came out. Her legs crumpled and Annie fell face forward in the middle of the market street she knew so well. Sheila, terrified witless, ran away screaming her head off to find Billy.

Annie was taken to hospital where she was examined. 'She'll be all right,' the doctor told Billy, 'but she has had a terrible shock.'

'Oh, Mum, I'm sorry, I should have told you before,' wept Billy.

Annie sat up in bed and stared at him with a stony eye. 'Well, I knows nah, don't I?' And from that time on she never mentioned Emily again, but she became feeble and would sit outside the house on a chair just staring into space. Losing Emily and her little ones had been the final blow.

Finally the dark clouds parted and the blue skies appeared; the Allies were at last winning the war. Then came Victory night when it seemed as if all of London had gone wild and they had a big street party. Annie still sat outside her house, but her limbs had stiffened so she made little attempt to go far. They all danced a knees-up, and even Sheila wore a coloured paper hat. The horror of the blitz and the buzz bombs was soon forgotten.

They had lit a big bonfire and weird shadowy figures careered around it but Annie sat dreaming of those who would never return. 'Well, fank God I've lived to see this day,' she said, albeit sadly.

Sheila, who still seldom spoke, said shyly, 'Maybe our Amy will come home now.'

Down in the village of Ashmullen, they also celebrated the Allied victory with a big party on the green. Nancy was there with her little girl, Heather, who was now a year old. She was as dark as Nancy and Dick were fair, and her parents worshipped her. The night that Heather had been born Dick had got drunker than he had ever been in his life. He and all the farm hands had poured gallons of Devon cider down their throats. Dick was a happy man. Nancy seemed to have settled down and loved her role as a farmer's wife.

But there were quite a few farewells that summer. Dick's aunt Edie went off to live in Florida, taking Dick's father with her, for the benefit of his health. Nancy had all the rooms of the old farmhouse redecorated, and polished all the copper and brass until everything shone clean and bright.

Nancy always referred to her husband as 'my old Dick', much to the amusement of Amy.

'Why *old* Dick?' she laughed. 'He's only two years older than you.'

'Oh, you know what I mean,' smiled Nancy, 'he's so sweet and so slow.' And now there was genuine affection in her voice.

Amy was fourteen. She had grown tall and had a pretty

freckled face. Her hair was cut in a page boy bob with a heavy fringe which hid the scar on her forehead. Amy was actually feeling a little disgruntled, for Captain Trelawny, Miriam's husband, had returned from the war, and Amy did not like him one bit. 'He barks like a blooming dog,' she told Nancy. 'And he's ancient! Much older then Miriam. "Gel!" he shouts at me, "bring up my tea, quickly!" I told him I'm not a servant and he don't like me one bit.'

'Perhaps you should go home to London, Amy,' said Nancy. 'Or, better still, come and live with Dick and me.'

Amy pulled a sullen face. 'I won't leave Miriam and she doesn't want me to go,' she protested.

Nancy sighed. For Miriam had recently confided in her about her own plans for the future.

'But you can't stay on, Amy,' she said gently. 'Just between you and me, Miriam is going to Jack in Canada. But for heaven's sake, don't say I told you so.'

Amy stared at Nancy aghast. 'She wouldn't do that,' she cried in a low, frightened voice.

Nancy raised her eyebrows. 'It's no good you getting upset, Amy. What I said is true.'

'Well, then, I'll go with her,' declared Amy truculantly.

'Now, you have to be sensible,' the sensible Nancy said. 'Now that you've left school, you'll have to get a job and you can't expect strangers to support you.'

Amy screwed up her face in grief. 'I don't want to grow up, Nancy,' she said plaintively. 'I've been so happy here.'

'Well then, stay,' replied Nancy, 'and come and work for Dick on the farm. But you do know that Mother hasn't been well since Emily and her kids got bombed. And there's only poor Sheila left to look after her.'

Amy put her hand on her chin and gazed obstinately into space. 'If Miriam don't want me, then I'll go home,' she said, 'but I won't leave till she tells me.'

Nancy shrugged. 'You're going to have to learn that we can't have everything we want out of life. We've all spoiled you, I'm afraid, and that's a pity.'

Within two weeks Amy had made her decision. She would return home to London. Miriam seemed a little distracted and worried, and not concerned about Amy's future. And when she told Amy that she and the Captain were going to buy a smaller house as her husband was retiring from the army, Amy knew that whatever Miriam's plans were, she was not included in them. It was final. She put her arms around Miriam's neck and sobbed.

'I'll never forget you, Auntie Miriam,' she whispered through her tears.

'Now don't be silly, girl,' said Miriam. 'We're moving into a nice house in Devon near the sea and you'll come to me for your holidays and bring your young man. You are sure to find a nice one back in London.'

So Amy didn't know if Miriam was still planning to join Jack in Canada or not but she was pleased to have a standing invitation to visit her.

Amy kissed the pony, the cat, and the dog goodbye and Miriam put a tearful girl on the train for London, off to a new destiny. Our Amy had suddenly grown up.

Billy met her in London at the station and took her in his old van back to that old slum district where she had spent her early years. Amy had a very sullen expression on her face as she stared out at the busy streets and the big empty spaces where there had once been houses, but when she saw the bent, tired figure of Annie sitting on a chair outside the front door, she burst into tears. She dashed up to her white-haired mother and slung her arms around her.

As always Annie showed little emotion, she just patted Amy on the back gently. 'Now don't cry, gel,' she said. Her voice was tired. 'I must say, you've growed up a nice gel.'

Chapter Six

Rehabilitation

Annie squinted up at Amy through the haze of cigarette smoke. 'Bit taller than the other gels, I should say,' and she took another puff on her Woodbine. Going inside the house Amy stared in dismay around the untidy rooms, the rubbish on the floor and the table littered with used crocks. After all these years living with Miriam, she was quite unused to poverty and she was shocked.

Then from a dim, gaslighted corner shuffled poor Sheila. She had a woolly hat clamped down over her ears, and a grubby over-all draped untidily around her thin figure. Sheila's pallid blue eyes stared vaguely at Amy, unable to recognize her little sister after such a long time.

'Oh, it's Sheila!' cried Amy. 'Whatever's the matter with her?'

'Nerves got bad, that's all,' muttered Annie. Turning to Sheila, she said, 'Pull yer bleedin' self togevver, Sheila, it's our Amy come 'ome.'

Sheila's face twitched spasmodically but Amy ran to her and gathered her in her arms. 'Oh, poor Sheila,' she cried. 'What have they done to you?'

Sheila rested her head on Amy's broad shoulders and smiled a gentle smile as her sister cuddled her.

Annie sat down on a chair without saying a word. She had a glum expression fixed on her face as she sat puffing madly at her fag.

'I'll make tea,' said Sheila, delighted to be able to wait on Amy. 'We've got a nice cake from the milkman.'

Amy sat down and surveyed her future home in silence.

'It's no good turning up yer nose,' said Annie. 'This is all we got left of our 'ouse. It was bombed to the ground, yer know. I lost all me nice fings, I did, that night.'

'Never mind,' said Amy as tears filled her eyes. 'I'll get a job and buy you and Sheila lots of nice things.'

Annie gave a shrug. 'That'll help I suppose, but I never looks forward to noffink these days. Tonight you can sleep in wiff us.

Billy's got yer a camp bed but 'ees goin' ter do up the attic and then yer can go up there wiff Sheila. I needs a bit more room, I do, now that I'm disabled.'

Amy looked down at her mother's useless withered leg and love and pity welled up inside. 'It was about bloody time I came home, I think,' she said abruptly, and a strong urge rushed through her to make things better for her poor mother and sister.

So at fourteen, Amy got a job at Woolworth's and became the wage earner of the family. The hours were long and Amy had to stand behind the counter most of the day and was not allowed to sit down. It was exhausting but the thought of that wage packet at the end of the week kept her going. Most of the customers liked Amy. She was tall with ash blonde hair cut in a neat page boy bob. She had clean fresh-looking skin and a wide pleasant smile. And she was no fool; she minded her own business, and she never saw anyone shoplifting, though in this poor district that sort of thing went on all the time. On Friday evenings Amy would go straight home with her wages. She always gave three pounds to Annie and kept two pounds for herself. She tidied up poor Sheila and took her to the Britannia Cinema on Saturday nights. Sheila loved it. Back home the girls had pinned pictures of their favourite filmstars on the attic walls and Sheila would spend hours staring dreamily at these photographs of Clark Gable and Betty Grable with a beautiful smile on her face.

Sheila seemed to have improved since Amy had come home. She had filled out and now kept herself clean and tidy. Amy gave her some nice dresses and help to roll her hair into a neat style. She never allowed Amy to cut her hair. Amy learned this once when she had wanted to trim Sheila's ends, but Sheila had panicked at the sight of the scissors. Amy never tried again but now rolled up the blonde tresses for her, and put lipstick on her lips and powder on Sheila's shiny red nose. Sheila was thrilled. She loved Amy passionately. Every day, as soon as Amy got home from work, Sheila would be ready with a cup of tea for her, and took off her shoes and fussed around her. Annie actually felt a little jealous at times but her financial status had improved so much since Amy had come home and she was too wise to make any comment.

Sheila's housekeeping habits improved vastly. She swept, dusted and polished the two slum rooms until they shone with cleanliness, and she continued to care for Amy's treasures, peeping at herself in the nice hand mirror, pouting her lips like the film stars did.

Although Amy quarrelled frequently with Annie, she never did with Sheila. She was always so sweet, kind and gentle to Sheila that the older girl could do little else but improve. But Sheila was still very nervous and easily disturbed, and often had bad nightmares during which she huddled close to Amy in bed.

On such nights, as Sheila clung to her, Amy would lie awake and think of the fresh country air, and in her dreamy thoughts she could see the green fields and the farm she had come to love so much. And she would wonder if she would ever go back.

At Woolworth's she now had her own counter. She was bright and alert, and just the kind of girl the shop liked to train. She did not have that brash Cockney accent the other girls of that area had, she never swore and she took little notice of the lads. Amy enjoyed earning money. She liked to be smart, and to have nice clothes to wear, for she had good taste. But things were still a little hard to come by, but there was her older brother Siddy who would often help her out in that area, she discovered. Siddy had come down in the world a bit since the war years. He no longer ran his bar and his little Jewish bird had got married to Izzy Simons, who had a drapers shop in Pimlico Walk, at the far end of the market.

Although Sadie was married, she and Siddy were still in love and deep in the throes of an affair. Sadie was a nice, well-brought-up Jewish girl who had been in a boarding school during the war. Her father, Jack Goldman, decided it was time to get his daughter a nice Jewish husband and told her to stop working at the bar. Sadie obediently married Izzy Simons, a very respectable local man, and with a very bored expression served babywear and wool in Izzy's drapery shop. But she always had one eye down the street watching for Siddy to come visiting. Jack Goldman was a big shot down the market. He did not run off in the war, but had been an air-raid warden and kept his business going. His wife had been killed when their shelter was hit during that bad blitz when they had a stall that sold surplus wear, old army equipment and articles that had been damaged in the blitz. Now, after the war, Jack was doing well. He had two shops, one in the city and one in the market, and he was well liked and respected by the Cockneys.

238

He gave plenty of money to charity and had helped to build up the market after the war. That year he had become head of the traders' association which met weekly in the Coster's Hall, and ran raffles and had collections for the poor folk in the district. Jack liked Siddy, even though he wasn't Jewish, and he shut one eye if Siddy went up to see Sadie when her husband was travelling, trying to sell ladies' underwear. Jack employed Siddy in his shop and relied on him quite considerably. The two men respected each other and knew each other's secrets. Jack had a secret business which he had started when the Yanks were here – selling dirty pictures of lovely nude ladies. Recently he had progressed to hard porn, which he sold outside the Windmill Theatre in Piccadilly, and business was doing very nicely.

'Everyone to his own peculiar perversions,' Siddy would say. 'Meself, I wouldn't touch that stuff with a barge pole.'

Still, Jack and Siddy were good friends. With his short square shape and a big trilby hat propped up by extraordinarily large ears, Jack was a well-known figure down the market. Siddy with his long lank brown hair and sallow face was always joking and skipping in and out of the shop chatting up the girls.

Amy would often meet him on Saturday afternoons as she rummaged through the bargain rails to try to find an expensive suit, perhaps only smoke damaged, which could be cleaned and be an excellent buy. Siddy was sure to find anything she wanted.

'Ten bob to you, love,' he would say, and then give her five bob back saying, 'Buy Muvver a bottle of stout with that.'

But still Annie would not acknowledge her son.

Amy would often try to encourage her to make an effort. 'Take a little walk down the market, Mum,' she would say. 'You might meet someone you know.'

'No bloody fear!' Annie would retort. 'Might bash into that bloody Siddy. Crooked little sod.'

'Oh, Mum,' Amy would sigh. 'Siddy is all right. He works in a shop now and everyone likes him.'

'They don't bloody know him,' Annie would grouse.

Commodities were still a little short. Butter was still rationed, as was sugar. But every weekend a box of food was put on Annie's doorstep. Sheila would go down to get them, and there was Siddy with a wide grin on his face as he put his finger to the side of his noise. 'Stumm,' he'd say.

Sheila understood, 'Just been down to get the things from the milkman,' she would tell Annie.

'Don't run up no big bills,' Annie would sniff. 'Can't afford them.'

The secret was safely kept from Annie. In no way would she welcome Siddy in to her home; it was as if she blamed him for the loss of the rest of her family.

Amy became very fond of Siddy and they confided in each other. She felt quite sorry for him when he told her that he and Sadie really loved each other, but because of her religion they could not get married.

'Oh, it's all so silly,' said Amy. 'But suppose you give her a baby?'

'It's a wise child that knows its own father,' grinned Siddy, enigmatically. At that time Sadie was three months pregnant.

And so Amy grew wiser and not a little wary of the ways of the world. At sixteen, she had matured into a wordly young woman, who knew how to dress and behave. She now had a new job working in a big West End department store where she was to be on a training programme until she was eighteen. Amy loved her new job. Carefully dressed each morning, she would get on the bus, walk down the street wearing neat little gloves and carrying a rolled umbrella.

Sheila would wave goodbye to her. She would have got up early to make Amy's breakfast which she had then served to her as well.

Annie changed very little in those last two years, though her arthritis slowed her down increasingly as it crept up to her hip. She would sit on a chair outside the door most of the day, for it was so painful to move, and she quarrelled incessantly with Emmy, Billy's wife, who lived downstairs with Billy and her two children.

It was mostly the little boy they quarrelled over. Emmy was terrified of Sheila because she was so peculiar, and she did not like her children to go near her. Whenever Sheila sat on the stairs and talked sweet nothings to the little boy, Emmy would dash out and snatch him up and run inside with him.

This behaviour infuriated Annie who would hurl insults at her daughter-in-law. 'All right,' she would yell, 'we ain't goin' ter bleedin' eat 'im.'

240

Then Emmy would complain to Billy, who worked hard on the transport and came home very tired, and did not want to get involved in any arguments. He usually tried to dodge Annie and seldom went upstairs to visit.

Amy was rarely affected by such scenes. 'Been playing happy families again?' she would comment after some noisy fracas.

But all this came to an end when Billy changed jobs and went to work for a frozen food firm in Chelmsford. He and his family moved out of the downstairs flat and a West Indian family moved in. Sheila was absolutely petrified of them, even though they were perfectly nice and friendly. There was only one toilet in the house which was downstairs next to the kitchen occupied by the West Indians, so to go down those dark smelly stairs to the toilet became too frightening for her. Someone always had to go with her. If Amy was not around, she would sit doubled up in pain and terribly constipated waiting until her sister came in from work to accompany her.

One evening, when Annie was dosing poor Sheila with liquorice powder, Amy suddenly became very annoyed. 'Why I put up with this place, I really don't know. They're building new council flats down in Shoreditch. I'm going to write and put our name down for one.'

'Won't get one,' moaned Annie. 'Got a long waiting list, they have.'

'Well, I am not staying here,' declared Amy. 'You'll just have to go with Sheila to live at Nancy's and I'll get some lodgings up west near my work.'

Sheila blubbered and Annie nagged. There was no way she was moving out to live in the country again. And poor Amy trying hard to keep the home going was at her wit's end.

When Siddy saw her looking so harassed, he was worried. 'What's up, sis?'

She confided in him. 'It's the conditions we live in,' she said. 'There are just too many of us in that house and Sheila is terrified of the West Indians who have moved in. We deserve a better place to live, and I have to find something.'

Siddy looked at her thoughtfully. 'I've only got a little dump meself,' he said. 'You know, sometimes I'd like to live in a house with the family, but I know it's no good crying for the moon.'

'There's not many of us left now,' said Amy. 'What with

everyone all over the place. And to think we were a great crowd, us Flanagans, when we were kids. We ruled the street, we did.'

And that was how they eventually got a nice council flat down at the other end of our market. It was not a sky-high block – it was just three storeys high and they were given a ground floor flat because of Annie's disability. It was spanking new and there was even a small patch of grass outside where Sheila could walk about safely.

Amy threw caution to the wind and immediately treated themselves to a three-piece suite and a carpet, all on hire purchase, to be paid back weekly from her wages. But they were at last happy and comfortable and very close to each other.

Nancy and Dick came on a visit with their little girl, as did Lily, and Letty came to see them before she left with her new husband for Canada. Amy organised a little celebration to show off their new home. Siddy sent beer and wine, though he did not come in, but his sisters went out and talked to him outside. They kissed and cuddled him there, for there was still a lot of affection left in this sadly depleted family.

Chapter Seven

Courting

At seventeen Amy was a handsome young woman, who dressed and carried herself well. She had kept the smart clipped accent she had copied from Miriam who had always moved in posh circles. During the week she worked hard but every Sunday was spent at home with Annie and Sheila. Sheila always cooked a roast with baked spuds and a pastry for afters. She had become quite a good cook but Amy and Annie always had to watch out for her because the slightest disturbance could cause her to drop dishes and upset saucepans.

Later in the afternoon Annie would sit out on the green chatting to the old folk who lingered there too. Mostly they nattered about the blitz and harked back to the good old days when all the small streets had criss-crossed the market and had been a big community in which everyone knew each other. But those days had flown by. All around high-rise flats had been built and in those post-war years many of the East Enders did return to the areas they knew so well, even if the war had changed it all so much. And certainly the East End's criminal element was still there; but now tucked away in those modern little boxes. At one time the criminals had openly ruled the area.

'There used to be old Janey Richard,' Annie recalled. 'She wore a man's cap and a big sacking apron rolled up over her arm. She'd go straight into old Scheiderman's shop, nick a joint of meat and hide it in her apron. Old Scheiderman used to jump up and down with exasperation but he never dared do or say anything in protest.'

Annie's eyes gleamed with delight at the memories. 'Then off Janey would go to unhook a nice pair of kid's pants hanging outside Long and Doughty's,' she continued, 'and that's the way Janey did her shopping all the way down the market. Not one penny would she spend.' Annie would tell this story with glee.

The old lady listening to Annie would cackle with glee. 'Yes, those big boys, the heavy mob, were always just behind her.

Nobody had a chance with the heavy mob guarding her.'

'Disgusting old woman. Don't tell me about her,' Amy would mutter if she overheard these reminiscences.

'Ah,' replied Annie, 'but there's many a poor sod arahand 'ere remembers 'ow kind she were. And she put many a meal on their table an' boots on their nippers' feet. When she died it was a real splendid funeral, with a great big wreaff from the neighbours inscribed to "the Angel of Hoxton, our Janey".'

And thus Annie would spend her time talking about the old days in the East End, and clearly revelling in them. But she would never dwell on stories closer to her heart or talk about her beloved kids, like Emily, lost with her own children in the war. The hurt was too deep for her to recall. No, her memories dwelt on the Cockney characters of the past. 'And they're still there, Amy,' Annie announced jubilantly. 'Saw two of them brothers only yesterday, going to the pub. They must 'ave been inside, 'corse they was mixed up wiff that Yank's murder wot happened just up the road, it did.'

'Oh, stop it, mother!' exclaimed Amy in her poshest voice. 'I don't want to know about those low-class people.'

'Oh, hoity-toity,' called Annie. 'Yer might be glad of 'em yet, yer never knows.'

Sometimes on Sunday evenings Amy would feel rather low and depressed. She would remember how she used to cuddle up to Miriam on the big Chesterfield and hold her hand. She felt as if she was crying inside, but she did not understand the feelings she had deep down. She would stare at Annie's moon face surrounded by the haze of cigarette smoke and look at Sheila slumped in the armchair with her mouth open and her face devoid of all expression. This was a hard life, Amy thought, for the hundredth time. She didn't mind it so much now, and their situation had certainly improved. They had a nice bathroom and she had her own bedroom and the flat was filled with pretty things that she had bought for it. But was this all there was to life? It would be nice to have someone to cuddle her, and wine and dine her, just as they did in the films. But the reality of it was that she kept her nose to the grindstone at her job. She now travelled each day on the tube, being squashed twice daily in that train with hundreds of other people on their way to work and no time to talk to each other. Their only thought was to fight for a place to straphang. The tube train went back and forth from East End to West End taking Amy to the posh department store where she still worked. Nowadays Amy worked on the cosmetic counter which, along with the expensvie perfumes and soaps, sold bright fripperies to please the rich, bored young ladies who spent their time idly shopping each afternoon. Bright silk scarves were hung artfully on stands, while earrings and perfume bottles were placed in tasteful displays on the glass counters. Customers were encouraged to take a nice squirt of perfume to test its fragrance, and Amy in a friendly but precise voice would persuade them to buy. She had become an attraction to that counter, with her carefully cut blonde hair and just the right amount of costume jewellery to go with her black dress.

One afternoon, as she was rearranging the silk scarves, an unusual type of customer hovered at her counter. He was a tall slim young man, casually dressed, and with dark auburn hair which stood up on end as if it had never been brushed properly. He had a wide grin which revealed a set of perfectly white teeth and he smiled as Amy looked on in astonishment as he picked up one of the test bottles and squirted a spray of perfume into the air.

'Do you mind?' Amy snapped. 'That is very expensive perfume.'

'No, darling,' he said still with a grin. 'I just wanted to see if they worked. Don't use it meself.' He put the bottle down and continued to hover while Amy tried to ignore him and went back to arranging the scarves.

With hands in his pockets the young man looked her up and down, then finally said in broad Cockney. ' 'Ow much is them, then?' He pointed to the bottle he had squirted.

'Seven pounds each,' replied Amy very coldly, knowing that he wasn't interested in buying.

' 'Ere, I didn't wanna buy the bleedin' store,' he said, and slouched away.

Amy flushed scarlet and felt quite uncomfortable. She comforted herself by deciding that the man was just a nasty character to be ignored.

Wednesday afternoons, Amy got off work because she worked late on Saturdays. As she sat on the tube the following Wednesday wondering how she would pass the afternoon, she was suddenly aware of this same rude young man sitting opposite her. He had stretched out his long legs in front of him and was gazing mischievously at her.

' 'Ullo, doll. Got an' 'alf day, 'ave yer?' he asked.

'It's none of your business.' returned Amy very annoyed, and feeling a blush creep up her neck.

The man lurched over and sat next to her. Amy stiffened, absolutely petrified.

'It's okay,' he said. 'I ain't goin' to interfere wiff yer. I'd just like to get to know yer, that's all.'

Amy stared at him. There was some cheeky look in those greeny grey eyes that suddenly made her giggle nervously. She tried to stop herself but couldn't.

The man grinned even more. 'That's it, doll, cheer up, 'ow far yer goin'?' he asked.

'To Mile End,' Amy replied, looking down at her hands coyly.

'Funny, I could a' swore you was an East Ender in spite o' that posh voice.'

Amy smiled. She was feeling a little more relaxed. 'How come you are hanging around the West End all day?' she asked boldly.

'Noffink else to do,' he said. 'I'm waiting for a ship. I'm just goin' dahn to the pool office to see if I can get back to sea. I'm just pretty fed-up hangin' abaht 'ere,' he said. He hesitated for a moment and then looked at her eagerly. 'Why not ger off at Tower Bridge wiff me and we'll walk over the bridge and 'ave a cuppa by the gardens? It's just the day for it.'

Amy paused. It was indeed a lovely day and this young man seemed very friendly. 'Oh, all right,' she said. 'Why not?'

Why or how she made that decision she would never know but suddenly finally she found herself walking over Tower Bridge with a handsome young man who took her hand gently in his and squeezed it. A shiver of excitement ran through her veins. Amy had never felt anything like it. They stopped for a while on the bridge and looked down the great river.

'The Pool Office ain't open yet. It'll be open after lunch. Let's sit dahn and wait.'

They walked on and sat on a bench in the Tower Gardens and talked about themselves and their experiences during the war. It turned out that Jimmy Spinks, as he introduced himself, was one year older than Amy.

'I was in a bad boys' school and I kept running way. Finally I got on a boat in Liverpool – I lied abaht me age – and was on the convoys. It was a good life if a bit dangerous one. They calls me Sparky,' 'cos I got on the radio deck.'

Amy found herself very interested in him. 'Where did you grow up?'

'Befnal Green,' said Sparky. 'Me family got blitzed. Me muvver and me sister was killed, so there's only me left. Never 'ad a farver that I remembers.'

Amy squeezed his hand in sympathy. After all, her own father had died when she was very young.

Sparky suddenly got to his feet, he bent down and gave her a swift kiss. 'Okay, darlin',' he said, 'I'll just pop over and register for another voyage and then we'll go out an' 'ave a good time.'

While Sparky went off to the Pool Office, Amy sat demurely on the park bench. She could not think what had got into her. What on earth was wrong with her? Why did she not get up and trot off home, when surely by now Mum and Sheila would be worrying about her?

Sparky came back. His long shadow fell on the path as he stood smiling and looking down at her. 'Well, I done it. I got four days now 'fore it takes orf,' he said. He held out his hand to her. 'Come on, let's 'ave a cuppa.'

They sat by the river in the summer sunshine eating sticky buns, drinking tea from paper cups and watching the kids playing on the pleasure boats. They walked hand in hand around the Tower looking at the ravens and the red-coated, stern-faced, Beefeaters, and the hordes of tourists.

'I've been all over the world,' Sparky said. 'I've been to New York, Ottawa and San Francisco, and they ain't got nuffink like this out there. Our London was somefink really worff 'angin' on to. It often amazed me,' he continued, 'how they knocked out all our slum 'ouses and killed the poor people. Why didn't they get this big place like the Tower and St Paul's or Buckingham Palace? I think 'cos they was bloody scared. They just chucked dahn their bombs and ran, the bastards.'

'Oh, Sparky, don't swear,' said Amy.

Sparky roared with laughter. Catching her in his arms, he swung her in the air. 'Oh, I finks yew are the cutest little bird I've ever met, an' I'm goin' ter spend ev'ry minute of the next three days with yer.'

'. . .,' gasped Amy. But the force of his kiss silenced her. She had

247

never been kissed on the lips before but this was the most exciting thing she'd ever experienced. She let herself relax in his arms and between kisses, she murmured, 'I can't stay out late because of Mum and Sheila.'

'I'll take yer 'ome early tonight,' he said, 'but tomorrer and the next days I tells the time yer go 'cos yer goin' aht wiff me.'

Amy smiled. She liked his authoritative tone. And so in the cool of the evening, they walked all the way back to Shoreditch, chatting nonstop. He kissed her again before they parted, and he said, 'Don't let me dahn, will yer, darlin'?'

Annie and Sheila were in a terrible state when Amy finally tripped in at nine o'clock. There were dog ends everywhere, because Annie, in her anxiety, had just smoked cigarette after cigarette and dropped all the ends on the floor. In the corner Sheila was sobbing hysterically.

'Oh, what's all this about?' asked Amy. She was rosy cheeked and her eyes were shining. 'I've never stopped out before. It was my half day.'

'You should 'ave told us,' grumbled Annie, 'Fair upset poor Sheila, it has.'

'Oh, some girl had a birthday party,' said Amy. 'Now shut up and let's have some supper. Tell you what, I'll treat you to fish and chips – coming with me, Sheila?'

Sheila had stopped sobbing but she stared sadly at Amy and shook her head.

'Well,' said Amy impatiently. 'You make the tea and lay the table. And stop snivelling,' she snapped. 'I'll go round the chippy.'

Later that night as she lay in bed, Amy thought of those delicious deep kisses and the strength of Sparky's arms as he had held her. Oh, she felt so happy. She could hardly wait for the next day when she would see him again.

Next morning she dressed with extra care. 'I'll be late,' she told Annie and Sheila. 'Don't wait up. I'm going to the pictures in the West End with a girl from work.' The lie came easily.

Sheila pouted her lip. 'Can I come?' she asked.

'No, love, it's too busy up there. I'll take you to the Britannia Cinema on Saturday.'

Amy sighed as she travelled to work. It was clearly not going to be easy having a boyfriend with Annie and Sheila being so possessive and dependent on her. But then a little voice nagged at her and suggest that Sparky might not turn up anyway and all her newly stoked emotions would be frustrated.

She did not have to worry. At the end of the day, as the shop was closing, he arrived, dressed in a very smart suit and holding a box of chocolates under his arm. 'I booked us in for an early show so we can get out in time for a meal and a drink,' he said.

They went to Leicester Square cinema, but they didn't see much of the film. Their kissing became so very passionate and intense that even the chocolates got hot and sticky.

'Let's get out of 'ere,' said Sparky. 'I need a drink.'

They stood in a dark doorway holding each other tight. Amy felt the heat of his body through her thin summer dress, but she felt no fear.

'Look what you've done to me,' he joked.

When Sparky had cooled down, they went to a pub. At first Amy was reluctant to go in.

'I've never ever been in a pub,' she said.

'Oh, Amy,' he cried. 'There're so many things you ain't never done. Well, this one I can handle,' he laughed as he guided her into the pub. 'You needn't drink anyfink 'eavy. Wat abaht a shandy?' he asked. She nodded, so Sparky ordered a shandy for her and a pint for himself.

Amy felt strange and far away but drank the cool drink.

Sparky said, 'If I wasn't goin' away, I'd ask yer to marry me.'

'But you just met me,' said Amy, amazed.

'Well, I know I want yer and I ain't never felt like this abaht a bird, 'specially one like you, Amy. I can't believe you ain't never done it.'

'Oh, Sparky, don't talk about it,' Amy's face flushed scarlet with embarrassment.

He cuddled her tight. 'Yer haven't done anyfink really bad yet, Amy, but darlin', I will teach yer to luv' me but yer gotta belong to only me and it don't seem fair me goin' orf and leavin' yer. So I promise to behave meself, until I comes back and, oh darlin', yer must be there waitin' for me.'

Amy got home at midnight. Before she left Sparky again they kissed passionately near her home. And this time Amy knew she wanted him as much as he wanted her, but she pulled away before they went too far. 'I must go in, Sparky,' she whispered. 'I'll see you tomorrow, darling.'

So almost weeping with joy, young Amy crept into bed that night. As she settled into the cool bed, she heard Annie's gruff voice call out. 'Is that you, Amy? Hope you bolted the bloody front door.'

Chapter Eight

Her Man

That last night before he sailed, Sparky took Amy to a party. 'We're goin' to me mate's house,' he said. They went down the back streets of the East End to a small house where the seamen were saying goodbye until next trip.

It was a good party with plenty of drinks and 'knees up'. Amy had relaxed a little and drank gin and orange. At the end of the evening, the other guests were slowly leaving to go home, and Amy was feeling a little drunk. She lay on the settee in a happy, dreamlike state with her Sparky. The hostess said a hasty goodnight, turned out the lights and left them alone in the room.

Amy pressed close to Sparky, feeling his strong muscular body. 'You can do it, darling,' she whispered, 'if you want to.'

'Do you?' asked Sparky, surprised by her boldness, but he did not give her a chance to change her mind. And so Amy surrendered her virginity to Jimmy Spinks. He was her man, the first and last one, as far as she was concerned.

Very early in the morning as Sparky walked her home, Amy had cried a little.

'I'll be gone six weeks, Amy,' Sparky said, 'but you can write to me at this address.' He handed her a piece of paper. 'We will get married when I come back. I feel sorry about last night,' he said. 'I never wanted to do that to a lovely gel like you, but I promise I'll come back for you.'

'It was the most wonderful happening in my life,' answered Amy enthusiastically, 'and I'll wait for you because I love you.' So they had parted.

When Amy got home, Sheila had to come creeping down the hall to let her in quietly so that Annie would not know she had been out all night.

Amy had hugged her sister. 'Oh, Sheila, I'm so happy. I've fallen in love.'

It didn't take long for Annie to learn about Sparky. She was not impressed. 'Soppy cow,' she muttered, 'mooning over a bloody sailor. Got a girl in every port, they have.'

Amy frowned. 'Not Sparky,' she insisted. 'He's mine.'

Siddy was pleased to hear that Amy was courting. 'But you take care, ducky, and if anyone tries to take liberties with you, refer them to me. I'll get the boys to beat them up.'

'What boys?' asked Amy impatiently. Sometimes Siddy's secret life puzzled her. 'I'm going to get married when Sparky comes back,' she told him.

Siddy looked at her affectionately. 'Don't be in such a hurry, sweetheart. Marriage is not all it's cracked up to be.'

Siddy had had troubles of his own recently. Izzy had quarrelled with Sadie and she had fled to Siddy asking him to run away with her. But Siddy was too afraid of her father Jack who told him in no uncertain terms that it was a bad idea. 'Now pack it up, Siddy, my boy,' he said. 'Sadie is a Jewish gel and she's got her own family so don't spoil it for her.'

Siddy knew that Jack was right. He told Sadie to go back home and then spent his time at the dog track or down Petticoat Lane on Sunday mornings where he would sell balloons or any sort of cheap stuff from Jack Goldman out of the suitcase. The coppers continually moved him on but he made a lot of odd friends. The end had come to the surplus stores, so Jack Goldman concentrated more on his porno book shop in the West End. But here he met trouble, for the coppers up West were a little more nosey than the good old friendly well-bunged East End ones and often came to turn over the shop. When they did this Jack would toddle off with his suitcase full of porn to a new hiding place till the coast was clear.

So far Jack and Siddy had kept out of trouble but Siddy knew it was risky – mainly for Jack. 'It's like sitting on the edge of a bloody volcano,' he would remark to his mates. 'Something's gonna blow soon and if they get that dirty old sod he'll go down, that's for sure.' He did not confide in Amy over such matters. She was just his little sister who would never understand the ups and downs of a market trader's life. She would never understand him and his ways.

Meanwhile, Amy went happily to work and began to buy herself pretty underwear from the store, where she was allowed a discount. She whispered to the other girls that she was going to get married soon.

'Why, Amy?' said the staff manageress when she heard. 'You have only just met him. Why don't you wait till you know each other a little better?'

'Oh, I don't think he will wait, and I couldn't bear to lose him.'

The manageress was a worldly woman but was not going to interfere. She shrugged. 'Well, I wish you luck anyway, Amy.'

Those six weeks for which Sparky said he would be away turned to eight. The time dragged by and for Amy the period he was away was very long indeed. She put his photograph beside her bed and wrote long letters to him. A picture postcard arrived from Canada. Sparky had written in a very untidy scrawl and did not have a lot to say, but Amy's heart beat excitedly every time she looked at it.

Sheila watched Amy these days with a very worried expression on her face.

At last one evening, as the store closed, Amy suddenly gasped and rushed towards a tall, tanned, red-headed figure crying, 'Oh, Sparky! You came home!' Her work mates looked at each other and smiled. They were all a little surprised.

Amy was over the moon. She felt as if she was walking on air. They sat on the tube holding hands and Amy thought her heart would leap from her breast as Sparky talked about Canada, and all the places he'd visited, the wonderful cities with lots of space and how nice it was in the autumn, with the sun still shining even in October.

'That's what I would like to do,' Sparky said, fired with enthusiasm. 'Marry you, darlin', and get us a nice place out there.'

'My sister, Letty, is in Ottawa,' Amy said timidly. 'She went there with the WAAF's.'

'All the better. We'll save up and go stay with her. I'll get a job out there.'

It all sounded very nice but Amy was afraid even to think about it. She was already feeling nervous about introducing Sparky to Annie and Sheila. How would they react, especially when he talked about taking her away from them?

Now she began to enjoy a regular sex life with Sparky. They made love whenever they could – at parties, in doorways, in the park and even in the sitting room when Annie was in bed and Sheila sound asleep. Sparky had no home. His home was a sailor's club since he had had no regular residence since the war and depended on the generosity of his many mates. He was a popular fellow for he was generous himself and a very good entertainer. He played the piano and sang rude sea ditties in the pub, and sometimes he would dress up and do a fat woman act at parties. Everyone loved having him around.

As it turned out, Amy need not have worried about bringing Sparky home and introducing him to her mother and sister. Like everyone else, they adored him. There had never been so much laughter in that little flat. He charmed everyone and teased Annie, calling her 'Fanny Annie', and tickling her big bunion which stuck out of her carpet slippers.

'Me name's Annie Flanagan,' Annie would protest, unable to suppress her giggles or her delight at having so much life around her once more. She took to Sparky in a flash. 'He's a real cough drop,' she told Amy approvingly one day.

To Sheila Sparky was also very kind, stuffing her with the crisps, sweets and lemonade which he brought home from the pub. 'Who's goin' to be a good girl, then?' he would say, holding up the goodies in the air just for a frustrating moment before handing them over. Once she had the booty, Sheila knew what to do. 'I am going to bed now, Sparky,' she would say.

Then Annie with a great grunt, and perhaps burping from the two bottles of stout inside her, would go. 'All right, give us a hand up,' she would say. 'I'll have an early night.'

Grinning broadly, Sparky would escort Annie to her bedroom door always keeping up his banter. 'Let me come with you, love,' he'd whisper. 'I'll keep you nice and warm.'

'You cheeky bugger!' Annie scolded him, but always with a nice warm smile. Seldom in her whole life had Annie had so much attention.

When the others were safely in bed, Sparky would hold Amy in his arms and waltz her around the room. 'That's it, darlin', now the night is ours,' he would laugh.

Sparky was often still sleeping on the settee early in the morning when a weary Amy got ready for work, but he would walk as far as the tube station with her.

Amy would kiss him goodbye with passion. 'Don't sit in the pub all day, will you, Sparky?'

Never the less he always did just that, what with all these mates of his who were still ashore and spending their shillings, backing

254

horses and playing cards. This lazy side of Sparky's character did bother Amy at times, but every time she saw him outside the department store waiting for her at night her reservations would disappear and her heart always skipped a beat. Sparky was such a fine fellow – clean and neat with a healthy glow to his skin, a tall, lithe figure with those fine white teeth. She could never reject him; he was her man.

The marriage was often discussed but the details were still not entirely settled.

'We would have to find somewhere to live first,' said Amy one day when they were talking it over once more.

Sparky frowned. 'That's not going to be easy. Couldn't we pack in with old Annie? We could get spliced at the registry office and then I'll do another couple of voyages to get some money in the kitty. After that we can try to buy our own little house.'

The discussions rarely got further than that but Amy felt that she was already having a hectic honeymoon and so there did not seem much point in worrying too much about it. Although Sparky had a room at the sailor's hostel he spent most of his time at Annie's place anyway.

'I expect the family would like me to have a nice wedding,' said Amy, on another occasion, 'and my sister could come and I'd have my nieces for bridesmaids.'

'You'll 'ave wot yer want, darlin',' said Sparky generously as they lay on the settee. He nibbled her ear and brushed his tongue along her neck. Amy's skin tingled with delight and she shivered gleefully as she snuggled up tight.

Sparky stroked her hair. 'We really tick over, you and I,' he said approvingly.

'I'm afraid sometimes that I'll get a baby,' she said in a low, anxious way.

'If you do then we'll get spliced,' Sparky said lightly, 'but meantime, darlin', it's time for me to make another voyage as I have run out of dough. I'll sign on for the Middle East. They're lousy ships but the pay is good and the voyage not too long.'

Amy was silent. He was going away again with nothing settled and clear cut.

So early in November, Sparky sailed away and a silence descended on the flat. All three women were affected by Sparky's absence. Annie sat puffing mournfully at her fags and Sheila snivelled and became quite despondent. And, of course, Amy felt utterly alone. But she decided to work with a will and earn all the commission she could on her sales to save up for the wedding. She wrote to her sisters Nancy, Letty and Lily and told them that she was getting married in the spring. She even ordered a white dress from the store.

Sparky had been gone about three weeks when Amy began to get worried that she might actually be pregnant. When she thought about it, her feelings swung up and down. On the one hand it would be so nice to have a baby but where on earth would they all live? Also – and this was very important – she would not be able to get married in her white dress. Would Sparky come home in time? Oh, suppose something happened to him! Poor Amy found herself full of these woes and worries, though she always kept them to herself. Sometimes she noticed Annie staring at her suspiciously but she did not dare say anything to her mother.

A few weeks before Christmas Sparky arrived on the doorstep. He was a little thinner but still full of beans and, of course, loaded with presents for them all. That first night, when the rest of the house was asleep, Amy confided her worries to him expecting him to be angry. But Sparky's reaction was quite unexpected. With a muffled whoop of delight, he undid her dressing gown and pulled up her nightdress.

'Stop it, Sparky!' Amy protested, wriggling around angrily.

But Sparky knelt on the floor and placed his ear on her bare stomach. 'Hullo, son!' he whispered, 'your daddy is home.'

They both burst into fits of laughter.

'Hush,' said Amy, 'you'll wake Mum.'

'Not with all that rum inside her, we won't,' said Sparky. 'Now, darlin', let's make more love and give 'im good nourishment.'

'Oh,' sighed Amy, 'you are terrible, and not a bit romantic.'

'Me? I finks I'm very romantic,' said Sparky, pressing hot lips on to hers.

It was soon obvious that she was indeed pregnant. She cancelled the white wedding dress and told everyone that the big wedding was off. She never said why but most of them guessed.

Just one day before the wedding Siddy got arrested. Sparky heard the news on the grapevine.

'What for?' demanded Amy when he informed her.

'Well, you won't like it, but they say he was trading in porn.'

'No, not Siddy! I'll never believe it. But for gawd's sake, don't tell Annie.' Amy was appalled because she was very fond of Siddy.

But it said in the papers the next day that the police had entered a shop in Soho that dealt with dirty books.

A very determined Amy went marching down to Sadie's shop to find out what was going on. Sadie was sitting there looking very haggard and her eyes were red. 'I'm truly sorry,' she said. 'Siddy carried the can for my father, you know. That was Siddy's way. We knew the police were on to us and Siddy said, "He's an old man, Sadie. I can take a spell in the nick, and he can't.".'

'Oh, the silly bloody fool,' declared Amy, 'and I wanted him to give me away at my wedding.'

'Not a lot we can do now, love,' Sadie said sadly. 'I suggest you get on with your own wedding and good luck. I'm going to see Siddy, he's on remand in the Scrubbs. I'll tell him you sent your love,' she wiped her eyes and kissed Amy on the cheek. 'It's a lousy thing to have happen at this time,' she said woefully.

'Well, I suppose things happen the way we make them happen,' returned Amy unsympathetically, 'but thanks all the same.'

Siddy's plight was put to one side as the wedding festivities took over.

Amy and Sparky got married on New Year's Day at the local registry office. Amy wore a nice blue suit that Siddy had come by and even though it was not a white wedding, it was certainly a noisy one. Annie's flat was full to bursting two days before the great event and for two days after it with the succession of Sparky's mates and their wives, who brought presents and congratulations with them. The night they got married they cleared the pub for the Flanagan's wedding festivities. Nancy and Dick came with their young daughter, Billy and Emmy with their two boys. Then late that night two tall six foot soldiers appeared in the form of the twins, who flew in from Germany. There was a telegram from Letty in Canada, and one from Lily who was out in Malaya nursing the troops.

Annie was in her element. Dressed up in a new silk dress and real shop hair-do, she sat at the head of the table in the place of honour as her family began to gather about her for the first time in years.

Even Joe appeared just as Annie began to wonder if he would.

He strode into the pub, a tall, upright man with white hair and a tanned face. Marching across the room, he swept his little sister up in his arms. 'Congratulations, little Amy,' he said. 'I left Maureen and the kids with her mother in Cork. Must celebrate our Amy's wedding, I told myself.'

And, celebrate he did, along with everyone else. Those celebrations went on for days, back and forth to the pub with all guests kipping on the floor of the flat.

Amy and Sparky spent their first night of marriage in the spare room of one of his many mates' houses but then they went back with Nancy and Dick to Ashmullen the next day, leaving the family still celebrating.

Down in Ashmullen, Sparky charmed the local villagers who all remembered Amy as a little girl and were delighted to see her again now. Nancy had made a fine comfortable home of the old derelict farm house. Her husband Dick was still very sweet and very slow. He had become quite fat and jolly. He worshipped his daughter Heather. She was a small and dark child with long black curls. Amy thought she was very spoilt and watched how she twisted her father around her small finger.

'She's a little monkey, Amy remarked to her elder sister.

Nancy smiled indulgently. 'She's very sweet really. In fact, she's rather like you when you were young,' Nancy added. 'I don't suppose I'll have any more children so we give her a good life to make up for my own childhood.'

Amy glanced at her wondering why Nancy should be so sure there would be no more children, but did not pursue the matter. She changed the subject. 'It's so lovely down here,' she exclaimed. 'Almost just as it always was. I've been up to the Cedars and looked over the gate. I can't believe that Miriam isn't there any more.'

Nancy smiled sadly. 'There aren't many people in this world like Miriam Trelawny.'

'Have you heard from her?' asked Amy, suddenly feeling bad not to have kept in touch. 'How is she?'

'Well enough,' replied Nancy. 'She and her husband have a cottage in South Devon. We write and phone each other occasionally. Captain Trelawny is not in very good health and seems to be a bloody devil to live with. Miriam doesn't deserve that.'

Amy nodded. 'I'm sorry if she's not happy.' Then she paused.

'Do you think that I am going to be happy, Nancy?' she asked, looking up with a look of such innocence that Nancy had to smile.

'Well, you've got the man you wanted, so now it's up to you to see that it works,' she said, looking at her shrewdly.

For those few days in Ashmullen Amy was so happy she could not believe it was happening to her. In spite of the freezing weather, she and Sparky walked across the heather-covered moors for hours. The air was fresh and invigorating and her heart could never have felt more lifted.

Wrapped up in his thick coat Sparky put his arm around Amy's shoulder as they stopped to stare at the bleak but magnificent view. 'Great, isn't it? It reminds me of Canada, you know. You'll love it out there.'

Sparky hadn't mentioned Canada for some time, and Amy was surprised. She frowned. 'But, Sparky, what about the baby?' she asked. 'I can't go out there till it's born.'

'Why not?' asked Sparky. ''Avin' a baby is nothin'. They do it all the time., Just look at yer Mum, she 'ad you on a bus comin' back from the 'oppin', or so she tells me.'

Amy blushed. She hated to be reminded of Annie's bawdy tales. 'I won't go till I've had her.'

'Whatcher mean, her? It's a boy!' exclaimed Sparky. 'A big bouncing son.' He picked her up and ran along with her bouncing in his arms.

'Oh, Sparky, be sensible,' she begged. His boisterous irresponsible ways worried her sometimes.

Their honeymoon over, they returned back to a cold dismal winter in London, where they packed in with Annie and Sheila who had to sleep with Annie so that Amy and Sparky could occupy the other bedroom. Not that Sparky took up much space. All he had brought with him from the sailor's home was a sea bag full of underwear, a few shirts and toilet accessories and his best suit on a hanger. 'That's all I got to worry abaht,' he said. 'Lived out of a bag for years,' he boasted. 'I'm used to it. Noffink will worry me as long as yer wiff me.'

Amy was determined to get their own place. Since Annie's was a council flat and technically they were not allowed to have lodgers, Sparky should not have been living there. Not that anyone would have squealed. But Amy had to go by the book and she

259

told Sparky that she had put her name down for a council flat, now that she was a married woman.

'What for?' asked Sparky. 'Just another couple of good voyages and we'll be able to get out of this dump as soon as we get the fare to Canada.'

'I don't want you to go back to sea,' protested Amy. 'Stay with me till the baby is born and get a job. There must be some other things you can do.'

'I can't do me own job,' said Sparky a bit huffily. 'I'm one of the best radio operators there are, but it's a specialized job at sea, and not easy to break into in civvy street.'

'What about the telephones?' declared Amy, determined to hold him in England.

Seeing the desperate look in his wife's eye, Sparky relented. He pecked her on the cheek and squeezed her. 'For you, dear, I'll try anyfink, but whether I can stick an eight-hour job in an office, I'm not sure.'

Delighted to have been able to influence him, Amy hurriedly got application forms for jobs in the Post Office and various other big companies, carefully filled them in for her man.

Sparky hung around and tried for the jobs that came up but nothing came of any of them. Each time he never got through the first interview, there was always some silly reason why he missed out.

Things were difficult. Each day after work Amy would come home a little tired to Sheila's weak tea and Annie's grousing, and find Sparky out in the pub. She was beginning to show quite a lot and already had given her month's notice.

Sparky was now completely broke except for his dole money. Still he did not get a job. The only bright event during that period was that suddenly they were offered a council flat in the same block as Annie's. It came just at the right time. Amy was feeling very unfit and could hardly wait to retire from her job and get off her feet as her legs had swelled badly.

Sparky also suddenly had some good news, too. 'Got a chance to get on the Hamburg run,' he said. 'I'll only be gorn three weeks at a time. We'll take the flat and go and get a nice lot of gear on the 'ire purchase and set up a swell 'ome. I'll get good pay and you can stay at 'ome.'

Heartened by the fact that some money was coming Sparky's

way, Amy set about getting their flat ready, buying a cot and making a nice nursery. The next few weeks were hectic but by the time Sparky set off, they were moved in and settled in to their new home.

Sparky came home from the ship for one week out of every four. He earned good money and was very happy. But at home he always attracted a string of mates who aggravated Amy now. When Sparky was at home, he and these men sat having boozy gatherings in her flat every Saturday night with Sparky always popping off somewhere else at a moment's notice. He would return home very merry and generous to her, loading her with goodies. Amy liked the presents, but the excessive boozing between trips annoyed her, particularly since Sparky seemed to spend all their money on drink and would borrow back whatever he had given her to save, just before going back to sea. Still, she loved him, and in no way would she complain about him. Occasionally she would nag at him a little but he just covered her face with kisses to keep her from complaining. 'Oh, little Amy, how I love you,' he would croon.

So Amy would tell herself, 'I have nothing to grumble about – he's my man .'

Chapter Nine

Visiting

Amy was expecting her baby any day now and every morning she popped in to see her mother. Amy was a little bit afraid of the pregnancy, a new thing happening to her, and did not like being alone during these last days. It suited Annie who liked having an audience and in her usual tone was chatting about something she had recently heard out on the green.

'This woman I met was so posh, "Anyone heard about what happened to Mother Rain?" she asked us. "Wot?" says I.'

"I am doing research for a magazine" she says, "it's on freaks. I heard Mother Rain was quite an unusual person."

"Oh, yes," says I, "pigs' trotters she 'ad for 'ands – seen 'em meself in the chip shop. Used ter put 'er change in a kind of little pocket in 'er paw."

"How interesting," says she.

"Well,' says I, "that ain't all – 'orses 'ooves she 'ad, and all the kids would chase 'er to lift 'er skirt 'cos it was rumoured she 'ad a long tail. And as gawd's my judge, she was ever so old. Why, me muvver said she was around in 'er days but she disappeared in the blitz, she did." She wrote it all down, this posh woman did, so I says, "It used to be said that it was 'cos 'er muvver 'ad a lot of men." And d'yer know wot? She larfed and said, "It don't sound like men with the pigs' trotters and a donkey's tail." Now, wot d'yer fink of that? "Well," says I, "we know abaht 'er – us folks in 'oxton – she lived 'ere wiff us." '

Amy's child was kicking lustily in her belly and suddenly it seemed to turn in the womb. 'Oh, for God's sake, Mother,' she snapped, 'be quiet, keep your horror stories to yourself.'

'Miserable cow,' grumbled Annie, lighting another Woodbine.

Then Sheila dashed to the door as Sparky came rolling over the green. To see Sparky was the heyday of poor Sheila's life. Amy's husband staggered in with a small dog tucked in his pullover. Holding it up by the scruff of its neck, he laughed, 'Look at this scruffy old mop I got for yer, Sheila, darlin', it's called Bridget.'

Sheila squealed with delight and took the terrified little dog into her arms.

Amy stared at Sparky in astonishment. There was lipstick on his face and on the collar of his shirt. The stench of whisky hit her as he collapsed heavily into the armchair.

'What you doin' 'ere, Amy?' he asked. 'Thought you'd gone to bed.'

Sheila was fondling the dog and pouring it a saucer of milk.

'Why do you call it Bridget?' Amy asked dryly. 'That can't really be its name because it's a male.' Her tone was acid for she knew that the barmaid who worked in the pub Sparky frequented in Bethnal Green was called Bridget.

'Yer all right, darlin'?' Sparky asked, looking at the worried expression on her face.

'Of course I am all right,' Amy snapped. 'And if you are fit enough to walk, I'd like to go home, if you don't mind.'

Sparky was concerned even in his drunkenness. He wanted to cuddle her as they walked to their flat but when he tried she pushed him away. Never before had she disliked her Sparky, but tonight she hated him.

Early the next morning she was in labour in the maternity wing of the local hospital. At midday she gave birth to a big bonny girl. She knew that Sparky would be disappointed but she didn't care. Still angry with him, she actually felt glad, that in some way she had got her own back on him.

But when Sparky arrived at the hospital that afternoon all neat, clean and perfectly sober, he looked delighted. He kissed the baby gently and affectionately and said, 'We got a lovely gel, Amy, isn't she pretty? Wot we gonna call 'er?'

Amy's anger disappeared at the sight of Sparky as the proud father. 'You choose,' she said, feeling supreme happiness once more inside her.

'How would you like Rachel?' he asked. 'It was me muvver's name.'

'It's all right,' said Amy, 'but I thought it was a Yiddish name.'

'Not on yer nelly,' he laughed. 'Me muvver were Welsh and real chapel,' he added defensively.

That was the first time she had ever heard him talk of his own family, and they sat holding hands till visiting time was over.

'You're not disappointed because it's a girl?' she asked timidly.

'Nah!' scoffed Sparky in his Cockney manner, 'we still got plenty of time to make a bleedin' football team.'

Amy smiled. There was no one like her man. Sparky was so happy-go-lucky and full of generosity and warmth. So what if he went off the rails occasionally? What man did not?

Now Amy was a young mother and settled down into a regular pattern of life. Every day she would take the baby for a walk in her pram and wheel it around to Annie's. Annie still sat on the seat outside on the little square of grass each day, always on the look-out for someone she used to know and with whom she could gossip.

Sparky had gone back to sea and, left alone, life, Amy thought, was pretty dull. The baby had to be fed on time, and the nappies washed. It was all very monotonous.

One day when Rachel was three months old, Amy had a long letter from her brother Siddy and a visitor's card to go down to see him in the open prison on the Isle of Wight where he now was.

Sparky happened to be at home when this letter came, and he was very insistent that she go and see Siddy before he had gone back to sea. 'Go and visit the poor sod,' he said. 'I know how lonely yer can get for the sight of yer own folk. Go and visit the poor sod.'

Amy liked the idea but didn't know if she could go. 'But what about Rachel?'

'She will be all right for one day with Annie and Sheila,' Sparky reassured her.

Rather nervous about the whole project, Amy went to visit Siddy after Sparky had gone back to sea. It was the first time she had left her baby but prayed that Rachel would be all right. She had given strict instructions to Sheila about bottles and nappies.

'Can't tell me anyfink abaht babies,' jeered Annie, 'had firteen, I did.'

Amy knew that her mother would nurse Rachel on her lap most of the day and that by the time she came back the baby would be thoroughly spoiled and crying for attention all the time. But there was nothing else to be done, so Amy accepted it. So, wearing the nice blue suit she had worn for her wedding (and which Siddy had got her), Amy went on the tube to Waterloo Station. She already had a ticket and a special concession, which put her right away with several other young women standing at the barrier waiting for it to open. Some had small children with them and tense expressions on their faces. Amy noticed that they naturally split up into little groups; some were smartly dressed while others were ragged and poor. But they all got in the same end of the train.

'Going to the Island?' asked one shabby woman with two small children.

'Yes,' replied Amy.

'Get used to it. I've gone it for two years now. He gets parole soon, and I'm not sorry it's over.'

Amy was amazed at the woman's ability to talk about her husband's situation so freely. To her it was a quite disgraceful thing to happen to one.

'Who you got in there? Your husband?' the woman asked her.

'No, my brother,' replied Amy. 'And this is the first time I ever did this.'

'I've never missed a visit and all my husband does is give me the third degree when I get there. He even pumps the kids to find out if I've been going out and leaving them.'

'Oh dear,' sighed Amy but not too sympathetically. She would never put up with that sort of life, she thought to herself, feeling rather superior.

Just as the train started to pull out of the station, along the corridor came a lively old lady who was obviously well known. Small and sturdy with nicely set iron-grey hair, she wore a black coat and dress and was adorned with several long gold chains from which a locket and a Star of David hung. She looks rather prosperous, Amy thought, watching her with interest.

'Hullo, Dolly,' everyone smiled and greeted the old lady as she went along the compartment.

'Hullo, ducks,' she replied in a lively tone. 'Another month gone round, then.' She moved on down the train stopping to gossip here and there until she reached the very smartly dressed bunch who sat together. 'Just going down to get a drink at the bar,' she told them. 'Coming, gels?'

The women all got up laughing and went with Dolly on down the corridor to the bar. That was the last Amy saw of them on the train.

Once on the ferry from Southampton, Amy avoided the

shabby woman because her kids were playing up and their noise gave her a headache, so once the ferry docked on the Isle of Wight, she was not sure where to go to next. She stood amongst a crowd of other travellers, some with suitcases, buckets and spades and a line of kids all going on their holidays. But in what direction did one go for the big prison way out on the island? Just as she stood there, a taxi went past with those four smart women in it. Another taxi followed and it slowed down as a voice called out: 'Waiting for a cab, love? Ger in here. We're going in the same way.' It was the old lady who had been so popular on the train.

'Which one you going to?' she asked as Amy got in the taxi.

When Amy told her, she grinned a crooked grin. 'Oh that's the open nick, I'm going to Parkhurst, so you'll be getting out before me.'

'Oh, there's more than one, is there?' Amy commented, trying to be sociable.

'Yes, love, three all told. Some worse than others. This must be the first time you came.'

Amy nodded.

'Me, I been doing this a long time now,' Dolly chatted cheerfully. 'Got three boys and there's always one of them in bloody trouble. Still, never mind, good boys to me, they are, and while I'm able I won't neglect them. Two of 'em are twins and they usually get nicked together, but this time only Morry is inside. He was always a bit highly strung – got a bad temper, and that's what gets him in trouble.'

Amy listened with interest, thinking that there was a lot of Annie in this old gel. They were similar in many ways except that Dolly was so lively and active and did not seem to mind that her boys got in trouble. That certainly wasn't the case with Annie and Siddy.

'Who you going to see? Don't I know you?' Dolly peered at Amy.

'Don't think so,' said Amy. 'I was evacuated all the war, but now I live in Shoreditch. It's my brother Siddy I'm visiting.'

'Not Siddy Flanagan?' Dolly cried. 'Side-kick of old Jack Goldman? Well, fancy that.'

Amy blushed. She was not sure she wanted to be associated with all this criminal activity. 'Yes,' she said quietly.

But the old lady jawed away, 'Used to be a mate of my eldest son, Reggie.'

'Did he,' said Amy, rather haughtily.

But the old lady did not bat an eyelid. Out of her coat pocket she pulled a packet of peppermints. 'Have one,' she said holding them out to her. 'I like to have a peppermint before I go in. I don't let them know I've had a drink with the gels. You get used to it you see, love. I've been up and down the country visiting all the nicks, I have. I like to make it me day out. You see them nice smart women I had a drink with on the train, did yer? Well, they'll be old ladies by the time their men get out. Come from around your way, they do. Twenty years some of them got. What do you think about that?' She sat back in her seat, sucking a mint and rolling it around her tongue.

Amy did not reply; she felt a little sick.

'Here you are, that's your stop, good luck, cock,' called Dolly as Amy climbed out. 'See you again.'

Amy found herself outside a pair of massive iron gates. A uniformed policeman stared coldly at her as she produced her pass. After checking it, he allowed her to go in through the gates into a large courtyard. Along the path, young lads idled about with brooms in their hands and others sat outside huts in the sunshine. It seemed to Amy that there were whole armies of them, just sitting their lives away. What a depressing sight.

Siddy was in the visiting room. With an exclamation of delight, Amy went towards him, her arms outstretched, to greet him, but he waved her off. 'Hullo, darlin',' he smiled. 'Yer mustn't touch me in case old Bill sees yer. Sit down and let's have a good long chat.'

Amy looked him over. He seemed very well and healthy. He was clean and had a short haircut which suited his long lean jaw, and he wore washed-out blue overalls.

'If you brought me anything don't give it to me yet,' he whispered. 'I'll tell you when.'

'I got some fags,' she said.

'Good,' said Siddy with that devil-may-care grin. 'Seen Sadie?'

'Occasionally,' replied Amy. 'And someone said her father had gone away somewhere.'

'Done a runner, eh? Got the wind up,' said Siddy. 'Never

267

mind, time's passing fairly quickly and I got a few pals in here. How's Sparky and the baby?'

So they talked about the family and agreed that it was better not to let Annie know too much about anything. Or big brother Joe, who could be hard on a loser.

The journey back to London was uneventful. From the prison Amy found herself a cab easily enough and at Southampton got into another part of the train, away from the smart gels who meandered back and forth to the bar chatting in loud voices as if they never had a care in the world.

Amy was very glad to get home. It had been a long day and a tiring journey. She was just glad to have had the chance to talk to poor Siddy even for only an hour, and the lively fast talk of old Dolly stayed in her mind.

The baby was sound asleep, well tucked up in her pram by Sheila. As usual, Annie was dozing, but she woke up soon enough. 'You look done in,' she said as Amy sat in the chair. 'Fancy going all that way and spending money to see that crooked sod. I wouldn't cross the road to see him, I wouldn't.'

'Oh,' sighed Amy, 'you don't change much, do you, Mother?' Collecting her baby, she wheeled her home across the dark green. She tucked Rachel into her cot and climbed into her own bed clutching Sparky's photograph. 'Oh, I do wish you would stay at home with me all the time,' she whispered as she kissed it.

On Sparky's next leave, he was full of beans and ready to make love as usual. But Amy pushed him away. 'No,' she said, 'it's too soon, the baby is only twelve weeks old.'

But Sparky said, 'Amy, my love, me mates tell me it don't matter. Some women starts another one at three months.'

'Well, not me!' said Amy. 'I'm certainly not going to lumber myself up with a lot of kids like my mother did.'

'Well, you please yerself,' said Sparky slightly annoyed. Without another word, he got dressed and went out visiting his mates.

Amy sat down on the bed and cried her eyes out. What was she going to do? It obviously wasn't a good idea to hold out on him like that. He was too popular with the birds and she could lose him if she was not careful. Thinking carefully, she decided to change her tactics.

'Let's prevent me having another baby for a while,' she said to him later. 'If you want to save up to go to Canada, it will be better. And I might get a job later on and let Annie and Sheila mind Rachel for a few hours a day.'

Sparky was quite happy with this suggestion, so they made up and spent a happy week together. They left the baby with Annie and even went out to the theatre up west. The play bored Sparky stiff but Amy was thrilled at the star performances.

'We ought to do that more often, Sparky,' she said afterwards.

'Not if I knows it,' retorted Sparky grumpily. 'I was so dry, couldn't 'ave spit a tanner.'

'Well, they had a bar, didn't they?'

'I had to fight my way through all them toffee-nosed sods to get a rotten warm 'alf of bitter,' he grumbled.

It was just not his scene, and Amy had to face that. But apart from such incidents they were a fairly happy couple. He loved small Rachel and whenever he was home he would wheel her out in the pram and would stand talking to the neighbours for hours. He still had many friends who were always pleased to see him. Amy never sought after that kind of social hospitality, and had few friends. Her closest confidantes were Sheila and Annie, and she seldom stood gossiping. She always carried herself proudly and walked very sedately, when she walked, nicely dressed, down the market.

'That's Siddy Flanagan's sister,' the Cockney traders would comment. 'Fancies 'erself, don't she?' Married to that young Sparky and he's a bit often away, they tells me.'

Had Amy come down to earth it might not have been such a big shock to her when Sparky fell in through the front door at two o'clock one morning beaten to a pulp, with a big gash in his head and his arm broken.

Worried sick, Amy put a towel around his head and gave him water.

'I'll be all right, love,' he said. 'I was just in a bit of a car crash.'

Amy ran to the doctor's surgery and dragged the reluctant doctor out of bed to attend to Sparky, whom he sent off to the hospital immdiately to get his head stitched and his arm set.

And so began six weeks of nursing Spark back to health. The accident made him miss his ship and he was not likely to be able to sign on for quite a while, so they had to live on his sick pay. Amy was struck by how very vague Sparky was about his accident.

'Who was driving the car?' she asked.

'One of me mates,' replied Sparky evasively.

'Did he get hurt too?' she asked. 'Whose car was it?'

Each time she asked questions he told her a different version of the affair until, very frustrated, Amy finally said to Annie one day: 'Here we are practically broke and Sparky has been injured. I'm sure he could get some compensation because of the accident.'

'Don't be such a silly cow,' scoffed Annie. 'The boys done him up.'

Amy stared at her in amazement. 'What boys?' she demanded.

'Don't ask me,' returned Annie, looking away. 'We don't mention names dahn 'ere but I was told by someone on the green that 'e got a bit cocky in one of their low-down clubs, so they set abaht 'im.'

Slowly but surely her mother's words sank in and a harsh light revealed a sordid aspect of her life that she had always ignored. With her head in the clouds always looking upwards, she had had illusions about her life. She would constantly think about Miriam's home with the antiques and beautiful furniture, the big brick fireplace, and the lines of books. At times she had dreamed that they would live in a place like that too, and that Rachel would even have a little pony when she got older. But now all those illusions were shattered. Her dreams came crashing down like a house made of cards. The problem, she decided, was the area. Sparky wouldn't hang out with the wrong types if they lived somewhere else. They had to get out of this gutter, that was the next thing to do. But how?

First she decided to tackle Sparky's drinking, and she started by refusing to give him money to go out with his mates. Sparky grumbled about this a lot but Amy was not going to listen.

'Listen,' she said, 'if it wasn't for your drinking habits, you wouldn't have got into a bother with those villains in the first place. It's time to stop.'

'Well, you know what it's like when a fella's away from home,' whined Sparky. 'It's the life at sea – all booze. And so when yer get ashore yer can't help yerself.'

'Right then,' said Amy with determination, 'don't go back to sea. You must try to get a job. I've decided that I'm definitely going back to work to save up money, too, and I definitely don't want no more kids for a few years yet. I'll not let you pull me down into the gutter, there's too much of that going on around here anyway.'

Sparky knew there was no point in putting up any resistance when she was in such a mood. 'Okay,' he said, 'don't argue. We'll do what's best. I'm nearly finished with the therapy at the hospital, so I'll find something to do. In the meantime I'll help Annie and Sheila mind Rachel, if that will please you.'

So Amy went back to work in a big store in the city. It was an old-fashioned sort of shop which dealt a lot on credit, but the wages were good and Amy did not have far to travel.

Sparky was still having trouble moving his arm so he had to go to the hospital for physiotherapy every day. He would wheel Rachel round to Annie's before he went for his hospital treatment and Sheila took over watching and playing with the baby while Annie sat outside in the afternoon amusing herself and her cronies with that neverending 'good old days' gossip. Then in the early evening Sparky would go to the pub to have a drink, but only one half. 'It's all I can afford,' he would say, 'but I like to see me mates.'

Amy worked eight hours a day. She had always been a little solemn but now, as she entered her twenties, her face had assumed a rather hard expression. She seldom relaxed and had little time for anyone but Rachel. She even became quite impatient with Sparky and often cross-questioned him on how he had spent his day. She loved him but the pressures on them were so great and he still had done nothing about getting a job himself.

Sparky was usually quite tolerant of her questioning, but one day he completely lost his temper. 'Wot the 'ell is this, the effin Gestapo?' he yelled at her.

'No need for that kind of language,' Amy replied haughtily.

Even though they had very little of it, Amy was very careful with her money and would not waste a penny of it. That way they managed to get through the bad winter. And at last Sparky got a job. It was only a weekend job in car sales near where he used to live. 'One of me mates,' he told her, 'is gonna give me cash in 'and, no questions asked, it will be a help.'

Amy agreed and accepted the idea of spending Saturdays and Sundays alone if it meant bringing in money and adding to their savings. Gradually her dreams came back again and the motivating force in her mind was a picture of that nice house in the country. One day they would have it. . . .

Sparky was earning a bit now and seemed to bring home quite a lot of presents for Amy and Rachel. There'd be a short fur coat or some nice glassware, which someone, he'd say, was selling cheap. Amy remained blissfully naive of the details and divorced herself from East End life. She did not visit Siddy again but she did know that on his release from prison Sadie had been outside to meet him and that together they had fled to somewhere up north.

Late one evening, as Amy and Sparky ate their tea, they heard the tramp of heavy feet on the steps outside the front door. Suddenly there was a heavy thump and some policemen rushed in and grabbed hold of Sparky.

Amy was stunned. It was like a nightmare. Through a blur, she watched Sparky struggle and protest but the police stood firm and announced, 'You are under arrest.' The words were still ringing in her ears as they carted Sparky off to the police station.

Amy took her baby and ran over to Annie who, for once, was kind and sympathetic. 'The bastards,' she said, 'he ain't done nuffink. Someone's set 'im up, they 'ave. That's 'ow it is around 'ere, they can't bear to see yer gettin' on, they can't,' and she wept with Amy who was too scared to go home.

In the morning one of Sparky's dodgy mates came looking for Amy. 'Got a message from Sparky,' he said, 'you're not to worry, and that he never did anything. Old Bill are holding him for a few days, 'cos they are after the real villains, that's what.'

'But what's it all about?' asked an agonized Amy.

'Well, it's a big showdown at the garage, there's been some dodgy insurances, and buying of hot cars. It's nothing to do with Sparky, it's the guys who run it.'

'Well, then, why doesn't he tell them?' demanded Amy in bewilderment.

'It don't work like that, missus,' Sparky's mate tried to explain. 'It's just that it's a big deal and the old Bill will hold him to get the big guys. He's coming up in court in the morning. He said you're not to go 'cos he don't want you involved.'

'Oh dear,' she wailed. 'What can I do?'

'Nothing. They will acquit him. Old Bill knows Sparky's just a mug; they don't miss a trick.'

'But who are those criminals?' cried Amy. This conversation was above her head.

'Well, missus, don't ask me, and if I was you, I'd stay out of it.

Sparky will be home, you can count on it. It's his first time in trouble so they can't hold him long.' With that, he put on his checked cap and went on his way.

Alone in her flat Amy sat weeping, and was just too miserable to even think about going to work. She sat there feeling as if she had not a friend in the world. Where were all her brothers, Siddy, Billy and Joe? No one wanted to know.

Annie, however, came up trumps. She was so kind and thoughtful. Somehow she understood Amy's heartbreak. Amy who had always thought of her mother as a very cold unsympathetic woman, could hardly believe how kind she was being, making Sheila go and get the meals, helping to cook and being very maternal. 'Don't go home, Amy,' she said, 'stay 'ere wiff us.'

Amy leaned on her and wallowed in the comfort she offered. They spent many happy hours chatting out on the green. 'You're better off staying wiff me,' Annie said. 'Yer never knows how them bleedin' crooks will turn, yer can never trust 'em. Mind you, they won't get past me,' she added with belligerent pride.

'Depends if Sparky grasses,' said the gossipers.

'No, he won't do that, he's a very fine, principled boy, my son-in-law,' said Annie with pride.

In fact, Sparky was held for three months. The police knocked him about a bit in an effort to make him talk but there was no evidence of him being in any way a party to this insurance fraud, so they eventually acquitted him. Sadly, Sparky came home a very bitter disillusioned lad with a seething hatred of coppers that would never leave him.

During those three months that Sparky was on remand, Amy's savings had dwindled to almost nothing. On his return, Sparky got a loan from a mate of his and bought an old lorry. He began to do some freelance transport and started making a fair living. Amy stopped work and stayed at home. She and Sparky grew very close again and she began her second baby. Sparky was delighted. 'Maybe I'll get a son this time, I can't keep on being so unlucky.'

But the stars were not in his favour. Amy had another girl. Sparky welcomed the baby but Amy knew that his heart had been set on having a son. Life settled down again; they were all together and getting by. For the time being Amy knew that she

273

had to accept that this was to be her existence and so she might as well get used to it. Besides, the council flat and the two babies took up most of her energy and she had little time for dreaming nowadays.

Poor Annie was getting old. Her health was deteriorating and her legs getting worse. One day Sparky brought home a wheelchair for her and after that Sheila was often to be seen pushing Annie along with Sheila's little dog sitting in Annie's lap yapping at everyone who passed.

Amy was most pleased about the change in Sparky. He was no longer irresponsible. He seldom went out drinking but was a good family man and worked hard to build up a good business.

'I'll own a fleet of lorries before I am finished, love,' he would tell his delighted wife. And Amy was very proud of him.

Chapter Ten

No Escape

By 1956 the East End of London had changed radically. Big rebuilding programmes had injected new life to this run-down, badly blitzed area bringing shops, supermarkets and high-rise flats for a new generation, instead of the slums that had been there before.

Amy's life went on just the same, though they lived more comfortably with a better flat and nicer furniture. It was still not too far from Annie and Sheila so that Amy could pop over each day to help Sheila get Annie out of bed and onto her seat on the green. Annie's limbs continued to stiffen and it was difficult for her to move about, but mentally she was fine. She was always ready to chat about this and that, and once she started on the good old days it was a job to stop her. With snow-white hair and a blue woollen cardigan, she was a well-known sight on that green in Shoreditch. Every day it seemed that more and more people she knew returned home to their grass roots after the war and its aftermath, like migrating birds, to the old haunts of their youth. Annie was always delighted about this and would say excitedly, 'Guess who I 'ave just met, Mrs So and So, you know, 'er daughter married that fella', you know who, 'er 'usband got killed in the war . . .'

Amy would pretend to listen but her mother's chatter would go in one ear and out the other. While Sheila pranced around and played ball with her dog Ben, Amy would sit back and let herself be flooded with her old dreams of living in a great big house in the country with a log fire.

Sparky's transport business had done well. From a small company it had gone slowly from strength to strength, expanding until it was a large international concern. It was quite an achievement, particularly in such a short time, and he was proud of it.

He gave Amy good money and took her and the children to the seaside once a year, but otherwise he had little time for them, always staying at the office late in the evenings to catch up with the growing paperwork. He now had a lot of lorries and other drivers working for him. He worked very hard but some of his old habits remained. He still liked, for example, a Sunday morning drink with his pals and would go to the pub off Brick Lane to meet them, leaving Amy, as always, alone to cope with the kids.

Amy's feelings about Sparky were confused. She did love him and she was delighted by the way in which he had struggled out of the gutter and become a man of substance, but there was always a remoteness about him, a barrier, she could never break through. But he was so good to Annie and Sheila, and was an excellent father to his daughters, and materially a good husband. She felt that she should count her blessings; she could do no better. Certainly from the outside they were doing well, and Sparky was always keen to show Amy off as his wife. Whenever they went to one of the many flash parties given in the neighbourhood, he insisted that she be the best dressed woman there and wear all the jewellery he had bought her.

But whenever Amy mentioned the idea of a little house in the country, Sparky would say: 'One day, Amy, I'll quit and we'll go off to Canada, I promise. Just be patient, darlin'.'

'I don't care if I never go to Canada but I'd like to bring the girls up in a nice area,' Amy would say timidly.

'What the bleedin' 'ell is wrong wiff the East End?' Sparky shouted one day when she said this. 'Why all the brains and the money is down 'ere and I'll get my share of it if it kills me.'

And Amy would retire back into the shell she had built up around herself, knowing that it was hopeless to argue.

That year a pale, washed-out and very dejected looking Siddy returned home. Amy bumped into him on a Sunday morning in Petticoat Lane, where he was selling very unreal-looking gold watches from a suitcase.

'Oh, Siddy,' she cried, 'why didn't you let us know you were back?'

'Wasn't sure you would be interested,' shrugged Siddy despondently. 'Not now that Sparky's Jack the lad.'

'What do you mean by that?' Amy demanded defensively. 'Sparky's worked hard and got a good business going. Don't begrudge him that.'

'Sorry, sis,' replied Siddy, looking sorry and humble.

'Well, from now on you come to Sunday dinner with us.'

276

decided Amy. 'I suppose you're in lodgings.'

'Yes,' said Siddy, closing the suitcase with a bang. 'Now I gotta move – old Bill's coming along. See you Sunday next week.'

'Three o'clock is dinner,' said Amy, giving his hand a little squeeze as he dodged off.

'Poor Siddy,' she said later to Sparky, when she told him she had seen her brother. 'He looked right down on his luck.'

Sparky glanced at her, and she was disturbed to see that his eyes had a hard, unfeeling look about them. 'Okay, so what did he want?' he asked.

'Oh, Sparky!' cried Amy. 'You're getting real mean and very hard. Poor Siddy. Well, he's coming to Sunday dinner next week and he don't want anything from you. He's just coming to see his own family, that's all.'

Sparky noticeably relaxed and then smiled charmingly. 'All right, darling,' he said with a sigh. 'Do as you wish.'

The following Sunday, Amy cooked roast beef, baked spuds and batter pudding, and Sparky brought in bottles of beer. Siddy arrived looking very thin. He huddled pathetically by the big fire.

'Oh, Amy, there is no place like home,' he said. 'And you sure got it set up nice here.' He looked around the flat appreciatively.

Sparky quietly poured out the beer but made no comment. To his mind, Siddy was a lame duck. Amy loved lame ducks but Sparky had no time for them.

'Sadie ditched me,' said Siddy as he scoffed his dinner. 'Wasn't her fault – her old father put the arm on her.'

'If she had really loved you, she would have stayed with you,' said Amy.

'I don't blame her,' replied Siddy defensively, 'after all, Jack's got an inn out in the country, so they tells me, and now Sadie and her old man run it. Jack lives with them now that he's retired. He got me duffed up and dumped in an alley down the Lane, he did,' he added bitterly.

'Rotten old devil,' said Amy.

Later, when Siddy had left, she confronted her husband. 'Now, Sparky, you got to help Siddy. You give him a job or I'll know the reason why,' she said.

Sparky's lip set with grim humour. 'Thought you said he was to stop out of trouble, not to buy it,' he said.

Amy stared at him. 'Oh, don't be funny,' she said. 'You see to him or I'll be very annoyed.'

So Siddy got a day job in Sparky's yard. Sparky had not been at all keen to employ him, but he knew that it would make Amy very happy, so he was prepared to take him on.

Thus, in that typical Flanagan way Amy looked after her brother Siddy. He found himself new lodgings but spent most mealtimes in Amy's flat.

Annie was most incensed to learn about this. 'Bloody mad, you must be, takin' that Siddy in. Sparky don't really want 'im in the yard, he's bloody trouble, that Siddy, like some bleedin' Jonah, he is.'

'Oh, what are you talking about, Mother? snapped Amy impatiently. 'Siddy has had a bad deal and you certainly haven't helped him by your attitude.'

'Don't say I didn't warn yer,' cried Annie, as aggressive as ever.

Sparky's business continued to grow. Siddy turned out to be very useful about the place and he certainly knew how to keep a still tongue in his head. So, after that difficult start, he and Sparky got on quite well together.

A big racket was going on in dockside London at that time and the lorry owners were all involved. The Big Boys, as the crooked element were known, still ran the vice and crime of East London and all had their little men working for them in their small clubs and pubs where many of the rackets went on. This latest racket was that of hijacking lorry loads so that the owners could put in false claims to the insurance company, and get compensation. The gangsters would then call for their slice of the cake, having dispersed the booty via the well-concealed channels run by the old war-time black marketeers.

This sort of thing went on all the time but as far as the rest of the residents of the East End were concerned, what went on in gansterland was not their business. The art of living down there was keeping your nose clean.

That Christmas Annie's twins arrived home from the army. It was their last leave before they were to be demobbed. They had volunteered to join the Hong Kong police, so it was hallo and goodbye. Annie welcomed them warmly. They stayed at her flat and slept on the floor in sleeping bags. Amy cooked for them and gave them a big party on Saturday night. The twins regaled them all with juicy indecencies about their lives in the army. They told one story about how they had both courted the same girl and when she got pregnant she did not know whom to blame when she came up to identify the man. 'Thought she was seeing double,' they guffawed.

Amy did not think this very funny, at all, nor the other stories of their escapades out East, 'keeping the wogs in order' as they put it. She thought it all a bit distasteful but did, nevertheless, put on a good party for them. Halfway through the evening, the twins went down to the pub to get extra beer, and in no time at all, a big fight had started which went on until after midnight when the police finally arrived and arrested the twins, who had actually started it.

Amy had to take her rent book down to the police station at Old Street to bail her brothers out. Sparky had missed the whole event, having had to go out, supposedly to pick up a lorry which had broken down. 'Who was they fightin' with?' he asked Amy when she told what had happened.

'It was those terrible Palmer twins that everyone is so afraid of.'

Sparky's jaw dropped. 'Oh no!' he exclaimed. 'A lot of bloody good the twins 'ave done me.'

'I don't know what you are talking about,' snapped Amy, 'and anyway, they are on their way back to camp now.'

'And, I hope they bloody stay there,' snarled Sprky.

'Oh, Sparky,' wailed Amy, 'why are you like that with my family? I sometimes think that you are jealous because you haven't got a nice big family of your own.'

She had touched a nerve. Sadly, Sparky picked up his little daughter Annie, and kissed her. She was known to him as Tosh. She had bright red hair and was very sturdy and very much a favourite with her dad.

'Who said I ain't got a family?' he said. 'Let's have another baby. Amy. Might get a boy this time.'

'No, thanks,' replied Amy. 'Not till we move out of this rotten slummy street.'

Later that year Sparky suddenly said to her. 'Written to Letty lately?'

'Well, I do owe her a letter but now with Rachel going to

nursery school and me helping out at Mum's every day I don't seem to get a lot of time.'

Those hard bright eyes stared at her across the table. 'I didn't ask for a long comment about the family,' he said harshly. 'Write to Letty and tell her we are coming out for a holiday. Ask if she can put us up.'

'Oh, Sparky, oh, that's great!' cried Amy excitedly.

'Well, I am not too sure yet, but keep it under yer 'at. I don't want anyone else to know about it – not Siddy nor Annie, no one. You understand that, don't yer, Amy?'

'Oh yes!' she said, but she didn't. Why all this secrecy about a holiday abroad? But she kept her promise to him. All that spring he was often bad tempered and quite often drunk at the weekends. Amy felt sure that he had more on his mind than he was prepared to share. She wrote to Letty, who replied immediately to say that she was delighted and that they could stay with her whenever they wanted.

Now they did have a date. 'July, but stay stumm,' Sparky told Amy. 'I'll see to the tickets and everything. You just collect up your and the kids' gear.'

Of late Sparky had been very close with one of his drivers, a big, loud-mouthed fellow called Tom Evans. Amy could not abide him. They had been at a party one weekend and Tom Evans was there with an extremely young blonde. She could not have been more than sixteen. Amy remembered this girl being born to a family who lived down their street. Her parents had moved the family out of London soon after the blitz started. So to see this lovely child, who everyone called Bubbles because of her blonde curls and her sweet dolly face, was quite a shock to Amy. 'What's he doing with her?' she muttered to Sparky in a low voice. 'Why, his daughters are older than her.'

Sparky said, 'That's Tom's business, he's left his wife, packed in with her, so I've been told, so keep yer mouth shut, and don't let him hear you talking like that. Bubbles is no angel. She ain't nothing like she looks, I can assure yer.'

Amy was quite disgusted by the sight of this little blonde girl, who still lisped like a child, cavorting about the room swinging her hips and wobbling her breasts while the tough-looking Tom Evans drooled over her. At one point, when Bubbles lay back in her chair with her legs spread wide showing her thighs, Amy felt

280

she had seen enough. 'Pull your clothes down, love, all the men are getting a good view,' she said tartly.

Bubbles sat up and stared insolently at her, 'You mind your own bloody business. People like you ain't got much to show.'

As Amy retired to the kitchen in a fury she could hear Bubbles' silly immature voice ringing across the room, 'Who's she then? Old bent nose – some sort of prize-fighter?'

Amy instantly demanded to be taken home. If there was one thing that upset her it was any reference to the bend in her nose. 'I'll give her prize-fighter,' she raged at Sparky. 'She can have a bunch of fives from me any day, saucy little cow,' she said when they got home.

'Don't go on so, Amy,' said Sparky. 'The kids that are coming up now are different in more ways than one to us.'

'You're not kidding,' declared Amy, 'and that old Tom Evans ought to be shot for carrying on with her.'

Sparky grinned. 'Someone might do that yet.'

'Oh,' said Amy impatiently. 'I'm not coming to any more of your bloody flash parties.'

'You won't have to,' said Sparky. 'Get them glad rags in a case. We're off to Canada next week.'

Amy packed excitedly and sent a wire to Letty. At the weekend, Sparky brought home a big pile of account books from work and burned them one by one on the kitchen fire.

'What are you doing?' asked Amy in bewilderment.

'I'm getting out,' said Sparky. 'In fact, I've already sold out. Don't ask me too much, but Tommy Evans is taking the business over. Siddy still has a job, so don't worry,' he added hastily.

'Mean to say that after all those years of hard work you sold out to that rotten Tommy Evans?' Amy could hardly believe what she had heard.

But Sparky came and cuddled her close. Tears came to her fine eyes. 'Don't bother your pretty head, darlin',' he cajoled. 'Come, let's get the kids together. We're off tomorrow – I've got the plane tickets.'

'But what about Annie and Sheila?' cried Amy. 'And how long are we going for?'

Sparky sighed. 'For once in your life, Amy, think of me. I've been saddled with your bloody family too long. Now I'm getting out.'

'But, it's only a holiday, isn't it, Sparky?' she asked anxiously.

'Yes, if you like,' he mumbled and started to empty the whisky decanter into a glass.

Annie was very annoyed to discover that Amy was planning to disappear for a while, and even more annoyed that she couldn't say how long she was going for.

But Amy herself was not at all sure what was happening to her. She gave Sheila some of her dresses and make-up and told her to take care of Annie.

It was all a big rush. The next minute Sparky arrived in the car outside and tooted his horn for Amy. 'Ain't he coming in to say goodbye?' cried Annie in despair.

'Mum, the kids are asleep in the back and Sparky's asked you not to talk and not to say where he's gone.'

'Oh,' Annie's big mouth drooped down at the corners. 'Trouble, eh!'

'Oh, no, Mum,' said Amy impatiently, but she leaned down and gave her a sudden big hug before running out to join Sparky.

They drove to Heathrow Airport and boarded the plane for Canada. Still Amy was not sure if she was doing the right thing. It was very unpleasant, that journey, a long flight on the crowded plane. The kids were very restless and Amy, who had never flown, was extremely nervous. Sparky drank steadily all the way over and said very little. He just kept checking his watch all the time. It was very long and tedious.

Fortunately, Letty was at the airport to meet them. Amy had not seen her sister since she had left Ashmullen for the WAAF's but Letty had grown into a very lovely mature woman. Her husband, Frank, was a tall, healthy looking man who was a schoolmaster. Right away, he got along with the little girls. Tears of happiness were shed as they drove out to Letty's suburban home outside the town. It was a very smartly furnished house high up on a hill surrounded by tall pines. In the distance they could see a big lake.

'It's just like Ashmullen,' said Amy.

'Yes, that's why I'm so happy here,' said Letty. 'But, how fortunate you are, Amy, to have such lovely children. I don't take after mother – so far there's no sign of a child.'

After a few days with Letty and Frank, the family all settled down. Sparky cheered up and was more of his old charming self.

They went out on picnics and life was one round of exciting things happening.

The months flew by, and Amy began to get a little concerned. 'I wonder if Sparky has booked our return flight,' she said to Letty one day. 'We can't abuse your hospitality for ever.'

But Letty's eyes darkened with sadness. 'Oh, Amy, don't you know? He's staying on. He's asked Frank to help him find an apartment and he is going to apply for a work permit. I thought this was all agreed between you.'

'Oh, my God, what a dirty trick to play on me!' Amy cried.

'Well, it seems he has his reasons,' said Letty very quietly.

'Well, he had better bloody tell me them,' said Amy in a fury.

Sparky made no excuses and did not deny that he had intended to stay from the beginning. 'I shall see if it's possible,' he told her.

'But, my God! Why didn't you say so? Poor Mum and Sheila, and what about Siddy?'

'Here we go,' declared Sparky rolling his eyes. 'But just you take a look at this.' He pulled from his pocket an evening paper and there, spread across the front page, was a big story from London of how the police had smashed a racket in the East End and arrested two Palmer brothers for a whole catalogue of crimes, including murder. The big racket concerning the hijacking of lorries had been exposed. There were pictures of Sparky's old yard and poor Siddy, looking very depressed, standing in the entrance. 'Quite a few arrests have been made,' Amy read in disbelief, 'and the police were still looking for important witnesses.'

'What is it all about?' she stared at Sparky in bewilderment.

'You wouldn't understand,' he said, 'but they had the arm on me for years.' He smirked. 'Now I've left them all holding the baby.' With a grim smile, he folded the paper and put it back in his pocket. 'So, Amy, you understand that we stay here, like it or lump it, my love.'

Amy sank down into a chair. 'Oh, Sparky, what on earth will they do to you?'

'I don't know but I've certainly made a few bloody rotten enemies,' he said. 'But don't you worry, love, I've got enough money to set us up over here. Forget about home for a while, will you?'

There was no choice now. With the money Sparky had managed

283

to get away with, he bought Amy a nice house not very far from Letty. It was the house she had always dreamed of owning, with a big brick fireplace, a modern kitchen, and a grand view of that big lake. There was a convent school nearby so the two girls, neatly dressed in school uniform, went off to school there each day, while Amy spent her time polishing and painting her nice house. When the deep snow of the Canadian winter came down it wrapped them around warm and cosy in this new nest. And Amy found that she was happy. Although there was often a deep tug of remorse in her heart when she thought of Annie and Sheila back home, these were the most contented days of her married life.

Sparky was no longer called Sparky. Now he was known as Mr Tony Spinks, or just plain Tony. He had had several jobs, but now worked in a car-hire firm in the town which also supplied a car for them to use. So at the weekend Sparky would take his family on long trips into the deep Canadian forests.

The little girls readily took to their new life. They would play football out in the park and when there was deep snow, they went tobogganing down the hill. From the kitchen, Amy could hear the sound of their happy laughter.

Tosh was becoming quite a tomboy, while Rachel was a little more solemn, more like Amy. Since she had been going to the Catholic school, she had become very interested in religion.

Amy would watch Rachel, her long blonde hair hanging over her face as she wrote in her exercise book, and think it was the best thing she ever did for her family, to agree to leave the slum where she had been born.

Sparky, or Tony, as she now tried to call him, was very good to her and often wooed her to get pregnant again. 'Let's have another baby. This time I'm bound to get a son.'

'You have Tosh, she's more like a boy than a girl,' Amy joked.

'But I want a son,' insisted Sparky. 'I always have done.'

'Well, it's all in the hands of fate,' she said, 'for I don't seem to fall for children so easily as I did.'

Letty came to visit every weekend, and they all spent the holidays together. Letty worked in the local library and Frank taught at the nearby school. They were a hardy pair who loved the outdoor life. They frequently played tennis and took long hikes into the country, which Amy found very tiring. So she usually kept herself occupied at home with Rachel while Sparky joined the others on their hikes, taking young Tosh with him.

All in all they became a happy and devoted family, but Sparky was still restless. When the spring came, Amy and Sparky went down to walk beside the broad swift-flowing river. Huge lumps of ice still floated on the black water as they watched the long, low-built ships sail up to the arctic wastelands.

'There's a big world up there, Amy,' murmured Sparky. 'I'm only standing still here because you want it, but I can't do this forever.'

'Oh, whatever is wrong with you?' snapped Amy. 'I settled here because you wanted it. Don't uproot us again. I'll tell you, if I go anywhere, I'll go back home.'

'Over there is Detroit.' Sparky pointed towards the bridge, ignoring her remark about home. 'Once over that bridge you are in the United States, and that is a thriving place; there's money there.'

Amy gazed dismally over the bleak river to the skyscrapers of Detroit and longed to be back beside her big log fire. She had been aware for a long time that Sparky was restless and it worried her. A wave of homesickness suddenly washed over her. She was learning to like Canada but it was occasionally hard. Sometimes when she went shopping in the town, the flow of the traffic bothered her. And everything was so big – the shops and the streets all so widely spaced. It was nothing like those small slum streets of London.

It was during their second cold winter that Amy caught a virus which affected her chest. She felt pretty poorly and had to stay inside, unable to go out in the arctic conditions.

Sparky was very good to her during this time. He took the children back and forth to school and got books from Letty's library for her to read. He fed her with hot spiced drinks and cooked her hearty meals. But it did not seem to help. Slowly, Amy grew very thin and very depressed.

Sparky joined a sports club and went out in the evenings often leaving poor Amy sitting gloomily by the fire thinking of her mum and Sheila and poor Siddy. They all seemed so far away and she often wondered if she would ever see them again.

Then one day she got a long letter from Nancy which shocked her. Nancy wrote to say that Mum had gone into hospital and that they had taken Sheila away to be taken care of. On reading about this, Amy wept solidly for an hour.

When Sparky came home that evening, he comforted her gently. 'When the spring comes, you go on holiday back home,' he said. 'I'll try to save for it because you know we are only just getting by. All the money I had out here went into this fine house because you wanted it so much.'

'Don't worry,' snivelled Amy, annoyed by the sudden bitter edge to his voice. 'I'll be all right, I'll forget it.'

Yet the worry of Mum and Sheila was like a yoke on her shoulders. She could not get rid of it, and it weighed down on her constantly night and day. This concern added to her general feeling of homesickness and contributed greatly to her depression as she sat there so far away from home and the members of her family she loved.

Chapter Eleven

East End Troubles

At first Annie had been devastated when Amy wrote to tell her that she and her family were going to settle in Canada. Illiterate, she had not been able to read the letter herself, and had had to wait several weeks before her son Billy popped in to see her. He read it to her slowly.

'Don't surprise me none,' she said gloomily when he had finished, but inside she felt quite shocked. It *was* a surprise.

'Sparky was in a lot of trouble, I heard,' said Billy. 'Those rotten sods, them crooked brothers, was after him. Some says he grassed on them, and I'd not give tuppence for his life if he did,' said Billy.

'Oh well,' sighed Annie. 'Well, now they're all in Canada, so there's not much I can do. And I got Sheila to fink of.'

One day a fellow in a cap and muffler came and sat next to Annie as she sat out on the green. 'Hello, Annie,' he said.

'I don't bleedin' knows yer,' she replied grumpily.

'Yes, you do. I'm Siddy's mate.'

That was like a red rag to a bull to Annie. 'Sling yer bleedin' 'ook!' she yelled at him. 'Sheila, come and give us an 'and, I'm going in.' She pulled up her enormous bulk and waddled inside.

Poor Sheila flapped around every day after that peering outside to see if that bloke was there, because Annie said she would not go out if he was.

'E's a copper, I can smell 'em a mile orf,' she said. 'Ain't gettin' me ter talk. Not on yer nelly.'

Siddy had been arrested and tried. He got a suspended sentence and was now out and living in Amy's flat. Tommy Evans had gone down for two years, but the Palmer brothers brought in a clever crooked lawyer to fight their case. He got them acquitted but they had to pay heavy fines for their part in the lorry insurance racket.

'There is no such fing as bleedin' justice in this bloody country,' snorted Annie when she heard the verdict.

'It's just as well Amy and Sparky gor aht. The East End ain't safe while those Palmers is still around, I assure you.'

Indeed, fear and violence continued to skulk in London's back streets. A new generation of tough kids had grown up since the war as the gambling clubs and the strip clubs came to the fore and now a new kind of evil reared its ugly head. Once drink had been the worst problem but now it was drugs. There was a lot of money to be made so the racketeers did not care how many lives their activities might destroy. The drug trafficking began in those low-down clip clubs in the West and East End, run and organized by the big time crooks as they peddled their wares and made a fortune.

One of the victims of this racket was the young Bubbles, who Tommy Evans had set up in a nice flat in South London, with strict instructions to stay out of the East End until he had done his time. He warned her that he would do for her should he hear that she had got involved with another guy.

Bubbles was only eighteen, immature, hot natured and psychologically hooked on cannabis. She drove a big red car which Tommy had left behind and which could be seen every night parked outside Amy's old flat while Bubbles spent the night with Siddy.

'Sheila!' Annie would say. 'Put yer 'ead rahnd the corner and see if that car is still there.'

And Sheila, like a scared rabbit, would come running back a few minutes later to tell her it was.

'There!' Annie would declare. 'Told yer about that Siddy, didn't I? Never was no good, he wasn't. I don't know why Amy let 'im live in 'er flat.'

But Sparky had paid six months' rent in advance to give himself time to get away, so Siddy had no immediate worries about that.

Annie would sit out on the green her mouth working angrily at the thought of what Siddy was getting up to with this blonde young woman. 'I knows 'er, I do,' she would mutter, 'and 'er muvver. Never was no good, she weren't. Used ter go dahn Aldgate after the men. Well, what's bred in the blood comes out in the flesh, so they sez, and that Bubbles will come to a sticky end, she will,' predicted Annie.

At the end of the six months, when the rent had run out, the council commandeered Amy's flat and all her furniture was placed in storage. Despite this, Siddy's romance with Bubbles continued, much to the surprise of the local inhabitants.

Siddy moved away into sleazy lodgings, and Bubbles worked in the strip clubs. Siddy always looked after her; he got her home when she was high on drugs and put her to bed. Once she was settled, he would then go around to his low down haunts to get a supply of this cannabis she was so fond of. And Bubbles spent. Bubbles spent all of Tommy Evans' money which he had stashed away.

For once in his life Siddy had someone of his own in this lovely wayward young girl. She played up to him and would lisp like a child, 'I love 'oo, Thiddy,' she would simper. 'Don't go and leave me will 'oo, Thiddy?'

Siddy stayed with her and she became the be all end all in his life. This romance was much talked about among the criminal element, and it was always treated as a joke, for in spite of Siddy's love for her, it was well known that Bubbles was promiscuous and that she liked old sugar daddies and just took them for their money.

When he got the news of their love affair, Tommy Evans, still in the nick, uttered threats to Siddy's life. But poor Siddy was infatuated and was just like a dog on a string; when Bubbles needed him, he was always there for her.

The affair ended abruptly when Tommy got a week's parole. He arrived to catch Bubbles at home and began to beat her up. She managed to run out into the street to get into the car to warn Siddy. But as she unlocked the car in that dark street, Tommy secretly got into the boot, and Bubbles in her upset state drove on without even realizing that she carried trouble to poor Siddy. As she ran up the steps of Siddy's lodgings, he came out to greet her and Tommy Evans dashed up the steps waving a big gun. As he came near, he fired straight at Siddy's lower parts and Siddy collapsed on the floor screaming. Evans dragged Bubbles down the steps, bundled her into the car and drove off.

Poor Siddy rolled around on the ground. The bullet had wedged in his private parts. An ambulance was called and in the hospital they had to remove poor Siddy's balls and part of his penis, so he really was in a bad way.

The next day, news of this incident spread like a bush fire around the neighbourhood.

'But who did it?' No one would say. Those harassed detectives

289

got no information out of anyone – it was all stumm, finger to the nose – and Tommy Evans was safely back in the nick having reported back in good time from his parole. No one seemed to know where Bubbles had gone, for she had disappeared into the endless web of vice that operated in the East and West End.

Not long after all this, Annie was sitting outside on the green, still gossiping about the old times, when Dolly Palmer came to visit her. The old lady dropped a box of chocolates in Annie's lap and said, ' 'Ullo, Annie, and 'ow are yer?'

'I'm fine,' said Annie. 'Wot d'yer want?' She was not very friendly.

'Oh, only to say I'm sorry about your Siddy. My boys send their respects to you.'

'Well, they can keep 'em to their bleedin' self,' said Annie, 'and I ain't got no son called Siddy.'

'What a funny woman,' muttered Dolly, as she went on her way.

'Don't know abaht that,' Annie said to another close neighbour later on, 'if anybody's funny, she is. Them bloody boys is a nuisance arahn 'ere, and she encourages 'em.'

'Fings ain't wot they used ter be, Annie,' said the wizened old woman sitting next to her.

'No, they ain't, and that's a fact,' said Annie. 'They tells me that our old street's now a block of bleedin' sky-high flats and all them old shops is gorn up that end of the market.'

'No,' said the old woman. 'Anderson the baker's still there and old Paget's son, he got a shop up there.'

'Oh, I 'members 'im, old Paget,' said Annie. 'Dead and gorn now, used ter go rahnd wiff a donkey and cart.'

'Nice man he were,' related the old lady, and so they went on and on, these memories of the good old days. The present day was getting too much for Annie, she had to hark back to the past. When Billy next came to see her he said: 'Mother, I think you should move out of this district. Come up our way, and you'll get a nice council house in the country.'

'What?' roared Annie. 'It took bloody Hitler and his bombs to move me aht of London and was I bloody glad to get back, so no crooks is goin' ter drive me aht.'

Billy retired from the fray, leaving his Nancy to try. All fresh complexioned and clean in her summer dress she arrived with a

290

basket of farm goodies for them. 'Mummy, dear, be sensible. You don't know what you are bringing on the family by your defiant attitude,' she pleaded. 'Look how they ran Amy out and what they have done to poor Siddy.'

'No, gel, go back to yer nice 'ome and little kid and leave me an' Sheila be,' replied Annie aggressively.

'You know you can come back to Ashmullen,' begged Nancy. 'Dick will get you a place of your own if you won't live with me.'

Annie lit a Woodbine and puffed at it angrily. 'Now will yer go? And, mind yer own business, me and Sheila are all right 'ere.'

'Oh,' said Nancy exasperated. 'You are a selfish old woman. What about poor Sheila? Why, she is not much older than I am but she looks like a middle-aged woman. All this tension is making her more nervous.'

'Leave me and Sheila be!' yelled Annie. 'And sod off! I don't care if I see any of yer, I'll get by.'

Nancy wrote to Amy about all this. 'It's quite hopeless,' she wrote. 'We can't budge her. She is more stubborn now than she was in the blitz, but I have done my best.'

Sometimes Joe, who was working in the oil fields, sent her a money order, along with a letter. Annie was unable to read the letter and just took out the money order and treated Sheila to the sweets, lemonade and crisps that she loved, and got herself plenty of stout and Woodbines.

There was not one line on Annie's brow even though she was often in pain from her arthritis. The smooth skin and halo of white hair remained with her, and still full of jaw herself, she would sit listening to the chat from old neighbours which kept her in touch with the old times.

One highlight of her life, every two weeks, was a visit to the hairdresser's, which she had done since Amy's wedding. There they trimmed and set her hair keeping it a lovely white with silver rinses. Sheila would push her along to the end of the market where Esther had a shop that had been there many years. Esther's parents had been the old-fashioned men's barber's shop with the long candy-striped pole outside the shop. This was when men did not use electric razors and liked close shaves. Old Manny Webb had cut hair in his shop which had been a hive of gossip all about the First World War. In the latest war, the bombs had disposed of his little shop and Manny and his wife had died in the Jewish Old

Folks' home. After the war, their eldest daughter, Esther, came back from evacuation and started up in a brand new premises and added a ladies' department.

Esther Webb was now in her sixties and had known Annie all her life. She was a nice and homely woman whose dumpy little shape bustled here and there across the shop. And as she worked she talked incessantly. A visit to Esther was a tonic to anyone bored and lonely and there were many that way in those high council flats. So Esther's shop was always busy, packed with long lines of old ladies sitting under driers or waiting to be attended to. Whatever they were doing, they chatted, relaying the news of the day and harking back to the old times before and during the war.

Annie was in her element there. Nothing would make her miss this trip to the hairdresser once a fortnight. Sheila pushed her mother along in the wheelchair and helped her inside. Then she would sit very quietly, her little dog, Ben, on her lap. Sometimes she would comb his coat and tie a blue bow on it. Everyone knew Ben, who snapped and snarled at strangers, but was friendly to anyone he knew and he liked. Sheila was never anywhere without him.

Esther would say: 'Come on, Sheila, let's make you look nice too. I'll cut your hair and perm it.'

But Sheila would shrink back into her seat shaking her head and staring in confusion all around her.

'Let 'er be,' Annie would say. 'She won't let anyone touch 'er. Only our Amy was allowed to do that.'

'It's a bloody shame,' said Esther. 'Your other gels are so smart, and poor Sheila looks about forty.'

Sheila would cuddle Ben, kiss the top of his head and make no comment.

During Annie's visits to her shop, Esther was wise enough never to mention Siddy. She would ask after Amy, Joe, Billy – anyone but Siddy.

So Siddy's accident was talked about in whispers and everyone shut up as soon as Annie arrived. But without the bright gossipy Esther and that nice hair-do, Annie would have found life a little tedious.

Then one bright summer day Annie was sitting outside in her wheelchair having just returned from the hairdresser's. 'Go and make a pot of tea, Sheila,' she said. 'Let Ben stay on me lap for a while, he's having a kip.'

Willingly as always, Sheila went inside to put the kettle on while Annie and Ben quietly dozed in the sun. Annie's hair was white and silvery shining brightly in the sun, her face still quite red from the heat of the drier. She did not notice the two lads lurking about on the other side of the green watching, as they often did – kids playing truant from school, out to nick from the cars or anything left on park benches. Suddenly they swooped, running past Annie, and scooping up the dozing Ben from her lap. They ran off down the road with the dog which yapped like mad in their grip.

'Oh, you sods!' screamed Annie.

At the sound of the commotion, Sheila came dashing out and ran after them. 'Ben! Ben! Don't take my doggie! Let him go,' she called.

The lads disappeared like the wind, laughing gleefully as they leaped over the high railings and disappeared with Sheila's beloved dog in their arms.

Poor Sheila stood screaming in frustration by the railings which she could not get over. Annie struggled to rise in panic and fell out of her wheelchair. There was no one around on the green. Most of the flat dwellers were out at work and the kids were all at school. Still screaming, Sheila ran back towards Annie who was now lying helplessly on the ground, but suddenly fell down in a fit in the middle of the green. Annie yelled frantically for help. At last a little old man came out from next door. Realizing what had happened, he helped Annie back in her chair, but she fell forward again, her mouth all twisted. She was unable to speak. He ran to the phone box and called the ambulance and the police. Both Annie and Sheila were taken to the hospital, but no more was ever heard of little Ben.

The whole district got roused up over this incident. Down at Esther's the customers all shed tears. 'Oh, she had 'er hair done only that day,' said Esther. 'It gave 'er a stroke, it has. They sez she can't utter a word.'

'Oh, gor blimey!' said one customer. 'Poor Annie, that's gonner upset 'er.'

As always, Billy was sent for. Nancy came, as did Lily, who was now a big busty woman and the matron of a home for deprived children.

Annie just sat up in bed and stared apathetically at them.

Sheila had first been sent to a psychiatric hospital because of the screaming nightmares but now had been returned to the general hospital. But they could not really cope with her there so she was sent back to the psychiatric hospital. In the end Annie was sent home and Lily stayed a while to clean up the flat and organize the home-help, such as meals-on-wheels. But she could not stay for too long. 'I have my own group of children to think of,' she said.

No one bothered about Sheila. No one even visited Sheila. Poor Annie would sit mouthing silent words which seemed to say: 'Where's Sheila?' But no one could cope with her, it was all too much for them all.

In the end Nancy wrote to tell Amy the bad news.

Back in Canada, Amy's depression had not lifted. Sparky could not put up with it any more. 'Right,' he said one day. 'Go home, if you like, but leave Tosh with me.'

There was no question in Amy's mind of splitting up her family. 'Come home too, Sparky, it's all blown over now. Let's get back to where we belong.'

'Look, Amy, I'd have to sell this house. I can't just walk out on it, and I will need money to start again in England.'

So the arguments and debates continued until one day when Sparky placed a wad of notes on the table. 'I quit my job,' he announced 'and got a bonus. Go take a plane home now if you want to.'

'What about you, Sparky?' sobbed Amy.

'Look, I've decided to stay and sell this 'ouse, and then I'll work my passage home on the boats. I'll get across that bridge to the States and go home that way. It will be easy to get a job on one of the Atlantic Liners. It may take longer but like that I'll not bring too much attention to myself, just in case they have a contract out on me.'

Amy held her head in distress. 'How can I leave you? How do I know you will come home?'

'Well, doll, you will have to trust me, won't you?' said Sparky with a smile.

The following week Amy said goodbye to Letty and Frank, and Sparky, who was putting the house up for sale and selling all the furniture. He was to stay with Letty until he had completed the deal. He stood there at the airport with the wind blowing across the tarmac, ruffling his red hair which he now wore much longer so it had begun to curl. Amy glanced over his long lean healthy body in the casual shirt and tight jeans which had become his normal mode of dress, and she smiled sadly at him. 'I'll be waiting for you, Sparky,' she said quietly.

The plane took off and Amy was on her way home at last.

It was a more comfortable flight this time as the plane was not crowded, and Amy managed to get a good rest. She sat staring out into that wide air space. The fluffy clouds down below looked like a snowfield and way up there in the blue empty void it was all so peaceful. Suddenly she was a little girl again and Miriam Trelawny was sitting next to her, her soft hand holding hers. Her soft voice was saying: 'Now, Amy, be a good girl, Auntie Miriam is here.'

Amy woke from her reverie with a start. It was now night time and the air hostess was pulling down the blinds. 'Have a good sleep,' she said. 'I'll wake you all for breakfast.'

Amy's little girls were facing her, cuddled up close together. Amy looked tenderly at them; there was a sweet smile on Rachel's face.

Suddenly a pang of fear ran through Amy's body. All at once she felt afraid that something might go wrong and they would never meet up as a family again. It ruined her night. She could not sleep but instead tossed uncomfortably in her seat, sweating and biting her fingernails.

In the early morning, when the dawn shed a pink light on all the other sleeping passengers, the stewardess brought Amy a cup of tea. 'It won't be long now,' she said. 'We will be landing in twenty minutes.'

Amy had never felt so grateful in all her life.

Chapter Twelve

Coming Home

It was raining in London when Amy came home. The shiny wet pavements and the stiff breeze blowing off the Thames seemed to bid her welcome. The children were tired, but uncomplainingly helped to carry the bags. They travelled by bus into the West End, then by tube to the East End. By the time they neared home they were all very weary, trudging along dragging two heavy suitcases. It was very comforting for Amy to spot Annie's flat just before it began to get dark. There were no lights on but the front door was on the latch. Amy pushed it open, and switched on the light, then went inside.

Annie sat slumped in her wheelchair in the middle of the sitting room. Her head had dropped against her chest. She was dozing and the whole place looked as if it had been hit by a tornado. There were empty bottles everywhere, cigarette ends overflowed the tin stuck in front of Annie's wheelchair and an overpowering stench of urine and bad food permeated the air. It was all a dreadfully squalid scene of neglect. Amy stood still, gasping for breath. Her two little girls who had crept in behind her looked around and started to giggle.

Annie slowly raised her big head. Her hair, no longer a silvery white, was just a kind of dirty grey.

'It's Amy, Mother,' Amy cried. 'I've come home.'

As Annie stared at Amy, her mouth worked but no sound came, and tears poured down her faded cheeks.

'Oh, Mother,' exclaimed Amy. 'What have they done to you?' Tears fell down her own cheeks as she put her arms around her mother and cuddled her. Pointing to the bedroom, she said to her wondering children: 'Go in there and unpack. It's auntie Sheila's room. You can tidy it up for her.'

Amy made Annie a cup of tea, washed her face, helped her to the toilet and found clean knickers for her. Poor Annie had just sat and wet herself, it being too difficult to propel herself to the bathroom. She was indeed very feeble. Amy nagged all the time.

'How could they leave you alone all day? Wait till I see that Billy.'

Annie just wagged her big head pathetically, her mouth moving wordlessly. But Amy could tell what she was trying to say. 'Sheila, where's Sheila? Bring her home, Amy.'

'Yes, Mother,' replied Amy reassuringly. 'Tomorrow I will do just that. Now you relax. I am staying with you,' she consoled her. Annie's wrinkled hand grasped hers so gratefully.

The little girls were having fun in Sheila's room and put on the old portable gramophone, which Amy had brought back from evacuation and which Sheila had taken such good care of. The strains of that old record came drifting out, 'Amy, wonderful Amy,' and filled the whole flat. Annie gave a twist of a smile and touched her ear as if to say, 'I don't speak but I can hear good.'

The next day Amy went to the welfare and complained bitterly in an effort to get Sheila out of the hospital, and about the conditions in which her mother was left to live.

The welfare people were apologetic but explained that Annie was awkward and would not allow the flat to be cleaned up or let anyone in to wash her.

Amy would not listen. 'It's a bloody disgrace, is all I can say, it might be your mother to be treated like that some day. You get your bloody wages, so do your job. And I want my sister Sheila sent home.'

They told her that they weren't sure if this request would be possible to meet as Sheila had deteriorated in the hospital.

'I'll go and see for myself then,' stated Amy, marching out smartly.

Back at the flat she told the girls to stay and look after Granny, and then she set off by train to Essex to see Sheila.

It was a soul-destroying sight that met Amy's eyes at the hospital. There was Sheila crouched beside her bed, her hands over her face. The ward was very overcrowded, the windows were barred and the floor was bare. The beds were packed close together and it was impossible to escape the weird antics of the disturbed patients.

Amy and the authorities argued at length about Sheila. They said she had to be examined but in the end Amy had her way.

At first Sheila did not know Amy and would not look at her. The young nurse roughly pulled Sheila's hands away from her face. 'She is very different you know.'

But Amy's sturdy shape almost pushed the nurse over as she shoved her out of the way. She pulled Sheila to her feet and cradled her in her arms. Sheila started to sob heart-brokenly. 'Don't cry darling,' said Amy. 'Amy's here, you remember.' And Sheila put her arms about Amy's neck and repeatedly kissed her.

'Take me home, please take me home to Mother,' Sheila whispered.

'I will, darling, where are your outdoor clothes? Come on, we'll see the matron. No one's keeping you in this terrible place any longer.'

After a big battle with the staff Sheila was eventually allowed to go home with Amy. They travelled back by train. Amy got a taxi to the station and Sheila was supremely happy. She did not say a word; she just sat staring at her beloved sister Amy.

Amy wanted to scream she was so angry at the injustice of it all. Poor sweet Sheila who wouldn't hurt anyone, shut up in that grim asylum. 'Some one is gonner pay for this,' she vowed.

When they finally got home, Annie was over the moon with joy to see Sheila at last. Her wide grin appeared on her face once more as she held her daughter to her bosom and her mouth worked as if she had so much to say but could not tell them.

And so part of the family was reunited under one roof.

Amy called the council in to clean up the flat, and arranged for a nurse to come each day to help wash and dress Annie. She got sheets and an allowance to feed them, and all the commodities and welfare facilities needed to take care of Annie. She did not leave a stone unturned in her battle to get what they were entitled to.

During the day the girls went to a local school and Sheila and Annie sat out on the balcony, while Amy cooked them all good nourishing meals. She was now so busy there was no time to think of Sparky or what he was up to.

Sheila and Annie developed a kind of sign language between them, so that Sheila was able to transmit to Amy all Annie's needs. It worked very nicely. Slowly Sheila got some of her confidence back. Amy would tuck her up each night with one of the girls' toy dogs which looked a little like Ben and leave the light on for her. Sheila had told Amy that in the hospital they had always turned the lights out, something that terrified her ever since that shelter disaster.

Bravely Amy coped with Annie and Sheila in addition to her two little girls. Her sister Nancy came visiting, bringing with her a big basket of farm produce and home-knitted woollies for the girls. Emmy, Billy's wife, sent sweets and toys. Even Lily turned up, leaving a gift of money for them all. Each one in turn Amy lashed with her tongue, blaming them for the neglect of Sheila and their mother.

'But Amy,' pleaded Nancy tearfully, 'she is so obstinate and won't do anything for us.'

'Well, you seldom came by to see her,' declared Amy.

Nancy burst into tears. 'Oh, don't pick on me now, Amy.' she sobbed. 'I'm so upset about poor Miriam – she was like a big sister to me.'

'Why? What is wrong with her?' asked Amy, a little surprised.

'Oh, I was going to tell you,' wept Nancy. 'She got killed in an air crash. The same day as you came back, she was flying to Canada. She had lost her husband and was at last flying out to join Jack. He had a ranch out there and had waited all those years for her.'

Amy's big brown eyes widened in horror. 'Oh, no!' she cried. 'Not our Miriam!'

'It's true!' said Nancy. 'Dick rang up the airline. They told him that the plane crashed off the Newfoundland coast. There were no survivors.'

Through Amy's mind flashed that strange dream in which Miriam had seemed to be so near to her in the plane when she was coming home. She covered her face with her hands. 'Oh Nancy,' she wept, 'and she came to say goodbye to me.'

Sadly the sisters comforted each other, and even the unemotional Lily was distressed when she heard the news of Miriam. 'Miriam was like a mother to us all,' she said. 'We had little love from Annie, so that's why we are a little careless now.'

Annie was in bed in the next room and she banged violently on the bedside table with the stick.

'Oh, there she goes,' said Lily. 'I don't envy you your life, Amy.'

Amy smiled. 'She hears everything. She can't utter a word but has earholes on sticks.'

Rachel and Tosh giggled. 'She is always so funny, our granny,' they said in unison.

When the sisters returned to their own homes, Amy felt very

down-hearted, but she coped with her family to the best of her abilities and as far as the money she got from the welfare would go.

At night she went her rounds. She covered up the little girls who slept in the single bed next to Sheila. Sheila would lie cuddling her toy dog in her arms, her mouth open as she snored noisily but peacefully. Then she would go in to see Annie who would still be sitting up in bed puffing her fag. 'Put that out, it's bedtime,' Amy would say firmly. 'I am going to put out the light.'

Annie always grimaced in a kind of grateful smile, and she held Amy's hand as she kissed her goodnight.

Amy knew she was needed but once she was alone, her mind began to be tormented with questions. As she made up her own bed on that old put-u-up in the sitting room, tears would pour down her cheeks. 'Oh, Sparky,' she wept, 'where are you? This waiting is driving me mad.'

All night long she tossed restlessly. She missed his strong body beside her at night and his noisy antics as he played with the kids or sung and whistled all the time. Would their lives ever be the same?

One day, when morning dawned, she heard the latch on the door rattle. Thinking it was the milkman, she got up, pulled on her dressing-gown and opened the door. There stood a tall young man in a dark blue sailor's outfit. He had a seabag slung over his shoulders and wore horn-rimmed specs. He dropped the seabag, put out his arms and grabbed her. 'Oh, Amy, darling, you sure are a sight for my weary eyes.' Amy sighed as she sank into his arms. Sparky was home once more.

Great was the excitement when the rest of the household rose. Sheila was very excited and kept grinning. Rachel kept jumping up and down and little Tosh never left her father's lap. Annie was got up and wheeled into the sitting room very early, while Amy cooked eggs and bacon for them all, leaving her no time to talk to her returned husband. Sparky looked so different. He had lost weight, he wore his hair long and it curled up at the nape of his neck, and he had grown a moustache to match his long ginger sideburns.

That evening, the atmosphere was a little quieter. Annie was in bed. Sheila was in her bedroom playing Ludo with the little girls, and Sparky and Amy were alone at last. He pulled Amy down on to the settee beside him. 'Oh, Amy,' he said, 'how I've missed you all.'

Amy gently stroked his untidy hair. 'Take off those specs, Sparky, it don't look like you.'

He removed his glasses and kissed her passionately. 'I wear them as part of my new image – like it?' he asked cockily.

'No,' she said, cuddling close to him. How she was enjoying his lovely male smell of fresh skin laced with tobacco. This was her man: how had she managed without him?

As his hands roamed urgently over her body, he whispered, 'Where do we kip?'

'Oh here,' she said. 'There's nowhere else, but wait until they are all in bed.'

So Sparky and Amy became true lovers once more on that same old settee where they had done their courting. Annie could be heard snuffling and twisting about in her bed and Sheila let out frightening little cries throughout the night. But the world was theirs; they were lost in the land of lovers.

By morning, Sparky, in his shirt sleeves, served everyone tea in bed and was his bright breezy self. Before the girls went to school, he stood them together and said, 'Line up.' Then with a serious expression on his face, he said, 'Now it's stumm.' He put his finger to the side of his nose.

'Yes, Dad, stumm,' the little girls replied.

'You don't go telling the kids at school that your dad is home, right? Because I'm on a special secret mission for the government, savvy?'

'Oh yes, Dad,' they cried, and went off to school giggling at the excitement of it all.

'But why does your return have to be a secret?' asked Amy later that morning.

He cuddled her. 'Look darling, these bastards might have a contract out on me. I don't trust them. I've got enough to start again – but this time it's on the level, I ain't getting mixed up with the big boys again – no siree! I have learned my lesson.

Amy looked a little afraid and put her arms about his neck. 'Oh, don't scare me, Sparky, don't spoil it all.'

'Well, doll, it must be faced. Why do you think I took so long coming back to you? I was trying to fox them. Didn't want no reception committee waiting for me.'

301

Tears poured down Amy's cheeks. 'Oh Sparky, don't tell me it's as bad as all that?'

'No, not really, but you can never be sure, Amy. They are a bloody evil lot, you know, and it don't take a lot to get on the wrong side of them. After all, I did clear out and leave them holding the baby. But don't worry, love, the best place is home and we will get by.'

For a while Sparky only went out when it was dark. Even then he wore a black trilby hat and a long black overcoat, avoided the trouble spots and most of his old mates.

Every time he went out, Amy would wait anxiously for him to come home, when she would throw herself into his arms. They were so loving and so sweet to each other that it seemed that they had begun another honeymoon in that warm nest with Annie, Sheila, and the two girls. The flat was very overcrowded but there was plenty of love and warmth and happiness within.

But after about three months of this fugitive existence, Sparky came back one night to tell Amy that he had got a little business started. He had rented an arch near Liverpool Street Station where he was going to repair electric faults on cars, and buy old cars to do them up and sell for profit.

Amy looked anxious.

'It's quite clean, and no one knows me. I'm Tony Binks from now on. We'll stick it out here until we get enough money to buy a house in one of those new towns and take Annie and Sheila with us.'

He was generous and so considerate to her family, how could Amy not agree and trust him as she would do all her life?

Then began a peaceful year. The little business thrived but never did too well. Amy took a part-time job in the baker's shop in the market. Sparky bought and sold his cars and became quite famous at doing repairs. His training at sea had given him useful skills. Tony Binks, as he was now known, was a real wizard with old cars, repairing and refurbishing them and then selling them at a profit. But unfortunately because of his generous ways he often got knocked and rarely paid, but all the same, he made a fair living and they all seemed quite content, though there was never enough money in the kitty to put a deposit down on the nice new house that Amy longed for. Eventually they settled for another council flat in the same block as Annie's but four floors up. It was a bigger and more spacious home. Sparky bought some new things and got Amy's old furniture out of storage. Life was not all sunshine and roses but farily content. Amy would pop in each day to see Annie who never got her voice back but was fairly fit otherwise, though still unable to fend completely for herself. Sheila was able to cope quite well because Annie did not sit out on the green any more but instead sat on the balcony when the weather was good, looking out towards the old places she used to know, and pointing frequently to the old square tower of the parish church.

It was while working in the baker's shop that Amy made contact once more with her brother Siddy. She was at first very disturbed to realize that the lean gaunt man who came in to buy a couple of rolls, a shabby, down-at-heel creature, was her beloved brother. He limped badly and wore very old shabby clothes. He was indeed, very down and out.

'Oh, Siddy!' Amy cried. 'What has happened to you?'

That old devilish grin appeared as he replied, 'I'm okay, sis.'

'But where have you been? Are you working? Why do you look so ill?' Questions poured from her.

'Can't stop, sis,' he said briskly. 'I'm helping out on the tater stall. See you later,' and Siddy limped off.

At three o'clock Amy finished work and went up to wait outside the school to meet the girls as they came out. She was feeling most upset about Siddy but when she mentioned him later to Sparky, all he said was: 'Can't carry the world on your shoulders, Amy. You do too much for your family already.'

'Oh, Sparky, he looked a proper down-and-out and limped along so badly,' she said sadly.

'Well, seems that they really nobbled poor old Sid. That's why he lost his privates. He has to wear a kind of plate down there, I gather. It's finished him with the women, it has.'

Amy felt sick. 'Oh Sparky, we must help him,' she begged.

'There's nothing you can do, and Siddy wouldn't thank you. Let him alone. He's got plenty of friends and I don't want him to know that I am home.'

'Oh, why not? You can trust Siddy.'

'Amy,' said Sparky, his voice suddenly hardening. 'After all I've been through I don't trust no sod.'

So Amy went back and forth to work, she often stopped to say hello to Siddy who hopped around the big vegetable stalls fetching and carrying for their owners. Sometimes Amy would slip him a packet of fags but that was all she could do. Much as she wanted to, she did not ask Siddy to come home any more, she was too afraid of Sparky. For if Sparky said no, it must be no.

Siddy was not bothered. 'I'm all right,' he told her. 'Got good lodgings, and all me pals are around here.'

There was no mention of that dangerous love affair with Bubbles or of Sadie, his lost love. To Amy it was as if Siddy was only a shadow of his old self.

One day a big story splashed across the newspapers when the beautiful blonde Bubbles had been found dumped in an East End alley, her fair body ripped open and her lovely face battered and bruised.

Siddy was grabbed by the police, and everyone was quite agog at this terrible murder. Bubbles had only been twenty years old and had grown up in the district; it was indeed a dreadful thing to happen.

But Sparky was a little alarmed. 'Blimey, I hope it don't bring old Bill nosing about down here. Siddy would not hurt a fly, so they'll let him out in no time. They just got to get some information from him.'

Amy was very worried for a while, but Sparky proved to be right. The police let Siddy out again once he showed that he had a good alibi.

'She was just a whore, that Bubbles,' said Sparky, 'and they finished with her, chucked her out into the dustbin. I've been told she was full of dope.'

'Oh, don't talk about it,' wept Amy. 'I never liked her, but I feel so wicked at what has happened to her.'

'Amy,' said Sparky, 'you know very little of what goes on out there, so let's keep ourselves to ourselves, shall we?'

Three weeks after Bubbles was buried they found Siddy's body on the railway line just outside Broad Street Station.

Amy and Billy had to go and identify him, but Sparky stayed out of the way. When Siddy was buried it was the grandest funeral that had ever been seen down the market, for the trades people had a whip round to see poor Siddy off great style. Huge wreaths and long lines of cars followed his cortège to Manor Park. The verdict was that Siddy had fallen over while trying to get across the railway line, as some often did, in a short cut from East to West. Therefore his was declared an accidental death rather than suicide. But Amy knew, Billy and Sparky knew, and all of Siddy's friends knew otherwise. Poor Siddy, who had never amounted to much and had been rejected by his own mother, went off in grand style nonetheless.

'Poor Siddy who had loved and lost,' Sparky said. 'Poor sod, he was a born loser, but at least no one can kick him in the arse now.'

Amy went with Billy in the principal mourners' coach, as they drove past the hundreds of people lining the roadside, she realized how few of them she knew. Some came in big limousines. She recognized the Palmer boys with their big heavily padded shoulders and smart suits, and their small black-clad mum between them. It was Dolly, the old woman she had met when she had visited Siddy on the Isle of Wight. The sight of them worried her. How deep had Siddy been with them? Then to her surprise, sitting in a big Rolls Royce, Amy spotted Sadie and her father. Sadie had grown very stout and was weeping copiously, while Jack Goldman, now a white-haired old man with his fur hat on top of his head, looked very serious. Then there were the various car loads of Siddy's market friends. The stalls had all closed for the day, as had the pub.

After the funeral, a noisy party was held in the pub, but Billy and Amy went back to Annie's house. Annie did not know where they had been and stared suspiciously at them. Amy wanted so much to tell her of the son she had rejected and of how well he had been loved in spite of all his troubles, but knowing Annie, she thought it was all better left unsaid.

'Let sleeping dogs lie,' as Sparky had advised.

Chapter Thirteen

I'll Wait For Ever

The building continued throughout the East End. The council were making huge improvements everywhere, and were now demolishing what was left of the old shops and houses, and building a new market in a covered arcade. Lots of the older costers objected but the council compensated them and moved them on to the new towns.

Esther the hairdresser was one of the first to go. She came to Annie one day bringing her a present, and the two women sat gossiping in a kind of sign language all afternoon. Annie had cheered up immensely since Amy's return but was still unable to speak clearly, so when Annie and Esther came to a point when they couldn't understand each other, Sheila would step in and translate what Annie wanted to say. Otherwise Sheila sat peacefully crocheting lots of round woolly hats, some of which she wore. She had a different one for each day. Sheila's hats were the joke of the family. She presented them to her nieces and nephews, who never ever wore them, and all the hats eventually ended up on some stall at a charity fair or a jumble sale down in Dorset or up in Chelmsford. Nevertheless, this hobby kept Sheila quiet and content and everyone bought her skeins of wool or gave her old jumpers to unpick to make more woolly hats. Sheila, in some ways, found herself in her element looking after her mother. She liked to be needed, but could not be expected to go far from home; sometimes just a walk to the chip shop would terrify her.

But Amy thought this was a blessing. 'It's just as well Sheila doesn't go out much,' she said. 'The area is fast becoming fairly dangerous. The old folk we knew are not there any more.'

Sparky remarked, 'Be patient, doll, one day we'll make it rich and move to the country, but at the moment it is all graft and I have to stay near my work.'

Amy plodded on with her own work, spending the mornings in the baker's shop, and the afternoons with Annie. Her little girls had grown quite independent of her. Tosh had her sports and

Rachel her studies. Both girls had chosen their own kind of friends. Tosh's friends consisted of all nationalities and all colours – black, white or brown. As long as they could skip and jump or play netball, they were her pals. Rachel was inclined to stick to one nice girl whose folk owned the baker's shop.

As the years went by, life for Amy did not change. She had reached a point when it did not matter any more. Sparky was still very good to her and whenever he made a lot of money, he bought her gold bracelets and diamond rings. 'Keep them safe,' he would say. 'They can always be pawned if we are ever broke.'

Recently Sparky had begun to make some more friends – 'smart-alec guys', as Amy called them, who liked fast cars and night clubs. Often Sparky would get taken out on stag nights or when some young fellow was getting married.

Amy did not mind, but she would say: 'Don't get mixed up in anything dodgy, will you, Sparky?'

'No, love, I've learned my lesson,' Sparky would assure her. 'I am Tony Binks now, superman with cars and much appreciated. The old Sparky died a sudden death.'

For some reason a cold shiver went down Amy's spine. 'If it wasn't for Mum and Sheila I'd put my name down for a council house out in Essex. I get afraid of this place sometimes.'

'Amy!' he cried, forgetting what he had said about moving to the country. 'My little Cockney gel, this is where you and I belong. We proved it, didn't we, by coming back? So let's dig in our roots and make ourselves a fortune until the bloody taxman chases us out.'

Amy smiled. Sparky was always so full of humour nowadays, she could not be angry with him for long. But, in fact, slowly and surely Sparky was being lured back to his old haunts; he even took to going for a Sunday lunchtime drink at his old pub in Brick Lane.

Amy would warn him. 'Mind what you are up to. Don't get thick with those crooks again, will you?'

'The brothers have all gone for the big time up west now,' Sparky told her. 'Trans-Atlantic deals are what they are after, not little tiddlers like me. It's the big fish they hook these days.'

Even though Amy found herself worrying inwardly, it was nice to see Sparky happy and his confidence restored. He started to wear smart clothes and aftershave, and went off for his nights out whenever he fancied them.

On Sparky's nights out, Amy would go with the girls to the cinema and on her return would sit with Annie and Sheila. That she was sometimes very lonely she would not admit, but she took good care of herself, dressing carefully and very smartly, and having her hair done every week. She was only in her thirties but she was slowly becoming 'her indoors', as they called a woman who was very respected but played no part in the deals that were set up in pubs and clubs by the sharp male East Enders. Occasionally there was a social occasion, a wedding or an engagement party, to which Amy had to go and be the best dressed one there. She would wear all her fine jewellery, and Sparky would be very proud of her, twisting her around and saying, 'Gee! you'll knock all those lads for six when they see you, my lovely Amy.'

Despite Sparky's flattery, Amy was conscious of her defects and did her best to disguise them. She kept her figure and had a rather haughty bearing. Her smooth ash blonde hair was cut in a dainty little fringe across her forehead in order to hide her scar. And at these occasions she was very proud to be admired as the wife of Tony Binks, that astute, much-sought-after businessman.

It was on one night after one of these parties that Sparky had said: 'Oh, life is just great for us now. I'm not sorry I came back, but one thing that is still missing in my life, is that son I never had.'

'I don't think I want any more children, Sparky,' Amy said quietly. 'It will mean losing that nice little job if I have a baby to look after.

But Sparky frowned. 'Fuck the job, Amy! It's me you will look after.' With that, he unzipped her fifty-quid party dress and carried her to bed. 'From now on, you are my lovely woman and we will make love while we are young and healthy. We're going to have as many kids as I can get.'

'Oh, no Sparky,' protested Amy, but her voice was lost as his lips pressed down on hers, and that lovely thrill of being close to her man, who so badly wanted her, overcame everything else. From then on, Amy's life was a constant honeymoon. Sparky showered her with gifts. Every night he brought home bottles of brandy and boxes of chocolate. They would sit around their big coloured television and get sloshed, and once the little girls were in bed, they too would go to bed for a night of love.

Amy bloomed. She was happier than she had ever been, though she kept telling herself that such contentment could not last. Always inside, she felt a feeling of apprehension. Often Sparky came to meet her at lunchtime, wearing his greasy old overalls and driving an old banger. He would pick her up from the shop after work saying: 'Come on, darling, let's have a little session before the kids get home from school.'

'Oh, Sparky, you are getting so sexy,' Amy would say but her heart was beating with excitement at the thought of his strong arms around her. And he was so good with the children. Whenever Rachel got sulky, demanding to have some expensive thing such as some fancy shoes to be like her friend, Sparky always gave in and bought them for her. He played football on the green with Tosh on summer evenings and arm-wrestled with her on the rug in the winter. Amy would say, 'You are encouraging her to be a tomboy, Sparky.'

'Well, it's a tough old world she is going into, and she might need those muscles,' he would reply with a laugh.

Every day it seemed Sparky was happy whistling and singing and bustling with energy. One day, on a Sunday morning, he came home looking quite excited. 'Guess who I met down the pub?' he said.

Amy, serving lunch, paused to listen.

'Tommy Evans,' he said.

Amy nearly dropped the plates.

'Oh no!' she cried, 'Not Tommy Evans! I heard he moved to Harlow.'

'Well, he has, but he comes up now and again to have a prowl around the old places. He's back with his wife and kids and been going straight. Now he does long-distance lorry driving – goes right out to Germany and France.'

Amy put Sparky's dinner in front of him with an unsmiling face. 'All I can say, Sparky, is that I don't know how you can even speak with him after what he did to poor Siddy.'

Sparky's eyes gleamed in temper. 'Now Amy,' he said, 'your Siddy asked for that, knocking off Tommy's bird and doing in the money he had stashed away while Tommy was in the nick.'

'I don't believe that,' Amy said obstinately. 'And what about that poor girl who got murdered? For all we know, Tommy Evans did that.'

'Oh, for Christ's sake, shut up!' Sparky pushed his dinner away impatiently. 'Don't go on about something you know nothing about. I'm going to bed.'

So for the first time in many months Amy did not join him but sat watching the film of the week on the telly and having a little snivel whenever she thought of poor Siddy.

After that exchange, Sparky continued to be a little cool towards her, and on Sunday mornings she would now often spot the portly shape of Tommy Evans hanging about waiting for Sparky, and watch wistfully as they went off down to the old pub together. Sparky would always return in the evening much the worse for drink.

Amy did nothing. It was no good arguing with Sparky once he was set on something. Every Sunday she looked over the balcony to watch Sparky greet Tommy Evans, she felt very afraid, but she did not know why.

A month later she had some wonderful news to tell him which brought them close once more, pushing Tommy Evans to second place. Amy discovered she was pregnant.

Sheila giggled and hugged herself when told about the expected baby. She was so happy it might have been her baby.

Annie shook her head at the news. 'Boy this time,' she said in her own kind of language which they had all begun to understand. It was so difficult for Annie to pronounce the words, but the speech therapist called once a week and Annie was improving vastly. She had begun to say simple words and enjoyed the attention she was getting.

Rachel was not sure about the new baby at all. 'It will be a bit embarrassing when my friends find out,' she muttered.

But Tosh was very pleased. 'Won't it be great to have a brother?' she exclaimed.

Sparky laughed and whirled her around. 'That's it, Tosh,' he roared, 'you really cracked it.'

Amy gave up her job without complaint and lived peacefully through her period of waiting. Sparky was as good as gold but was eaten up with his own shady kind of business. 'Got to get a bit of money in the kitty,' he would say. 'We're going to have a big family.'

The shady figure of Tommy Evans stil lurked around but nothing would induce Amy to acknowledge him. She heard in the baker's shop that he had moved back into the district and had a council flat in Hackney Road.

'I don't know what you got against him, Amy?' Sparky would say.

'He's a real villain,' she would reply. 'It makes me feel cold every time I see him.'

'Well,' grinned Sparky, 'ain't we all? But he's me mate and that's it.'

In spite of this, Amy was fairly content. She would sit out on the balcony with Annie in the afternoons during that summer knitting little woollies while Sheila crocheted no end of little white bonnets.

Annie would sit sucking a sweet in quiet contentment until the little girls came out of school. Then Amy would go home to get Sparky's dinner ready. It was a calm and placid existence and Amy wanted for very little.

At Christmas the family got together as everyone came visiting. Annie sat like a queen surrounded by presents from her children – from Joe in Dublin where he now ran a hotel, the twins in Hong Kong in the military police, and Nancy and Lily and Letty – in Canada – and all her grandchildren.

Amy was happy for her because Annie had had a hard life and now it seemed that it was all good things happening to her at last.

As New Year approached, Sparky said, 'There's going to be a big party on New Year's Eve around at me mate's house in Stepney. Get yer glad rags on, Amy, we'll go together.'

Amy was five months pregnant and beginning to show. 'I don't think I feel like it,' she said. 'Anyway, I won't be able to get a dress on, I've got so big lately.'

A sudden flash of temper lit up Sparky's green eyes. 'Now, Amy, you get going, or else go and buy another dress – one of those maternity fings. You got the money and I want you with me. I'm going to let some folk see that I am a man of substance and expecting a son.'

'Oh, all right, but I don't care about your crooked friends or what they think,' said Amy defiantly, 'I'll just go if you want me to.' The next day, New Year's Eve, Amy popped out to the market and bought a nice full flowing dress and had her hair done. She sent the little girls around to Annie's and then she and Sparky got dressed up for the party.

It was about six o'clock and she was just putting on her coat when someone whistled from down below.

Sparky went to look over the balcony. 'Wait a tick, Tommy, and I'll come down,' he yelled.

'Where are you going?' Amy asked in astonishment.

'It's just Tommy. He wants to go up the road for a quick drink. I won't be long. And I need some ciggies to take to the party anyway.'

Tears of disappointment filled Amy's eyes. 'Oh Sparky,' she said, 'don't go now, I am all ready to go out.'

'Won't be a tick,' he said, struggling into his smart jacket. 'Sit down and rest for a few minutes – it will do you good.'

Within moments, he had slipped out of the front door. Feeling very frustrated, Amy sat down heavily and wept, but in the manner of many pregnant women, she quickly dozed off in the armchair and woke up sometime later feeling extremely cold. She switched on another bar of the electric fire and looked around for Sparky. There was no sign of him. He had not returned.

Bleary-eyed, she looked at the clock on the mantelpiece. It was eleven o'clock. Surely he had not gone to the party without her, that was not like him. She went out on to the balcony just as a noisy reveller passed by underneath, singing and dancing as he celebrated the New Year.

'Oh, Sparky,' Amy cried. 'How could you have gone without me?'

She made herself some coffee and watched the New Year celebrations on the television. As she watched the film of young folk jumping into the fountains in Trafalgar Square and of the police breaking up the fights around them, she felt very glad not to be out there but safe in her own home instead, and she hoped that Sparky was not getting into trouble. The bells tolled in the New Year, one, two, three. . . . Amy listened with a heavy heart and she suddenly felt very lonely, as if a kind of emptiness had entered her heart, a coldness that never left.

At one o'clock she was just thinking about going to bed when the telephone rang. Oh, that's Sparky to say he's not coming home, she thought, I expect he is staying the night with his mates.

But it was the voice of a strange woman. 'Is that Tony Binks' wife?' she asked.

'Speaking,' said Amy.

312

'Well, dear, don't get too upset but I've got bad news for you.'

'Yes?' Amy's heart was thumping. Now she was sure that Sparky was in the nick.

'I am Tommy Evans' wife. He just came home in a terrible condition saying that Tony had been shot up and that three men took him off two hours ago.'

'No!' cried Amy. 'It's a joke – don't try and frighten me.'

'I am sorry, dear, but it's true. I'm in a 'phone box and must go back to my Tommy. He's in a bad way.' With that, she rang off.

'It can't be true. What shall I do.' Panic-stricken, Amy ran over to Annie's flat, but everyone was in bed and the lights were out. Then she changed her mind and went home again. Sparky would turn up, she was sure. He would get home somehow.

She sat waiting and waiting through that long, long lonely night with a strange silence all around her.

At eight o'clock in the morning she looked through the telephone book and rang round all the places and people that Sparky knew. Most of them were kind but not very helpful. 'Go to the police, Amy,' some said. Others told her to try the hospitals. It was only from the mate who had given the party that she got some positive sort of help. The lady of the house said, 'I'll send me brother Harry over to take you round to Tommy Evans' place. He knows where Tommy lives.'

Harry soon arrived in a big flash car. He was a big broad fellow who looked like a villain. 'I'm 'Arry Brahn,' he introduced himself, 'a pal o' Sparky's. We ran togevver as kids in the blitz. If 'es in trouble, mate, we will find 'im, and them bastards can settle wiff me.'

Amy didn't know if he was just trying to impress her, or what, but she was so tired and she had to hope that he could help her. He took her straight to Tommy Evans' house where they found Tommy crouched in an armchair, still shivering with fright. 'They got him,' he said in a husky voice. 'He walked right into it. You know Sparky, no one worried him.'

'Who got him? Why?' demanded Amy.

'Don't know,' replied Tommy. 'I seen a van and I dived under a parked car. I never saw their faces – just the glint of a gun.'

Harry said: 'Come on, Amy, we'll try all the 'orspitals.'

He was a kind calm man and very considerate. Amy leaned on him even although he was a complete stranger to her.

They tried five hospitals and had no luck at any of them. When they left the last one, Harry said, 'It's no good, Amy, it's ol' Bill now or nobody but I'll get aht o' the picture if yer don't mind. I ain't actually got a clean slate meself and don't want to get mixed up in this. It's a big deal and I ain't no grass.'

With her face swollen from the tears she had shed, Amy rang the police station. 'My husband did not come home all night,' she said 'and I've heard he's been shot.'

The sergeant made a joke of it. 'Oh, he will turn up. He's probably sleeping it off somewhere.'

Then she heard a voice in the background which seemed to check him, and the more cultured voice of a detective came on the line. 'Can you give me his name and address and I'll see what I can do.'

With a sigh, she gave him the details and then put down the 'phone. She sat back and rested her head on the back of the chair feeling woe-begone and not knowing which way to turn. Suddenly there was a ring at the front door bell. She stared up in shock. Outside were two men and a uniformed policeman. 'May we come in? We have news of your husband.'

Amy opened the door wide. The uniformed policeman planted himself on the doorstep but the two plainclothes men walked in 'Do you mind having your flat searched?' they asked. 'We are in search of stolen property. Are these your husband's spectacles?' One of them placed Sparky's horn-rimmed specs on the table. They were cracked and broken. 'Is this the shirt your husband was wearing?' they asked, producing a piece of a blood-stained shirt. They put it on the table and added two spare buttons that had either fallen off or been pulled oft.

'Oh, yes!' cried Amy. 'Where is he? Where's Sparky?'

'Well,' one of them said ponderously, 'that we don't know, if you don't.' He wrapped up the items with care and put them in his pocket. 'We have a report from a witness who saw the shooting. He was in the public bar which your husband had just come out of.'

'Where was it?' she asked, feeling now numb with shock.

'In Chester Street.'

'Oh, my God!' cried Amy, 'that is Sparky's favourite pub.' She fell down in a faint.

When she came round she was in bed and a neighbour was with

her. 'Oh, Amy, we are all so sorry they got your husband last night, the bloody gangsters. Have this nice cup of tea, dear.'

Amy stared at her in disbelief but suddenly they heard tramping of feet down the hall, and men with cameras burst into the bedroom and started taking pictures of Amy sitting up in bed. Horrified she hid her face with her hands until a hefty policeman came in and turfed the newspaper men out of the flat. He bolted and barred the door and came back to assure her that they had all gone.

'Oh my God! What is going on?' Amy asked.

'Not to worry, Ma,' said the policeman. 'The news broke in the papers, that's all, that your husband has been murdered and they are looking for his body.'

Once more Amy burst into tears, and a policewoman came in to bathe her eyes and talk soothingly to her.

Amy tried to push her away. 'Get out of my house!' she cried. 'Go away!'

'Now dear, stay calm, don't get excited,' the policewoman said.

Two more detectives came and systematically searched her house, moving every ornament, opening every drawer and reading all her personal letters.

By now Amy was sitting in her armchair by the fire shivering in terror. As she watched them, she sat waiting, expecting and hoping to see Sparky come dashing in and throw all this lot out. But Sparky never came. There was no sign of him.

The newspapers had a field day. 'Small-time crook killed by East End gangsters,' they wrote. 'Body not yet found. Police appealing for witnesses.'

For thirty-six hours, Amy's flat was overrun by different people, all strangers she did not know. Than at last on Monday, Nancy arrived with Billy. They locked up the flat and took Amy round to Annie's but still the busybodies hung around staring up at the windows. The news boys prowled about talking to anyone who would talk to them, ever ready with their cameras, and each newspaper had its own version of the story. But still there was no body.

The police came back to the flat and took away what was considered evidence – all Sparky's business books and a few of his personal possessions – while Amy crouched in Annie's flat, afraid to show her face at the window.

Brother Joe came over and even the twins got special leave and went up to Scotland Yard. But they all caused nothing but trouble telling the law how to do their job.

During those long months of waiting, the family was very supportive but only the wide boy Harry was of any real help to Amy. He had been genuinely fond of Sparky, and he talked to Amy quietly in his gruff voice, of the days when as boys they were young tearaways in the London streets, and Amy liked to listen to him.

When the time came she went into the London Hospital to have her baby and gave birth to a boy who was the splitting image of Sparky. He had the same fair complexion, and a tuft of red hair stuck up on end. Though wild with delight at getting a boy, Amy was also sad.

Harry sent her flowers and came to see the baby.

'Sparky wanted a boy so much,' Amy said to him. 'And now he will never see him.'

Harry was always optimistic. 'Don't be despondent,' he said. 'If I knows Sparky 'e will turn up like a bad penny when it's all blown over. They ain't found no body yet.'

To Amy's astonishment, down the ward one day came the small active figure of Dolly Palmer. She was still dressed in black and carried a bunch of flowers and some grapes in a basket. Amy held on to her baby and stared aggressively at her.

Dolly placed the flowers and fruit on the bed and stood looking at the baby. 'Well, it's the image of him. My boys send their regrets,' she said.

'I don't need no sympathy from them,' replied Amy sharply.

'Well,' said the old lady, 'my boys ain't as black as they are painted, but one thing I'll tell you, gel, is that they don't know where he is, either. Well, good day to you and good luck to your bonny son.' With that, she toddled off down the ward.

Amy screwed up her brow anxiously. 'What did all this mean? Was Sparky still alive? Oh, please, God, it was true. Oh, come home, Sparky,' she wept. 'Come home to your lovely son. I'll wait for you, I'll wait for ever.'

When Amy came out of the hospital she went straight to Annie's, for she could not face that flat without Sparky. The windows had been broken and the front door latch had been forced. She had not been back long before the newspapermen came back offering her big money to tell her story of her life with this small-time crook who had reached the big headlines.

Amy could not stand it. She gathered up her baby and prepared to go down to Nancy's farm in Ashmullen where her little girls had been staying for protection. Amy was thin, white, gaunt, and very harassed and felt as if she had no true friends but her family.

Harry Brown offered to drive her down to Ashmullen to prevent her from having the strain of that long train journey. Amy was extremely grateful that this big, gruff, down-to-earth man was indeed proving to be a true friend of Sparky's. 'Don't worry, 'ave a good holiday,' he told her. 'I believe Sparky will turn up and 'e will know where ter find yer. Don't worry abaht yer flat, I'll sort aht any bastards wot comes a snoopin' arahnd.'

Amy managed a wan smile, for Harry was quite able to do what he threatened, she was very sure. The rough tough background of his youth had built into him a very strong yet curiously unaggressive character. 'I can't thank you enough, Harry,' she said when he was ready to go back to London. 'I'll try to settle down here for a while till something turns up, one way or the other.'

At the village everyone wanted to see the baby. Nancy was completely over the moon with delight. And Amy was pleased to see how well her little girls got on with Heather, their cousin.

For a space of time there was a little peace in Amy's mind, but she frequently watched the road from the farmhouse window hoping against hope that Sparky would find her. When the postman came she was always the first down the path to greet him gazing despondently at the correspondence. One letter from Letty in Canada gave her slight hope. 'We all know that Sparky was a tough, hard-living man,' she wrote. 'He will go to sea and then make his way back here and as soon as he does I'll be the one to let you know.'

It was all very pleasant, her family support, yet, in spite of the police search and her ever-watchful family, not a sign or sound of Sparky was seen or heard. He had only a few pounds in his wallet, so how could he escape? These thoughts she turned over and over in her mind but there were no answers.

Each day her little son, Tony, grew more and more sturdy and became increasingly spoiled. And each day she worried about Annie and Sheila, whom she had left behind. It was cosy and

317

comfortable at Nancy's but Amy felt like a lost soul. No longer did the wide moorland impress her or the rich country scene delight her. Even the comfort of Nancy's farmhouse was lost on her. It was as if her heart had died.

Chapter Fourteen

The Wrong Man

When Sparky went out for a drink with Tommy Evans on that cold New Year's Eve, he did not notice that his friend was a little edgy. Tommy was wearing a smart pinstripe suit and a wide trilby hat. He puffed at a big cigar with nervous apprehension.

'Quiet tonight, ain't it, Sparks,' he said casually.

His tall, red-headed mate looked down at him with an amused glint in his eyes. 'It will soon liven up when the pubs open,' he told him. 'Anyway what's up? Got a hangover or just the bleedin' creeps?'

'Nah, just a bit unsettled, that's all,' replied Tommy, looking back and to the side like some wily old rat.

'Well, cheer yer bloody self up because I am taking Amy out tonight. We'll get some cigs and have a pint and then I am goin' 'ome.'

'It's all right,' shrugged Tommy, 'might go home early meself. Let's walk to the main road and cross over to Brick Lane and have a drink in the Black Horse just for old time's sake.'

'Please yerself,' said Sparky, stretching out his long legs and walking at a quicker pace.

They went through the small alley which they knew so well, into the High Street, then across the Main Road to Chester Street, to their own local where they usually had drinks on Sunday mornings. They went in and had two drinks, treating each other. Sparky bought two packets of fags to take to the party.

Tommy Evans still seemed a little on edge, frequently watching the entrance as if expecting somebody.

'Right,' said Sparky, downing his pint and banging the glass down on the counter, 'that's me lot. I'm goin' 'ome now. Yer can stop if yer wants to. Good night guv'nor,' he said to the landlord, ''appy New Year, I'm orf.'

But Tommy Evans quickly finished his drink and almost gasped for breath. 'I'll come with yer,' he said urgently.

They stepped outside into the dark street. A pale moon slid in and out of the clouds making deep shadows all around. It was as silent as the grave. Suddenly a van cruised past them and a voice called out, ''Ere, I want yer!' There were three men inside the car, one driving and two in the back, their hats pulled well down over their faces. In that lonely street the voice echoed out, and a Cockney voice said again, ''Ere, we want yer, mate!'

Sparky would take no nonsense from anyone. He stared back at them. 'Well, what the bleedin' 'ell d'yer want?' He stepped forward towards the van which had pulled up at the kerb with its engine still running.

The air was suddenly split with the croak and a glint of a gun showed from the back. Without uttering a word, Tommy Evans dived under a nearby parked car. His mate Sparky spun round with a dreadful cry, his hands waving in the air, as a bullet creased his forehead, spun over his head and hit the pub window. The glass blew in with a great crash. From inside the van, a hand held the gun, and another gruff voice could be heard crying, 'Fire low, you silly sod. Get 'im in the legs.' And another two bullets whizzed out of the van and in a second Sparky was writhing in pain on the blood-spattered pavement. The van started up again and a big fellow climbed out to look at Sparky. He stepped back in surprise. 'Oh, Christ, yer silly git, it ain't 'im. Quick, get 'im in the back before they all come out o' the pub.'

So Sparky's limp body was dumped into the back of the van which then sped away.

When they had gone Tommy Evans wriggled out from under the parked car. Getting to his feet, he started running as fast as his legs could carry him in the opposite direction.

The guv'nor came out of the pub to have a look, and the customers, who had previously been crouching down inside, too terrified to move, stood around talking excitedly. It had been just like a scene from a gangster film. They agreed, no one could believe it had happened. Outside, the guv'nor looked down at the blood-splashed pavement, at Sparky's specs that were smashed into two pieces and at the pieces of Sparky's shirt torn away as he had been dragged into the van, and knew that what had happened was serious. 'Get going,' he said to those who crept out to look. 'Don't touch anything, I'd better get old Bill.'

The sergeant was sitting having a cup of tea at Old Street nick when the guv'nor came in to report what he had seen and heard.

320

He had been expecting trouble but not so early. He put on his jacket and came down to the pub to investigate. 'It's usually when the pubs turn out that they start,' he said, picking up Sparky's specs and wrapping them up along with the torn bits of shirt.

'Who was he? Anyone know him?'

No one answered. In this part of the town even if you knew something you never divulged it. It did not pay to know anything, the repercussions were too great.

The sergeant questioned a few bystanders who quickly disappeared and then decided that there was not much more to be done at that point. 'Oh well,' he said, 'something will turn up by morning.' And he went back to finish his cup of tea at the station.

The van careered swiftly over Southwark Bridge heading for the south side of the Thames – Over the Water, as the Cockneys put it. Inside, the young lad with the gun shivered and vomited. 'What yer goin' to do?' he asked. 'He's bleedin' all over the place, I can't take it.'

'Dump 'im outside the 'orspital,' suggested the driver.

'Nah! too risky, they might see the number plate.'

'Well, he ain't dead, is he?'

A pathetic moan came from Sparky who was huddled on the floor of the van. 'All me effin' upholstery is goin' ter be ruined,' moaned the driver, slowing down. 'Where to nah?'

''Ere, turn down the next alley,' the big fellow ordered. 'It leads to the wharfs beside the river. I'll take a quick shifty at him. If 'e ain't dead we 'ad better finish 'im orf and dump 'im in the river. Then we'd better blow 'cause yer ain't done wot yer was paid ter do and they ain't goin' ter like that.'

The van turned down into a remote alley just past the bridge. It was very lonely down there – all the stores and warehouses were closed for the holidays. The river looked cold and icy as they got Sparky out of the van and dumped him down in a dark spot.

Sparky had stopped moaning now and was lying very still.

''E's snuffed it,' said the big fellow. 'Stiff as a bleedin' board, he'll be soon. Right, now give us an 'and and chuck 'im in. He'll float dahn on the tide.'

With a terrific heave, the driver and the big fellow threw Sparky's body into the Thames.

'Now get the effin 'ell outa 'ere down the Brighton Road. We gotta lay low for a while now.'

As they sped off into the night, the cold green river gathered Sparky up with a deep gurgle as it flowed out to sea. But predictable as the River Thames is, the tide drained out very quickly that night and washed Sparky's body up into the grey muddy banks by the underground warehouses that lined this part of the river. As the river flowed by, it rolled Sparky over and over in the thick mud until he was unrecognizable as a human being. Then with a big swoosh, it pushed him down a big hollow, and his seemingly lifeless body was rolled down into a cellar where it lay still.

At twelve o'clock the bells welcomed in the New Year. The population started to meander out of the pubs and danced in the streets, as people made their way over the bridge to get to Trafalgar Square where the celebrating was going on around the big Christmas tree. Everyone was ready to party all night. Car loads of revellers went over the bridge, youths shouted and cheered, and young lovers paused to kiss. No one noticed the pathetic mud-covered body which now rested down there in a hollow on the river bank below.

One of the last revellers was a derelict old woman. She was very short and wide because of the layers of extra clothes she wore. Shopping bags held all her possessions and bottles frequently popped out of them. She carried one bottle of booze in her hand and she would stop every now and then to take a swig at it. On her head was a battered green beret under which her grey hair stuck out around her wizened wrinkled face. But Sophia, or old Soaky, as the Cockneys called her, was feeling very happy as she sang, 'Show me the way to go home. I'm tired an I wanna go to bed,' in a cracked voice waving her bottle at the passers-by. ''Appy New Year,' she called and shouted, but they did not respond. Old Soaky hurled a string of four-letter oaths after them but she was such a well-known character in that part of London that no one took much notice of her. Cursing all the time Soaky climbed down the long dangerous wooden steps that led to her hideaway by the river bank. She took a few steps in the mud and then fell over the helpless body of Sparky. 'What the effin' 'ell?' she cried, putting her hand out and feeling his face. 'Oh crikey, a stiff!' Trembling, she lit a match and gazed down at him. 'Ah, the poor young sod. Too young ter chuck 'imself in the river.' Then her hand felt inside his jacket and she pulled out the mud-soaked wallet. 'Cor! seven quid,' she gloated as she counted the sodden notes. 'I'll put 'em on the pipes to dry, and I'll get a few bottles tomorrer to see me frough.'

With surprisingly agile movements she climbed up the steps to a deep recess under the bridge where the hot water pipes from the power station were situated. It was here that old Soaky slept, with just a few sacks and a bit of tarpaulin for the damp nights. Setting down her bottle, she put her loot along the pipes to dry and looked down at Sparky's lifeless, muddy shape. 'Oh, crikey,' she muttered, 'how can I look at him all night? I'll cover 'im up and let old Bill find him in the mornin'.'

She dragged down a piece of tarpaulin and rolled Sparky loosely in it, and pushed him under the place where she slept. Then with a sudden afterthought, she poured some of her whisky between the stiff blue lips. The liquor made a kind of gurgle as it went down. 'Oh well,' she said taking another swig herself, 'mustn't waste it. It won't do him no good, poor little sod, will it?'

Soaky returned to her nest and settled herself down for the night. In no time she was sleeping soundly and her drunken grunts and snores waffled across the murky, fast-flowing waters of the River Thames.

When morning dawned the tide was up and washed the sides of the warehouse. Soaky awoke feeling warm and dry in her hide-away. She lit her little oil stove and placed a big enamel mug full of water and tea leaves on it to make a 'brew up'. As the cold morning air settled in, she began to feel a bit damp and shivery.

'Never mind,' she muttered to herself, 'a nice drop of whisky in me tea will soon pull me togevver.'

As she sipped her hot tea, she was startled by a strange sound. It was a kind of dull moaning sound. Was it the wind? Or the river boats? Then she remembered that poor stiff under the bridge. She hopped down quickly to look at him. To her horror she saw that his eyes had opened, and he now stared vacantly at her. 'Oh my gawd!' she cried. 'The poor sod ain't dead.'

She went back up to get her mug and returned to hold it to Sparky's stiffened lips. He was soaking wet because the river had washed over him in the night. 'Gotta get yer outa there,' Soaky murmured. 'Wait a minute.' She pulled and pushed with all her might. She was quite strong for an elderly woman but then Soaky was not as old as she looked. Her way of life had prematurely aged her. So with much effort she managed to drag Sparky to a high dry spot, near the pipes that crossed the river. With her hand she wiped the mud from his face, and poured hot, whisky-laced tea, down his throat. There was blood on his head and a piece of his ear missing. 'Had a nasty fall, ain't yer?' she said conversationally. 'Wasn't drunk, was yer? Naughty boy.' She undid the tarpaulin and wrapped her own bedding around him talking to him all the time. 'Silly boy, fancy getting fed up with life at your age. Don't know what the world is coming to.' She explored his lower parts, and there she found a deep wound in his thigh. It was still bleeding slightly. 'Oh dear, who done that? Nearly knocked yer cock off, yer have.'

Soaky lifted up her skirt. Underneath the top dress she wore another half a dozen. For if anyone kindly gave her a dress, Soaky would wear it till it fell off her. She tore away some white material. 'Now, that's a nice calico, that is,' she said. 'I'll wet it and make a bandage. I'll soon get you fixed up, my lad, and then you can go home to your muvver. There ain't a lot of room for two dahn 'ere.' All the time, as she dressed his wound, Soaky cackled and nodded her head like some comical puppet in the theatre. She washed and bathed Sparky's body and bandaged his thigh. 'Nice looking boy,' she said. 'Real red hair, something like my Johnny. Bleedin' Germans killed my Johnny,' she said bitterly. 'Oh, the bastards!' She grabbed her bottle of whisky and began to drink. 'I'll sit right here next to yer to keep yer warm,' she said, 'but it ain't bad dahn 'ere. Look at me central 'eating . . .' she giggled, pointing to the pipes.

Sparky's eyelids flickered occasionally and his lips were now less blue. He twitched every now and then but there was no other sign of life in him. 'I'll get a nice loaf and a bottle of milk and make yer some nice sops,' she told him. 'Better get out early, in case they catches me.'

Off Soaky went, hopping along like a little dog out on a spree. First she went to the factory where the milkman left three pints for the watchman. She eyed out the land and then quickly pinched one of the bottles. 'That'll do.' Then off she went down past a little grocer's shop where the shopkeeper was so busy putting out his wares that he did not notice the quick hand that whipped away one of the wrapped bread loaves which had just been delivered.

Off went old Soaky back to her hideout, where she boiled the milk and soaked the bread in it. 'Now, some nice sops,' she cried, ramming it down Sparky's throat. He began to cough and splutter.

'That's it, luv – corf it up,' cried Soaky. 'Get all the bloody Thames outa yer lungs and this sops will do yer good.'

New Year's Day was quiet after the festivities of the night before. At midday Soaky went on the prowl again, going to different pubs where she hoped to get treated. Then she spent some of Sparky's money on a bottle of whisky. When she got back to her hideout, it was getting dark, and Sparky still lay wrapped up in the tarpaulin with a pile of sacks over him. She wiped his face with her hand, and wet his lips with the whisky. 'Come on, cock, we're gonna have a party, you and I.'

Soaky sat beside Sparky drinking from the bottle and getting very drunk as she sang all her favourite Cockney songs. She had brought some drinking straws back from the pub. Filling the mug with milk, she added some whisky and stuck the end of the straw in his mouth. 'Now, luv,' she said, putting the other end of the straw in the mug, 'sup it up, it will do you good.' Slowly, those dry lips of Sparky's began to draw down the fluid, and the colour came back into his ashen cheeks. Soaky wrapped him up warm and rolled him nearer the pipes before continuing with her drunken revelry till late into the night. Still no sound came from the body wrapped inside that bundle of sacks. He just had his eyes open and he stared vaguely about him. The warmth and the hot drink were beginning to heal his body but there was no cure for his mind; although that bullet had not penetrated his brain, it had damaged it.

Old Soaky took good care of him, and no one bothered them. The police and the watchmen were quite aware of the existence of old Soaky but they knew she would not bother them for long. For old Soaky was what was known as a 'traveller'. She came in on a bender and then would disappear to Kent for the summer, when she would work, picking fruit and such like. That had been her pattern of life since the war, when she had lost both her son and husband in a matter of weeks.

So Sparky lay in Soaky's underground cellar while the police were dragging the river and searching all around the wasteland for his body. They pulled in the three criminals but finding no

325

corpse, they had to let them go. Someone had grassed that they had taken money from the big boys to carry out a contract but then had mucked it up. They would have felt safer in prison because the vengeance of the East End gangs was something to be avoided.

Tommy Evans sold his story of his narrow escape to the newspapers and received a large sum of money which he used to fly off to South America with his family.

But Amy, poor sad little Amy, was left with nothing. She came back from Ashmullen, to her flat with her three children, still watching and waiting for Sparky to come home.

Chapter Fifteen

Old Soaky

The Thames tide rose and fell, and the flotsam and jetsam of river rubbish piled up high on the tow path as old Soaky went back and forth, her old wellington boots squelching through the mud. She was keeping a wary eye open for anything that might be of use, that had been washed up by the tide. Occasionally she found coins or a bit of jewellery but lately her luck had been out. Added to this problem was the responsibility she had towards that poor sick lad whose body was still up under the wharf. When sober she would stare at him dejectedly wondering what on earth she should do about him. It never occurred to her that the whole country might be searching for him. For old Soaky never read newspapers, she only collected them to keep her feet warm at night.

One morning, just as she was grabbing the pint of milk off the watchman's doorstep, he opened the door swiftly and pounced on her. 'Gotcher!' he hollered. 'You wicked old cow! Stole a bottle of milk from me every day this week, yer did.'

'Owa'' Soaky yelled. 'Let me go! I'll give yer the money for it, honest, I will. Yer don't expect a poor old body like me to go chasing after the milkman, do yer?'

'Now, old Soaky, you just get yerself outa' 'ere,' the watchman said. 'Yer get orf on yer travels or I'll get ol' Bill ter move yer aht.' He hovered over her, a big man in a blue uniform with silver buttons.

'Nasty old sod,' yelled Soaky, 'all the bleedin' same, yer are, when yer 'as a uniform on. I knew yer when yer didn't 'ave a pot to piss in.'

The man softened a little. 'Well, get on yer way,' he said. 'I ain't havin' you pinch me milk to feed them wild cats.'

'I only wanted a nice hot cuppa,' she whined, 'me throat gets so dry in the mornings.'

He reached inside his hut and handed her half a bottle of milk. ' 'Ere y'are, that's wot's left of yesterday's, but I warns yer, it's the last time. Yer had better get on yer way tomorro'.' With that, he disappeared into his hut and banged the door shut.

Jubilantly, Soaky lopped off very quickly back to her hideaway clutching her half a bottle of milk.

Sparky was now propped up against a brick wall. He still had a kind of twisted expression on his face but there was a little more colour in his cheeks. His eyes looked vacant as he stared around him.

'Pooh!' Soaky cried, 'wot a stink! Done it again, 'ave yer? Never mind, I'll soon clean yer up and then I'll make yer some nice sops. Does yer good that does.'

Later she sat mournfully stirring the bread and milk beside the small oil lamp, a melancholy expression on her wrinkled face. 'Pity I got to move on, she reflected. 'Just as I was getting used to havin' a bit of company. I wish yer could speak to me, son, then I might be able to find someone who owns yer.' She patted Sparky's head as if he were a stray dog. 'Shame I got to leave yer, 'cause if they chases me outa 'ere I'll be put in an institution. Yer wouldn't like that, would yer?' she queried, but nothing came back from that expressionless face.

'If I leaves yer 'ere, yer will die. That's just as well, I suppose,' she added in a very depressed manner, 'because you, poor boy, are in a very bad way. But old Soaky ain't like that,' she said getting up and cheering up. 'Help each other, is my motto and gawd help them wot gets caught helping theirselves.' She gave a little titter and proceeded to shovel Sparky's breakfast sops down his throat. Then she wrapped him up warm and rolled him closer to the hot water pipes. 'Now yer a nice clean boy. Have a nice little snooze, old Sophia won't be long.' She spoke tenderly to him as if he were a baby. Seeing Sparky settled, she then toddled off along the riverside, walking on the tow path with her head bent, her eyes searching the ground in the hope of finding something valuable. Then she made a sudden detour up a flight of steps to an old tavern called the Tugboat, the back entrance of which led down to the river. It was here that a few remaining lightermen gathered to drink and talk among themselves. There were still some old barge owners and some descendants of the ancient watermen who ferried folk across the Thames long before they built the bridges. Yet some still plied their trade along that now almost deserted river. One such man was Jack who now sat in that sleazy bar contentedly puffing his pipe. He wore a sea cap on the back of his tousled head and beer dripped off his beard.

''Ow are yer, Jack?' asked Soaky sliding in beside him. 'Thought I'd find yer 'ere. I saw your old barge, the *Mary Lou* out in the river.'

'Gor blimey! Soaky, what do you want?' Jack cried. 'Thought you had passed over.'

'Naw, naw!' grinned Soaky. 'I'm still alive and kicking. Got enough to treat me? Only half of scrumpy, that will do.'

Jack beckoned the barman to bring Soaky a drink. The barman brought the cider and slammed it on to the wooden table, glancing at Soaky with the utmost suspicion.

But Soaky was unperturbed and swallowed her drink with gusto. 'I want to ask yer a favour, Jack,' she said.

'Out with it,' Jack said, giving her a shrewd glance from under his heavy great brows. 'If it's money I ain't got any. Doing very badly these days.'

'I was goin' to ask yer to take me 'ome on yer barge,' Soaky said.

Jack guffawed. 'What, on the old *Mary Lou*? Can it, Soaky, you go home on the road, like you always do.'

'Not this time, Ben I can't, and you often did me a favour in the past.' She nudged him with her elbow, 'And I done you a few, too.'

'Oh, blimey, Soaky, now that was twenty years ago and you was a lot different to the old bag you are today.'

'Oh, well, soon forgets, yer friends do, when yer need them,' Soaky said dropping her head gloomily.

'What's the idea of wanting to go down the river? It's miles out of yer way,' Jack said in a puzzled manner.

'I got a passenger,' Soaky explained. 'A good friend of mine, been on a big bender and got awful complications.'

'It's time you packed all that up, Soaky,' said Jack, 'at your age, too.'

'Naw, naw, nuffink like that. He's a young lad, I knows him well, I'm goin' ter take him back to his muvver,' lied Soaky.

Jack stared at her even more suspiciously. Then he said: 'All right. Six o'clock is high tide. You'd better be there, 'cause I won't hang about.'

'Thanks, Jack,' Soaky said as she lopped away with her old

wellington boots flopping against her legs and her little green beret clamped down tight over her wispy grey hair. She talked loudly to herself as she made her way back across the main road. She called in at the off-licence for a bottle of whisky and took swigs from it as she went along home to her nest under the bridge. Sparky still lay huddled by the hot pipes, wrapped in tarpaulin. Soaky poured the neat whisky down his throat, and he coughed and spluttered with some vigour.

'Good,' said Soaky. 'Now that means yer getting better. Now, we are going to the country. It's very nice down in Kent, I spent a lot of my young days down there, I did. Got me own 'ome, I 'ave, down there. I only comes up to town for a little bit of excitement. Now, yer be a good boy while I'll wrap yer up nice and warm and get yer ready.'

Buried in the debris lying around them she found a length of rope which she tied around the old overcoat and tarpaulin that Sparky was wrapped in. 'Now I got to get yer down the river,' she said. 'And I got an idea.' Off she scampered, looking this way and that like a wary stray cat. In no time at all she had found what she had in mind. It was an upright trolley that was used to carry the loads from the lorries. But it was too early to pinch it yet, while it was still light. She returned to her hideout and waited. At five o'clock, when it was dark, old Soaky made off with the trolley. She dragged poor old Sparky along by the rope tied round his middle and, with surprising strength, hoisted him on to the trolley to which she firmly tied him. The whisky seemed to have knocked Sparky out. He lay with his mouth and eyes closed. Soaky picked up her over-flowing shopping bag and hooked it over the handle of the trolley. 'Good, 'ere we go. Back to the nice countryside – that will do you the world of good, Boysie.'

Pushing and shoving, she manoeuvred the trolley down the incline to the river, and then on to the tow path and under the bridge. The tide washed around her feet, and the trolley's wheels got stuck in the mud. But she did not give up. Valiantly and with great effort, old Soaky managed to push her load towards the Tugboat tavern. At last the shadowy shape of the *Mary Lou* loomed out of the mist. A lamp shone out and a husky voice called to her: 'Is that you, old Soaky?'

'Aye, aye! Captain,' she called back jubilantly, giving the trolley a final push to get it along the gangway where the old barge lay heavily laden with cargo.

'Oh, blimey!' exclaimed Jack. 'What have you got there?' He came forward to help her, peering down at Sparky with caution. ''Ere, he ain't dead, is he?'

'Of course he ain't,' snapped Soaky. 'I wouldn't waste me bleedin' time 'umping 'im back 'ome if he was.'

Between them, Sparky was unloaded and carried down the gangway to a small cabin where a wood stove burned. Inside, the air was quite smoky but very warm.

'I'll put you down at the cement works in the morning. That suit you?' asked Jack.

'Right!' replied Soaky, getting out her bottle. 'Now I'll have a little kip.'

All through the night the barge chugged through the deep river mist moving with the tide towards the backwater where Soaky came from. And throughout the night, Sparky lay motionless on the bunk while Soaky dozed boozily beside him.

At dawn Jack threw an old sea boot down the gangway to wake her up. 'Stand ready,' he called 'going inshore.'

There was a loud grating sound as the *Mary Lou* rocked precariously against the sea wall. Jack hitched the barge to the bollard with a rope. 'I'll help you get him ashore,' he said, 'but gawd knows how you'll get on from there. But that's not my business. And don't you pester me any more, Soaky, I'm right fed up with yer.' He was half joking as he said this.

'All right,' Soaky said. 'Get us ashore and I'll do the rest. I ain't only a pretty face, yer know.'

Jack grinned into his beard. 'Yer a rotten old baggage now, Soaky, but you wasn't too bad when you was young and I first knew yer.'

Slowly they hauled Sparky's helpless body ashore and laid him down on the frosty grass. Then Jack untied his barge and sailed on down the Thames Estuary to a place where the Medway and the Thames joined each other in a race for the sea.

Soaky lay beside Sparky watching the red dawn streaking the sky as the sun came up over the sea. 'Soon be daylight, Boysie,' she said conversationally to the unconscious lad, 'and I'll find a way to get yer 'ome.'

Soon the world was awake. The birds sang their early morning song and over the green marsh the cattle began to low. Still Soaky

331

sat patiently waiting for someone to turn up and transport her to that little old shack in the woods where she lived most of the summer.

Soaky's story was a sad one. She used to be known as Sophia Irene Browne, a tidy lively little Cockney woman who came down to Kent during the war with her teenage son, while her husband was out East in the army. At first, Sophia lived in a tied farm cottage with her son, Johnny, and worked in the fields and orchards. But within a year, her husband was killed out East and Johnny had left to join the navy. But he, too, was soon killed, drowned before his nineteenth birthday. After this double tragedy, Sophia went on the booze. She drank very heavily and it was not long before she was pushed out from the farmer's cottage. It was then that she packed her lot in with old Silas, a notorious boozer, who was a good deal older than she. Silas was hooked on his own homemade brew. He made wine that was extremely potent and lived in a rickety little shack in the woods. He worked his own land, paid no rates or taxes, and he made no contribution to the war effort. When Sophia from London shacked up with old Silas it became the joke of the village, but nevertheless, Silas and Sophia seemed to get on very well together. In the summer Sophia worked at the fruit picking and Silas grew his own vegetables and kept chickens. They would get drunk together on Saturday nights and could often be seen swaying home arm in arm through the country lanes.

After the war Sophia stayed on living with Silas in the old shack. Their way of life was still not all it could be. They had a hole in the ground for a lavatory and a long walk down the lane to fetch fresh water. But it was exceptionally beautiful up there on top of the hill where the emerald green forest rolled down towards the sea, away from the troubled world. There was no one to worry them, and no one to care for but each other. When Silas had sat in his old homemade chair and drank his last glass of rhubarb wine, Sophia had been devastated, but after his death she stayed on in the shack getting rather more derelict and drinking more frequently than before. There were no proper deeds to the shack or to the land around it, for Silas had dug it out of the forest and squatted on it for so many years that no one bothered. The shack stood empty whenever Sophia went off for a big booze-up in London, but the locals knew that Sophia would return in the spring like a migrating bird. Having earned the name of old Soaky, she was accepted in the neighbourhood as an eccentric.

Soaky's return this year was on the early side. A frost was still on the hedgerows as she sat on the edge of the marsh with her silent companion waiting patiently for someone to transport them both up the hill to her little shack.

She did not have to wait long. Along the lane came the crippled farmhand Jim, in a shaky old wagon, tossing out bales of hay to feed the cattle.

'Jim!' Soaky hailed him.

'Well, I'll be buggered if it's not old Soaky,' laughed Jim. 'What are you doing down here so early in the morning?'

'Trying to get up to me shack. Will you give me a lift, Jim?'

'Well, it's a bit out of me way, but I'll do it,' he replied generously.

'Got me son with me,' she said. 'I'm bringing him down for a breath of fresh air.'

'Thought he went down at sea?' asked Jim.

'Naw! Just got knocked abaht a bit, but he still ain't well. Going to look after 'im, I am.'

'Well, let's hope he will be all right,' said Jim, looking down at Sparky's lifeless body.

'I'll get 'im on 'is feet, I will,' said Soaky.

'Going to be a bit lonely up there for you in this weather,' remarked Jim.

They pulled Sparky into the wagon amongst the hay bales, and set off. 'No,' said Sophia as the shack came into view. 'I'm used to it, I've slept in a lot worse places than that, I have.'

When they reached the shack, Jim, being a very kindly lad, helped Soaky to carry Sparky into the shack. They had to fight their way down the weed-covered path and through the tangle of blackberry bushes that grew around the shack. Inside, everything was covered with cobwebs.

'Well,' said Jim as he dumped Sparky on the bed. 'I wish you luck. I'll be off now. I got a long day's work ahead.'

'Soon get a nice fire going,' said Soaky, when Jim had gone. 'Ain't it nice to be 'ome? Got plenty of logs out there to last me till the spring.'

Soaky lit the fire and in no time the wooden logs were blazing

333

brightly. She put the ancient iron kettle on to boil and covered Sparky with lots of blankets.

'That's it, Boysie,' she said, 'sleep it orf – that's the best cure for everything.'

She settled herself in the rocking chair by the fire, pulled out her bottle and continued to take swigs from it. 'Said yer were me son, I did. That will soon go round the village,' she muttered on. 'Bloody nosey lot they are, down there, but my Johnny wouldn't mind. He'd like his mum to have a bit of company, wouldn't you, love?' She looked up at the dusty picture of a smiling sailor boy. She sighed deeply and began to doze a little.

Suddenly she woke with a jerk and sprang into action. 'Now then,' she said determinedly. 'You've got a lot of work to do, you have, Soaky.' With great vigour she began to dust down the cobwebs from the corners. She washed the cups and saucers and rummaged in the cupboards for things to eat. 'Wasn't a bad old bloke, Silas. Still got some homemade jam, he made, and honey from 'is bees and wine from 'is fruit. Always was busy, he was. I was fond if 'im, I was, so you be a good boy,' she chattered on to Sparky, 'and me and you will spend the summer 'ere in this lovely fresh air.'

She pulled back the ragged curtains to reveal the splendid view right out across the Thames Estuary. All around them the forest was quiet with just the hush of winter. The frost hung in silvery threads on the boughs and a little robin puffed himself out against the cold and hopped about on the path.

'Well, now, 'ere's that old robin, cheeky little sod, come to welcome me 'ome,' said Soaky with great satisfaction as she watched him. She was very glad to be back.

Chapter Sixteen

The Kent Woods

Slowly the beautiful spring came to that part of Kent bringing great beauty as it had done every year. Under the bushes sweet violets grew and the primroses came back to life, their green shoots poking through the moist earth with tiny golden buds about to give birth. This was the time of the year that old Soaky always looked forward to. It gave her renewed life. This year she pranced about the neglected plot pointing out to Sparky such things as the growth of the wallflowers.

Sparky now sat just inside the door of the hut, well wrapped up in a lot of old woollies.

'There y'are, Boysie,' she said. 'Them daffodils is showing through the ground. Old Silas planted them when he was young and every year they comes back up, just like me,' she would titter.

Although Sparky could not completely share the joke, there was a response from his twisted face and a kind of lightening up of his fish-like eyes.

'That's it, Boysie,' Soaky said kindly, 'get that nice fresh air in your lungs. You'll soon feel better.'

There was indeed a vast improvement in Sparky. He would point to his mouth if he wanted to eat or drink and to his lap if he wanted to urinate. Then Soaky would get out the wide-necked bottle and help him. 'Now be a good boy,' she would say. 'No bed wetting tonight, eh?'

There was also a definite change in Soaky herself. Soon after their arrival she had said: 'Now I'll put a nice big pot of hot water on and me and you will have a wash. We're going to burn all these dirty old clothes. I got some nice frocks put away down here, and I think Silas' old clothes should fit you a treat.' She had washed Sparky and dressed him in old pyjamas and made him stay in bed. The old stone fireplace glowed all night as she had stoked it up with logs, and the high pointed roof gathered in the heat. Soaky had then washed herself and, quite unashamed, stood in the firelight naked as a jay bird. 'I'm a crooked old body now but I used to be nice and slim, I did,' she informed Sparky.

The next day she made a fire in the garden and burned all their old clothes along with the garden rubbish.

And the days were spent, when she wasn't drinking, cleaning up her little patch and making the place comfortable for her and her newly adopted son, Boysie.

With a plentiful supply of homemade wines the two of them stayed put until the spring came round. Sparky's condition continued to improve but there was no chance that he would ever really be normal. Their relationship was a good one; he was to her husband and son, and she to him a mother. They both needed each other in this wilderness, amid the dark forest overlooking the wild marshlands. They grew close and made the best of what life had left to them.

Jim the farmhand often came by to leave them cans of fresh water and occasionally milk. And Soaky went out onto the little plot that Silas cultivated and dug up potatoes, carrots and onions. 'I'll make us a nice stew tonight, Boysie,' she said to Sparky. 'Won't have no meat in it, but vegetables does yer more good.'

When spring proper came at last and the paths were clear, Soaky put Sparky in old Silas' chair and for safety's sake tied him in tight. 'Now, I'm going down the village,' she explained, 'to see if I can draw me old age pension. I do that every year. Be a good boy and I'll bring you back some sweets.'

A kind of nodding of Sparky's head was all she got, but it was clear that he understood her.

Soaky pulled on Silas' old trench coat, jammed her green beret down over her grey hair and, in her floppy wellingtons, set off down the lane carrying an empty shopping bag. As she made her way along the muddy woodland paths, she hummed a little tune to herself. The birds hopped around repairing their nests and a mating black bird sang his courting song. There was not a sight nor sound of another human. It was nature at its best and most wonderful high up on the green hill overlooking the sea. Slowly down the hill she went, noting with satisfaction the glowing patches of wild flowers through the fresh green grass as she left the shadow of the great oak trees and went on through the apple orchard in the direction of the square Norman church tower, the centre of the village.

The village was a very old settlement, situated at the end of the marshland, which hit the Thames shore. Soaky had seen many changes in the place since she had first discovered it – new houses and bungalows had appeared and the population had grown, but it had not lost that rural touch. Every year it lay low and silent under the winter snow and every year it would return to life when the spring came round. As she crossed the village street, villagers who knew her called out: 'Hallo, you back, Soaky?' or 'How's tricks, Soaky? Still up in the woods?'

To some she replied but to others she did not.

'Cheeky sods,' she would mutter. 'Knew you when you were snotty-nosed kids, I did.'

In fact, everyone had known for some time that Soaky was back, for Jim had quickly spread the word that she had returned but that this time she had brought her wounded son from the mental hospital and was looking after him.

This last fact had puzzled those of them who cared to think about it. 'I don't believe it,' said some. 'Didn't her son go down on the *Renown*? And that was more than twenty years ago. He must be an old man now.'

'Well, I don't know who she's bloody got up there but let's help the poor old gel,' said one kind-hearted villager called Ted Hazel. 'I'll pop her in a couple of rabbits when I go up there shooting.'

Soaky was given a fairly warm welcome by the villagers who generally did not really care for the woodlanders who squatted up there in the woods.

At the Post Office, Soaky handed in her pension book. It was a tattered, dirty object that went with her on her travels.

The cashier told her: 'It's out of date, Sophia. We'll send for a new one for you. In the meantime, you can get credit if you want it.'

Soaky filled her bag with provisions, not forgetting to slip in a bottle of her favourite brand of Scotch, and then went off to the Victoria, one of the three pubs in the village. The governor took one look down his slate. 'All right, Soaky,' he said, 'on the slate then but only two, mind you.'

Soaky had her two scrumpy ciders and then trotted off to the Bull, where the same thing happened, and then on to the Evening Star. Afterwards, she wove her way down the village street, staggering a little as she humped her heavy shopping bag over the shoulders. Her old back bent but her feet were still firmly on the ground when she made her last port of call at the Merry Boys, a small inn just outside the village on the edge of the wood.

Miss Smith, the proprietor, stared at her in an unfriendly way. 'Soaky,' she said, 'I can see that you've filled yourself up in the village, and now you want to scrounge drinks from me.'

This sort of welcome always set Soaky off. She waved her fist aggressively and her language became very strong. 'I ain't no bleedin' scrounger,' she shouted. 'I pays me way, I do. Got a sick son up there, I have. Fought for the likes of you, he did.'

Miss Smith moved back as Soaky advanced belligerently.

But sitting in the corner of the pub was an old friend of Soaky's, the Donkeyman. Big, broad and red-faced, he stood up. 'Sit down, old gel,' he roared. 'I'll get you a drink. While I got a penny in me pocket, you can always have a drink off me.'

Soaky sat staring boozily at him. 'Old Donkey,' she slurred. 'It's good ter see yer still around.'

Miss Smith retired from the fray as Donkey and Soaky got together with half a dozen drinks talking of old times. 'No toffee-nosed sods around then, eh Donkey?' laughed Soaky, knocking back another whisky.

As a boy, Donkey had looked after the string of donkeys that worked in the local quarries. The donkeys were no longer worked but the name had stuck. Now retired, Donkey, kept a few of the beasts on his plot of land and drove a little donkey cart around the village. If anyone got drunk and was unable to walk properly, Donkey was always there ready and willing to get them home through that dark wood. If by chance he was the one who was too drunk to see, it was just as well that the little donkey knew its way home.

At the end of the day, a very jolly Soaky went home singing, 'Oh, I do like to be beside the seaside,' lying on her back in the donkey cart.

The lights in the shack were not on when she arrived home. Sparky still sat tied to the chair by the fire which was almost out. Soaky very drunk and very contrite, waved the bottle at him. 'Never mind,' she muttered, 'have a little drink with me, Boysie.' She poured the neat whisky down his throat and then, after stoking up the fire, she lay down on the rug to sleep it off.

338

Spring gave way to summer and Jim brought up some laying hens that someone did not want and a white rabbit for Sparky, who just sat and stared at it most of the day. Soaky went out fruit picking and was away quite a time.

Sparky was now able to move a little and could help himself to the sandwiches and drinks that Soaky left within his reach. Soaky would return every afternoon at three o'clock, loaded with cherries and blackcurrants, or whatever fruit she had been picking that particular time. In the fields they rather liked old Soaky.

'She's a good worker in spite of her boozing,' the farmer said to one of the other pickers. 'But I must say there seems to be a good improvement in her this year. She comes to work regular and she don't have the big hangovers now.'

'She's drinking much less since she had that lad up there,' said one woman.

'I'll send him some homemade cake tomorrow,' said another.

Soaky settled to a kind of regular pattern of living and made many friends who gave her little luxuries to give to her 'son' – cakes, sweets, a home-knitted pullover. They were only little things that they, being only workers, had to give. On Sundays Soaky planted the garden and tended her vegetables and tomatoes. She cleared the undergrowth around the shack and repaired the chicken house in which were two hens and a cockerel. The big apple trees produced huge green apples in the autumn and the blackberries grew in abundance. She kept herself well occupied, making fruit jellies and jam, and never worried about the outside world. There were no more trips to town, just her and Boysie and the little old shack. Occasionally she did go on a bender whenever she got fed-up and then she would go down to one of the locals to fill herself up on cider until she started singing and dancing and then the old Donkeyman would give her a ride home.

The newspapers still occasionally carried headlines of the terrible East End crime that had shocked everyone early in the New Year, of the body that was never found and of the three men accused, because someone had grassed. Then there was the news of the men's acquittal because no body had been found. None of these things bothered old Soaky. They passed her by. She simply was not interested, living her own rural life with Sparky, or

Boysie, as she called him. Whenever Soaky was a little high on homemade wine, she would give Sparky a few glasses too. He would rock his head from side to side and give a kind of giggle. Soaky would hold his hand and sing. 'When Johnny comes marching home, hurrah!' and rock his hand up and down and indescribable pleasure showed in those rather lifeless eyes.

The summer had been glorious that year, with the sun beating down on them every day as they sat in the garden. Then the leaves of the trees turned, colouring the entire hill with reds and browns and greens. When winter came, it was back beside the big log fire once more. And Soaky did not feel the urge to travel up to London as she usually did. She was settled in her shack. 'You and me, Boysie, lives the life of bloody Riley up here in this lovely place,' she said. 'I'll never ever want to leave, now I've got you to look after.'

Chapter Seventeen

The Last of Old Soaky

After five idyllic years living in the woodland shack with Soaky, Sparky had come a long way. He was now physically quite strong but still quite mentally retarded. He was able to walk a little and talk in a strange kind of gabble. He listened attentively a lot, and he was a very happy boy. He could feed the chickens and keep the fire going, and was now quite independent in his personal hygiene.

It was Soaky who got Bill Dunkley, the old blacksmith, to come up and give Sparky a hair-cut and a nice close shave every now and then. Bill was very useful to all the people like Soaky who squatted in the wood. His smithy was next door to the Merry Boys Inn, where he shod horses and often sheared the sheep in between times. He cut the small boys' hair and shaved their dads and also kept a betting book. So if anyone wanted a bet on the big race it was just next door to the pub. He also had a telephone, which was a moneyspinner for him, because he did a roaring trade with the woodlanders who were not on the phone.

Although they could not be seen easily and each was as isolated as Soaky's, there were in fact around thirty or forty little home-made shacks in that deep wood, and they carried on over the hill and all down the lane. Each one was an individual property with its own design and its own way of life. It was a secret way of living and staying away from the authorities.

The woodlanders dug into the moist earth to produce fine vege-tables, and they grew wonderful roses in the clay soil. Some kept bees, others had a pig or two, and everyone had geese or hens, and lots and lots of fine apple trees.

The story was that this woodland community had begun way back after the First World War when Lord Darnley, whose family had owned all this land since the days of James I, and who was a modern and generous young lord, had bequeathed a plot of land in Parrot Wood to any soldier returning from the war on condition that he cultivated it. A fee of one pound was charged with an option to purchase a deed, though most of the old folk never bothered. They just built shacks and farmed their plots and lived happily ever after. Many children were born there and the old folk stayed on and on as other families came to the woods when the Second World War began, just to get away from the blitz, and so the woodland community was formed. After the war the younger descendants took over these shacks as weekend places and came down with droves of kids, had bonfire parties and spent their holidays wandering the woods. But they were disapproved of by the local council. The young Londoners cut the grass and went fishing and shooting for a couple of days before returning to town for the week. It was a kind of mixed group. But still the old folk clung to the derelict shacks they could no longer look after. The buildings were all very primitive. There was no running water and the shack dwellers had to walk the whole length of the lane to get water from the stand-pipe at the end of the road. Some trundled barrels to collect it, while others wore old-fashioned yokes on their shoulders with a bucket attached on each side and then staggered breathlessly back up the hill with their supply of fresh water. It was all a unique and strange way of life but quiet happiness hung in the air. When they did chance to meet the neighbours would greet each other warmly, or they would leave a little present of flowers and fruit outside your shack.

Unfortunately, like most beautiful spots, the condition of the woods came to the attention of the modern district council who had severely neglected it for many years, calling it 'unadopted land'.

For years they had ignored the old folk who had lived through the winters up there suffering so much hardship – too feeble to fetch water or chop wood – that many were found frozen stiff each spring. It was unadopted land and no business of the county council, but nevertheless, peace and beauty reigned. There was the lovely dawn chorus high up in the trees in the summer, and the nightingales always sang sweetly; the blue jay nested there and many tiny blue tits flew in and out of the clinging ivy trails. The wild life was quite prolific and the bluebells carpeted the woods in the spring. There was an indescribable beauty up there on that green hill which led down to the Thames marshland. It was there that black-and-white geese migrated from colder climates to fill the small pools. And it was here that the inhabitants were able to go out to collect their Sunday lunch. It was an idyllic way of life that had gone on for many years and, as far as the woodlanders were concerned, that would go on for ever.

But the ideas in the village were very different. Down in the Merry Boys Inn the locals talked of farming and sailing and they disapproved of the shanty farms in the woods. Then a rumour began to circulate that a compulsory purchase of the woodlands was to be made. Men wearing soft hats and carrying notebooks snooped furtively around the shacks but got little satisfaction. Then Medway newspapers started a big campaign about the woodlanders with articles about the bad conditions of the people living in the woods.

'Goin' to chuck us out the woods, Soaky,' said Donkeyman one day. 'Where will you go?'

Soaky was lolling, well-boozed, in the back of the donkey cart. 'What will I do? Me and Boysie's all right hup thar. Wot do I want an 'lectric light for? Gor a nice tilley lamp, I 'ave.'

'They say it's 'cause we ain't got a proper lavatory,' said Donkey.

'Ger away,' yelled Soaky. 'Gets a nice lot of stuff out of the old lavatory. How yer gonna grow things w'out it?'

Donkey gave a loud guffaw. 'Heryar, Soaky, back 'ome again,' he said, pulling the donkey to a halt.

Soaky staggered out of the cart. 'Let him come up here,' she roared, 'that council man, and I'll give him what for. Bloody nosey parkers, that's what they are.'

Then it happened. The council announced in the paper that they were about to place a compulsory purchase order on the eighty acres of the woods to run a new road through to the village. At the Inn that Saturday night they were all full of this news.

'Just as well,' one of them said, 'get all them old blighters out of them woods, it will.'

'It'll be good to have a bus service in to the town,' said another.

But not everyone felt that way. There were the weekenders who loved their woodland shacks and spent much time and money renovating them. Then there were those, like old Soaky, who knew no other way of living and were just content and happy to while away the seasons in that wonderful forest that ran over the hill down to the sea. Anyone who owned the land and could produce documents to prove it was instructed to contact the council but not many were forthcoming having hidden in this remote spot and resented interference from the authorities for so many years.

The council had its way and one by one they picked off the squatters and gave them a few hundred pounds and a place in the old folks' home. There were heart-rending scenes from some who had young families and tried hard to stick it out. But in the end they were defeated.

Soaky was oblivious to most of what was going on around her. She still went her merry way, and she and Boysie stayed by the fire into winter, filled up with homemade wine and kept each other company. Soaky never received letters, so when the postman puffed down the path one day and handed her a buff-coloured envelope, she waved it around in the air 'This ain't for me, I don't have no letters,' she declared.

'Well, it's got your name on it,' replied the young postman emphatically.

'Well, you can bloody well take it back, cause I don't want it,' said Soaky.

The postman turned back down the lane and Soaky threw the unopened letter after him and it fell on the ground and got trodden into the mud and forgotten. Such incidents happened several times that winter.

In the spring when Soaky was out and about again there were a lot of old faces missing down in the Merry Boys Inn.

'Where's old Donkey?' Soaky demanded of Miss Smith.

'Gone to live in town, replied Miss Smith. 'Him and his missus is in the old folks' home.'

'Whatever for? yelled Soaky aggressively. 'He was hail and hearty, same as me.'

'They took the money the council offered them and then the council pushed down his shack.'

'I don't believe it,' declared Soaky in horror.

'It's true, Soaky,' said Miss Smith. 'Haven't they made you an offer yet?'

'Offer? What offer?' yelled Soaky.

'Well, I'm being pushed out too,' Miss Smith said. 'They are going to pull this place down and build a school up here.'

'I don't believe yer,' sniffed Soaky, swallowing down her glass of strong cider.

344

'It's a fact. I'll be gone by the end of the summer,' said Bill Dunkley, the blacksmith.

Bleary-eyed, Soaky stared around the room. 'Yer havin' me on, ain't yer?' she declared.

The others knew that there was no persuading her so they just shut up and stopped trying to convince her that what they were telling her was true.

'No one's gettin' me out of me old shack,' she declared. 'Left that to me, old Silas did. Me and Boysie is all right up there.

So Soaky ignored the warnings of the other woodlanders but each day as she went to get water the people gathered around the tap to talk of the end of the woods and as she passed them many of the old places looked desolate and empty with no children playing in the plots any more.

One day a big bulldozer arrived and pushed down most of the small shacks, uprooted all those lovely elms and left them dying in the hot sun.

Seeing what was happening Soaky started swearing revenge on everything and everybody, the lane rang with her bad language. 'Bastards!' she cried. 'Poor old trees. Leave us alone, you bleeders, we ain't goin' ter move. You go to hell!'

The workmen only laughed at her causing Soaky to swig more whisky from the bottle she had just bought.

And now it was assumed that the council had won and the woodlanders had lost. Even when Soaky went to draw her pension, they asked: 'Where are you moving to, Sophia?'

'Me? I ain't moving!' Soaky yelled. 'I'm staying in my little old shack and I'll defy anyone that tries to get me out.'

As the other shacks gradually disappeared, Soaky barred her gate and stared suspiciously at anyone who came down the path. Young men from the council got huge tufts of wet grass aimed in their faces and jugs of water thrown over their heads. 'I'll get the bleedin' gun,' Soaky would shout at them. 'I'll fix yer.'

Sparky sat outside the shack enjoying each scene with a fixed grin on his face. Soaky got very confused. She supped all that was left of the wine and forgot to cook the dinner. Having finished all the drink in the house, she went down to the village for whisky. First she went into the Victoria and then the Evening Star, and then on to the Bull, declaring to one and all that no one would budge her and Boysie from their shack. When she staggered along to the Merry Boys Inn, it was getting dark and the lights of the well-loved inn seemed so very far away that she sat down at the foot of a great oak and dozed off. The revellers came out of the inn singing as they wended their way home. The glow worms cast a strange green light; an owl hooted and the moon sank into the clouds. The woods were silent. Soaky slept on through the dark night and as the cold mist came over the marshes she tried momentarily to move but she couldn't. She lay back, still and helpless, and she gently closed her eyes and passed wearily off into a more peaceful world.

Jim found her the next morning as he went to tend the cattle. He rang for an ambulance which had to come from the nearby town. Before the ambulance arrived, Soaky was carried into the Merry Boys Inn and laid out on the old wooden table in the bar. They straightened out her old limbs but there was no sign of life left in her.

'Poor old gel,' they said. 'She was so worried about having to leave that old hut. That's what done it.'

'Here, what about her poor son?' someone said. 'He is up there all alone.'

They went up to the shack and took Sparky back to town into hospital while the ambulance took old Soaky to the mortuary.

The next week, when Soaky lay buried in the churchyard among her old friends, the council came and bulldozed down her shack, trampling over her beloved roses and uprooting her apple trees. The old shack in the woods just disappeared.

Only those who had known the woods remembered old Soaky and no one bothered about Sparky, who had been put away in that hospital for the mentally disturbed, way out of sight of the town.

Chapter Eighteen

Still Waiting

For a long time after Sparky disappeared, Amy continued to feel in her heart that he would walk in one night, whistling a merry tune, and scoop her up into his arms in that boisterous manner he had. She suffered, long, sleepless nights and the long, lonely days and still there was no news of her man who had walked out for a quick drink and a packet of fags and never returned. Over and over in her mind she would trace the circumstances of that New Year's Eve, but she could never come up with a clear picture of what happened.

Her new baby, Tony, thrived and grew into a fat little toddler. Amy became very morose and bad tempered, dividing her time between Annie's flat and her own, always on the look-out watching and waiting.

Amy's two young girls had their own hobbies and their own friends. Her family seemed to have lost interest in her, but one good friend was always there. That was the wide boy, Harry, Sparky's old pal. It was Harry who took Amy out for drinks and repeatedly gave her advice. 'Pack it up, love,' he would say. 'Start living your own life, I'll stick by you and the kids. I promise to go straight. In fact, I have had an offer of a regular job. It's up to you, Amy, for myself I don't care. I'll remain a freelance but if you want me I am here to look after you and Sparky's family.'

Amy just could not make up her mind. She certainly liked Harry. He was common and real working class, short and with a dumpy, hairy body. He had been born and bred on the streets, just like Sparky, and he lived a dodgy sort of existence. But he always seemed to have money and was very generous with it. The baby loved him and called him Dad, but both Rachel and Tosh were resentful of him. No one on earth would ever take the place of their dad. A big enlarged photograph of their father hung on the wall in their bedroom and a book of photos of the good days in Canada was always on view.

Amy missed a man in her bed. Sparky's warm body sometimes

347

seemed to come to her in the night, and it would seem so real that Amy would get up and look around the flat, quite expecting to find him. So she didn't succumb to Harry for a long time. When the boy was five, he was still courting her, much to the annoyance of the girls, who treated him with such scorn.

One Saturday evening when Harry called to take Amy out, he told her that his sister, with whom he lived, was emigrating to New Zealand.

'What will you do?' Amy asked.

'Find lodgings, I suppose,' he replied. 'I've got an elder brother who went out to New Zealand before the war. He's now got a meat-packing business and has done very well for himself. My sister has been thinking of going out there for a long time. It was him who got me my job in Smiffields, he does a lot of business wiff them.' For a year now Harry had held down a regular job at Hay's Wharf, his strong sturdy body humping huge carcasses of sheep. He earned good pay which he spent very generously on Amy and her children.

Amy stared solemnly at him. 'All right, Harry,. everyone knows that you and I are going around together. You might as well pack in with me, but I won't marry you, not until the seven years is up. If Sparky should come back before that time then it will be finished between us.'

Harry grinned. 'It would be the finish of me too, if the old Sparky what we used to know came back, but fair enough, Amy. I'll take good care of you. You'll have no need to work or get social welfare. I can afford to look after you and the family.'

And so began a new phase in Amy's life. Harry's strong arms went around her at night and took away those terrible nightmares. And not having to do her part-time job any longer she had more time free for Annie and Sheila. Mostly they were happy, though the girls would not take any notice of Harry. They were now almost teenagers and stayed out late going to discos. Sometimes Harry tried to give them paternal advice. 'Look 'ere,' he would say, 'you mind who you mixes wiff. In this part of town you could land plenty of trouble.'

'You are not our dad,' they would reply saucily.

Harry was a kind sort of man and this kind of talk hurt his feelings deeply. But there was nothing he could do about it. However, little Tony loved him and Harry bought him plenty of

348

toys and played with him and enjoyed taking him outside all dressed up in smart clothes.

'Harry's a real dad to Tony,' Amy said to Annie. 'The boy worships him.'

Annie nodded her head vigorously: She still did not speak but was very alert watching everything that went on about her, and she still ruled poor Sheila with a rod of iron. Sheila had become quite thin and pathetic looking and she spent her days fetching and carrying for Annie, though she never seemed to mind. She was always in that dream world of film stars and garish magazines that she could not read but loved to look at and cut out the glamorous pictures from.

Life went on at an ordinary pace for our Amy. Now she had a man again, and he was a good man, though very homely. Harry liked to sit in and watch the television most evenings, though occasionally he would go out to watch a football match or a film. But mostly he was happy at home with the family

Amy had never yearned for a bright life, so she mellowed in the warmth of this man's love who left her with few worries. She took less care over her appearance, growing and dressing more plainly as she tried to shift the hurt that every now and then still stabbed her like a knife in her heart. Nothing had been heard of Sparky, her true love, for seven years, and the police had stopped looking for him.

Tony went to school, Rachel went off to live in a flat with her boyfriend who worked at her office, and Tosh went off to teacher training college. Harry took on his role as head of the family with relish. 'Let's move to a nice place, Amy, and send Tony to a good school. I can afford it.'

But for Amy it was the same old reason. 'I can't leave Mother and Sheila,' she said. 'They depend on me.'

So Harry gave in but he did get Tony into a good prep school anyway, and paid for it out of his own pocket. 'I never stood a bloody dog's chance when I was a kid, so let's give the boy a good start,' he said.

So at eleven years old, Tony went to a big private school in the City. Harry took him every day and brought him home in the evenings and sat for hours trying to help him with his homework, while Amy passed away her time wtih Annie and Sheila.

Annie had spent some time lately in and out of hospital. She had a chest complaint which caused her a lot of trouble in the winter months. During this time, Sheila spent many hours going back and forth to the hospital carrying bunches of flowers or bags of sweets, scurrying along on her thin, spindly legs. During Sheila's visits she often noticed another person at the hospital, a small, black-clad figure who seemed to carry the weight of the world on her shoulders. It was old Dolly Palmer whose husband was dying of cancer. All her three boys were now away in prison, and she looked a tragic little figure as she trotted from prison to prison and then to the hospital. Everyone respected her, and all past crimes were forgotten, because that is the way of the East Enders. They would ask her: 'How are you, Dolly? How is the old man?'

'Oh, he is still lingering,' she would reply. 'Not much hope, I'm afraid.' She would stop by to say a word or two to Annie who sat up in bed gasping for her breath and pointing out of the window at the old church tower which was the only remaining structure still standing from the old days. She would turn to Dolly and give her a big smile.

'I know, Annie,' Dolly would say. 'There's not much left of the old place, is there?'

It was while she was watching that window that Annie passed on. A peaceful smile spread across her face and miraculously at the last moment her voice came back as she said, quite clearly: 'Hello, Emily.'

Amy was standing beside the bed cuddling the weeping Sheila and could scarcely believe what she heard, for Emily was that lost eldest daughter who had been killed with her children by the bombs.

Annie's funeral was a big East End affair and all the family came. Letty and Lily came with their families as did the twins, and Joe and Billy. Thus all the Flanagans gathered together for the first time in many years to see their mother given a splendid send-off. The long line of carriages and all the market traders stood still to Annie's memory and many remarked on how that nice big well-dressed family that represented her now had once been the poorest lot of kids in the district.

After the funeral they all went home, back to their nice respectable lives, leaving only Amy and poor Sheila still in this slum place.

Sheila was completely lost without her mother who had ruled her life; she had very little left of herself. As far as Amy was concerned, there was only one thing to do. 'Sheila will have to come and live with us,' she told Harry. 'She won't be happy with anyone else.'

Harry gave a deep sigh but gave in graciously.

So Sheila moved in and certainly was a problem. One thing she liked was to keep busy, so she would constantly fiddle around washing the dishes, and not very well either. Harry, who had been the dishwasher for quite a time, was thoroughly put out.

Sheila's humming also annoyed him intensely. It was a continuous, tuneless hum, that Sheila sang all the time when she was happy, and it interfered considerably with Harry's television viewing. In no way were Sheila and Harry compatible; they were at cross purposes all the time.

Amy always sided with her sister during any of these confrontations, another fact that made Harry exceedingly cross. But Amy was not going to give way. Harry was not going to rule her life, particularly when he was not even her husband. Amy and Harry began to pull apart and he spent more time and effort on the boy, Tony, taking him on Saturdays and Sundays to films and football or down Petticoat Lane. Tony was growing into a tall slim lad, so much like his own dad. And he also had that quiet humour that Sparky had possessed.

The area had quietened down a little but was still a dangerous place to be after dark, for young unemployed boys hung around in gangs and fought each other viciously. It seemed that a new kind of criminal was replacing the old heavies, most of whom had died in the nick. The police had formed a vice squad a few years back with which they had really cleaned up the town. The Palmer brothers and their associates had all gone on down with long sentences for various crimes.

When Tony was about thirteen and doing very well at school, something suddenly happened to shake that East End community. Some fellow in the nick had turned Queen's evidence and crimes previously unsolved had come to light. One was the story behind the disappearance of Tony Binks, known to the underworld as Sparks. The news hit the newspapers and television screens. So, one evening, as some big shot expounded his theory on the old crime, young Tony sat looking at the photographs of his real dad as they were displayed in bright colour on the telly.

Amy got up and turned the telvision off but Tony stopped her. 'Hey, Mum,' he said. 'That's the same photo that's in Rachel's photo album and he's got the same name as mine. Who is that man?' he demanded.

'I don't know,' said Amy as tears welled up in her eyes. 'Go to bed now. You need to get up for school in the morning.'

He obeyed, good boy that he was, but he was no fool. He was a studious lad with a good education, and he knew how to do research. He read the newspapers and the old newspaper cuttings which he found in an old suitcase belonging to Tosh. He even confronted Harry one day. 'Are you my father?' he demanded, 'or is it that bloke who's supposed to have been murdered by these gangsters?'

Harry could not lie but he held down the situation very well. 'No, lad,' he said. 'That was your real dad and he was my best mate. If he is still alive somewhere I know he would want me to take care of you.'

Tony put his arms around Harry's neck warmly. 'You are the only dad I know,' he said, 'and that is all right with me.'

From then on there seemed to exist a barrier of coldness between Amy and her son. It puzzled her. She could not define it but she always felt it was there.

This led to more trouble with Sheila, who liked to go to bingo on Friday nights with Amy, but Harry was now insisting that Amy stayed home with him and Tony to help improve the situation between mother and son.

Amy was between two fires: her fondness for Sheila and her allegiance to her lover and son.

'Let Sheila go alone,' said Harry, 'she knows the way.'

Uneasily, Amy gave Sheila money on Friday evenings to go to bingo which she did manage to do perfectly well. Amy went to meet her on the way home when it got dark. One night when she met her, Sheila said, 'I'll get the fish and chips.' They usually bought fish and chips after a night at bingo.

'Are you sure? Will you be all right?' asked Amy, half delighted and half alarmed by Sheila's sudden assertion of independence.

Sheila nodded vigorously.

'Then I'll go home and put the kettle on.'

352

Back at the house, Amy waited for quite a while and Sheila did not return. Tony and Harry were deeply engrossed in the football match on television, and she did not like to disturb them, but she began to get very worried. Eventually, she said timidly, while looking out of the window, 'Sheila's a long time. 'I'll go and see if she is all right.'

'No, I'll go,' said Harry with a sigh, getting up and putting on his jacket before going outside into the cold night air. There was no sign of Sheila in the fish-and-chip shop where they said she had been in and out half an hour or more before. Harry stood bewildered looking out over the darkened park. Suddenly he heard a little groan and stumbled quickly towards it. There he found poor Sheila lying half-unconscious on the grass, her clothes ripped and her body covered with blood.

Harry picked her up and, as he ran with her towards the house, she came round and started to scream hysterically at him, hitting out at his face. In her confusion, she did not know him. Harry ran into the house, where he laid her down. 'Ring for the police,' he said to Amy. 'God knows what they have done to her, poor soul.'

Amy tried to calm Sheila, but she just uttered those dreadful piercing shrieks. It was only the hypodermic needle of the doctor that finally silenced her.

The police arrived and examined the spot where she had been attacked. Her handbag had been turned inside out, and the fish and chips were scattered all around. Someone had heard her screams and seen three youths running away. But if they were the culprits and what they did to her only Sheila could tell, and her poor distressed mind could not cope any more.

So once more the newshounds came down on Amy. Harry chased them off and little articles appeared in the papers raking up old sores and the past including all the details about her husband's disappearance and the fact that she was now living with another man. Sheila's attackers were never caught and she stayed in the hospital for a long time. And in that time she became very withdrawn.

As much as she wanted Sheila home, Amy knew that it would be hopeless because every time she saw Harry, she started to scream. For some reason the sight of him brought that terrible nightmare flooding back.

'Oh, my God,' cried Amy, 'what else can happen to me?'

'Let's get married, Amy,' Harry said one day. 'Even if only for the lad's sake – he knows it all now.'

'I'll think about it, Harry, but I have enough to worry me at the moment,' replied Amy.

Harry looked sad but in his kind, steady, gentle manner he did not push the subject.

The problem of Sheila was uppermost in Amy's mind. She had promised her mother that she would take care of Sheila, so she could not leave her in the hospital and in no way would she settle down with Harry!

For a year Sheila stayed in the mental home and Amy visited her regularly. She would weep so many tears over her sister that even young Tony got a little fed-up with it all.

Then Harry said: 'Amy, this is the last time I'll ask you, but if we get wed we can go out to stay with my sister Marge in New Zealand. She is doing very well out there. It'd be just you and me and the boy.'

Amy stared at him aghast. 'But what about Sheila?' she asked in horror.

Mild generous Harry suddenly lost his temper and they started to quarrel violently. 'Fuck Sheila!' Harry cried out loud.

Amy hated bad language. 'There's no need for that,' she replied frostily.

Then Harry let loose his feelings. 'For Christ's sake, Amy. What am I here? I have worked my fingers off to look after you for ten years now, and you still treat me like the flaming lodger.'

'Well, if you don't like it, you know what you can do,' she retorted, her temper welling up inside.

'Yes, I do and from now on it's time to make a decision, I'll take that job in New Zealand and if you won't come, you can stay here.'

'My son stays with me,' she challenged him.

'Okay, you know how I love that boy, so chuck dirt at me. But I warn you, Amy, I am off in the New Year whatever you do.'

'Oh, go and leave me alone,' yelled Amy. The very mention of New Year always had a bad effect on her.

Amy went off to bed to weep her heart out. 'Oh, Sparky,' she sobbed into the pillow, 'if you are alive, come back to me. I love you, and no one will ever replace you.'

But only the silence of the night answered her, because for the

354

first time in ten years Harry had got drunk and lay sleeping on the sitting-room floor. Tony had got up in the middle of the night and covered him with a rug.

Amy's sister Nancy, now a plump, contented woman, visited Amy just before Christmas, and when she heard Amy's tale of woe she said: 'Why don't you just forget Sparky and marry Harry? He is a good man and good for you.'

'He still wants to go to New Zealand,' Amy snivelled, 'and I had enough of going to Canada. Why should I leave everything behind for him? And besides, if Sparky ever came home he would not know where to find me.'

'Oh, don't be so ridiculous,' cried Nancy impatiently. After that, she gave up on Amy and returned to her comfortable home.

On Christmas Eve it was Lily who visited. She was big and husky, unmarried and sort of mannish. 'You must be mad, Amy,' Lily said, when she heard what had been going on. 'Why not go away? It will be a new life for you out in New Zealand, and that's the best way to forget.'

'Well, I have still got Sheila to worry about,' insisted Amy.

'Oh, shut up!' said Lily impatiently. 'Sheila will never be normal, and you and I know that, just as Mother did.'

'Well, she is still our sister,' said Amy.

'Look here,' said Lily with authority, 'if you like, I'll have her down with me. I am matron at the home now and those kids of mine would be company for her. It'll bring her out of herself.'

'Oh, no, not disturbed children,' said Amy.

'Amy, my kids are deaf and some are dumb but they are deprived in the way that we were. It will be good for Sheila. I'll send a note to the hospital and have her there for Christmas.'

In the end Amy agreed, so she had a very quiet Christmas with just Harry and Tony.

Tony was becoming quite a radio addict. For Christmas Harry had bought him a shortwave radio and some radio equipment, including a set of headphones. This headphone set Tony wore a lot, walking around with them on so as not to hear Amy and Harry bickering with one another.

At New Year, Amy got moody, as she always did, and started to moon over Sparky's photo with big tears in her eyes. Earlier that evening she and Harry had had another argument about going to New Zealand, and Harry was fed up. 'I must be bleeding crazy,' he said, 'ten years now I've lived with Sparky's sodding ghost.' With that he had flounced out of the house.

Amy picked up a novel to read, in an effort to occupy her mind and show that she did not care, while Harry walked the deserted streets outside thinking of the days long gone when he had romped the streets with Sparky. He realized that it was in the street he now walked that Sparky had been gunned down, never to be seen alive again. It was quiet and he felt a little creepy but his footsteps guided him along the same route. It was eight o'clock and the lights of the pub, where they used to drink, shone out in front of him. He pushed open the door and went in. It was very quiet in there, for this had once been the haunt of gangland but now it had changed hands and had become deserted as the Asians, who didn't drink, moved into the area. Then three men entered the bar. They were a little drunk. They ordered drinks and sat down shouting at one another.

Idly Harry stood up at the bar listening to them. One was a portly fellow dressed in good clothes and smoking a cigar. He swaggered up to the bar and ordered brandies in a loud voice. The other two were typical East End youths. They were dressed in leather jackets and jeans and had strange haircuts. Their leader's voice rang out across the room boastfully. 'This is the pub I used to use when I was one of the lads,' he declared. Then he lowered his voice. 'As a matter of fact,' he continued, 'this is where I had a last drink, me and me mate Sparky, before they got him.'

Harry could not believe what he was hearing as that loud voice continued in its boastful manner. 'Oh, those were the days, bang! bang! And that was yer lot. After me, they was, but gets old Sparky and he's never been seen since. Them what done it are all inside now. That was fourteen years ago but it don't seem that long,' he added in his raucous voice.

'You mean they did a murder here?' asked one lad.

'Just outside this bloody door, mate,' declared the fellow in a loud manner.

Harry stared straight at him. Of course, it was that bastard Tommy Evans who had set Sparky up. He was supposed to be in South America. A wave of red hot temper suffused Harry. There he was, the fat sod sitting down there boasting about what he had done to Sparky. It was because of that fat sod that Amy had such an unhappy life. Without a word, Harry leapt forward and grabbed the fat man by the throat.

356

Tommy Evans was taken by surprise, as Harry jolted his head back straight through the plate glass window. All hell was let loose as the young lads jumped into the fray attacking Harry.

Tommy Evans rolled about on the floor gasping for his breath with a huge gash in his neck while Harry fought off the other two ruffians. Harry was strong but eventually they knocked him down and out, and were still busy kicking his ribs when the old Bill burst in upon the scene.

Amy had put down her novel and began to think about going to bed. There was not much to stay up for. Young Tony sat idly watching television when the phone rang. He answered it eagerly for he was missing Harry who did not often go out and leave them like that.

Amy was yawning and about to rise to go to bed when Tony returned from answering the phone his face very white and set. 'Mum,' he said, 'our Dad's got himself in trouble. That was the station sergeant. Dad is under arrest and said to go down in the morning to Old Street Station.'

Tony looked so forlorn that Amy rushed to him and held him tight. 'Oh, the silly great sod,' she said. 'Got himself drunk, I suppose. Wasn't in his car, was he?'

Tony shook his head. 'No, I saw him walking towards the main road. He was ever so fed-up, Mum. Poor old Dad.' Tears were about to fall from those greeny grey eyes, so like Sparky's.

But Amy's courage came to the fore. 'Serve him right,' she declared. 'It won't hurt him to spend a night in the nick. We'll bail him out in the morning. In the meantime I'll make a nice cup of cocoa and we'll turn in for the night.'

Early the next morning she was down at Old Street Police Station. She was on her own, having told Tony to stay in bed. 'I'm used to this,' she said. 'But I don't want you mixed up with all those drunks down there.'

When Amy saw Harry she was very dismayed. His head was bandaged and there were bruises all over his face. A large copper hovered over him as he sat looking very sorry for himself.

'Why won't they let me bail you out?' demanded Amy. 'What on earth have you done?'

'I duffed up Tommy Evans,' he said in a whisper. 'Sorry, love.'

Amy's face went deathly white. 'But I thought he had gone abroad.'

'So did I till I heard him boasting that he set Sparky up. Then I couldn't control myself,' said Harry.

Amy stared morosely at him. 'Oh, here we go, it's going on forever.'

'They won't let me out because Tommy's in a bad way. You see I pushed his head through the pub window.' Harry looked both proud and sheepish about what he had done.

'Oh, my God!' cried Amy, holding her head in her hands in alarm.'

'Look, try not to worry, love, and make it all right for me with Tony. Reassure him. I'll get by and there's money in my post office book if you need it. Just bring it in and I'll sign it. I expect I'll go on remand to the Scrubbs but try not to let it get you down.'

Amy walked out of the police station with her head in a whirl. When would all this end? Was there no place to hide? It was bound to get in the papers and what with Tony at that posh school, it did not bear thinking about.

The next six weeks were hell on earth for Amy and no one came forward to help. A snide little reporter who was at Harry's hearing followed Amy home and tried to put his foot in the door. 'Tell me your story,' he said. 'You are Mrs Binks, aren't you, the wife of the notorious criminal who disappeared and whose body has never been found?'

'Go away!' screeched Amy hysterically trying to jam the door against him.

As they struggled over the door, Amy suddenly heard a yell from the reporter as Tony, arriving home, swung his foot up and hit the little fellow where he felt it most, causing him to drop his notebook and send the camera spinning. Tony's face was flushed with rage as he cried out: 'Now piss off and leave us alone!'

Amy was astounded. Here was Sparky reincarnated in young Tony with his red hair and glaring eyes. As the reporter retreated, they bolted and barred the door and windows and took the phone off the hook. But it was too late. The daily papers had published an article about her and Sparky and the Sundays collected up a lot of old dirt.

Amy and her fourteen-year-old son clung together in their trouble. He told her that he was not going back to school after the holiday however hard she tried to make him go.

'Mother,' he said, 'you just don't know those toffee-nosed sods. They will never let me live it down. No, thanks. When it's all blown over I'll get a job but in the meantime I'm here to look after you and stand by our Dad, because if that bloke Tommy Evans dies, he will go away for a long time.'

'Oh,' sobbed Amy, 'what have I done to deserve all this?'

'All I can say, is that you are a born bloody loser,' said Tony in a hard voice.

Amy looked at him in shocked surprise but then a tiny grin spread across her face. 'Well, I suppose you would call it that.'

Harry came up for trial and Tommy Evans appeared in a wheel-chair, his head all bandaged and his neck plastered. He had a top lawyer working for him. Evans, the lawyer said, had been having a peaceful drink when he had been viciously attacked without warning.

The defending lawyer brought forth the mitigating circumstances and Amy's life was tossed back and forth across the court by these hard legal minds. The fact that Harry and Amy were only living together and not married, and that there was no evidence that Tommy Evans had done anything outside the law meant that Harry ended up with two years inside for breach of the peace, causing damage to the pub and causing grievous bodily harm to Evans. He got only two years because he had not been in any trouble for ten years and he was sent to an open prison.

As they listened to the sentence, Tony sat beside his Mum, his face hard, white and bitter. Harry cast a long look at him and winked in his direction.

Amy was allowed to say goodbye to Harry before they sent him down. Peering at her through a window covered with wire mesh, Harry's eyes were red as if he had been weeping. 'Take care of yourself, love,' he said. 'Don't waste your life on me, but whoever you get let them be good to Tony.'

'Don't be silly,' snivelled Amy. 'I'll wait for you. Both Tony and I, we said we would and we mean it.'

Chapter Nineteen

The Awakening

It was not easy to take the fact that Harry was in prison, but life had to go on. Amy still had her fine son to consider. He came first before everything else. She had clung to him and brought him up with love and care. Harry never came between them. Her girls could look after themselves now but there was still poor Sheila. Amy had promised her mother that she would look after her afflicted sister, and she would never go back on her word. She wondered if she had done the right thing in allowing Sheila to stay so long with Lily at the home for disturbed children. Now that she was alone again she would go and bring Sheila back home to live. Tony had taken this news fairly casually when she had mentioned it to him, as is the way of the young folk.

Tony now had a job with an electrical firm and doing very nicely, and he was also going to evening classes to finish his studies.

Harry wrote to them regularly from prison. He was allowed to write one letter a month. 'Please don't bother to visit me, Amy,' he often wrote. 'It is a long way to come. But if you do, don't ever bring the boy because I don't think I could bear to have him see me cooped up here in the nick. So let's leave it for a while, shall we?'

Amy would have happily gone down to see Harry, just as she had done for poor Siddy, but she respected Harry's wishes and just wrote to him and sent him the little extras that he was allowed. She felt quite lonely and bored, and began to think about getting herself a job, as money was running low. She was still getting offers from the newspapers to tell her side of her story but she hated them so much that she did not succumb. The first thing she had to do was get Sheila back, but when she set about doing that she received a very rude shock.

It had been four months since she had seen Sheila and now the spring time had come. Lily had often telephoned Amy to say that Sheila was doing very well and was being a great help in the children's home. But when Lily told Amy that she had also arranged with the mental hospital to let Sheila stay permanently, Amy was not at all pleased. She got herself ready and went down to Sussex to see for herself. She found the journey tiring. She had travelled very little of late and, now turned forty, she was beginning to feel her age.

Lily's children's home was a big white house with a lovely garden. Small children played outside on swings and roundabouts while others sat very still on a big long balcony.

Amy found Lily in her office. Her sister was as big and busy as ever. 'Nice to see you, Amy,' she said. 'Sorry about our little bit of trouble.'

'Trouble is my middle name,' said Amy dryly.

'I'll send for some tea,' replied Lily without a trace of a smile. That close family feeling they had once shared had gone. It had faded away with the years.

Sister Lily had always been a bit of a bully, and Amy had always preferred her sister Emily, and this well-built, well-spoken lady in the stiff starchy uniform seemed quite unfamiliar to her.

Lily sat back at her desk busily writing reports. 'Sorry,' she said. 'But I must dash these off quickly. Then we will have our cup of tea.'

Feeling very depressed, Amy sipped her tea. 'How's Sheila?' she ventured.

'Oh, she is fine,' beamed Lily. 'You won't know her. She spends her time helping me with the younger children, and I got her on a course of tablets which are stopping those convulsions. We'll go out and find her, shall we?'

Amy sat there feeling a little confused. She did not want to share Sheila with Lily like this. Sheila had been the little lame duck that she, Amy, had always looked after. Sheila was part of Amy's very own existence. But she did not say anything.

After tea they strolled around the grounds and came upon Sheila sitting under a big oak tree. She was dressed in a pretty blue summer dress and was cuddling a fair little child close to her side. They both sat listening to a young woman who wore horn-rimmed glasses and whose hair hung in long pigtails.

'Oh, there they are,' declared Lily, 'and that is our therapy teacher with her. Sheila adores her. It's a strange coincidence, but her name is Amy, just like yours.'

361

Seeing her afflicted sister Amy advanced eagerly towards her but Sheila looked up and seemed afraid. 'No, no!' she cried, putting up her hands to shield her face.

'It is Amy, darling,' Lily said. 'Amy's come to visit you.'

But Sheila did not respond, and Amy almost sobbed with grief.

Sheila got up and ran towards the therapy teacher who put her arms around her. 'There's nothing to be afraid of, Sheila,' she said. 'It's your sister Amy come to see you.'

But Sheila clung to her frantically, grabbing her tightly with her fingers. Amy, the teacher, moved toward the house. 'I think I'd better take her inside,' she said. 'It's too much of a shock for her to see you again, I'm afraid.'

'Sheila!' roared Lily. 'Stop being so silly! This is our Amy.'

But Sheila just covered her face with her hands and clung to the teacher.

Tears were now pouring down Amy's cheeks. She could not believe that Sheila did not recognize her. 'But I thought you said she was getting better,' she gasped, staring at Lily.

Lily shrugged nonchalantly. 'Well, she is, but you don't understand, this is her world now and the other Amy has taken your place in her disturbed mind.'

'Oh, no, I can't believe it,' wept Amy.

Lily gave her a good thump on the back. 'Now cheer up, Amy,' she said. 'You don't have to worry about Sheila any more now that she has found peace of mind, so why disturb it? Come, let's go in and have a drink, my dear. I deal with these cases all the time and the mind is a very strange thing.'

'Do you think she will ever come home to me?' asked Amy with anguish in her voice.

'No, my love,' said Lily. 'Leave her here. It's the best and kindest thing to do. These things take their own direction and all that slosh and sentiment we were brought up with does not help. When she lost Mum she clung to you, but then Harry came along and she lost you to him. So now you had better leave her alone. Come on, let's have that drink,' she said more gently, now acknowledging Amy's sad face.

In Lily's office they sat drinking a couple of gins. 'Stay for dinner,' Lily urged her.

'No,' said Amy. 'Please ring for a cab. I want to go home.'

As she travelled home in the train, Amy turned the day's events

362

over and over in her mind. Was she sorry that Sheila did not want to see her any more? She could not decide. But she did know that Lily had turned into a hard-hearted bitch. She made her mind up there and then that she did not want to see her sister, Lily, for a very long time to come. She would tell Tony of this meeting with Lily but she would not tell Harry, for she knew without a doubt that he would only laugh at her. She was sorry that Sheila did not need her any more and really could not believe it still, but, looking on the bright side, at least she would not have to worry about Sheila's welfare any more. She was basically having good treatment and she certainly seemed happy. What had happened would have to remain her own private sorrow, tucked away in her heart with the rest of her sadness.

Now ahead of her she had two years of comparative freedom. There had to be some reason for struggling on, and she supposed she had better find it. Tony was trying to grow up fast, and detaching himself from her increasingly. The two girls did not even bother to write to her. Rachel was too busy with her own family and Tosh – well, God knows where she went when she left university. How strange and lonely Amy felt. She was very glad to be home, to dream around the fire.

That night was strange and restless. She lay half asleep and tossing, when suddenly she heard whispering in her ear and there was Annie, her mother. Annie was young again, and wearing a bright scarf over. her dark hair. And then poor Siddy appeared, just as she had seen him dead. And then came the tall, ginger-haired Sparky. Amy tried to move but her limbs seemed paralysed. She tried hard to get up but still could not move; she tried to call out but no sound came. She lay in her bed, sweating with fear, but after a while her muscles relaxed and she returned to normal. She switched on the light and from then on felt too frightened to go back to sleep.

'Oh dear,' she sighed, 'what is happening to me? I'd better go to the doctor in the morning.'

The next day the local doctor gave her some pills. 'It's nervous strain,' he said. 'You must keep occupied. Why don't you go out to work? Then you will get a sound night's sleep. Your problem is caused by worry, and you have certainly had your share of that.'

So Amy began to write after jobs, but there were many young folk out of work and it was not easy for a person of her age to find employment. One day she saw an advertisement in the paper for women who could sell and work on commission. At the interview they explained that it was promotional work and that after training she would move around with a team. She would need to be able to drive a car, they told her, but while training it was not necessary.

'Its sounds exciting,' said Tony when Amy informed him that she was on the short list for this job. 'Why don't you take Harry's car and learn to drive?' he suggested. 'Take driving lessons right away. I'll treat you.'

Amy smiled. 'It's all right, son, I can still afford that,' she said, touched by his offer.

Amy got the job, and so it was that she pulled her socks up. She got her hair cut and permed in a nice short style, bought a smart suit and went daily to the city by tube to do her training. In the evening she had her driving lessons. The effect on her spirits was marvellous. She made friends with other young women and slowly regained confidence in herself. The smart slim woman who walked briskly to the station each morning was more like the old Amy but with a quiet poise she kept her past to herself. She was like the survivor of a great battle, living only for her son, and still in her heart for the day when Sparky would return to her. But in the meantime there was poor Harry stuck in the nick. She felt guilty about him. In some ways it was her fault, she believed. She should never have involved him in her life. That was the heavy feeling of guilt she carried so she must not desert him. Occasionally she did go to visit him down on the island where many East Enders had resided in the past. These trips to the Isle of Wight were often the highlight of her social life.

Harry was a tough little man and prison life had made little difference to him. He joked with her on these visits and sent his love to Tony saying, 'Tell the boy to keep his nose clean and not get tangled up with the law. They've got some vicious little sods down here these days.'

Amy brought him all the news and gossip of the East End. He loved to hear it all. 'They buried old Dolly Palmer last week,' she told him one day.

'Go on!' exclaimed Harry. 'Some blokes are going to miss her. She must have visited every nick in the country chasing after them twins of hers.'

'Yes, she wasn't a bad old girl,' agreed Amy. 'They say she was very generous to the wives of the boys in prison – not that she was short of a few bob. Those villains she brought up took good care of her.'

'Ah, well,' said Harry philosophically, 'even us tough boys remember and love our mums.'

'Buried her in style, they did,' said Amy. 'TV cameras and film stars were there and her boy Terry was even allowed to attend – with the cuffs on, mind you, and old Bill in attendance.'

This amused Harry; he roared with laughter. 'Well, who would have thought our street would get so famous?'

Amy suddenly turned serious. 'Will you get pardoned next year, do you think?'

'I bloody hope so,' said Harry. Wistfully he added. 'Do you really want me back home, Amy?'

'You know I do,' she told him warmly.

Harry gave her a big grin. 'I'd kiss you,' he said, 'but that bloody screw is looking at us.'

The prisoners and their visitors were allowed to sit and chat but were absolutely forbidden to touch each other in case a visitor slipped something to a prisoner.

With Harry being so chirpy she enjoyed her visits to him. Now she was visiting him once a month, going down on the train, where she met other prisoner's wives. Some brought young children with them. It seemed to Amy that each time she visited, the wives were younger and there were more and more children who screamed blue murder when it was time to leave their dads behind. It was such a pity, she thought, that this army of young men was locked away like this when in her young days they would have all been in the forces fighting for survival. Now, in this open prison, they stood in bored, pathetic droves, dotted along the pathway, standing with brooms and shovels in hand as they pretended to keep busy with one eye on the visitors arriving, in the hope of seeing someone they knew.

Amy would look at them and sigh. Was there no other way of punishing these offenders? This way only punished their families as well. The young women had to be mother and father to their babes and struggle along on the money they received from the welfare state. Amy's sad brown eyes would watch the young girls talking to their husbands and bouncing their young babies on their laps as they pretended to be cheerful so as not to depress their caged men. Amy, *she* knew their heartbreak, for she felt as if she had spent all her life waiting in one way or another – first for Sparky, now for Harry. She supposed she must be raving mad, but this was all life had given her, so she had better make the best of it.

In her new job she was now 'out on the road', as they termed it. She had passed her driving test and drove herself around the suburbs selling various commodities to the shops working on a good commission basis. She had great confidence in herself now.

Tony was doing a part-time course in electronics, like his dad. He was a wizard at this kind of thing. He had become very interested in computers and now had his room rigged up like a miniature radio station.

Now that she was happier and more satisfied, time passed quickly for Amy, and her terrible past began to fade. Harry would be home soon after the New Year, so she did not mind having to wait to pick up the threads of their life once more. But to her dismay Harry seemed to have had other ideas. In his last letter he had written to say that his sister Marge had written to him and asked them to go out to New Zealand when he got out of the nick. 'I think it will be a good idea, Amy,' he wrote. 'New Zealand is a fine country with plenty of opportunities. I will not get my job back and don't fancy being out of work.'

Amy was very angry when she read this letter. 'Well, after sticking by him while he was in the nick,' she raged, 'now he wants to go off to some forgotten land.' Canada had been enough for her. No way would he pull up her roots again. It was the East End for her till the day she died. She wrote a letter back to Harry. Her tone was cool. 'No, Harry, definitely not. I now have a good job and in no way will I jeopardize that. My home is here.'

When Harry read her letter he sighed a deep sigh, but he did not mention New Zealand again to Amy in any of his letters. But as the year rolled on, be became keener and keener on the idea as his sister's encouraging letters continued to arrive. In every letter Marge would point out the advantages of emigrating to New Zealand. She wrote that her husband was now the overseer of a big meat packers and would welcome his skill and give him a good job anytime. 'Leave it all behind, Harry,' she wrote. 'The East

End has not been all that good to us. We lost Mum and Dad and our sister, and now you have been towed into trouble. Come out here with me and make a new start.'

This last letter decided Harry. If Amy would not come with him, he would just have to go alone to New Zealand. Maybe Amy would get wise afterwards and follow him out there later.

It was a terrible blow to Amy when Harry told her of this decision but in no way would she give in and leave Tony. 'Do me a favour,' she said. 'I won't go. I had enough of being abroad in Canada with Sparky. I was so homesick then that I nearly went mad.'

'Oh, grow up, Amy,' Harry said gently, 'that was a long time ago.'

But Amy was quite adamant and very annoyed. She even missed a visit deliberately to the prison just to make him change his mind, but Harry's mind was made up.

'My sister and brother-in-law will pay our passage out and find me a job,' he told her. 'What chance do I stand out there?'

He pointed at the prison gates. 'When I get my release I'll just be standing on the bleeding corner all day with all the other out-of-work hoodlums.'

'Oh, well, Harry, please yourself,' shrugged Amy. 'I'll get by.'

Chapter Twenty

The Return

Greatstone is a busy little town with narrow roads and plenty of heavy traffic making its way to the coast. Amy was always a little nervous in strange places, her grass roots feelings were so strong that when she was a mile or so away from the East End she would begin to panic. This was her last visit to Harry, for he would be out in January.

The Welfare for Prisoners' Wives organization ran a coach from the train station which deposited them all outside the prison gates but this time Amy had declined the coach. For once she just could not bear to watch the young mothers and their whining children, and she wanted to make her own way there alone this time as she gathered her strength to give him her final and definite answer for the New Zealand plan. She had to make it clear once and for all because the last thing she wanted was to have him secretly hoping that she would change her mind.

As she came out of the station her head ached with the tension of travelling and the worry about this ultimatum. She had to wait some time for a bus out to the open prison, so she decided to go and get a cup of tea in the meantime. She crossed the road and headed for the big Army and Navy store. It was a lovely big shop and reminded her of her first job she had as a sales lady. It was then that she had first met Sparky. She sat in the shop's cafe sipping her tea and dreaming of those days long gone. It was many years now since Sparky had disappeared. She accepted at last that he would never come back to her now, but she still mourned him deep in her heart. His memory was like a knife left sticking there; and in no way could Harry have replaced him.

Today she decided she would reorganize her life. Let Harry go out to New Zealand. She had a good job now and could well support herself. It had not really been an easy decision because Harry had been so good to her and Tony. There was a nervous sweat on her brow as she clutched her hands around the cup, but she collected herself, placed the cup in the saucer and swept off through the store, her tall slim figure passing on to the store's gaily decorated counters.

In two weeks it would be Christmas. Balloons and streamers swung from the ceiling, and everywhere there were dainty Christmas lights. A large and beautifully decorated Christmas tree was on display in the centre of the main hallway and the sight of it comforted her. She would be lonely this Christmas but she might visit one of the family. She began to look at the presents on the well-laden counters and came upon a display of pretty silk scarves. She fingered the soft silk and again her mind went back to that special day twenty years back when she had sold silk scarves at her first department store. She then noticed a little bit of confusion going on around her, as a large crowd of disabled men and boys went through the shop, accompanied by a couple of uniformed nurses and minders. They were out on their annual Christmas shopping spree, and were all very noisy and excited about it. With their bent crooked legs and misshapen heads, they milled around her and the counter, and she stood back nervously. Then along came a retinue of bathchair patients – poor unfortunates who were unable to walk at all. Amy tried not to look and stood still fingering that silk scarf.

Suddenly there was a strange animal-like wail and a long thin skeleton of a man with sparse red hair almost fell out of the bathchair and grabbed hold of her legs. His red-rimmed eyes rolled as if in a fit, and he jabbered excitedly like a monkey. His grasping hands dug deeply into her flesh and held on to her as she tried to pull away. Horrified, she looked down at this twisted man in a bathchair, and the world suddenly swirled before her. For a brief second she thought this creature was Sparky, and she gave a frightened gasp and fell sideways, almost collapsing on top of this horrible thing who still clutched desperately at her skirt.

The nurse and shop assistants ran to her aid and she was carried half-unconscious into the staff room, while Sparky was slapped and put back upright in his bathchair. Then the party of patients went hurriedly on its way.

When Amy came round, the nurse was offering her a drink. She was very apologetic and asked if they should get her a doctor. Was she all right? Did she know why she fainted? They fired questions at her but all Amy could see was those red-rimmed rolling eyes of the mentally disabled man.

369

'We do not understand what happened. Boysie is usually so good, and well-behaved,' said the young woman in uniform trying to explain her patient's behaviour. 'We wondered if it's possible that he recognized you or something, or did he have a fit and cling onto the first thing handy? They do, you know.'

Unable to speak, Amy looked up at the nurse in dismay and just shook her head.

'Well, we have sent him back home to the hospital. He has been with us for a very long time,' said the nurse.

'Who is he?' Amy stammered out at last.

'No one knows very much about him. All we know is that his mother always looked after him and he came to us when she died. Here's the address of the hospital to write to if you wish to make a complaint.'

Amy gazed at the card in a daze. She turned and said: 'Please, will someone get me a taxi? I have to visit someone.'

As the old taxi rattled along the country road, she tried to collect her wits. No, it was not possible, it had been her own imagination, she told herself. That poor devil had just fallen out of his bathchair on his own. He had a fit. She had to put it from her mind. Perhaps the strain of all she had been through of late had been too much for her. Now she began to cry and heavy tears poured down her cheeks. What should she do? 'Oh my God,' she wailed, 'how much more can a heart and brain stand?' She had to escape, and there was only one way – into the arms of the warm, comfortable, caring Harry.

Harry was very pleased to see her. They walked about the prison grounds together, wrapped up against the cold. Under his coat, Harry wore a faded blue shirt and jeans. He looked very fit. He put a finger close to her eyes and wiped her cheek. 'You have been crying, matey,' he said. 'What's wrong? Tell Harry.'

Amy clung to him. 'Oh, it's all right,' she said. 'I'm depressed about you going away, that's all. And I shall be so lonely at Christmas this year – that is the worst time.'

'Well, my love, I have got news for you,' he cried jubilantly. 'I'll be home the day after tomorrow and we will be able to have Christmas together. I got me remission so at last I'll be free of this place. And there'll be no more bird for me, I'm definitely going to New Zealand. Oh, Amy,' he said, clasping her hand, 'say you will come with me and I'll be the happiest man alive.'

370

Amy held his roughened workingman's hand and closed her eyes to try to forget the nightmarish incident. 'Oh, Harry,' she said. 'I feel safe with you, and I can't live alone any longer. I'll sell the furniture to pay for my fare and come to New Zealand with you.'

Harry hugged her with delight and swung her round. 'You've changed your mind somewhat. Ever since I mentioned the idea you've said you'd die rather than live anywhere outside the East End.' He chuckled loudly, and his eyes twinkled.

'Oh, Harry, please don't laugh at me. My mind is made up. Even if Tony will not come with us, I'll still go. I've had enough of this country, after all, and I want to leave it all behind.'

'That's me gel,' said Harry giving her a rough kiss.

Once Harry was home from prison, he and Amy got busy packing up and putting all the furniture up for sale. Amy was surprised to discover that she had no regrets now. All of a sudden she could not bear to think back to the past, and she had a strong and sudden urge to go forward.

To her surprise and pleasure, Tony wanted to join them. 'I might as well,' he said. 'After all, Harry is the only father I've ever known and I would miss him. And there are good prospects out there and times are getting very bad here in England. Even a good education is no guarantee that I would get a job.'

All packed and ready, Amy took a last look from the balcony of her flat, looking away over the roof tops towards the tower of the old church. 'Goodbye, Mum,' she murmured. 'It's all changed now. You would not like it here now, either, so I am going to a new life.'

And so in March, Amy, Harry and Tony sailed away on a ship to the other side of the world, never to return to the East End again.

Chapter Twenty-One

Boysie

The hospital staff were all very concerned about Boysie, who was a general favourite with staff and patients alike. He had been with them now for four years and had gradually improved enough to make friends with the other patients and do little tasks to help the nurses.

Nurse Helen was particularly attached to him and had tried patiently to teach him to write his own name, but so far she had not accomplished much. But she did have quite a warm feeling for this poor unwanted man who needed friendship so much. They all called him Boysie because the local folk in the woods had told them that was what he had been called by the wretched old woman who claimed him as her son. Nurse Helen knew his story quite well and whenever she was on night duty and he was unable to sleep, she would sit by his bed and talk to him. 'I am from Kent,' she would say. 'I know those lovely woods where you came from. I used to go up there on my bike when I was at school.'

Boysie would grimace in reply and a sudden glint in his rolling eyes would tell her that he understood what she had said.

Helen had been brought up in the medical profession. Her father was a country doctor and her mother an ex-nurse. Helen herself never made the grade at the school because she hated to study and loved the free fresh air, preferring pony riding and biking in the woods to books. So she neglected her school work and did not obtain the medical degree her parents had wished for her. Yet Helen was content. First she did child nursing and had then progressed in stages to the psychiatric hospital where she was now. She did not mind in the least that she was not a doctor. The pain and suffering of these disturbed patients were to her like that of little puppies or kittens. She had to fuss and care for them. At twenty-two years old, she was a fair-haired, good-looking young woman and so full of happiness that a peaceful halo seemed to surround her. There was no doubt that she had found her rightful place in life. For the two years she had been in Greatstone she had got very attached to Boysie and he had improved under her care. But now, after his outing to the town, he lay in a coma. After seeing Amy, he had gone into a fit and had never recovered from it. But no one seemed particularly concerned about him now. The doctor's attitude was callous. 'He will never be cured,' he said. 'It might be the best thing just to let him slowly fade out.'

Helen was incensed about this attitude. She quarrelled with the other nurses and was in trouble with the sister. She tried to rouse Boysie and refused to keep giving him the sedatives prescribed for him. Eventually she was pulled up before the matron for disobedience of the hospital rules. The matron tore her off a strip and fined her. The meeting became so heated that in the end Helen announced that she wanted to leave. She left matron's room and was crying in the corridor when Dr Macgregor came by. They had trained in the same hospital but he was now an up-and-coming neurologist at a big London hospital. As Helen sobbed loudly outside matron's office, Dr Macgregor came up close to her. 'Tears?' he exclaimed. 'Not our Helen, our little sunshine girl? Who has upset you?'

Helen motioned towards matron's office door.

Dr Macgregor's eyebrows were raised. 'Oh, and what have you been up to?'

Helen liked him and was soon unburdening her soul to him. 'It's Boysie,' she said. 'He is in a coma and no one's doing anything to help him.'

'Oh, I see, you mean the young ginger lad?'

'Honestly, Dr Macgregor, I know he understands me, I am sure he does. I realize it is wrong to get personally involved with a patient but I can't help myself this time.'

Dr Macgregor patted her shoulder. 'Dry your tears and I will have a talk with matron to see if I can get some idea of the case. Now, cheer up, Helen, you are a wonderful nurse, and I'm sure they would hate to lose you.'

The next morning Helen was more her old self. She had been taken off Boysie's case and was in another ward but she noticed with satisfaction that Boysie was getting a thorough examination by Dr Macgregor, as well as the hospital's medical officer. And she was delighted to learn that he had been taken off all the drugs.

One evening she crept in to see Boysie. He just stared in front of him, his eyes glazed, and he obviously did not recognize her. The nurse on duty told Helen that he was at least sleeping more peacefully than he had before and 'he is going off to London tomorrow,' she added.

'Oh?' cried Helen, a little dismayed. 'Why?'

'They think they can operate on his brain. There seems to be some pressure there. They might even cure him and then he will be almost normal again.'

'Oh, how wonderful,' cried Helen.

'Of course,' said the nurse, 'it's a chance in a thousand. It's more likely to finish him off at the start.'

Helen dashed off to the lavatory to have another weep but in her heart she felt lighter. At least the doctors were going to try to do something about him, she thought, and not just let him lie there and die.

The next day, Boysie was taken away to the Brook Hospital, the most famous place in London for brain surgery.

While he was away, Helen moped around and rang the hospital twice a day, but she never got much information out of them because it was a new kind of treatment and the results would not be clear for some time.

Six weeks later Boysie came back to his old hospital. He looked quite different but he was still very confused.

Helen had wept many tears over him but the doctors were confident. Apparently they had taken part of a bullet out of his brain and were amazed that it had remained there for so long. No one could enlighten them as to how the bullet got there in the first place but they guessed that it was from some sort of shooting accident in his youth. There was no one able to tell and no one to care – only Helen, who was more determined than ever to get through to him. The matron was more sympathetic to her now and left her alone.

Slowly as the spring came round, Boysie improved. He sat up and grinned at her, and when she pushed him around the gardens to show him the first primroses, he seemed very pleased. He even tried to say something. As he struggled to get out the words, Helen put her ear close to his mouth. To her amazement and delight, she heard him whisper: 'Soaky. Woods. Flowers.'

Each day Boysie managed a few more words. Soon he was

having speech therapy classes and physiotherapy, and gradually he learned to walk again. Tall, thin and stooping forward on a frame, he soon learned and before the next Christmas had come around, the improvement in him was amazing. He had put on weight and with the help of a pair of large spectacles he managed to focus his eyes. Helen was so happy for him. She bought him sweets and knitted him a pullover and she protected him from the more violent patients. She felt that he was hers; if it had not been for her interference they would have let him die. No mother could have been prouder of her boy than Helen was of her patient Boysie. He now would sit in the recreation room nodding his head to the music on the radio and trying, in an odd strangulated manner, to sing a song.

'Oh, look at him,' said Helen. 'He can hear the music and is really enjoying himself.'

But still in her heart she was worried. For if Boysie continued to improve at such a rate they would send him away to some other place – a permanent home for the disabled. She was not sure she could face losing him, she had become so attached to Boysie. Despite that concern, Helen was very happy. The following year she worked very hard for her sister's cap and obtained it. Her parents were rather surprised at her success for she had always been such a happy-go-lucky child but now had become very serious minded. Helen went home to Sussex occasionally to see them and always talked of this hospital and the marvellous recovery of one patient known as Boysie who now worked as a part-time porter and lived in the hospital.

'Daddy,' she said, 'it is nothing short of a miracle. You would never recognize him from what he was like. He has developed so well. He still has trouble with his speech and does not recall his past but we are great friends and he is very attached to me. I do feel very responsible for him.'

Her father pulled a long face. 'You are twenty-three years old, Helen,' he said, 'and it's time you found yourself a partner, but I'd rather you didn't fall for one of your lame ducks, one of your mental patients.'

'Now, that is very unkind,' Helen replied as her face flushed indignantly. 'I will bring Boysie down to meet you.'

'Don't bother,' her father replied sarcastically. 'I have plenty of disturbed patients of my own.'

Weeping tears of anger, she later told her mother about this conversation. 'Take no notice,' her mother said gently. 'He just works too hard. Bring your friend to visit us if you want to.'

'No, I won't,' said Helen, 'for if Daddy is unkind to him, it will undo all the good we have done.'

Helen put a stop to her visits home on her Sundays off, and instead she went walking in the country with Boysie. He had now put on weight and had grown into a fine figure of a man, with broad shoulders and a mop of bright red hair. He wore a nice tweed suit but he still dragged one leg a little when he walked. Helen soon corrected this drag with a good walking stick she bought him.

'For your birthday,' she said, holding it up towards him.

He grinned and shook his head, indicating that he did not have a birthday.

'Yes, you have,' said Helen, 'it is a certain day a year ago when you were very ill and then came back to life.'

They sat on the park seat and he shyly put an arm around her. Helen leaned her head on his shoulder. They were so happy and peaceful together.

'Don't you remember anything about your past life?' she asked him.

'Yes,' he nodded, pointing to his head and then his mouth, as if to say, 'I do but cannot say.'

'Oh, poor darling,' Helen kissed and fussed him. 'Next Sunday we will go on the bus to those woods where you came from. Would you like that? And if you remember anything you will tell me. All right?'

Boysie took her hand to his moist lips and kissed it.

'Oh, Boysie,' Helen giggled. 'You are becoming a real Romeo. Come on, let's get home to tea.'

Hand in hand they strolled back to the hospital as happy as any two people could possibly be.

Boysie had his own little room at the hospital and a light job as a porter plus three meals a day. Everyone seemed to have forgotten that he was once a patient. He was now big and strong and a great help with the more disabled patients. As far as the hospital authorities were concerned, Boysie had become part of the fittings, that is, to all except Helen, who fell more in love with him each day.

The next weekend, Helen kept her promise. They packed a picnic basket, and caught the bus into town to take them out to the woods where Sparky had come from. They got off at the end of the road, it was a lovely summer's day. Flowers bloomed everywhere, and birds sang a song of welcome as they strolled up the hill to the woods. On one side of the road were some brand new bungalows, and Boysie shook his stick at them.

'Oh, dear!' said Helen, 'they have started to build on the land. What a pity, it was so lovely up here when I was at school.'

They continued up the long lane to the top of the hill where there was a wonderful view of the point at which the Thames and Medway met. The two rivers gleamed in the sunlight and ships sailing up the river to London or out to the wild empty sea looked like tiny toys.

'Oh, it is lovely up here in spite of the building going on,' exclaimed Helen. 'Do you see anything that you can remember, Boysie?'

Boysie just shook his head and began to investigate the picnic basket.

After they had eaten they lay down side by side and looked up at the swallows flying around overhead in the lovely blue sky. Most of that lovely green forest had been destroyed. Great oak trees lay still on the ground dry and perishing in the hot sun and there were large gaps in the woodland where it had been cleared.

'Oh, what a shame,' said Helen but Boysie had got excited and was pointing to a piece of old rope attached to a fallen tree.

'You remember this?' It *did* mean something. 'Oh, it is so exciting, darling, tell me about it?' Helen cried.

They sat on the fallen oak and kissed as lovers. Then Boysie showed her that this piece of rope had once been Soaky's washing line. That much he recalled.

'Was she your mother?' enquired Helen gently.

He shook his head.

'You are a good bit older than I am,' she ventured. 'I often wonder if you had a wife and family?'

Boysie suddenly looked sad and then said in pure Cockney: 'Yus, I did.'

Helen smiled. 'Oh, Boysie, what English you speak! It is not very good.'

But Boysie had got very excited and was now pointing towards the river. Helen stood beside him and held his hand, a puzzled frown on her brow as she tried to work out what he meant. Suddenly she knew. 'Down the river to the town, to London town!' She turned to him, her eyes lit up with excitement.

Boysie grabbed her hand and held her close. He was getting very agitated.

'So that's it, darling,' said Helen. 'You are not from Kent woods but London. Well, that is marvellous, but it will have to do for today.'

But Boysie wanted to continue holding her. He kissed her repeatedly on the lips and would not release her. Helen moulded her body to his for a moment as she realized that he was now a true man and that he obviously wanted to make love to her. She held him close in return. 'No, darling,' she said gently. 'I have not done that yet, but if I do it will be with you. But not now. Be a good boy and let us go home.'

Boysie smiled happily. 'I . . . love . . . you,' he said slowly but very clearly.

As they went down the hill he whistled a catchy tune which Helen recognized. 'Maybe it's because I'm a Londoner that I love London so.'

'Oh, it is so marvellous,' she cried. 'It's all slowly coming back to you.'

As time went by their relationship became more intimate. Boysie improved with each passing day, but Helen discovered that he had a perverse kind of humour and could also be very jealous and have bad temper moods. But normally he was just very happy and very willing to help anyone who needed it.

The doctors were delighted with his improvement, and one even expressed the opinion that he thought Boysie might one day remember very clearly who he was and where he came from.

After this good report Helen was slightly worried. The two of them were now very involved and very much in love. She had once even mentioned marriage and Boysie had smiled a really nice smile as if to say that as long as she stayed with him he would do what ever she wanted. His sentences were short but to the point, so they had no difficulty now in communicating. But he was still shy and awkward with others. Helen continued to worry. Suppose he suddenly found out who he was? He must have had

378

some background. The doctor had stated that he was well past thirty-five or might even be forty, and she was just twenty-five. He must have lived with someone somewhere. Worried, she turned it all over in her mind, hoping that the truth would never be revealed. It would not bring pain and trouble.

'Boom' 'Boom!' Boysie suddenly said one day. 'That's it, bombed, my mother down our street.'

'Was she killed in the war? Is that what you are trying to tell me, Boysie?' Helen asked cautiously.

He nodded emphatically.

'So you definitely came from London,' she said. 'Perhaps we had better continue our search for your identity,' she said without enthusiasm.

Boysie stared at her thoughtfully and then took off his big specs. 'No, no,' he cried, 'I stay with you.'

'All right, my love,' she said, fondling his mop of hair, 'if that is what you want, I'll leave the hospital and we will get a flat and live together.'

This pleased him. He said, 'I am strong, I'll work for you.'

'I am sure you will but in the meantime we will lay our plans and go away together.'

No one was surprised when Helen left the hospital. She had been very lucky and landed a position as district nurse with a cottage thrown in with the job. It was in a remote village way down in Surrey.

A week later Boysie suddenly discharged himself from the hospital. Helen met him in town and they travelled down together to their cosy love nest. And as far as the population of the village was concerned, Boysie was the district nurse's husband.

The roses around the door and the pretty garden in front of their new home soon became Boysie's pride and joy. It gave them great happiness and they felt that they had left the tumult and the cares of the outside world behind.

The years passed very quickly in that remote country cottage which they had called Shady Nook. It was now a real home. Helen had two children and had become rather plump but her nature was still very sunny. She rode her bike leisurely around the country village in her neat nurse's uniform with her big black bag strapped to the handlebars. She visited the old and the sick and often the poor just to bring a smile, sustenance and words of comfort. Sister Helen was well known for her generosity and was very popular in the village.

'Strange man, that husband of hers,' the gossips in the pub would comment. 'Never holds a complete conversation. If you ask him anything he just says, "Ask the wife". Mind you, he's a nice quiet man, and good looking, too, but a lot older than her.'

Peace and contentment seemed to exude from Shady Nook. The roses round the door flourished and the flowers in the front garden bloomed in profusion. Boysie, the withdrawn, ginger-headed man tended them with love and care, and he also grew vegetables out in the back garden. Quietly he went about his work. His red hair shone bright in the sunshine and a nice bushy moustache gave him a sober appearance. The world outside did not bother him for he had found complete happiness in these late years. He also did little electrical jobs and was getting very good at them.

Helen was impressed by his skill. 'I often wonder if you once studied electronics somewhere,' she said, 'you are so good at that kind of work.'

'Oh well,' said Boysie. 'I don't remember, so what does it matter?'

Helen put a big notice on a board at the front gate outside. It read: 'Electrical repairs done. Plants for sale, and seasonal fruits.' Thus with her own salary on top they fared very well. John and Jennifer, their two children, grew up strong and carefree. They fished in the stream and went for long walks over the hills with Daddy. He was the be all and end all of their young lives. He was always at home while Mum was often busy and out of the house at odd hours.

Boysie had forgotten the bad days and was now living a full life. There were still times when he was very slow and stood staring into space as if there was something on his mind which he could not recall. But Helen was the bright and breezy one, doctoring him up and saying, 'No, my love, no looking back, only forwards.'

Then one day when Johnnie was six and Jennifer four, Helen suggested an outing. 'It would be so nice to give the children a day out. Let's go up to London for the day.' They rarely left the village, so this was a real treat.

There had been a royal wedding recently and the town was still flood-lit. The West End was a gay land bright with decorations, and quite a sight to see.

'London?' said Boysie, a little amazed.

'Well, it will be nice for the children to see it,' replied Helen. 'Most of the villagers have been up there.'

'As you wish, dear,' he said.

On Sunday morning they set off. They caught the excursion train to Victoria Station, and the kids were extremely happy and excited. Helen and Boysie were nicely dressed and looked like a very handsome respectable couple from the country.

They walked to Trafalgar Square where they fed the pigeons and Boysie carried Jennifer shoulder high down Oxford Street mingling with the tourists. It was fairly quiet because all the shops were closed.

Suddenly Boysie said brightly. 'It's Sunday, let's go down the Lane.'

'What lane?' asked Helen in her ignorance of London.

'Petticoat Lane,' he said decidedly. 'Come on, kids, we'll go down the tube.'

The escalators and the underground trains were an added thrill for the children.

'It's nice in the smoke, ain't it kids?' said Boysie with a laugh.

As they went out into the East End streets, a strange mood seemed to have possessed him. They milled among the crowds in the busy market. Helen felt a little nervous and held firmly on to her purse in case it got stolen. They hung about the stalls laughing at the Jewish traders and their Sunday patter. When the kids bought coloured balloons from a wizened old man, Boysie called to him, 'Hullo, mate, how's tricks.'

Helen looked concerned. 'Do you know him' she asked.

'No,' said Boysie, 'but I just felt like saying hello.'

'Did you used to live here, Daddy?' asked John, staring in wide-eyed wonder at the stall full of toys.

'No, but I used to play about down here on Sundays with me mate Harry and we used to get two bob each for helping to pack the stalls up when the market closed.'

'How funny,' giggled the kids. They were certainly enjoying themselves.

But Helen looked a little pale. Inside she felt sick. It had not been a very good idea, this East End trip, she thought. Boysie might recall his past life and she might lose him.

But Boysie seemed so full of beans and it was hard not to be happy for him, and he strode through the back streets holding himself upright and very alert. He stopped in front of an old pub that was now closed down. The windows were barred up, and Boysie stared at it in a puzzled way. Then he turned and said: 'Come on kids, I'll find the place where I used to live.'

With Helen trailing slowly along behind, and holding his kids' hands, Boysie strode along through the maze of odd little streets, alleys and high-rise flats. He looked around very intently until they came to another smaller market. Here the road ran over a small rise with an island in the centre of the road. 'Look,' he said, 'this is it, Whitmore Road. We used to run races down there to the old church and back again when I was a kid.' Again he stood still and looked solemnly around him. There was no trace whatsoever of the old street. There was not one house or person left to reassure him. Tears flooded his eyes as he put his hand to his head. 'It's no good,' he said miserably. 'It's all a blank void, but I am sure this is the place.' He shook his head in grief.

Helen put her arms around him. 'Hush, darling, don't look back. Let's only go forwards. I'll call a taxi and we will go home to Shady Nook.'

Boysie nodded and smiled at her. Then hand-in-hand, they turned and walked back slowly towards the tube station.